Vengeance of a Stolen Soul

Abigail Bowen

Disclaimer
This story is fiction. The characters, places, and events
are either from my imagination or used fictitiously. Any
resemblance to real people is coincidental.

Unless you recognize yourself as a villain. Then…
maybe do some soul-searching, sweetheart.

Edited with love (and brutal honesty) by **Sarah Dean**
Cover design by **Lesia S.**

Heads up
This book contains:

- **Explicit sex scenes**
- **Foul language**
- **Violence, blood, and death**

Consider this your warning… or your invitation

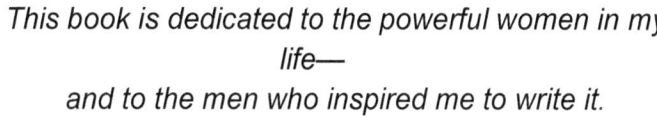

This book is dedicated to the powerful women in my life—
and to the men who inspired me to write it.

Chapter 1

The ER lights buzzed brightly overhead, making my eyes ache as I worked. I pressed the heel of my hand into the center of the kid's chest and counted under my breath.

"One, two, three, four..."

He couldn't have been more than sixteen. He had blood on his face, gravel in his hair, and his pupils were blown wide.

Dr. Porter barked over my shoulder, "Another dose of epi. Now."

"On it," someone said, already moving.

I kept going. Each compression shook his entire body. His chest felt like paper under my hand, fragile and folding in all the wrong places.

The room was tight with tension, crowded and quiet all at once, the kind of silence that only lives in the seconds before death.

The boy's mother was still in the hallway. I hadn't looked at her face. I couldn't. But I could still hear the sound she made when we'd pulled her out of the room, right after the monitor flatlined.

That scream. It tore through the halls like grief made audible, sharp enough to leave a mark.

The monitor let out a sharp beep. Then another. A slow, stumbling rhythm, but a rhythm.

He was back.

The mother pushed past the curtain, tears still on her face, and let out a choked sob when she saw him alive. She didn't ask permission. She just went to him, pressed her forehead to his, whispering something only he could hear.

I turned away.

Dr. Porter moved in. I stepped back, bracing one hand against the counter, letting my pulse catch up to me. The adrenaline lashed through me, hot and sour, but there was something else riding its tail... something cold and electric that didn't belong.

It wasn't just adrenaline. It wasn't exhaustion or shock.

It was panic. But not my own. It shot through my chest like cold fire, making my lungs tight. My skin prickled. I swallowed, trying to find air that didn't seem to exist. My vision tunneled, the world flattening into blurry shapes and noise. I don't know how long it lasted. A second? Ten?

The overhead lights flickered. One gave a pop like a firecracker and shattered, spraying glass onto the tile.

"Jesus Christ," a tech muttered. "That's the second one this week."

I straightened too fast, blinking hard, forcing air into my lungs. My whole body buzzed, nerves firing wrong, like electricity under my skin.

"You okay, Lena?" Anna, a nurse I'd worked with for a couple of years, asked. Her blonde ponytail was frizzy at the ends, her scrubs wrinkled from the late shift.

I nodded, but my hands were still trembling.

The room was already resetting. Machines hummed, and footsteps and voices moved on to the next emergency.

I told myself it was just the moment, that being so close, his fear had settled into my skin.

But I still couldn't help feeling that something was off. And that whatever it was, it didn't come from the chaos of the code. It came from me.

I slipped out of the trauma bay and into the nearest staff bathroom, closing the door behind me. I leaned over the sink, bracing my hands on the edge, trying to slow my heartbeat. The panic had faded, but its echo still clung to my ribs. My skin felt too awake, too thin. I looked up.

I don't know what I expected to see. With the way the panic had hit, I thought I'd look different. Fried, maybe. Like a cartoon character who just stuck a fork in a socket.

But it was just... me.

My ponytail was half undone, long waves of strawberry-blonde hair falling loose around my face. Sweat clung to the hair at my temples and along my hairline. My skin looked pale, freckled across the bridge of my nose and cheeks, a little blotchy from the heat of the ER. Bright blue eyes. Same as always.

Nothing looked different.

But it felt like something should.

• • •

I was driving home just after midnight. The sky was black—no stars, no moon. Just a sheet of darkness that stretched over the rooftops.

I pulled into the driveway on autopilot and shut the headlights off, the engine barely making a sound. The street was still. No lights coming from the other houses. The whole block felt like it was sleeping. Even the air didn't bother to move.

But our porch light was on.

Michael always left it on for me, even though I told him not to. "It's a waste of power," I'd said once. He kissed my forehead and said, "It's not about the light. It's about you knowing where home is."

I stared at that light for a few seconds longer, then killed the engine and stepped out.

Ashmore, Maine, wasn't much. Wide streets, aging storefronts, more churches than stoplights. No movie theater. No real nightlife unless you counted the two bars everyone rotated through on weekends like a ritual. People called it quiet. Peaceful.

Our house sat at the end of a cul-de-sac, nestled behind a row of tall sycamores. It wasn't big, but it had charm— weathered brick, white trim, flower beds that held the remains of plants I'd tried, and mostly failed, to grow.

The front steps creaked in two places. The ivy along the porch railing had declared war on the siding years ago and never let up. We trimmed it back every few months, and it always came back stronger. I kind of respected it.

It was the kind of house you chose when all you wanted was peace. Not silence exactly, but the kind that wraps around you at the end of a long day and says, you're safe here.

And for a while now, it had felt like home.

I stepped inside and shut the door behind me, the familiar weight of it clicking into place. The entryway opened into the living room. A pair of my boots leaned against the wall, half-tucked on the mat. The couch was soft and a little slouched in the middle, with the quilt from my mom folded over the back.

Our mismatched coffee mugs cluttered the table, next to an old paperback I'd been trying to finish for weeks. The hardwood floors creaked under my steps, except where the old woven rug softened the sound. The hallway led to the back of the house where the kitchen sat with open shelves, chipped counters, and a table we kept saying we'd replace but never did. The stairs curved up from the far wall, narrow and old, with a railing Michael had reinforced after I slipped on it once last winter.

Upstairs held the bathroom, our bedroom, and the tiny office we mostly used for laundry overflow. Nothing fancy. Just enough. It wasn't perfect, but it was ours.

I didn't realize how tense I'd been until I smelled the coffee and heard his voice calling from the kitchen.

"I made coffee!"

I followed the sound of his voice, my feet carrying me past the living room and down the hallway. He stood at the counter when I stepped into the kitchen, turning toward me with a warm smile.

"Decaf, before you yell at me," he said, lifting the mug in his hand.

Michael Brant was thirty-one and unfairly attractive. He was barefoot, wearing sweatpants and one of his old gray hoodies. Somehow, it looked better on him than anything tailored ever could. After almost three years together, I'd stopped being surprised by how effortlessly he wore comfort. He was tall, broad-shouldered but lean, dark blond hair that curled slightly at the ends. His jawline could cut glass, but his smile was soft. Those gray-blue eyes always felt like they were reading me without judging.

"I wasn't going to yell," I murmured, even though I kind of was.

He grinned. "You always yell when I make coffee after midnight."

"Yeah, but you're the one who starts alphabetizing the spice rack at 1 a.m. like a man possessed," I retorted.

He handed me the chipped blue mug Sarah gave me when I was in nursing school, the one with faded cartoon lungs and the phrase "Breathe, Bitch."

It made me laugh when I needed it most. Still did.

Coffee was my weakness—the smell, the ritual, that first sip. It grounded me better than sleep ever could.

I took a long drink. "You make it right," I said quietly.

Michael leaned against the counter, watching me like I was something delicate and valuable. "I remember how you like it. I always will."

My chest ached… just a little.

"You're quiet," he said. "Rough shift?"

"Yeah," I said after a moment. "We had a teenager come in. He was in a car accident. He almost didn't make it."

"Jesus," he murmured. "I hate knowing that's what you're dealing with while I'm watching bad documentaries and waiting for the dryer to finish."

He crossed the room and rested his hands gently on my hips.

"Come on," he said. "Let's get you to bed."

Michael took my hand as we climbed the stairs to our room. The house was quiet, but the noise of the ER still rang in my bones.

I stepped into the bathroom and peeled off my scrubs, dropping them straight into the hamper. The shower hissed to life, steam curling against the glass as I stepped under the spray.

I let the water run hot, hoping it would rinse off the tension, the sweat, the memory of that boy's chest caving under my hands. I washed slowly, like if I scrubbed hard enough, the panic would go too.

When I came out, Michael was brushing his teeth. He handed me my toothbrush, already waiting with toothpaste. We brushed in tandem, bumping hips like we always did when space got tight. He kissed my shoulder as I pulled my hair into a loose braid and changed into an oversized t-shirt.

I climbed into bed and tugged the blanket up, trying to shake off the night still clinging to me.

Michael slipped in beside me, his body warm and solid. He pulled me close, hand resting on my waist. "You okay?"

"Yeah," I lied. "Better now."

He didn't push. He just kissed the back of my neck and whispered, "I love you."

And I whispered it back.

I stared at the ceiling long after his breathing evened out, listening to the rhythmic tick of the old clock on the dresser. The house creaked in the usual places. A pipe groaned.

Normal.

But the longer I lay there, the more the room felt... off. Cooler and thicker. Like the walls had constricted around me while I wasn't looking. I sat up slowly, careful not to wake him. The room was dim, lit only by the low amber light slipping through the curtains.

That's when I noticed it.

The mirror on the far wall—Grandma's old antique one, the one I couldn't bring myself to get rid of—was fogged over.

There was no reason for that. No shower. No change in temperature. Nothing.

I got up and crossed the room, goosebumps crawling down my arms. My fingers hovered just an inch from the glass. Then, barely audible, like a memory pressed between layers of time, I heard it.

A whisper. My name.

"Lena."

I snapped back, stumbling a step.

I blinked and the mirror was clear.

My chest rose and fell too fast, air scraping in shallow pulls.

Michael stirred behind me in the bed. "Everything okay?"

"Yeah," I said, voice thin. "Just... got cold."

He sat up slightly, rubbing the sleep from his eyes as he looked at me, really looked at me, like he was searching my face for something I didn't say. "Do you want me to grab another blanket?"

"No, it's fine," I replied.

He didn't press. Just reached for me and pulled me gently into his arms, tucking the covers around us.

"Come here," he murmured. "I'll warm you up."

I curled against him, letting his warmth seep into my skin. It should've made me feel better. Safe. But I still couldn't shake the feeling that something had reached for me in the dark.

Sleep came, eventually. But it wasn't peaceful.

Chapter 2

I woke up to an empty bed and the smell of coffee drifting up the stairs. Michael was already gone.

Probably one of his tech client meetings, startup something-or-other. His schedule was weird, but the pay was good and the flexibility even better. I'd stopped asking what he actually *did* a long time ago.

There was a note waiting on my nightstand, folded once and written in his annoyingly perfect handwriting:

Didn't want to wake you, you looked peaceful. I made coffee because I know you're not human without it. I love you, in case you forget today. —M

I smiled and laid there for a second longer, holding the note loosely between my fingers.

My eyes drifted toward the far wall, toward the mirror. It looked normal now. Just glass and silver trim. No fog. No voice whispering my name.

I told myself it was a dream. Stress, maybe. My brain doing weird things after my rough shift. But a part of me didn't buy it.

I set the note down and dragged myself out of bed.

I brushed my teeth, splashed water on my face, and swiped on a little mascara, just enough to darken my lashes. I didn't bother with anything else. The eyes were doing all the work today.

Then I tugged on a pair of worn jeans and the first t-shirt I found that didn't have holes in it. My style wasn't anything fancy. Casual, comfortable, and usually covered in cat hair.

I gave myself a quick once-over in the mirror. I'd braided my hair while it was still damp last night, and now it was doing that uneven, frizzy wave thing it always did. I twisted it into a loose bun and called it good enough.

At twenty-eight, I'd long since made peace with the body I lived in. I hovered around five-seven, average enough to blend in, tall enough to reach the top shelf without a stool. I wasn't runway tall or rail-thin, but I had curves where I liked them and a body that felt like mine. Comfortable and strong in the ways that mattered.

Downstairs, Biscuit, our long-haired gray cat and reluctant roommate, was already on the kitchen counter, yowling dramatically and flicking her tail like I'd kept her waiting for hours. I scratched behind her ears and poured her food.

The coffeepot was still steaming. Naturally. Michael probably programmed the damn thing to stay warm until Armageddon.

I poured myself a cup and leaned against the counter, sipping slowly while watching Biscuit devour her breakfast. The warmth helped a little. Outside the window, the sky was overcast but bright, the kind of gray that made everything feel both calm and restless. I stood there for a long minute, letting the silence settle in, trying not to overthink the strange weight still clinging to the back of my mind.

I shook the thought off and reached for my phone, scrolling through texts and ignoring work emails. One new message made me snort into my mug.

> **Sarah:** *Food and coffee? I need caffeine and to bitch about a man who deserves to step on a Lego.*

God, I loved her.

Sarah had been my ride or die since sophomore year, when she transferred into my high school and sat next to me in chemistry. A total accident that turned into everything. We survived school, bad exes, worse decisions, and an almost-arrest in Vegas we never talk about. She was the one person who could always cut through my bullshit with a single look, and the only one who knew just how deep my cracks ran without needing me to say a word.

I grabbed my keys and headed out.

She was already sitting at our usual spot when I walked into the café, back corner near the window, where we could see people but not be seen. Her tan skin glowed in the light, sunglasses on like she was hiding from paparazzi, and she was aggressively stirring a latte with a tiny wooden stick like it owed her money. She wore a soft pink top tucked into high-waisted skinny jeans, paired with simple black flats. She was effortlessly pretty but still practical. Dark waves framed her face, brushing her shoulders, and even behind the sunglasses, I could practically see that her espresso-colored eyes were narrowed like she was mid-rant in her head and saving the best part for me.

A half-eaten cinnamon roll sat on a napkin beside her, and her oversized leather tote slouched in the chair next to her, no doubt stuffed with paperbacks, red pens, and whatever poorly-written fantasy novel she was tearing apart this week. Editing books paid her bills, but roasting them was her true calling.

"Wow," I said, sliding into the seat across from her. "You look like a woman on the edge."

She lifted her sunglasses just enough to glare at me. "He left me on read for two days, but posted an Instagram Story of his omelet with the caption *"Rise and grind."* She threw up a hand. "And the omelet had *raisins* in it! Like, who does that?"

I blinked. "Sociopaths?"

"You know what I realized, Lena? I'm not mad that he ignored me. I'm mad I almost fell for someone who puts dried fruit in hot eggs on *purpose*."

I laughed and grabbed a menu I wasn't going to use. "Tell me everything."

I flagged down the barista and ordered a coffee while Sarah launched into a full play-by-play of her latest almost-relationship. Apparently, his name was Jake. Or Jax. Or something that sounded like a guy who vaped indoors and called his mom "dude." They'd been texting for two weeks, and he'd already managed to commit two red flags and one beige one.

I leaned in, intrigued. "Which one's beige?" I asked between sips of coffee.

11

"He owns a snake. Voluntarily. No trauma. Just likes snakes."

"Oh no."

"Yeah. And he named it 'Viper.'"

"Oh *no*."

She sighed dramatically, then grinned. "But he's hot. So I'll give him one more chance to disappoint me."

"Excellent. Stay toxic."

She pointed at me with her straw. "Hey. You haven't given me a real update in, like, forever. How's the ER? How's Michael? How's your beautiful but emotionally stunted sister?"

I hesitated just a fraction too long.

Sarah noticed, because of course she did. "Uh-oh."

"It's fine," I said quickly. "Everything's fine. Michael's... Michael. The ER's exhausting. And my sister and I are, you know. Us."

Allie had always been a force. She was four years older, shorter than me, but somehow still managed to seem like the taller one in every room. Light brown hair, always perfectly styled, not a single strand ever out of place. She was the kind of woman who made people sit up straighter without realizing why, and she wore control like perfume. A psychiatrist, of course, because God forbid she *not* know exactly how the brain worked while also being impossible to read.

Sarah leaned in, resting her chin on her hand. "You miss her?"

I did. God, I did. But missing her wasn't the same as fixing things. Our parents' deaths split everything open, leaving Allie and me drifting in our own pain, too raw to reach for each other, too angry to say the things that might've stitched us back together. After the accident, it felt like we were caught in two different storms, each of us just trying to survive without making it worse for the other. But silence... silence grows teeth. And it bites harder the longer you let it linger.

"Of course I miss her," I said.

"But?" Sarah pressed.

I sighed. "But we're both too damn stubborn to admit we were wrong about anything. Especially after we lost Mom and Dad. Grief like that… it just makes everything messy."

She gave me a knowing look. "I get it."

We let the quiet settle between us for a few beats.

"I'm just saying," she mumbled through a mouthful of cinnamon roll, "if you ever want to trade your emotionally exhausting life for mine, I'll swap you a red flag man-child and a snake named Viper."

I grinned. "Tempting."

We stayed there for another hour, tucked into our corner booth, trading stories, sarcasm, and overpriced café food. Sarah ordered a second latte she didn't need. I laughed more than I expected to, and for a little while, everything felt normal.

Like the strangeness of last night had been nothing more than a dream.

After brunch, Sarah decided we needed to "walk off the carbs and judge other people's fashion choices," which somehow led us to wandering down a quieter part of Main Street lined with boutique shops, vintage clothing stores, and a few buildings that looked like they'd been forgotten by time.

One storefront caught my eye—a narrow place wedged between a tea shop and an antique map store. The glass was dusty, and the old wood sign above the door read: **Rowan's Books & Curiosities.**

Sarah grinned. "That place looks like it smells like incense and regrets. Let's go."

The bell over the door chimed when we stepped inside, and instantly we were wrapped in the smell of old paper, faded herbs, and something warm and woody like oak and clove. The space was cramped but charming, the shelves mismatched and tilting, the aisles narrow. Books were stacked everywhere. Some looked centuries old, others recent enough to still smell like new ink.

There were little trinkets tucked between the shelves—carved stones, antique pendants, even a bowl full of old skeleton keys. A small sign above the register read: *No Photos. No Returns. No Coincidences.*

Sarah made a beeline for a display near the front, then let out a loud, dramatic gasp. "Oh my god. Lena. *Twilight.* Hardcover. Original covers. It's like our teenage fangirl ghosts just screamed."

I snorted. "We were insufferable."

"We were iconic," she corrected. "I wore a Team Jacob shirt to gym class for an entire semester. I had no regrets."

"You still don't," I shot back.

She snapped her fingers. "Exactly."

I wandered deeper into the store while she lovingly flipped through pages of glittery vampire nostalgia. There was something comforting about the place. The smell reminded me of my grandmother's attic, where I used to help her sort through boxes she refused to throw out.

Then I felt it. A pull, deep and low. Like something inside me had just turned its head to listen.

I stopped in front of a shelf half-hidden behind a hanging curtain of beads. One book stood out. It was bound in deep green leather, no title, no markings. The edges were worn, and the cover looked soft from too many hands. I couldn't explain why, but it felt… familiar. Like I'd seen it before.

I reached toward it.

"Lena," Sarah's voice cut in close behind me. I jumped.

She held up a used copy of *Vampires and the Single Girl* with a smirk. "Weird little book cave or not, I feel like this is peak literature."

I glanced back at the green book, something about it tugging at me again. But I let my hand fall.

"Nah," I said, backing away. "Not today."

We wandered a little more, debated the ethics of love triangles, and made fun of at least six questionable book covers before leaving the store.

It was the kind of day that should've felt normal, and it almost did. But under it all, beneath the laughter and the comfort of familiar streets, something still hummed.

14

Tucked away. Waiting.

Chapter 3

The sky was dark by the time I got home.

My bag was full of overpriced chocolate I didn't need and books I probably wouldn't read, except for the one I kept thinking about and didn't buy.

Michael was in the kitchen, humming a tune I didn't recognize as he stirred something on the stove. He was wearing one of those soft, perfectly worn t-shirts that somehow made him look both relaxed and put together. He had no business looking that good while stirring sauce, like some domestic god who didn't know it.

"Is this what it's like to be spoiled?" I asked, setting the bag on the counter.

He turned, smiling. "It's called basic love and care, babe. You should try it sometime."

I rolled my eyes and reached past him for a spoon. "What is this?"

He gently swatted my hand away. "Dinner. Hands off. It's a surprise."

I scrunched my face. "Last time you said that, it involved quinoa."

He laughed. "Okay, fair. No quinoa. Just trust me, you'll like this one."

He set two plates down on the table—pasta, roasted vegetables, garlic bread that smelled like actual heaven—and poured us each a glass of wine like it was just any other night.

But there was something about the way he looked at me tonight. Like I was made of something breakable. Like he saw every sleepless thought and still wanted to stay.

We ate in comfortable silence for a while, the kind that comes from knowing each other too well. I kicked off my shoes under the table and let my shoulders drop.

"You seem lighter," he said eventually.

"Spent the day with Sarah," I replied. "Laughed too much. Ate things I shouldn't have. Got emotionally attacked by a *Twilight* display."

Michael chuckled, eyes crinkling. "You two are dangerous together."

"Honestly, it's impressive we haven't been banned from Main Street," I said.

He reached across the table and slid his thumb gently across the back of my hand. "I'm glad you had a good day."

And that's all it took—one look, one simple gesture—and suddenly I was back there.

Back to the first time I saw him.

It was just another shift. Just another hour of chaos in the ER.

Until he came through the doors, carrying a woman in his arms.

Blood soaked one side of her shirt, and Michael's own clothes were smeared with it. He looked panicked, but focused. The kind of calm that came from adrenaline and instinct.

"She walked into traffic," he said breathlessly. "I didn't see where she came from, I just saw the car hit her. I couldn't leave her there."

I remember how steady his hands were as he set her down. How he kept pressure on the wound without flinching. How he moved out of the way the second we took over, but didn't disappear.

He stayed. He sat in the corner of the waiting room until we stabilized her, asked for nothing, didn't make it about him.

Afterward, I brought him a cup of coffee.

"You okay?" I asked.

He looked at me, eyes bright with quiet gratitude, and gave me a warm, genuine smile. "I think so. Are you?"

I gave a tired smile. "Depends on the hour."

We talked for twenty minutes that night. And when I saw him again, a few days later at the coffee shop across from the hospital, it felt like fate.

18

I blinked, the memory still lingering like perfume on skin. I hadn't thought about that night in a while. How calm he was in the chaos, how he never asked for anything, just helped. I remember thinking, *That's all it takes, isn't it? Someone showing up when you don't expect it.*

And maybe that's why I fell so fast. He made it feel easy to exist.

Michael's voice pulled me back.

"You okay?" he asked gently.

I nodded, still a little dazed. "Yeah. Just remembering."

He reached for my hand again. "Come upstairs with me."

There was no pressure in his voice, just an invitation. But heat curled low in my stomach, spreading like a secret only my body understood.

Upstairs, the room was dim and warm. Michael closed the door behind us and crossed to me slowly, his gaze locked on mine. His fingers brushed my cheek, then slid back into my hair. He kissed me like he had all the time in the world—leisurely, deeply, as though savoring every second. I melted into it, into him. Everything else fell away.

Clothes hit the floor in pieces—his shirt, my jeans, both of us pulling at fabric like we couldn't stand the barrier between us.

His hands mapped me like he'd done it a hundred times and still hadn't discovered enough. His mouth moved over my skin, and when he said my name, it sounded like it was the answer to every question he'd ever asked.

I shivered, pulling him closer. His mouth traced slow, lingering kisses along my neck, the kind that made my pulse skip and my fingers dig into his shoulders. He lingered, his lips gentle against my skin, trailing lower with each kiss.

When his lips found my breast, he paused like he was memorizing the shape of me. My nipples tightened beneath the drag of his tongue, and heat pooled low in my belly—a slow, steady ache that bloomed with every careful movement.

His hands moved lower, tracing the curve of my waist, down to my hips, then gliding over my thighs like he was exploring me, like I was made for him alone.

The kisses kept tracing lower—across my ribs, my stomach—each one slower than the last, like he was savoring the path.

When he reached my lower belly, he paused, eyes meeting mine with a look that made my whole body tighten. Then he rose to his feet, hands slipping under my thighs as he lifted me effortlessly. I let out a gasp, arms wrapping around his shoulders as he carried me the short distance to the bed and laid me down carefully.

He knelt between my thighs, eyes never leaving mine as his hands gently eased my legs apart. Every part of me was bare and waiting, and then his mouth was on me.

The first stroke of his tongue sent a jolt through me, sharp and devastating in the best way. He moved slowly at first, tasting me like he had nowhere else in the world to be. Every flick, every circle was precise and patient like he knew exactly how to unravel me.

My hips lifted instinctively, chasing the pressure. The heat built fast, coiling low and tight until I was trembling, clinging to the sheets, his name slipping past my lips. I came with a gasp, the world shattering around me in waves of light and sensation.

He kept his mouth on me, tender and relentless, until the aftershocks left me trembling—hips jerking, hands fisting the sheets like I needed something to hold onto just to survive it. My body was still twitching when he finally pulled back, and even then, he paused to press one last kiss to the inside of my thigh.

When he looked up at me, his pupils were wide, lips slick, chest rising like he couldn't get enough air, or enough of me.

"Jesus, Lena," he said, moving up my body. "You're so fucking perfect."

And then he was above me, between my thighs, his body pressing into mine as if he couldn't bear the space between us a second longer.

"I need you," he breathed.

I pulled him to me, already dizzy from everything we were, everything this was. He kissed me hard, deeper than before. I could still feel the echo of the orgasm humming through my veins, but it didn't matter. I wanted more. I wanted him.

I wrapped my legs around his waist, pulling him closer, and he groaned against my mouth, like he'd been holding himself back for hours and couldn't anymore. He slid inside me in one smooth, slow thrust. Like he'd rehearsed it a thousand times in dreams and was finally where he was meant to be.

A moan slipped from the both of us. His hands framed my face, thumbs brushing my cheeks as if he needed to hold on to something real.

"Lena," he said, "you have no idea what you mean to me."

I didn't speak. I just held him tighter as he started to move.

It was slow at first—steady and deep, like he wanted to feel every inch of me, like he didn't want to miss a single reaction. My hands slid across his back, fingers digging in as each thrust sent sparks through me. The pleasure was intense, but it wasn't just that. It was the way he looked at me. The way he touched me. Like I was everything.

He kissed me through it—my lips, my neck, the curve of my jaw—never pulling too far away, never breaking that connection. Every sound he made was for me. Every gasp, every low, shuddering groan, every whispered promise.

"You're mine," he breathed. "You always have been."

The heat built between us—slow, then suddenly all at once, like a flame catching wind. My body tightened, back arching into him, and I felt him shudder as I came again, the rush crashing over me like a wave.

He followed right after, a raw sound tearing from his throat as he buried himself in me, every muscle drawn tight in release.

We stayed there for a while, tangled and breathless, our bodies locked tight. Then he kissed my temple, my cheek, the corner of my mouth. Little, lingering touches that were gentle and warm.

"I love you," he said.

Wrapped in his arms, with nothing but the soft rhythm of his breath and the warmth of his skin, I let the tension slide out of me.

Sleep came easily after that.

Chapter 4

I woke up before the sun, cradled in that hazy space between dreams and daylight, with Michael's arm slung heavy across my waist. His body was warm against mine.

For a minute, I didn't move. I just laid there, staring at the faint blue glow bleeding in through the curtains, listening to the tick of the clock. The sheets were twisted, still shaped by the way we moved the night before. I didn't want to get up. Not yet.

Michael murmured something in his sleep and pulled me closer, his face pressed into the curve of my shoulder.

I smiled. Not the kind I gave patients or strangers or people who asked how I was doing and didn't really want the answer. This one was unguarded and real. I let my eyes drift shut again, just for a little while.

Michael stirred behind me, his voice raspy with sleep. "You awake?"

"Barely," I replied.

His hand slid over my hip, fingers tracing lazy circles against my skin. "You were twitching a little last night. Dreaming?"

"Maybe," I said. "I don't remember."

I almost told him about the mirror and my whispered name. The way the air had felt wrong—thick and still, like something had stepped just out of sight. But the memory felt fuzzy now, half-dissolved in the softness of morning light and the comfort of his arms. And I didn't want to ruin a perfect morning.

Eventually though, we had to get up. He pulled on sweatpants and wandered downstairs to make coffee, and I took my time in the shower, breathing in the steam and pretending the world could wait.

After a while, the water ran cold. I shut it off, stepped out, and wrapped myself in a towel, steam coiling around my ankles. Towel clutched around me, I moved through the quiet hallway toward the bedroom, pausing when something caught my eye.

It was a box. It was tucked halfway under the bed, one of those old cardboard ones I hadn't touched since Grandma died. I didn't remember it sticking out before.

Maybe it got pushed out during last night's... enthusiasm.

I crouched, dragging it out with a grunt. Dust coated the lid. Faint handwriting, faded from age, still marked the top corner:

Margot's

My stomach twisted. I wasn't sure why. Maybe because I had forgotten it was there.

I sat on the floor, brought the box to my lap, and lifted the lid. The scent of lavender, parchment, and peppermint tea drifted up. It smelled like her in a way that made my chest ache. There were a few old photographs, crocheted doilies that she made herself, and a tiny vial of dried herbs sealed with wax. On top, there was a stack of letters tied together with a blue ribbon. I picked one up and turned it over.

It was a small envelope with *Corinne Moraine* scrawled across the front in Grandma's familiar script.

Corinne.

Grandma's oldest friend. The one who used to sit on the porch and drink tea, murmuring in that soft, steady voice like the world moved slower for her. I hadn't seen her in years. Not since Grandma died when I was fifteen.

They said she'd been admitted to a psychiatric facility not long after. Called it early-onset dementia, like that explained everything. Told me it wasn't uncommon, just one of those things that happens sometimes.

But Grandma had never mentioned Corinne being sick. Not once. And she would've. Wouldn't she?

The envelope trembled in my hands, but I didn't open it. I turned it over once more, then tucked it back under the ribbon like I hadn't touched it at all. I put the box back under the bed and rose slowly, still wrapped in the towel, still not sure if the chill on my skin came from the morning air or from seeing her handwriting again.

I got dressed in a daze, not really thinking about it. Just jeans, a shirt, and hair up. Something about the letter clung to me, but I didn't know what to do with it.

By the time I made it downstairs, Michael had already poured two cups of coffee and was leaning against the counter, scrolling through something on his phone. He looked up when he saw me and smiled like I was his favorite part of the day.

"There she is," he said, holding out a mug. "Thought maybe I'd have to come rescue you from a shampoo-related tragedy."

Normally, I'd fire back something sarcastic. This morning, I just muttered a quiet "Thanks" and took a sip.

He watched me for a second, then tilted his head. "You alright?"

"Yeah," I said, too quickly. "Just tired."

He didn't press. Just gave a nod and leaned back against the counter like he hadn't noticed anything at all.

"Want breakfast?" he asked.

"Just coffee for now."

We moved through the quiet morning like we always did, a rhythm we'd built without ever really talking about it. He made toast he wouldn't eat. I fed Biscuit a little more than she needed. We passed each other in the kitchen like two orbiting moons.

But the name was still in my head.

Corinne Moraine.

And the letter I hadn't opened.

Michael was sipping his coffee like it was just another morning and not the edge of a cliff I couldn't see. "You working today?" he asked.

"Yeah," I replied. "Double shift. Covering for Erin. She's got a wedding or something."

He nodded, eyes glancing to his phone again. "Long day ahead, then. Want me to bring you dinner later?"

"You don't have to."

"I know I don't. But I want to."

I gave him a small smile. "Sure. That'd be nice."

"Alright," he said. He set his mug down and crossed the room, pressing a kiss to my forehead. "I've got a call in ten. You good if I head out?"

"Of course."

He looked at me for a second too long. "You sure you're okay?"

"Yeah. Just tired," I said again.

His thumb brushed my cheek like he was wiping something away that wasn't there. "Try to rest before your shift. Promise?"

I nodded.

He grabbed his keys, tossed a final glance toward the cat, and disappeared out the front door.

And then I was alone. The silence he left behind was immediate. I stood there for a minute, hands wrapped around my mug, watching the steam swirl and vanish.

Then I moved. Back upstairs, I knelt beside the bed and pulled the box out again. It didn't feel heavy, not in the physical sense. But something in it pulsed, like memory pressing against the edges of the cardboard.

I slid the ribbon off the stack of letters and picked up the one addressed to Corinne. My fingers hesitated over the seal. I didn't know what I was expecting. Instructions? Warnings? A confession?

I peeled it open carefully, unfolding the paper with hands that didn't feel like mine.

Grandma's handwriting curved across the page, familiar and elegant and just a little unsteady. My fingers brushed the ink like it might smudge. As if touching it too hard would make her disappear all over again.

Corinne,

I don't have much time left. We've both felt it coming, haven't we? That slow unraveling in the bones, the breath, the magic. It's not something you

26

can outrun. And I'm not trying to. But I need to make sure she's taken care of.

Lena will need you one day. And when the time comes, she will need your guidance more than anyone's.

I've done what I could to keep her safe. It was never meant to be forever, only long enough to give her the chance at a life untouched by certain dangers.

When it begins, she'll be scared. She's always been so practical, so grounded. She won't believe it at first. You'll have to be patient. Gentle, but firm.

She doesn't know what she carries. She doesn't know what we've kept from her. I did it to protect her, you know that, but I also knew the truth would find her eventually.

When I'm gone, it's your turn. Guide her. Show her what she is. What she can be. Keep her safe until she can stand on her own.

And Corinne, if anyone tries to stop you, don't let them near her. Lena isn't just gifted. She's rare. And someone out there will want that power for themselves. Don't let them take it.

Watch for them. And trust your instincts.

Always,

~ Margot

I stared at the letter for a long time. The words blurred and reformed, over and over, as my brain tried to catch up to what my heart already knew.

Something was happening to me. Something old. Something buried. And Grandma had known. She'd planned for it.

And now… I had no idea what came next.

I folded the letter back along its creases, slower than I needed to, and stared at Grandma's name written at the bottom like it might reach out and steady me.

It didn't.

My hands were trembling again. I set the paper gently on top of the stack, then closed the box and slid it under the bed like that would somehow undo what I'd just read. Like I could shove the truth back into the box, into the dark, and pretend I hadn't seen it.

But I had. Grandma knew. Corinne knew. And now I knew too. Something inside me quivered, not fear exactly. More like a ripple. The faint scrape of something turning beneath the surface.

I stood up slowly, trying to will my limbs into steadiness. They didn't cooperate. I caught my reflection in the antique mirror and didn't recognize the look in my eyes. They were still blue. Still wide. Still ringed with the same dark circles that had been clinging to me for weeks. But something in them had changed. Like a door had opened, just a crack, and whatever waited behind it had started to wake up.

Chapter 5

The ER felt louder than usual. Not noisy, just... charged.

Every sound came in crisp and jagged, as if my brain had forgotten how to filter. The click of a pen, the echo of a monitor alarm, the sharp inhale of someone struggling to breathe in the next room.

It was just another shift I told myself.

I kept my head down, went through the motions. Charted, cleaned wounds, smiled when I was supposed to. I played the part of the RN I was trained to be. And for most of the night, that's all I tried to be.

Until Room Four.

The girl on the gurney couldn't have been more than eight years old. She was small, pale, and her chest was rising in shallow, erratic pulls. Her lips were tinged blue and her fingers twitched against the rumpled blanket.

Asthma attack, the chart read.

The room was already in motion. A respiratory therapist was setting up a nebulizer. Molly—my favorite coworker and the kind of nurse you'd want in a foxhole—snapped open a drawer, grabbing albuterol. Someone called for a pulse ox.

I stepped to the bedside, slipping the stethoscope into my ears. "Let's get oxygen on her," I said, voice steady. I leaned in towards her chest to listen to her lungs... and then something hit me.

It wasn't anything I could explain. It was like there was a warm thrumming energy that moved through my hands. My palms tingled and a sudden heat spread up my arms. It was soft, strange and wrong—no, not wrong. Just... unfamiliar.

I felt it *move*. Out of me and into the girl's chest. Her eyes fluttered. Her fingers jerked. Then she coughed, sharp and sudden. And the next breath came easier.

I yanked my hand back like I'd touched fire. The feeling vanished in an instant.

What just—I glanced around, heart pounding. No one was looking at me.

Molly was focused on the monitor, then looked down at the girl. "That was fast," she muttered.

The respiratory therapist blinked. "O2 sats climbing already?"

The attending physician looked up from the open laptop on the counter, brow furrowed. "Huh. Must've caught it right in time."

They all kept moving—adjusting meds, documenting vitals, resetting for the next wave.

But I couldn't. My hands still buzzed, the phantom heat curling under my skin.

The girl blinked up at the ceiling, no longer gasping. Like the whole thing had been a scare and nothing more.

I stepped back slowly, trying to steady the rapid drum of my pulse. *What the hell just happened?*

"Lena?" the attending physician said, glancing up.

I blinked. "Yeah."

I stepped back in, checked the monitor, adjusted the oxygen. Normal. Calm. Like none of it had happened. Just another moment in the middle of the shift. Except I knew better. Something had passed between us. And it didn't come from anything I learned in nursing school.

• • •

The next morning, I woke up with the hospital still clinging to me. It always did—the smell of antiseptic in my nose, the ache behind my eyes, the feeling that I'd forgotten something important but couldn't remember.

But this time, it was more than that. I kept seeing the little girl's face. The color returning to her cheeks. The way her chest had started rising more steadily.

And the warmth that had moved through me like it belonged to someone else.

I sat on the edge of the bed, hair a tangled mess, feet still bare. Biscuit hopped up beside me with a meow, curling into a loaf. I didn't pet her. I didn't move.

Michael wasn't in bed. I vaguely remembered him mumbling something the night before about an early meeting a couple towns over.

Eventually, I reached for my phone.

Lena: *You up?*

A few seconds later:

Sarah: *Bitch it's 6:43 am what the hell*

Lena: *Something weird happened at work.*

Sarah: *Weird how? Like "patient tried to shank me with a tongue depressor" or "weird" like capital W*

Lena: *Capital W. Something happened. I don't know what it means*

Sarah: *I'm making coffee. Come over. And grab donuts on the way.*

Lena: *Okay.*

I stared at the last message for a few seconds longer than I should have. Then I got up, pulled on a pair of black leggings and a loose-fitting shirt, and shoved my feet into sneakers. At the door, I hesitated, then grabbed one of Michael's hoodies off the back of a chair and tugged it on. A quick stop at the bakery for donuts, and then I was on my way.

Sarah's apartment always smelled like coffee, vanilla, and the faintest trace of the cinnamon candle she forgot to blow out half the time.

I walked in without knocking. She never locked the door when she knew I was coming.

She was standing in the kitchen wearing plaid pajama pants, an old hoodie, and a sleep mask pushed up like a headband. Her hair frizzed around her face. She was drinking coffee from a mug that said *"I survived another meeting that should have been an email."*

She blinked at me over the rim of her cup. "You look like someone who's seen a ghost. Or almost summoned one."

31

"I think…" I stopped, swallowed. "Something happened last night. At work."

She gave me a wondering look, but didn't say anything.

"There was a kid," I said. "She was there for a really bad asthma attack. She couldn't breathe. And I…"

I shook my head.

"I didn't *do* anything. I just… touched her. Like, normal assessment stuff. But it felt like something went through me. And then she could breathe again."

Silence.

"Like…" I huffed a laugh, but it broke halfway through. "Like I healed her. Somehow. With… I don't even know."

Sarah blinked once. Then took a sip of her coffee like she'd been waiting for this moment her whole life.

"Cool," she said. "Start from the top."

So I told her. About the little girl with the asthma attack. About how her breathing had been shallow and failing. How I'd touched her chest with my stethoscope and felt something spark under my skin like a hum, or a pulse, or a wave of warmth. I told her how it had moved through me and into the girl. How she'd started to breathe easier. How no one else seemed to notice anything strange, but I knew. I *felt* it. It wasn't normal. It wasn't medicine. It was something else.

When I finished, I took a long sip of coffee and waited for her to say I was being dramatic. That I'd imagined it. Or that I was insane.

But she didn't. She just watched me for a moment, then asked, "Are you sure no one else noticed anything?"

"No. She just… got better. And I pulled my hand back like I was burned. I didn't even chart it. I didn't know what to say. It's not the first thing, either. There's been other stuff."

Sarah's eyes widened. "Wait. What other stuff?"

I hesitated. "There've been things. Little things. Lights flickering and breaking in the ER. A mirror fogging up for no reason. I heard… something. My name being whispered. And I felt this panic in my chest, but it wasn't mine. It felt like someone else's fear."

I paused, then added, "And there was this book, at that weird little shop we wandered into the other day. Green leather, no title. I didn't even touch it, but... it felt like it was watching me. Like it was waiting."

Sarah blinked. "Jesus, Lena."

"I know how it sounds. I thought I was just tired, or cracked from work stress. But this... last night was different. It was real. I felt it happen."

She stepped around the counter and pulled me into a hug before I could say anything else. No questions. No judgment.

Just warmth.

"I've got you," she murmured. "Whatever this is... we'll figure it out."

I took a long sip of coffee, trying to find the right words. My fingers itched like they were remembering something before my brain could catch up. Then I reached into my bag and pulled out the envelope.

"I brought this," I said quietly.

Sarah raised an eyebrow, watching me place it carefully on the counter between us like it might break. "What is it?"

"A letter from my grandmother. It was addressed to her friend, Corinne. I found it yesterday in a box I hadn't opened since she died."

Sarah's gaze snapped between me and the envelope. "Did you read it?"

I nodded. "Yeah."

"And?"

"It wasn't about recipes or knitting or old memories." I paused. "It was about me."

Sarah didn't move.

"She knew something was coming," I said quietly. "Something in me. She kept it hidden to protect me, but it's always been there. And Corinne was supposed to help guide me when it started."

"And did she?" Sarah asked gently.

I shook my head. "No. She's in a facility now. They said it was early-onset dementia. But after reading the letter... I'm not sure it's just that."

Sarah reached for the envelope and turned it over carefully, like she expected it to hum or glow. "Do you think your grandma was...?"

"Magic?" I said quietly.

Sarah looked up. "Do you?"

I didn't answer. I didn't have to.

Sarah opened the envelope with the same care she'd use on something sacred. She unfolded the paper slowly, her eyes scanning each word like they might vanish if she looked too fast.

The silence between us stretched, filled only by the faint drip of her coffee maker and the sound of a neighbor's door down the hall.

"She wrote this for Corinne," Sarah said. "But it feels like she knew you'd end up reading it."

I nodded. "That's what scares me."

"She planned for this," Sarah said.

"What if I don't want it?" I asked. "What if I can't handle it?"

Sarah folded the letter gently and slid it back into the envelope. "Then we figure it out together."

I stared at her. "You don't even hesitate."

"Because I know you. And I've seen you hold your shit together through more than most people could handle in a lifetime." Her voice was firmer now. "And if Margot's right, if your powers are waking up, then it's already happening. You don't get to choose *if* anymore. Only *how*."

• • •

They say the internet has everything.

Turns out that's a lie.

After breakfast, if coffee and half a dozen donuts even count, Sarah pulled out her laptop and parked us on the couch like we were preparing for a research mission in a fantasy novel.

"Okay," she said, fingers poised dramatically over the keyboard. "Where do we start? Witchcraft 101? Ancient bloodlines? Sparkle-induced meltdowns?"

"Maybe... family magic?" I offered, pulling a throw blanket over my lap. "Or powers that come from inside you. Not spells or potions or whatever."

Sarah nodded and typed as she talked. "Okay. Bloodline magic... intuitive powers... emotional transference... Let's see what Google thinks of all that."

What we got was... not helpful.

One site had a glittery GIF of a howling wolf with text that read: *Your aura remembers past lives! Unlock your lunar lineage for just $44.44/month.*

Another had a forum thread titled **"My Cat Controls Weather."**

"I think Biscuit's been holding out on me," I muttered.

Sarah snorted. "Honestly, wouldn't even be the weirdest thing about her."

We kept digging through blog posts that referenced "lemur familiars," Etsy shops that sold "custom hex jars," and one particularly chaotic site that claimed you could absorb magic from moonlight if you danced naked and "opened your third eye."

Sarah leaned back with a groan. "Okay, I'm tapping out. Either this stuff doesn't exist or we suck at Googling magic."

"We're not going to find real magic on page three of Google, are we?"

"Nope," she said, shutting the laptop. "Which means we're doing the only logical thing."

I tilted my head. "Which is?"

She stood and pointed to me like a general issuing orders. "We're going out tonight. We're going to wear clothes that make us look like bad decisions. We're going to drink things with umbrellas. And we're going to pretend the world isn't quietly unspooling around you for like... four hours."

35

I blinked. "That's your plan to handle my awakening magical trauma?"

"Absolutely," she said. "You're running on coffee, anxiety, and ghost mirror energy. It's not sustainable. You need a reset. A normal night. No magic, no mystery, just drinks, music, and possibly regrettable dancing."

She pulled out her phone and started typing. "I'm texting Michael and telling him to meet us at the bar at eight. That seals it."

Then she grabbed her keys. "Come on. We're going shopping. I demand dramatic outfit montages."

• • •

The boutique Sarah dragged me to was one of those places where the lighting was suspiciously flattering and everything smelled like grapefruit and ambition.

Clothes hung from gold racks like curated chaos—lace bralettes next to faux leather miniskirts, silky blouses draped artfully beside sequined crop tops no one could wear a bra with. A disco ball turned slowly overhead, catching light from a neon sign that read *Hot Mess Energy* in cursive.

A sales associate with perfect eyeliner and combat boots gave us a nod of approval as we walked in. Sarah immediately made a beeline for a rack labeled *Weekend Recklessness.*

I hovered by the door, arms crossed. "I feel underdressed for just walking in here."

"That's the point," Sarah said, flipping through hangers with dangerous speed. "You're about to be reborn in retail."

"I don't need to be reborn. I just need something to wear for drinks."

"You need to feel hot. And slightly unhinged. Like a woman with a secret and really good thighs."

"I'm begging you to stop talking."

She grinned and tossed a hanger over her shoulder at me. I caught it before it smacked me in the face.

36

It was a dress. Midnight blue. Short. Fitted through the waist, with a neckline that dipped just enough to make me consider a backup sweater. The fabric was soft but structured and the thin straps crossed over the open back like it had been engineered to make people stare.

It was the kind of dress I'd reach for, then chicken out and pretend I grabbed it by mistake.

I held it up. "You want me to wear this?"

Sarah grinned. "I want your eyes to commit a murder. That color makes them insane."

"Sarah..."

She held up a hand. "Lena. You've been hiding behind baggy clothes and safe choices for too long. You need to remember you have legs. And boobs. And rage. Let's dress for all three."

I snorted. "You're the worst."

"I'm the best. Try it on."

The dressing room had the kind of mirrors that should've been outlawed, too bright and too many angles. I tugged the dress over my head and immediately regretted every decision that led me here.

It was tight. Short. Clung in places I usually hid and left very little to the imagination.

"Okay," Sarah called from the other side of the curtain. "Let's see it."

"I hate you," I muttered.

"That's not a no," she said.

I pulled the curtain back just a few inches.

Sarah's jaw dropped. "Holy shit."

I glared. "That's not helpful."

She yanked the curtain the rest of the way open and stepped back like she was witnessing a religious vision. "Lena. You look like a woman who buries secrets and bodies."

"That's not comforting," I replied.

"It's empowering." She circled me once. "That dress is doing God's work. Look at your waist. Look at your legs. Look at your boobs. Actually, don't. I'm jealous."

I crossed my arms, which just made the neckline worse. "It's too much."

"It's just enough," she said. "You don't have to pretend to be okay tonight. But you *can* pretend to be a badass. Sometimes the outside helps the inside catch up."

I looked at my reflection again. The girl in the mirror wasn't quite me, but she wasn't broken either. She looked like she might survive something.

I didn't say yes. But I didn't take the dress off, either.

"Okay," I said as I stepped back into the dressing room. "The dress stays. But I'm wearing my flat sandals."

Sarah looked personally offended. "Absolutely not."

"They're comfortable."

"They're also tan and orthopedic-adjacent. You look like a dangerous siren in that dress. You cannot complete the look with 'casual stroll through Target.'"

I sighed. "So what am I supposed to wear? Heels? I'll fall and die."

Sarah was already halfway across the store. "Trust the process!"

Five minutes later, she returned with a box like she'd just retrieved the holy grail from a backroom shrine.

She popped the lid and revealed a pair of strappy black heels that looked like they had opinions.

"They're going to kill me," I said.

"They're going to remind you how good it feels to own the room," she replied. "Try them on. Just one lap around the fitting room. If you fall, I'll pretend I don't know you."

I slipped them on, expecting instant regret but somehow, they fit. Like they belonged with the dress. Like maybe I did, too.

I took a few steps. Wobbled once. Straightened.

Sarah gave a slow clap. "Hot *and* coordinated. My work here is done."

I stared down at my legs, slightly taller, a lot more exposed, and felt something inside me. Confidence? Disbelief? Both.

"Fine," I said. "We'll get the shoes."

"Yes!" Sarah shot to her feet like she'd just won something.

Back at her place, we cranked the music loud enough to rattle the walls, raided her makeup bag, and took turns curling each other's hair like we were seventeen again and getting ready for prom.

Sarah twisted pieces of my hair into soft waves and misted it with something that smelled expensive before giving it a nod of approval. My makeup was bolder than usual—dark smoky eyes, a sweep of highlighter, and berry lipstick that looked more confident than I felt.

I gave myself one last look in the mirror. Not my usual jeans-and-sweatshirt reflection. This version of me had sharp cheekbones, killer lashes, and the look of someone who might actually believe she belonged in that dress.

And yet… she still felt like me. Just hidden underneath a little armor.

Sarah, meanwhile, looked like a red-carpet warning label. She had slick red lipstick, winged liner sharp enough to kill, and a crimson fitted dress that dared the world to keep up. She smiled at her reflection, then fluffed her curls with both hands like a lioness testing the wind.

The dresses we'd picked showed off our shoulders and with them, the matching tattoos we'd gotten years ago. Each one was a heart, bold in black ink, with soft watercolor shades bleeding around the edges like a painting come to life. Blues, purples, and hints of rose faded into one another, giving the design a weightless, almost glowing look.

While she fussed with her earrings, I pulled out my phone and fired off a quick message to Michael:

Lena: *Heading out with Sarah. See you there.*
Michael: *I'll be the one pretending I belong with the cool crowd.*
Lena: *Just a heads-up, the dress I'm wearing leaves little to the imagination…*

Michael: *I don't need to rely on my imagination.*
My tongue has tasted every part of your body.
But just so you know, I'm going to need to
stretch before I fight off the competition.
I smiled, just a little, and dropped the phone into my bag.

• • •

There were only two bars in town, and this was the nicer one, the one that pretended it belonged in a city with rooftop lounges and craft cocktail tours. Edison bulbs, reclaimed wood, and drinks with ingredients like "charred rosemary foam." It was trying too hard, but somehow, it worked. It was loud but cozy, packed but not claustrophobic. The kind of place that made you feel cooler just for walking in.

Sarah and I walked in side by side. Michael was already there, waiting at a high-top near the back. He stood the second he saw me. He wore a dark suit, clean and fitted, and the top of his shirt was unbuttoned just enough to make him look casual yet put together. His eyes swept over me. Not hungry or possessive. Just... reverent. Like I'd done something impossible by showing up like this.

We made our way toward him, my pulse kicking up just a little under his gaze.

"Wow," he said, pressing a kiss to my cheek. "You look…"

"I warned her," Sarah said. "I told her this look should come with a warning label."

Michael smiled, then pulled out my chair. "You're both dangerous."

A few minutes later, Sarah's date arrived. The infamous Viper Boy. Jax. Or was it Jake? Honestly, I'd forgotten to ask his real name.

He was average height, but still towered over Sarah's shorter frame. His light brown hair was long and his shirt had *Namaste in Bed* printed on it in block letters.

"So this is the famous Lena," he said, sliding into the seat beside Sarah and immediately throwing an arm over her shoulders. "Gotta say, I pictured someone… bigger."

Sarah rolled her eyes. "Don't be weird, Jax."

So Jax it is, I thought, a little relieved to finally know for sure.

"I'm just saying," he said with a lopsided grin. "For a nurse, she's kinda soft. Don't you have to, like, lift people or something?"

Sarah's eyes narrowed.

Before I could say anything, Michael leaned forward, calm and casual, but with an edge so clean it could cut glass.

"She's stronger than you'll ever be," he said, voice even. "You don't need to prove your worth by trying to chip away at someone else's."

Jax blinked. "It was a joke."

Michael smiled. It didn't reach his eyes. "Try a better one next time."

The moment stretched, tension thick as wet rope. Jax looked away first. Michael turned back to his drink like nothing had happened. Then, under the table, his hand found mine. I didn't say a anything. But I held on tighter.

For a while, the drinks flowed, the music thumped, and it almost felt like things were normal.

Michael ordered for me without asking. Not in a controlling way, but because he remembered what I liked. A raspberry mojito, extra mint. He leaned close when the music got too loud, brushing his fingers against my knee like he couldn't help needing to be near me.

Sarah and I laughed over a couple of disastrous Tinder stories, and even Viper Boy managed to be tolerable for a bit. He was charming in that try-too-hard, perform-for-the-group way. The kind of guy who thought calling the waitress "babe" was endearing.

But Sarah brushed it off. Rolled her eyes. Took another sip.

We played a few rounds of a bar card game someone had left on the table, one of those half-trivia, half-icebreaker decks meant to stir up conversation between strangers. Michael crushed the trivia questions. But when the game changed to guessing people's secrets based on nothing but vibes, I somehow won every round.

Sarah leaned closer, swirling the last of her drink. "You really *are* freakishly good at this."

I gave her a look. "Natural charm?"

She laughed. "More like spooky intuition."

I laughed, then nodded toward the guy by the jukebox. "That one? Definitely cried during *The Notebook*... and still texts his ex at two a.m.."

She cackled, leaning into me. "God, I missed this."

Me too.

For a few golden hours, I forgot everything—the mirror, the ER, the letter tucked into my bag. I was just a girl in a blue dress, drinking mojitos and trying to stitch herself back together with laughter and sugar-rimmed glasses.

Then things changed. It was subtle at first. The way Jax started leaning too hard into Sarah when she talked. The way his hand lingered too long on her hip. Then it got worse. He slid his hand up her thigh under the table, fingers disappearing beneath her dress like he'd earned the right.

Sarah went stiff. Her smile cracked.

"Jax," she said, sharply. "Stop."

He laughed. "Relax. You're the one who wore the dress."

"I said stop," she said firmly.

"You're no fun," he replied.

She tried to pull away but he gripped her thigh tighter.

And then Michael stood. He crossed the floor in a slow, steady stride, calm but coiled tight.

He stopped behind Jax's chair and placed a hand on his shoulder. From where I sat, it looked casual. From the way Jax flinched, it wasn't.

"I'm going to say this once," Michael said, voice smooth and quiet. "Take your hand off her. Right now."

Jax laughed, but it faltered. "It's not a big—"

Michael's fingers tightened and Jax winced.

"I said," Michael repeated, "take your hand off her. Before I break your wrist"

Jax yanked his hand back like he'd touched a hot burner on the stove.

Michael leaned down, low and lethal. "Next time you touch a woman without permission, you'll learn how fast I can make you regret it."

Jax's face went pale. He muttered something—maybe an apology, maybe a curse—and stood up from his chair.

Michael sat beside me again, his hand finding mine.

Sarah's voice cut through the air, clear and sharp. "Yeah, run along, *Viper Boy.* Go cuddle your snake and work on that personality."

Jax froze like he might say something, then thought better of it and left. The silence that followed wasn't awkward, just weighted, like the pause after a slammed door.

Sarah picked up her drink, took a slow sip, and looked at me with a dry smile. "So… this counts as another red flag, right?"

I huffed a laugh, still too stunned to do more.

"I hate guys like that," Michael said. "The ones who pretend it's a joke while they hurt you."

I looked at him, heart pounding. Not from fear. From awe. From the quiet, bone-deep feeling that this man would burn the world down to protect the people he loved. And in that moment, I loved him back so completely, it almost hurt.

Sarah let out a breath, then clinked her glass against mine. "Next time I say I'm giving a man a second chance, remind me of this moment and then slap me."

"Deal," I said.

A little while later, Sarah stood and brushed invisible lint off her dress. "Okay. I'm out. I've hit my limit for male idiocy tonight."

"You want me to come with?" I asked.

She shook her head. "Nah. I need a long shower and some quiet. But you," she said, pointing at me, "go home and let this man adore you. That dress deserves it."

We hugged at the curb. She kissed my cheek and whispered, "I've got you," before disappearing into her cab.

Another cab pulled up, and Michael opened the door. I got in. He followed, settling beside me, his hand resting on my thigh, thumb tracing slow circles over my skin.

"Let's go home," he said gently.

Maybe I didn't need answers yet. Maybe I just needed him.

• • •

Michael unlocked the door, held it open for me, and kissed the top of my head as I stepped into the dark living room.

I kicked off my shoes, but didn't move to turn on the light. I just stood there, wrapped in the afterglow of the evening— the drinks, the laughter, the hand on Sarah's thigh, the way Michael had looked at Jax like he could dismantle him without ever raising his voice.

Michael stepped behind me, his hands sliding slowly around my waist, his breath soft at my ear. "You look incredible tonight."

I turned to face him. "I don't want to talk."

His eyes met mine, deep and shadowed in the window glow.

"Okay," he said.

When I kissed him, it wasn't hungry or desperate. Not at first. It was tender. Sinking.

He kissed me back with that same quiet intensity. No rush, no demand, just presence.

His hands framed my face like I was something sacred, his thumbs brushing under my jaw as he kissed me deeper, slower. My fingers slid into his hair, curling at the nape of his neck as I stepped closer, needing all of him—the warmth, the solidness, the way he made the world feel small enough to hold.

He pulled back just enough to meet my eyes. "Bedroom?"

I nodded, already trembling.

He led me upstairs in silence, his hand never letting go of mine. In the bedroom, he turned on a lamp, and I stood there watching him, suddenly unsure if my legs would hold me.

Michael stepped to me, his hands gentle as they slid over my shoulders and down my arms.

"You're shaking," he murmured.

"I know." My voice was barely there. "I don't know why."

He tucked my hair behind my ear. "I do. "You've been holding everything in. Let me hold it for you now."

A sharp breath caught in my chest. I leaned into him, pressing my face to his chest as his arms wrapped around me.

We stayed like that, the world outside dissolving, until he gently lifted my chin. His soft lips found mine again

When we finally pulled away, he didn't say anything. He just looked at me, his gaze dark. And without a word, he began to undress me. The rhythm was slow, deliberate. A kind of quiet hunger threaded through every touch. He pulled my dress over my head and let it fall to the floor, his eyes dragging over me.

"You're fucking breathtaking," he said, a growl buried in the words.

His shirt came off next, then his pants. And when I reached for him, I didn't pull him to me. I dropped to my knees.

His breath caught. "Lena..."

He leaned back against the edge of the bed, letting me take the lead. I kissed down his stomach, then lower, trailing my hands over his hips as I wrapped my fingers around him, slow and sure.

He was already hard. Already pulsing in my palm. I leaned forward and flicked my tongue over the tip—just once, teasing—then took him into my mouth.

His groan echoed through the room. One hand slid into my hair, not pushing, just holding. I set a slow and deep rhythm, taking my time, loving the way his control slipped with every pass of my tongue. He said my name like it hurt, hips trembling beneath my hands.

"Fuck, Lena," he breathed. "You feel... God, I'm not gonna last."

I pulled back, locking eyes with him. "Then don't."

I took him deeper, faster, and he came with a broken gasp, his hand tightening in my hair, his whole body shaking.

I swallowed, kissed the skin just below his hip, and slowly rose to my feet. He looked at me like I'd undone him completely. Like I'd given him something no one ever had.

But I wasn't done yet.

"I need you," I said, the words trembling out of me.

He kissed me as he laid me back on the bed, his lips hot and lingering, his tongue sliding against mine with maddening patience. His hands moved over my body like he wanted to own every inch with his hands.

A sharp breath escaped me the moment his fingers slipped between my thighs.

"You're so wet for me," he murmured, mouth at my ear.

"I want you," I said, voice breaking on the last word.

He groaned, deep in his throat, like he was barely holding himself together.

He slipped a finger inside me, slow and deliberate, then another. I pushed against his hand, moaning, eyes fluttering shut.

The way he moved unraveled me completely. My hips lifted off the bed, chasing the rhythm of his hand, my fingers fisting the sheets as my release built in slow, shattering waves.

When I came, it wasn't quiet. I cried out his name, my body tightening around his fingers, thighs trembling, head thrown back.

He kissed his way down my body, licking across my stomach, my hip bones, then lower until his mouth was on me.

I moaned again, already too sensitive, but he held my thighs open and kept going, his tongue lapping at me like he was starving.

"Michael," I choked out. "Please—"

He lifted his head just enough to murmur, "Let me give you more."

He made me come again with his mouth. My vision blurred, my limbs loose and shaking. When he finally moved up my body, sliding between my legs, I was already undone. I ached for him. Every nerve lit up, begging for him.

He lined himself up and then pushed inside. A sharp cry escaped me. Every inch of him was perfect, filling me in a way that made my toes curl and my body arch into his.

He held still, letting me feel all of it, all of *him*. Then he started to move. Slow, deep thrusts that made my breath stutter. He kept his eyes on mine the whole time, like he was trying to see inside me. I wrapped my legs around his waist, pulling him deeper, harder. He groaned and dropped his forehead to mine.

"I love you," he said, voice raw with need.

The words caught in my throat, but I gave them back to him.

His pace picked up, faster now and rougher, but still controlled. Like he wanted to drive me crazy one thrust at a time.

I came again, shuddering around him, and that was it. He cursed low and broken, thrust once more, then stilled, pulsing inside me with a groan like I'd taken something from him he could never get back.

He collapsed beside me, arms pulling me close, our bodies still tangled, our breath still uneven. For a long moment, there was only silence.

And then, just barely above a whisper, I said it again.

"I love you."

His arms tightened. He didn't say anything, just held me like he meant it. The warmth of him, the rhythm of our breathing lulled me. My body ached in the best way. My eyes drifted closed.

Sleep came quickly.

I was back in Grandma's house.

Not the way it looked when she died, but how it used to be. Warm light spilling through the lace curtains. The scent of peppermint and something spiced in the air. The wallpaper faded, but familiar. The old clock ticking like a heartbeat.

And Corinne was there.

She sat in Grandma's favorite armchair, knitting something pale and fragile—a long, trailing thread of ivory yarn that kept unraveling almost as fast as she worked. Her hands moved steadily, rhythmically, even as her eyes stared into a place far beyond the room.

She looked older than I remembered, thinner. Her mouth moved as she worked, mumbling words I couldn't quite catch at first.

But then I heard it.

"Lena… Margot… Lena…"

Again and again. A chant, almost. A prayer unraveling in time with the thread.

There was a book on the side table with green leather and worn edges, the same one from the shop. It sat untouched, like it had been placed there for someone else to find. Corinne didn't acknowledge it. Her hands kept moving, stitch by stitch, like her life depended on it.

I tried to speak. To ask her something. Anything. But no sound came out of my mouth.

The mirror above the mantle quivered. I glanced up and saw a child staring back at me.

Me.

Seven, maybe eight years old. Braids, scraped knees, wide eyes.

I looked back at Corinne. And she was looking at me. Her knitting stopped. Her hands went still. Her lips moved again. Not mumbling this time, but clear.

"He's almost ready," she said.

My chest seized. I took a step back and the room cracked like glass. The floor split. The light vanished.

Corinne's voice echoed, sharp and hollow.

"He's almost ready."

Then everything went black.

I woke with a gasp, heart pounding, the sharp dream still behind my eyes. The words clung to me like smoke. "*He's almost ready.*"

I didn't know who *he* was. Or what it meant. But it felt like a warning.

My skin was damp with sweat. The sheets tangled around my legs. The space around me felt scorched, like something had just passed through and left ash behind.

Michael was still asleep beside me with one arm draped across my waist.

I didn't move. Not because I was scared, but because I didn't want to lose the quiet. The illusion of peace. The weight of his arm, the heat of his skin… it helped hold the fear back. At least for a little while.

The dream was still there. Grandma's house. Corinne's voice. The way her eyes had locked onto mine like she *knew* me. Knew what was coming.

And that book.

Chapter 6

The next morning, I lay in bed, staring at the ceiling. The remnants of the vivid dream clung to me. I was awake, but part of me still hovered somewhere else, caught in the echo of words I couldn't shake.

"He's almost ready."

A chill slid down my spine.

I slipped out of bed carefully, trying not to disturb Michael. My body felt slow, like it wasn't quite ready to rejoin the world. I dressed quickly, pulling on jeans and a light hoodie. Then I stepped into the bathroom, ran a brush through my hair and brushed my teeth.

Downstairs, the house was quiet. Biscuit looked at me from her perch on the windowsill but didn't move. I went through the motions on autopilot—grabbing the filter, scooping in the coffee grounds, filling the reservoir with water. The familiar scent started to rise as the machine hissed and gurgled to life. I leaned against the counter, impatiently waiting while watching the dark liquid drip steadily into the pot. When it was finally done, I poured a cup and cradled the mug in both hands. I wasn't really tasting it. My mind was still back in that dream.

I couldn't sit with it. Not today.

I grabbed my keys off the hook by the door, grabbed my phone from my pocket, and sent a quick text to Michael in case he woke up before I got back.

Lena: *Just needed some air. Be home soon. xo*

I hit send and slipped the phone back into my hoodie pocket.

I stepped onto the porch, pausing for a moment with the mug still in my hand. I set it carefully on the railing, turned, and walked to my car.

I got in, started the engine, and drove.

Twenty minutes later, I was pulling into the gravel lot behind Rowan's Books & Curiosities.

It looked exactly the same as the last time we'd walked in.

Dust on the windows. That crooked wood sign swaying just slightly in the breeze. The smell of incense and old paper.

The bell over the door gave its loud chime. No one appeared behind the counter.

I didn't wait.

I made my way past the shelves, around the curtain of beads, to the place I'd stopped last time.

The green book was still there. Exactly where I'd left it.

I reached for it slowly, half-expecting it to vanish when my fingers brushed the leather. But it didn't. The leather was warm beneath my fingers, the weight of it familiar in my hands in a way that made my chest tighten.

I opened it.

No title. No table of contents. Just a name written in elegant, slightly slanted script inside the front cover.

Corinne Moraine

I froze, staring at the name.

It was hers. This book had *belonged* to Corinne. And somehow, I knew it wasn't just a coincidence.

At the counter, a woman I hadn't seen before looked up from a half-finished crossword. She rang me up without a word and slipped the book into a paper bag. The bell over the door chimed behind me as I stepped back into the sunlight.

The book was real. And something told me... it was finally time to see her.

• • •

When I got home, Michael's car was gone.

A note was waiting on the kitchen counter, scribbled in his usual too-perfect handwriting.

Came downstairs to cold coffee and Biscuit
giving me side-eye. I've got a quick work thing
this morning (yes, on a Saturday. I'm as offended

as you are). Shouldn't be long. Miss your face
already. —M

I stared at it for a moment, then smiled despite myself.

I made a fresh cup of coffee and took it, and the book, to the kitchen table.

The green leather cover was familiar in my hands again, as if it had been waiting for me. I opened it slowly, letting the pages fall where they wanted.

It wasn't a normal book. There were no chapters. No structure. Just page after page of handwritten notes, scattered reflections, and odd little stories—some careful and almost poetic, others messy and nearly unreadable in Corinne's handwriting.

Some pages were written with patience—small observations about people she'd met, stray thoughts on how grief changes a person, notes about the soul and what it can endure. Others looked like she'd scribbled them quickly, words crammed into margins as if she needed to capture them before they vanished.

A few sections were blacked out. Not scratched or erased, but fully inked over as though someone had decided they were too dangerous or too painful to be read.

I kept flipping. Some pages mentioned marks. One entry stood out. Her handwriting was shaky, like her hand had trembled while she wrote it:

When the mark begins to rise, the soul must
be strong enough to hold it. If not, it may never
return. And without a soul... what remains?

I stared at it. Reread it. Over and over. There was no explanation. No follow-up. Just those few lines floating in the middle of a page, like it had scared even her.

The mark. I didn't know what it meant. But I knew it was tied to me. To whatever was waking up inside me. To why Corinne had mattered. Why Grandma had written her. Why the dream had shown me this book.

And then I remembered something from the letter. Grandma hadn't just warned Corinne to guide me. She'd told her to protect me. Because someone out there might want my power.

Suddenly, that line—the one about losing your soul—didn't feel like a metaphor. It felt like a threat. I closed the book gently and set it on the table, my coffee forgotten and growing cold.

Whatever this was, it wasn't a coincidence. And I needed answers.

• • •

The words from the journal still echoed in my head when I heard the key in the lock.

Michael stepped through the door, sunlight at his back, wearing a soft gray t-shirt and worn jeans that hugged his frame in that effortless way he always managed. A paper bag dangled from one hand, and he had that stupid, perfect smile like he hadn't just disrupted my entire morning by being gone.

"There you are," he said, dropping the bag on the counter. "You have no idea how hard it was to find that strawberry croissant you like. The one with the flaky top and the filling that gets all over your fingers."

He walked over and kissed the top of my head like it was the most natural thing in the world. And somehow, it was. He smelled like what I assume sunshine smells like—warm, clean, and just slightly unfair.

"Morning," I said quietly.

"Afternoon, technically." He looked at me, eyes scanning my face. "You okay?"

I nodded, too quickly. "Just thinking."

He didn't press. Just went to the kitchen, pulling out plates and whistling under his breath. He was casual, completely at home.

But the word echoed in the back of my mind.
Mark.

It meant something. I was sure of it.

54

We ate at the table, side by side, our knees bumping now and then. He told me about the guy at the bakery who tried to give him a cherry danish instead of the strawberry croissant and how he almost committed violence in my honor. I laughed with my mouth full.

After breakfast, he pushed his empty plate away and glanced out the window.

"So, I was thinking," he said. "Today's the day we finally fix that sad, lopsided porch swing."

I looked at him. "That thing hasn't moved since we bought the place."

"I know. It's tragic. But I'm a man with tools and mild overconfidence." He was already on his feet, reaching for the back door. "Come on, it'll be fun."

The sun was high and hot, the kind of brightness that made everything smell like wood and grass. Michael pulled out a toolbox I hadn't even known we owned, and we set to work. Or rather, he set to work. I mostly handed him things and mocked his tool-wielding technique. Still, it was nice.

While he wrestled with a stubborn bolt, I ducked into the garage to find a wrench. It was cooler in here. The air had a scent of old wood, oil, and totes of forgotten things. I ran my hand along the dusty shelves and stopped when something fluttered loose from behind a box of mismatched screws.

A photo. I picked it up carefully, brushing the dust away.

It was the four of us—me, Allie, Mom, and Dad—standing in front of the red rock formations at Garden of the Gods in Colorado. Allie had her hair in pigtail braids and was holding a melting ice cream cone. Mom had on sunglasses and her hair was pulled up in a messy, curly ponytail. Dad had his arm around both of us like we were going to blow away in the wind. I was wearing a tank top and grinning like a maniac, sunburn already spreading across my nose. It was summertime. Hot, dusty, loud with cicadas and road trip playlists. And happy. So damn happy.

I sat on an overturned bucket, holding the photo like it might crumble if I breathed too hard.

Mom had been a terrible singer and a wonderful cook. She used to hum while she chopped vegetables, even though it drove Allie insane. Her chili was famous in our little town. She could make a strawberry pie without looking at a recipe, and always claimed she had no idea how Grandma made hers taste like magic. "She probably used lard," Mom would say. "Or witchcraft."

Dad worked on classic cars in the garage every weekend, even when it was too hot and the mosquitos were out. He always smelled like oil and gasoline. He wore ratty t-shirts and played old rock albums too loud. He taught me how to change a tire and once let me name a '67 Mustang he rebuilt. I called it *Blue*, because... well, it was blue. Not my most inspired moment.

The day of the accident was hot, too. It was about three years ago. Allie had called me screaming. Or maybe I was the one screaming. I don't remember.

They said it was quick. A deer. A curve. No one to blame.

After the funeral, Allie and I didn't talk for weeks. When we finally did, we said too much. Or maybe not enough. I told her I was fine. That I didn't need anyone. She told me to go to hell.

And the truth is... I don't even remember what we were fighting about. Just that it felt like the end of something we never figured out how to fix.

Michael's voice drifted in from outside. "Hey."

I blinked, the memory fading. I slid the photo into the back pocket of my jeans and stood up, grabbing the wrench I'd forgotten.

"Coming," I called, my voice a little too tight.

Michael was kneeling by the swing, sleeves pushed up, dirt smudged across one forearm like a badge of honor. His hair was a mess. Still, he looked annoyingly attractive.

"You abandon me for ten minutes and everything falls apart," he said, holding up the bolt. "Weren't you supposed to get the wrench for this? What kind of assistant are you?"

"The kind that brings tools and emotional baggage," I said, handing him the wrench.

He grinned. "You really know how to keep things light."

We finished tightening the last chain together, him holding the swing steady while I leaned my full weight into the bolt. It creaked, but didn't give.

"There," he said, straightening. "Perfect."

"You say that now," I said, "but if I sit on it and eat dirt, you're taking me to urgent care."

"Fair," he replied.

I sat down carefully and gently started rocking. The swing held. Michael plopped down beside me and threw an arm around my shoulders. The boards beneath us creaked in rhythm.

The afternoon turned into a mess of paint splatters, crooked bolts, and bad jokes. That night, we sat on the porch swing like it had never been broken. The paint was still tacky in places, but it held our weight as we swayed gently back and forth, drinks in hand, Biscuit curled into a puddle at our feet. The sun was down, but the air was still thick with heat and the smell of fresh-cut grass. Crickets were starting up in the distance, faint and rhythmic.

Michael tapped his glass against mine. "To functional furniture."

I smiled, leaned into his shoulder. "Miracles do happen."

We rocked in silence for a while.

"I think I'm going to visit someone," I said finally.

Michael turned his head just slightly, waiting.

"I found an old letter," I went on. "From my grandma. It was addressed to someone named Corinne. I remember her, sort of. She used to be around when I was little. They were close and I guess seeing her name just... stirred something up."

He didn't answer right away.

"Where is she now?" he asked, his voice concerned.

"She's in a care facility across town. She has dementia."

Michael nodded slowly. "And you think visiting her might help... with whatever's been on your mind?"

I hesitated. "I don't know. Maybe not. But I keep having this feeling, like... like I'm supposed to."

He took a long sip from his drink, then set it down on the armrest beside him.

"If you want to go, you should. Just... be careful, okay?" He brushed a strand of hair behind my ear. "I don't want you to get hurt if she doesn't remember you. Or if it stirs something up."

I nodded.

"She might not," I said quietly. "But I think I need to try anyway."

Michael pulled me in tighter, kissed the top of my head.

"Then try," he said. "I'll be here when you get back."

Later, after the dishes were done and Biscuit had curled up on one of the kitchen chairs, I found myself back at the table with the green book heavy in my hands again.

Same page. Same line.

When the mark begins to rise, the soul must
be strong enough to hold it. If not, it may never
return. And without a soul... what remains?

I read it once. Then again. And again. It didn't make sense. Not really. But something about it felt loaded with meaning I wasn't ready for. Like the words were a warning and a promise all at once.

I didn't know what the mark was. Or what it meant for a soul to hold something like that. I closed the book carefully. And for a long time I just sat there wondering what, exactly, was coming.

Chapter 7

The rain started sometime during the night. I woke to the low hiss of it against the windows, the kind of steady, gentle downpour that made the whole house feel calmer.

Michael was still asleep beside me, one hand curled near his face, completely still. Biscuit had wedged herself between our feet, a little pile of warmth. I lay there for a while, listening.

Sunday. It felt like a day meant for staying inside. For coffee and slow mornings and maybe putting off the laundry for one more hour.

When Michael finally stirred, he stretched with a groan and reached for me.

"Still here?" he murmured, voice low with sleep.

"Unfortunately for you."

He grinned, eyes still closed. "Best thing that ever happened to me."

We got up late. Made breakfast in pajamas. Shared the last pancake like we were reenacting a hostage negotiation. Everything felt... easy.

Around ten, Sarah texted to say she was coming by, rain or not. She showed up forty-five minutes later with a dripping umbrella, a tray of coffees, and a giant blueberry muffin that she immediately claimed was for herself and no one else.

"Jesus, it smells like a bakery in here," she said, stepping inside and kicking off her boots. "I hate how domestic you two are."

"You're just mad I have a porch swing now," I said, grinning.

"You're damn right I am," Sarah replied.

Michael took her coat, gave her a dry towel, and played the perfect host. The two of them traded jokes like they'd been doing it for years. It should've felt weird, maybe. Watching my best friend and my boyfriend fall into such easy banter. But it didn't. It was ordinary in the best possible way.

We stayed in the kitchen most of the morning, talking about random things—bad weather, worse dates, whether a hotdog was considered a sandwich. Sarah and Michael were relentless with their opinions, and I mostly watched them, warm mug in hand, feeling like I was wrapped in something cozy.

Biscuit eventually jumped into Sarah's lap, claimed it like she'd paid for it, and promptly fell asleep. Sarah didn't even pretend to mind.

At some point, Michael got up to make more coffee, and Sarah leaned over, voice low. "Okay, but seriously. If you ever screw this up, I'm keeping him."

I rolled my eyes. "You can have him every other weekend and one major holiday."

She grinned. "Deal."

The rain kept falling outside, steady and calm. For a little while the world seemed to pause in the best way. And I let it.

A little while later, I went to the bathroom. I flipped on the light, shut the door, and caught my reflection… or I thought I did.

For one impossible heartbeat, it wasn't me. It was Grandma. Hair swept back in gray waves, her expression tight with something like worry. Like she'd been watching from somewhere far and didn't like what she saw.

My heart stuttered hard in my chest, a cold rush sweeping through my stomach. I blinked and she was gone. Just me again. I gripped the edge of the sink, searching the glass for any trick of the light. But there was nothing. No fog. No shadows. Just the echo of something impossible.

But I'd seen her. Or I thought I had.

I stayed there a moment longer, my skin prickling. Something clung to the moment, like a thread left behind and still tied to me. I ran my hands through my hair, trying to shake it off. Trying not to wonder why I suddenly felt like I wasn't alone.

I left the bathroom and went back to the sound of laughter and the comfort of pretending everything was still normal.

Sarah headed out mid-afternoon. She hugged both of us goodbye, promising to *"drag us out for some real fun"* next weekend because, apparently, we needed to be *"put to shame"* by her superior social life.

When the door clicked shut behind her, Michael turned to me, a grin still dragging at his lips. *"I like her,"* he said, and I laughed, knowing that *"like"* probably means *"adoring her but pretending to tolerate her."* I waved him off and we settled back into the kitchen.

I stood in the kitchen for a moment, then Michael joined me, leaning against the counter. His gaze was steady on me, like he could tell something was off.

"You okay?" he asked, his voice gentle but carrying an edge of concern. "You've been a little distant all afternoon."

I hesitated. There was a part of me that wanted to brush it off. To say *"I'm fine"* and move on. But something about the way he was looking at me made me want to tell him everything.

"I'm not fine," I admitted. "There's just… a lot on my mind."

He set his drink down and stepped closer, taking my hand to guide me to the table. "Talk to me."

I drew in a shaky breath. Everything I'd been keeping inside, all the questions that had been eating away at me, spilled out in a rush.

I finished telling him everything. The panic that wasn't mine, the fogged mirror, the book, the dream, the girl with asthma, the feeling of something weird inside me. When I stopped, I half expected him to look at me like I was crazy, like I'd finally crossed a line. Maybe even say something like *"It's all in your head."*

But he didn't. He didn't even blink. He simply took a breath and asked, "Do you feel different? Like something inside you is changing?"

I nodded. "Yeah, I do. It's like I'm waiting for something, but I have no idea what."

He didn't say anything right away. He just studied me, as though he was piecing together something I couldn't see yet.

61

Then, with a quiet, sure voice, he said, "I don't think you're crazy. I think something is happening to you, something you don't fully understand. But we'll figure it out, together. I'm not scared, Lena. I'm here with you. But... I need to know more. About what you're feeling. About what's changing."

He kept asking thoughtful and careful questions, as if he was piecing together a puzzle I couldn't see yet. Not to challenge me, but to understand.

I almost laughed, bitterly, at the thought. How many times had I second-guessed myself? How many times had I thought I was losing my mind? But here he was, asking questions not to challenge me, but to understand. To help me make sense of it.

My throat was tight. "I don't even know what to look for. What to do."

He took my hand and squeezed. "Don't worry about that right now. Just focus on how you feel. And let's take it one step at a time."

He paused, his eyes searching mine. "Have you had any more dreams like the one you had before? Or anything similar?"

I thought back. "There was that moment in the bathroom earlier... I thought I saw Grandma in the mirror. Her reflection, not mine."

Michael's brow furrowed, but he didn't look scared. He looked like he was calculating, processing the information. "What do you think it means?"

"I don't know," I admitted. "I can't make sense of it. It's all just... pieces. And I'm afraid of putting them together wrong."

He squeezed my hand again, offering a reassuring smile. "You're not doing this alone, Lena. I'm right here. You don't have to figure it all out in one go. We'll take it slow, okay?"

I nodded, the tightness in my chest loosening just a little.

We sat in silence for a while, just the sound of the rain filling the space between us.

Then Michael spoke again, quieter this time. "Whatever this mark is, we'll figure it out. Together."

I looked at him, the promise hanging in the air. I wanted to believe that. I wanted to believe he was right. But something still felt... off. Like I was on the edge of a cliff, and the only thing holding me back was the small, trembling hope that there was more to this than I could see.

After a few more quiet minutes, he turned to me again, brow furrowed slightly. "You still want to see Corinne, don't you?"

I nodded slowly, my gaze dropping to my hands, twisting in my lap.

"I think I have to," I said quietly. "It's like... I don't know what's happening to me, but Corinne might. Maybe she'll have some answers. I need to try."

Michael watched me for a moment, his brow furrowed as if weighing his words. "And if she doesn't remember? If she can't help?"

I looked up at him. "Then I'll just have to figure it out myself. But I have to know I tried."

"I'm not saying you shouldn't go," he said softly. "But... don't expect too much, okay? Corinne's not in a good place. I don't want you to be disappointed if it doesn't go the way you hope."

I nodded, grateful for his concern. "I won't. I just need to go."

• • •

I woke with a sharp jolt, heart pounding like I'd been running. My skin was damp, my throat dry. I blinked hard, trying to orient myself. The sheets clung to my legs, twisted tight. Michael lay beside me, his back to me, sleeping peacefully.

I didn't even remember what I'd been dreaming about, just that it had dragged me under and spit me out. I slipped out of bed and padded barefoot into the hall and down the steps. I didn't bother with the lights.

63

In the living room, I paused. The green book sat exactly where I'd left it, on the bookshelf tucked between a forgotten cookbook and a paperback with a cracked spine. I didn't reach for it. Instead, I grabbed my laptop from the coffee table and curled up on the couch. For a long moment, I just stared at the screen, my fingers hovering.

Then I typed: *Corinne Moraine.* A few clicks. A few filters. It didn't take long.

Meadow Hills Memory Care. That was the name. Clean website with soft colors. Stock photos of sunlit rooms and older women smiling over puzzles and flowerbeds. I stared at the screen, unsure what I was hoping to find.

There wasn't a picture of Corinne. Of course there wasn't. Just a phone number and an address. I clicked over to my calendar. Saturday. My next full day off. Five days away.

I didn't let myself overthink it. I marked it. Closed the tab. Shut the laptop. One step closer to whatever was coming.

Chapter 8

Saturday came faster than I expected.

Michael didn't say much that morning. He just watched me while I grabbed my keys and slipped on my shoes.

"You nervous?" he asked.

I shrugged. "A little."

He stepped closer and kissed me, then looked at me straight in the eyes.

"I love you," he said.

"I love you, too," I said back. "See you soon."

I walked out the door.

The roads were mostly empty and quiet. I kept one hand on the wheel, the other was fidgeting in my lap, tugging at a loose thread on my shirt. I didn't know what I was walking into.

Part of me was afraid I'd find nothing. That Corinne wouldn't remember me, wouldn't know anything about Grandma, or magic, or any of it. But almost worse than that... I was afraid she *would*.

By the time I parked, my stomach was a tight knot. I sat for a minute, staring at the building, just long enough to consider turning around. But I didn't. I got out, walked through the front doors, and gave my name to the woman at the desk.

A few minutes later, a nurse came to bring me to her room. She walked ahead of me, her sneakers making no sound on the polished floor. We passed a row of doors—most open, some closed—and the faint hum of a television drifted from somewhere down the hall.

"She doesn't get many visitors," the nurse said over her shoulder. "Maybe twice a year. A woman who says she's her niece."

I didn't answer. I didn't know what I expected from this visit, but the idea of someone else being here, someone who claimed to be family, left a quiet unease crawling under my ribs.

We stopped at the final room on the left. The nurse knocked lightly, then opened the door.

Corinne was seated by the window in a high-backed chair. She wore a pale, shapeless house dress and a faded cardigan that was slipping off one shoulder. Her thin frame was swallowed by the fabric. She rocked gently, her head tilted down, whispering sounds that almost formed words, but not quite. Her hands were folded in her lap, holding something dark.

My eyes caught it immediately. A small, oval object that was dark, smooth, and framed in what looked like wood. There were markings along the edge. It was ancient-looking. The nurse followed my gaze.

She spoke softly, with a small smile. "She's always carrying that around. Won't let anyone else touch it. Must mean something to her." She hesitated, then gently patted my arm. "I'll give you some time." Then she stepped out and pulled the door closed behind her.

The air smelled faintly of disinfectant. The walls were a dull beige—too pale to be warm, too dingy to be clean. A single window looked out over the back parking lot, blinds half-open. There was a twin bed tucked in the corner, neatly made with stiff hospital sheets. A narrow dresser stood across from it, its drawers slightly uneven, one of the handles missing.

There were no photos. No plants. No cards or flowers or signs that anyone else had been here in a long time.

I stayed near the door at first, watching Corinne from a distance. Her hair had gone completely white. Her frame looked smaller than I remembered, like the years had shrunk her. Wrinkles traced across her face, more than I remembered and deeper too.

I moved closer. Corinne didn't seem to notice.

"Corinne," I said, gently. "It's me. Lena. Margot's granddaughter."

Nothing. Just the soft, steady rhythm of Corinne's voice. A half-song, half-babble that repeated and looped.

I sat down in the chair across from her. Just a few feet of space between us. But it felt like a continent. I stayed there for a while, just… sitting. Letting the silence stretch. The murmur never changed. I'd come looking for answers. But all I found was a woman I barely recognized, and who didn't recognize me at all.

My eyes dropped to the object in her lap. It was a small stone, maybe the size of a silver dollar. It was dark and smooth, like river rock after rain. It sat inside a thin wooden frame, the edges worn down by time or handling. Carvings circled the border—old symbols, some still sharp, others faded like they'd been touched too many times.

I leaned forward, my fingers hovering just above it.

She won't let anyone touch it.

But Corinne didn't react. She just kept mumbling, her hands still. I reached out. Slowly. Lightly. Just a brush of my fingertips against the edge.

The stone made a sharp and dry sound, like porcelain cracking under pressure. A thin line split across the surface. A clean break, but not enough to separate it. Just enough to say, *something is happening.*

Corinne stopped moving.

My spine straightened without meaning to, every part of me suddenly alert. Nothing had changed in the room, but something had.

Then she lifted her head and looked straight at me. Her eyes met mine, clear and focused, cutting through the fog like they'd never been clouded at all.

"Anima toren… Vireth selan… Let the soul be unbound." Her voice was steady and clear.

We stayed like that for a moment, eyes locked. And then… it was gone.

Her gaze slipped. The sharpness in her expression faded. It was like watching a light dim behind her eyes. She slumped slightly in the chair, and the murmuring picked up again, as if the moment had never happened at all.

I didn't move. My brain was still trying to catch up—like reality had hiccupped, and something in me was lagging behind.

But I felt it. Something was happening inside me. It hit low in my spine and ran up through my chest. A jolt, fast and sharp, like lightning without heat. My fingers twitched. My breath caught.

It wasn't pain. It was something older than pain. Like a circuit had been closed. Like I'd been disconnected my entire life and hadn't known it, until something reached inside and flipped the switch. Like I'd been missing a limb I didn't know I had.

My fingers curled into the arm of the chair. I sat there, breathing, barely blinking. The surge passed, but I didn't feel the same. Everything felt sharper. The edges of the world. My heartbeat. Even the silence. Whatever had just happened, it hadn't been in my head.

I looked down at the stone, still cracked in Corinne's lap. She didn't seem to notice. She just kept mumbling, like the words had never left her mouth.

I stood slowly, careful not to disturb her. My legs felt unsteady, like I'd been sitting for hours instead of minutes.

I moved to the hallway. The building was still the same—TV murmurs, a phone ringing somewhere far off—but there was a tension I hadn't felt before.

I started walking. One step. Then another. That's when I felt it.

At first, it was just… a weight. Something low and aching in my chest. Like grief that wasn't mine.

I slowed. Another step.

It got worse.

A sharp sadness bloomed behind my eyes, sudden and overwhelming. Regret. Loneliness. Sorrow that tasted like metal in my throat. It wasn't mine.

More steps. And now pain… real pain. Heartbreak. Anger. Terror. Grief so deep it felt like it had soaked into the walls. A thousand fractured emotions clawing their way through my skin.

I pressed my hand to the wall. It didn't help. Everything in me screamed to stop walking. To curl in. To make it go away. But it didn't stop. It kept coming, every door I passed bled something new into me. My heart thundered. My skin buzzed. My thoughts scattered like glass.

It was too much. Too loud. Too raw. Too human. I felt like I was going to break.

The pressure built fast—inside my chest, behind my eyes, under my skin. Like something was pushing outward from the center of me, clawing for release.

My knees buckled. I pressed my hand harder against the wall, like I could anchor myself. But it didn't help.

Stop it, stop it, stop it—

And then I think I did break. Something rushed out of me in a violent surge that I couldn't contain. The floor shuddered beneath my feet. A deep, low vibration rolled through the walls. Lights flared. Somewhere behind me, glass shattered.

Down the hall, someone screamed. Then another. And another.

Pictures tore from the walls and hit the ground hard, frames splintering on impact. Doors slammed open. Staff shouted. Footsteps pounded like gunshots against the tile.

I ran. Down the hallway, past the nurses' station, straight through the front doors. Out into the open air, away from the screams, the broken glass, the impossible pressure still clawing at my skin.

I reached my car with shaking hands and fumbled the keys. My heart was still racing, my chest still tight, like whatever had burst out of me wasn't finished yet. I got in and slammed the door closed. I sat there gripping the steering wheel, too afraid to move. Too afraid to breathe.

I didn't know what had just happened. I didn't know what was happening *to me*. All I knew was that I needed to get out. I gripped the steering wheel tighter, forcing my breath to slow.

And suddenly, I wanted one thing.

Michael.

His arms. His voice. That steady look in his eyes that always made things feel okay. He'll know what to do. I just needed to get home.

But I couldn't move. I sat there in the car, frozen, hands clamped around the steering wheel like it was the only thing keeping me tethered to the world. My whole body buzzed like I was still vibrating from the inside out. Like my bones were humming with something I didn't ask for, didn't understand.

My breath came in short, sharp bursts. The windshield blurred in front of me, smeared with tears and panic and something deeper, something I didn't have words for.

I had *felt* them. Every raw, frayed emotion inside that building, like I'd opened a door and let a hurricane crawl inside my skin.

It wasn't just sympathy. This was more. Bigger. Wilder. Like something ancient had woken up inside me and didn't know how to be quiet.

God, what's happening to me?

I tried to think of Michael. His voice. His arms. The way he looked at me like I was something worth holding onto. He'll know what to do. He *has* to.

But even that thought felt thin now, too fragile to hold up under the weight pressing on my chest.

I gripped the wheel tighter, trying to steady myself in the shape of his name. Michael. Michael. Michael. The syllables beat like a drum in my head, chasing back the fear, the confusion, the stinging memories of Corinne's eyes suddenly sharp and knowing.

"Let the soul be unbound."

My stomach clenched. I didn't know what she'd done. What I'd done. What any of this *meant*. But whatever broke in that room... it broke something in me too. And I was terrified that once I got home, I'd never be able to put myself back together. Still, my hand moved to the ignition.

The drive blurred past in a mess of stoplights and static. My grip on the steering wheel never eased. Every bump in the road rattled through my bones like an echo of what just happened. By the time I turned onto my street, my entire body was shaking.

I pulled into the driveway, tires screeching as I slammed the gear into park. I ran up the sidewalk, almost tripping on the steps, and reached the front door. My hands shook so hard I could barely turn the knob. When it finally gave, I burst through the front door, sobbing.

The door swung wide behind me, left open in my panic— but Michael was there in an instant, coming from the hallway, eyes wide with alarm.

As he caught me, one hand still steadying me upright, I heard the soft click of him shutting and locking the door behind me.

"Lena," he breathed, arms wrapping around me. "What happened?"

I clutched at his shirt like a lifeline, pressing my face into his chest.

"I don't know," I said as I sobbed into his chest. "I don't know what's happening to me. I feel like I'm losing my mind."

"Shhhh," he whispered, rocking me gently. "It's okay. You're safe now. I've got you. Just tell me what happened."

"I... I don't even know how to explain it," I stammered, choking on the words between sobs. "One minute I was in her room. I touched this stone she was holding... and I felt something inside me. I don't know what it was. And then... God. These emotions just hit me. But they weren't mine."

I gripped his shirt tighter, crying so hard I could barely breathe. "There was so much pain, Michael. So much sorrow. I could feel it. All of it. Like I was drowning in it. I couldn't breathe, couldn't think. It was crushing me."

Tears streamed down my face, hot and relentless.

"It was too much. I felt like I was going to explode. And then... I think I did. Everything started shaking. The whole building! Windows shattered. Pictures were falling off the walls. People were screaming. I don't know how to explain it, but I know it was me. I was causing it!"

Michael stroked my hair gently, his voice steady. "It's going to be okay, Lena, it'll all be over soon."

And then—

Pain. A sudden, sharp burst in my stomach, like fire tearing through flesh.

I gasped, my whole body jerking. For a second, I couldn't even process it. I couldn't understand what was happening. I stumbled back, eyes wide, and looked down.

There was a knife sticking out of me... and his hand was on the handle.

I blink. Once. Twice. No. No, this doesn't make sense. My mouth opened, but nothing came out. I looked up at him, searching for the man I loved, the man I ran to, the one who held me.

But he wasn't there. His eyes were cold, narrowed with something sharp and cruel. The corner of his mouth lifted into a small, merciless curve.

"What...what are you doing?" I managed to say, voice shaking.

I looked down as the words left my mouth. My shirt clung to me, soaked with blood. Thick, dark drops pattered onto the floor, forming a small puddle.

He laughed softly. "Taking what I deserve."

"I don't under—" I choked on the words, then looked at him again, desperate for something familiar. "Michael?"

His expression didn't change. That cruel smile stayed plastered to his face.

My knees buckled, but he didn't let me fall. He lowered me carefully, like he was placing something exactly where he wanted it. The knife stayed in. His hand never left it.

"You have no idea how long I've waited for this," he murmured, straddling me.

Then I felt it. A deep, violent pull radiating from the knife buried in my stomach. Not pain, not exactly. It was worse. Like something sacred was being *ripped* out of me. Something vital.

I could feel it—myself—slipping away. Draining.

Michael watched me closely, his hand still gripping the knife, his voice was smooth. Almost gentle.

"I played my part perfectly, didn't I?" he said. "The doting boyfriend. The savior. The man you thought would never hurt you."

He tilted his head, watching me like I was something fascinating.

"You had to believe in me completely. Trust me with your soul. That was the only way I could take it. You were never anything more than a means to an end."

He said it like it was nothing. Like *I* was nothing. I couldn't move. Couldn't speak. My body was slipping away, piece by piece.

This isn't real. It can't be. Don't worry, I told myself. *You'll wake up soon. This is just a dream. Just a nightmare. You'll wake up soon.*

But the pain didn't stop. His hand was still on the knife. And I was still on the floor. Bleeding.

Michael's breathing grew heavier, almost trembling with exhilaration. His eyes fluttered closed for a moment—and when they opened again, they were brighter.

No… not just brighter. *Glowing.* A pale, silvery light pulsed beneath his irises like something alive. Something wrong.

"I can feel it," he said. "God, Lena… it's *pouring* into me." He let out a low, shuddering laugh, almost euphoric. "This… this is what power feels like. You have no idea what you've been carrying around inside you. And now it's *mine*."

"Fire," he breathed. "That one's strong. I could take over a city with that."

He tilted his head, eyes glittering. "Healing, too. Useful. Very useful."

Then he leaned in closer, voice lower, almost reverent. "And something else… something *deep*. I don't even know what to call it yet. But I will."

His voice became muffled, like he was underwater.

I couldn't feel my fingers. I couldn't feel *me*.

Michael leaned in and gently brushed the hair from my eyes. "You're doing beautifully."

Everything I am was slipping away…and I couldn't stop it. And the worst part? It wasn't a stranger. The man I trusted with my life, the man I ran to, was the one holding the knife. The one I loved more fiercely than I ever thought I could love anyone… was killing me.

Suddenly, a loud *bang* rattled the front door. Then again. Louder.

"Lena!" a voice shouted from outside. "Lena, are you in there?!"

Allie. My mind could barely register it, like I was hearing it from the bottom of a well.

Sirens wailed in the distance, growing closer. Michael's head jerked toward the sound, his face twisting with rage.

"Fuck," he snarled. "I'm not finished with you…"

He looked down at me, teeth clenched. "The rest will have to wait," he snapped as he yanked the knife free. And then he was gone. Just like that. He disappeared out the back door, leaving the front door trembling from Allie's fists.

The door crashed open.

"Lena!" Her voice tore through the room, hoarse with panic. She ran to me, slipping in blood as she dropped to her knees beside me.

"Oh my God—Lena. Lena, stay with me!" Her hands hovered then pressed on my stomach, trying to stop the bleeding. "It's okay. You're going to be okay. Just stay with me, okay? Look at me."

Her face swam above me, blurred and backlit by flashing red and blue outside. I tried to speak, but I couldn't. I couldn't feel the pain anymore. Just the cold. Allie's face was the last thing I saw.

And as the darkness pulled me under, one last thought echoed in my mind—*God… please don't let me wake up.*

Chapter 9

But I did.

I woke to the sound of beeping. I blinked slowly. Everything hurt. My ribs, my stomach, my throat. Even my skin felt sore.

I turned my head and saw them.

Sarah curled in a chair, knees hugged to her chest, her eyes red and swollen. Her hair was pulled into a messy ponytail, strands sticking out like she'd been running her hands through it for hours.

Allie stiff and pale, sitting upright like she hadn't moved in hours. Her dark blazer was rumpled and her hair was twisted into a low knot.

As soon as I made a sound—a rough, broken whimper—they were on me.

Sarah jolted upright, nearly falling out of her chair. Her hoodie was twisted around her wrists, expression crumpled with relief and panic. She grabbed my hand so tightly her nails dug in.

"Lena," she said, voice cracking. "Jesus, you scared the shit out of us."

Allie leaned in on the other side, one hand smoothing back my hair. "Hey. Don't try to move yet," she said softly but firmly. "You're okay. You're safe."

I tried to speak, but nothing came out. Just a strangled sob that rose up and split me open.

And then I couldn't stop. My whole body convulsed, pain blooming everywhere. I sobbed. Raw, ugly sounds that scraped my throat and left my lungs burning.

Michael.

I saw him do it. I felt it. But how could that be real? He held me. He kissed me. He said he loved me. And then he tried to kill me.

Sarah bent forward, wrapping her arms around me, cheek pressed to my shoulder. Allie pressed her forehead to mine, murmuring, "You're okay. We're right here. You're okay."

But I wasn't okay. I wasn't even close. None of this made sense. None of it fit. I loved him. He loved me. Didn't he?

You should have known, something in me whispered. *You should've seen it.*

I don't know how long passed before I could speak. Time felt sideways.

"Where…" My voice was broken glass. "Where's Michael?"

"He's here," Allie said. "In the waiting room talking to the police."

I blinked at her. Confused. Dread rising in my chest like bile. "You… called him?"

Allie nodded. "In the ambulance."

I shook my head violently, tears blurring everything. "It was him," I gasped.

They both looked at me, confused.

Allie's mouth parted. "Wait—what?"

Sarah drew back a little, her face going pale. "Lena… what are you saying?"

"Michael did it," I blurted. "He tried to kill me." More tears came, pouring from my eyes like poison spilling free.

Sarah took a step back, like the words physically hit her. "No… are you sure?"

Are you sure? The question echoed in my mind. Am I sure? Of course I'm not sure. Not in the way they mean. Not in the way that comes with clarity or calm.

My heart and my brain were screaming two different truths. One told me I saw his face, felt his breath on my cheek, heard the way his voice changed after the knife went in.

The other whispered that there had to be some mistake, and that Michael, the man who made me coffee and kissed my eyelids and held my hand through Mom and Dad's funeral, couldn't have done this.

But he did. I *know* he did. So why did part of me still want to take it back? Why did it feel like saying it aloud was making it more real, and less possible, all at once?

I looked at them, eyes wide, chest heaving. "He stabbed me. I came home after visiting Corinne. He hugged me, held me... and then he stabbed me. I saw his face. He smiled when he did it."

The words hung in the air and then something inside me broke. A sound escaped me—a sharp, strangled gasp that didn't even feel like mine. Because saying it out loud made it *real.*

Not a nightmare. Not a flash of pain in a blurred memory. He smiled. He *wanted* to do it.

My knees curled under the blanket, instinctive, like I could fold myself small enough to disappear. My hands trembled against the sheets.

What if they didn't believe me? What if *I* didn't believe me? Because somewhere in the aching hollow of my chest, I loved him. And now I was saying he tried to kill me. I wanted to drag the words back into my mouth. I wanted to scream them louder. I wanted them to disappear.

Tears spilled again, unstoppable. But it was true. God help me, it was.

The door opened before they could respond. A man stepped in, wearing a tie and slacks, a badge clipped to his belt. He was followed by a doctor with kind eyes holding a clipboard.

"Ms. Merrow," the officer said. "I'm Detective Alvarez. This is Dr. Hadley. I'd like for you to tell us what happened."

Hadley.

The name clicked just faintly. I'd worked with him once. Maybe twice. One of the rotating docs who filled in when we were short-staffed.

I wiped my face with the back of my wrist. "Michael attacked me. He stabbed me in the stomach and ran when he heard sirens. Allie got there just in time."

The doctor made a quiet note.

"Michael's been in the waiting room since you arrived," the doctor said gently. "He's... frantic. Worried about you."

"Don't let him in my room," I burst out, the words coming too fast.

Alvarez gave a small nod. "Can you walk us through what happened, from the beginning?"

I wiped away the tears on my cheeks. "I came home from visiting a family friend. Michael was there. I was upset. Then I started crying. He hugged me. And then he... he pulled out a knife and stabbed me in the stomach."

Silence.

"Did he say anything else?" Alvarez asked. "Any threats? Previous incidents of violence?"

"No. He was calm. Like he'd planned it. Like he was waiting for the right moment."

Dr. Hadley looked up, pen still. "How long have you felt emotionally distressed since your parents' passing?"

"What does that have to do with anything?" I snapped.

"Just trying to get a full picture," he said gently. "Michael mentioned you've been struggling. Have you been sleeping?"

"Of course I've been struggling," I snapped. "I was stabbed. By my boyfriend. And now I'm being interrogated like I imagined it."

Alvarez raised a hand, palms out. "We're not accusing you of anything, Ms. Merrow. But Michael did say he's been concerned about your mental state. That he's tried to get you help before, and that you've resisted."

"He also said you've become increasingly fixated on unusual beliefs," Dr. Hadley added. "Something about visions, magic, and voices."

My mouth fell open. "Are you serious?"

"Lena," Alvarez continued carefully, "just to clarify, is there any chance this wound was self-inflicted?"

The room spun.

I shot up in bed, ignoring the pain in my side. "You think I stabbed myself? In the gut? For what? Fun? Sympathy!?"

"We have to consider all possibilities," Dr. Hadley said. "Especially given the nature of the wound. It's deep, but clean. No signs of a struggle. And no forced entry."

Rage exploded behind my eyes. "You're not listening," I screamed. "You're not fucking listening to me! *He did this!* He *stabbed me!* And now you're looking at me like I'm some case file!"

They exchanged a look. That look. The one that said crazy without saying it.

"This is bullshit," Sarah snapped suddenly, standing so fast her chair tipped and clattered to the floor.

"Sarah," Allie said sharply, grabbing her arm. Her voice dropped into that razor-thin calm I recognized from growing up with her. The kind she used when she was scared.

She didn't speak right away. Her jaw clenched and her face went still. Then she turned and looked at me. For a second, she looked like she might cry. But she didn't. She swallowed it down, turned it into steel.

She believed me. But she was calculating now.

She squeezed my hand, once, then turned back to the two men, her voice like iron.

"I understand," she said. "I'm Dr. Allison Merrow. I'm a licensed psychiatrist, and Lena is my sister. I'd like to request discharge into my care. I'm qualified to supervise her recovery both physically and emotionally. I'll take full responsibility."

"Dr. Merrow…" Alvarez started.

She cut him off with a sharp look. "I'm also a mandated reporter. If I felt she was a danger to herself or others, you'd already know."

A pause. The cop glanced at the doctor. The doctor gave a slow nod.

"We'll approve it," Dr. Hadley said. "But she'll need follow-up care."

Allie nodded once. "Of course."

Alvarez stepped toward the door. "Dr. Merrow, if you wouldn't mind stepping out with us to finish the paperwork."

"In a minute," Allie said, eyes on me.

The cop hesitated, then gave a curt nod. He and Dr. Hadley stepped out and let the door fall shut behind them.

For a moment, the room was quiet. I turned my face toward the ceiling, tears sliding into my hairline.

"He made them think I did this," I whispered.

Allie exhaled. "They don't matter." She reached for my hand again. "We do. I believe you. And I'm not letting them take you."

Sarah leaned forward, grabbing my hand. "Screw him. You're not alone. We've got you."

A knock came almost immediately after. The door opened a crack.

"Hey, hon," came a familiar voice.

Molly. My heart lifted, then sank again.

"Got floated up from the ER today," she said, rolling in a cart with an IV bag and a laptop balanced on top. Her eyes glanced between the three of us. "Need to get your meds changed out."

Allie stood, smoothing her blazer. "I'll be back in a few. Don't let her fall asleep with her mouth open, she'll drool all over the place."

I almost smiled. Almost.

She kissed my temple and gave Sarah a squeeze on the shoulder as she passed. Then she was gone.

Molly moved quietly, checking vitals, swapping out the IV. Her hands were gentle, but her silence felt... off.

"How's the pain?" she asked softly.

"Tolerable," I lied.

She nodded and busied herself with the pump.

"Molly?"

She glanced at me but didn't really meet my eyes.

"You okay?" I asked.

She hesitated, then gave a small, tight smile. "Just worried about you. You scared the hell out of us."

"Yeah," I whispered. "I guess I did."

80

But something about her tone scraped at me. She wasn't talking like a nurse who believed her friend had been attacked. She was talking like…

"You don't believe me," I said.

Her smile faded. "Lena…"

"You think I did this to myself," I interrupted.

Molly's voice was soft and careful. "I think you've been under a lot of stress. More than a lot of people could handle."

My throat tightened.

"He got to you," I whispered.

"Nobody got to me," she said, shaking her head. "People care about you. That's all this is."

"This?"

"Getting you help," she said. "The kind you really need."

I blinked hard, trying not to break all over again.

She reached out and placed a hand lightly on my blanket-covered knee. "We just want you to get better."

Sarah moved closer, her eyes blazing. "You can go now," she said coldly. "Take your pity and get out."

Molly hesitated, then nodded. "Buzz if you need anything." She grabbed her cart and left the room.

I turned my face to the wall, the tears returning, silent and aching.

"He's twisting everything," Sarah said. "And they don't even see it."

I closed my eyes. Of course they didn't. Neither did I.

Chapter 10

I don't know how long I've been here.

Time had no shape anymore. Just sounds. The shuffle of feet in the hallway. The hum of machines. Every so often, the monitor would sound an alarming beep when my heart raced. Usually after the memory slipped in again.

Nurses came and went. They spoke softly and moved carefully. Like I was made of glass, and if they bumped the bed too hard, I'd shatter.

Michael never came into the room. But I could *feel* him. Through the walls. In the stale hospital air. Like smoke curling under the door, sliding across my skin and filling my lungs until I felt sick with it.

They told me he was still here. Still pacing the halls. Still asking for updates. Still pretending to care. That he'd been "beside himself" in the waiting room, crying and wringing his hands. Putting on a show. And everyone bought it.

Even the ones who didn't say it outright, they looked at me with that cautious uncertainty. The kind that wondered if maybe, just maybe, I'd done it to myself, and he was the poor, heartbroken man trying to save me. It was easier for them to believe that. Easier than the truth. That someone could love you and still try to end you in the same breath.

I didn't really sleep. I slipped in and out, never sinking fully under. Always one shallow breath away from remembering his smile as the knife slid in.

I started asking for more pain meds than I needed. Not to get high. Just… to float. To blur the edges of the hole I was falling through. I didn't want to feel. I didn't want to remember. I didn't want to exist.

Allie tried to get me to talk a few times. So did Sarah. I think they knew I wasn't ready. So they waited. Every time I opened my eyes, one of them was always there.

Sarah curled in a chair, her hands twisted in the hem of her shirt, eyes puffy and red. Allie leaning forward, elbows on her knees, typing furiously into her phone, her jaw locked tight like she was holding her entire body together through force of will.

But I saw it in their faces. They were afraid, too. Not of me but of what he did. Of what he could still do.

Michael was still in the building. Still breathing the same air. Still lying through his teeth to anyone who would listen. And somehow, that was allowed. That was fine.

At some point, I drifted off and when I opened my eyes again, I was alone. But I heard voices coming from the hallway. Raised ones.

Sarah's.

"I *swear to God*, if you even look in her direction again, I'll break your fucking face! You're lucky I don't set you on fire where you stand!"

My heart lurched. I pushed myself upright too fast, pain roaring through my side.

The IV tugged hard as I swung my legs over the edge of the bed, teeth clenched against the fire behind my ribs. My hospital gown was twisted and damp with sweat, and my fingers shook as I reached for the IV pole, using it to stand.

More voices now. Muffled and tight.

"Sarah." Allie's voice, sharp and controlled.

Then a third voice.

His. Smooth. Calm. Calculated. Just loud enough for others to hear. "I'm just trying to check on her. I haven't even been allowed in to see her. She's been through so much."

He sounded hurt. Confused. Like he couldn't imagine what all the fuss was about.

I shuffled to the door, every step a lightning strike of pain. My hospital gown clung to me, damp and twisted.

The hallway came into view as I cracked the door open. Allie stood between Sarah and Michael, calm but deadly. Sarah looked ready to ignite, fists clenched so tight her knuckles shone white.

And Michael…

Michael looked perfect.

Crisp button-down shirt, hair neatly pushed back, that same soft crease in his brow that used to make me feel safe. He looked like the man who brought me soup when I had the flu. Not the man who smiled when the knife slid in.

The second our eyes met, something in my chest twisted—hard. Because for just a moment… my heart *stuttered*. Like it still recognized him. Like it didn't *know* he was a monster. And that betrayal inside my own chest was somehow worse than the searing pain in my side.

"Lena," he said, stepping forward like we were alone. "Jesus, sweetheart, what are you doing out of bed?"

His voice was low and gentle. Practiced to perfection.

"You shouldn't be up," he said, eyes darting to Allie and Sarah like they were the threat. "You're still healing. You need to rest."

Then he turned slightly, pitching his voice so it would carry.

"I've been trying to see her since she got here. Just to make sure she's okay. But no one's letting me in. I'm not the enemy here."

A nurse passed at the far end of the hallway. She slowed, glanced over, then kept walking. Michael's voice rose just a bit more.

"She's been through so much. I just want to help. I've been trying to get her help for weeks. Ask anyone. I'm worried about her."

He sounded broken. Wounded. And I watched the nurse's head tilt, just slightly, like she admired his composure. Like he was the calm in the storm, not the storm itself.

Michael waited until the nurse turned the corner.

Allie stepped forward, voice cold and precise. "Michael, I know exactly what you're doing. And trust me. I'm better at it."

Michael's smile didn't falter. If anything, it widened. He turned to her, slow and lazy, like a snake tasting the air. "It's

85

almost adorable," he drawled, "that you think this is a game you can win."

Then his eyes swung back to me. And just like that, the smile died. His voice dropped, so quiet it was meant for only us. But all three of us heard it.

"Do you know what your face looked like when I did it?" He took a step closer, not bothering to hide the pleasure in his voice. "Like you finally understood. Like everything broke at once." He let out a low, pleased hum. "It was the most beautiful thing I've ever seen."

Silence.

Allie's fist twitched at her side. Sarah trembled, vibrating with fury.

And me? I stood frozen, my pulse crashing in my ears. He *loved* what he did to me. And he wanted me to know it.

Sarah lunged forward, snarling. "I'll fucking kill you—"

Allie grabbed her arm mid-swing, voice sharp with warning. "Not here."

Michael didn't move. He just adjusted the collar of his shirt, calm as ever. Then he looked at me one last time. His voice was almost playful.

"See you soon," he said softly. "Beautiful."

He turned and walked away, whistling under his breath. Like none of this mattered. Like I didn't.

I let go of the doorframe and the floor tilted under me. Allie moved fast, catching me before I hit the ground. I buried my face in her shoulder, words tearing out in a raw whisper.

"I meant nothing to him," I cried.

And that was it. The real wound. The deepest cut. He never loved me. Not once. Not ever.

Allie didn't say anything. Just held me tighter. When she helped ease me back into the bed, I barely felt the mattress beneath me. Everything inside me was numb.

Sarah stood frozen beside us, eyes red, her fists clenched and trembling. Her voice cracked when it came.

"He's dead," she hissed. "I don't care how. He's fucking dead."

Allie turned sharply. "Sarah."

"I'm serious," Sarah spat, wiping tears from her cheeks. "He comes near her again, I'll end him."

"I know," Allie said softly. "Me too."

She pulled the blanket over me, tucking it in at the sides like it was the only thing she could control. Then she pressed the call button.

A few minutes later, a nurse stepped in that I didn't recognize. Her eyes moved to mine, then to Allie and Sarah, taking in the atmosphere with a kind of wary compassion.

"She's in a lot of pain," Allie said. "She needs something to help her rest."

The nurse left and came back with a syringe. I don't know what it was. I didn't care. I barely felt the burn of it sliding into my vein. Just the warmth that followed. The soft pull at the edges of my awareness.

Sarah took my hand. Allie sat back down on the opposite side. The lights above me blurred. My heartbeat slowed. My body sank heavily into the bed.

And the last thing I heard before the dark pulled me under was Sarah whispering, "We've got you."

• • •

I woke to sunlight.

It crept in between the blinds, painting thin, gold lines across the blanket pulled up to my chin. For a moment, I didn't move. My body felt thick and heavy, like I was floating just beneath the surface of something I couldn't name. The pain was quieter. But not gone.

Sarah was curled in the chair beside me, arms folded across her chest, one foot tucked up under the other leg. Her head leaned against the wall. She was still in yesterday's clothes, her hoodie bunched beneath her chin, her mouth slack in sleep.

The room was quiet. But the door was open and from the hallway, I heard Allie's clipped voice. And another one that sounded familiar.

I blinked toward the open doorway, and saw Allie standing outside. Across from her was Anita Hall, one of the social workers. I knew her. I'd worked alongside her more than once. She brought in coffee on Fridays. Wore her hair in a tight bun and always asked about your weekend.

Now, she was talking about *me*. And her tone wasn't friendly.

"She's not stable, Dr. Merrow. You know that. She's disoriented, emotionally erratic, and there's still an active investigation into the injury. We can't just sign her out like this."

Allie didn't flinch. "She's alert, oriented, and her narrative has remained consistent. Her affect is appropriate to her current condition."

Anita lowered her voice, but I still heard it. "She says her boyfriend stabbed her. He says she's delusional. She's talking about... magic, Allie."

That landed like a fist to my stomach.

Allie's voice stayed even. "She experienced a temporary psychotic episode brought on by severe sleep deprivation. It's not uncommon. She's no longer showing signs of hallucination or disordered thinking. She's lucid and she's sleeping. She's not a danger to herself or anyone else."

Anita leaned in slightly. "Off the record? She looks like someone who's about to crack. And the attending agrees. Just seventy-two hours of inpatient observation. That's all we're asking."

I tried to sit up too fast, gasping at the sharp tug in my side.

Sarah stirred instantly. "Lena?"

I didn't answer. I was still staring at the door. Still hearing *inpatient*. Like I wasn't someone Anita used to laugh with over vending machine coffee. Like I was a risk now.

88

Allie's voice cut through, sharper than before. "She doesn't meet the legal criteria for a hold. She's sleeping. She's stable. And she's coming home with me."

Then another familiar voice joined in. I couldn't see him, but I knew it was Dr. Hadley.

"If you're taking her," he said, "I need your signature and verbal confirmation that you accept full responsibility for any crisis event that might occur."

"I already signed it." Allie's voice was flat, final.

A pause. Papers shuffled.

Sarah leaned toward me, whispering. "They're trying to admit you, aren't they?"

I nodded.

"Allie won't let that happen," she said. "Not on her fucking life."

And I believed her. Still, something in me twisted painfully. I used to trust this place. I used to feel safe here. Now they were trying to cage me because Michael knew how to smile better than I did.

Sarah sat beside me as the voices outside faded, her hand curled around mine like she was afraid I might vanish.

When the door fully swung open, Allie stepped inside. Her expression was tight, her movements sharp with barely contained fury.

"You're cleared for discharge," she said. "But they're dragging their feet."

She didn't need to say why.

"Dr. Hadley's co-sign wasn't enough," she continued. "They're calling in the hospital psych to do a final eval."

Sarah sat forward, eyes narrowing. "What the hell for? She's not crazy."

"I know that," Allie said, her voice on edge. "But after Anita's little crusade…" She exhaled hard through her nose. "They're covering their asses."

"Let me talk to them," Sarah said, already pushing up, half out of her seat.

"No," Allie said firmly. "You getting in their faces isn't going to help. Just give me time." She looked back at me, voice softening. "We'll get out of here soon. I think the psych working today is Dr. Mehta. He's worked with me before. He knows I don't make bullshit calls and I'm counting on that to be enough."

Sarah looked like she wanted to argue, but she didn't. Instead, she sighed and bent down in front of me.

"I've gotta run home," she said. "Grab some stuff, take a shower and change. But I'll be at Allie's when you get there."

She pulled me into a careful hug. I buried my face in her shoulder.

"I love you," she whispered.

I pressed my forehead into her shoulder. "Love you too."

Then she was gone.

Allie pulled a chair closer to my bed and sat beside me, smoothing the blanket over my lap while we waited. Every so often, she glanced at the clock, her fingers tapping against the paperwork in her lap with restrained irritation.

Finally, the door opened again.

Dr. Mehta stepped in, wearing a gray blazer and wire-rimmed glasses, his tablet already open in one hand. I'd seen him do a hundred psych evals in the ER. And now he was here to evaluate me. He offered a polite nod.

"Lena. I just need to ask you a few questions before discharge."

Allie stood.

"I'll give you privacy," she said. She paused and leaned down like she was adjusting my pillow and lowered her voice so only I could hear. "Say what they want to hear."

Then she stepped out, shutting the door behind her.

Dr. Mehta pulled up a chair and started clicking on the tablet. He went down the list of the usual questions. Mood. Sleep. Appetite. Hallucinations. Delusions. Self-harm.

I answered like a good, sane patient. Calm. Controlled. Appropriate affect.

Yes, I've been sleeping a little. No, I didn't feel unsafe. Yes, I understood what happened. No, I didn't think magic was real.

He thanked me for my time. Said I seemed "grounded and responsive." That there were "no current indicators for inpatient psychiatric care."

Which was their way of saying *we don't believe you, but we can't stop you either.*

And just like that, I was free to go. Still torn open. Still bleeding in ways no scan could show. But free.

Dr. Mehta left, and about twenty minutes later, Allie came back holding a small bundle of clothes—sweatpants and a baggy t-shirt.

"They'll be loose," she said. "Easier to move in."

She carefully helped me change and put my hair up into a loose ponytail. A nurse came in next. She removed the IV, checked my vitals one last time, and gave me that same polite, professional smile I used to give my own patients.

Then she rolled in a wheelchair. "All set," she said brightly, moving behind it. "Let's get you home."

But before she could touch the handles, Allie stepped in.

"I'll take her." Her voice wasn't unkind. Just... firm.

The nurse hesitated, glanced between us, then stepped back.

Allie looked at me.

"You ready?"

No. But I nodded anyway.

She guided the chair toward the door and just like that, we were leaving.

Allie wheeled me outside through the sliding doors. The fresh air was a quiet relief after the stale, chemical hush of the hospital. She opened the passenger door and helped me in without a word, then shut it gently behind me.

The car ride was quiet. I pressed my forehead to the window, watching the trees blur past. The world looked too normal. Like it hadn't noticed I was bleeding out just days ago.

Each bump in the road sent a flare of pain through my side. I didn't make a sound, but I saw Allie glance at me more than once. She didn't say anything. Neither did I.

When we pulled into the driveway, Sarah was already waiting on the porch. She looked fresh, like she'd finally showered and thrown on clean clothes. She was wearing jeans and a fitted black top. Even her makeup was done.

"Take it slow," Allie said. "We've got time."

I stepped out gingerly, the motion sending a sharp jab through my side that stole my breath. I bit down on it. Hard. Every step from the car to the porch felt like fire—small, stabbing reminders of what he'd done.

He kissed me. He smiled. Then he sank the knife in like it meant nothing.

Sarah reached for me when I hesitated at the first step. I shook my head.

"I've got it," I muttered.

I didn't. But I made it to the porch anyway.

"I brought your stuff," Sarah said, stepping forward. "And your gremlin. She's been pacing like crazy."

Biscuit let out a yowl from the screen door, like she knew I was finally here. I took a slow step forward, then froze.

"My house," I said a little panicked. "When you went back... was he there?"

If he could do that to me, there's no telling what he might do to her.

Sarah's expression changed. Just slightly. "No," she said. "And I brought Abel with me."

Allie, who had just stepped up behind me, raised an eyebrow. "Who's Abel?"

Sarah waved a hand like it was nothing, but I didn't miss the pink flush that rose in her cheeks.

"Old friend," she said. "He's a cop. He and I... had a thing. Once."

Allie shot her a sly look. "The one who got away?"

"The one I let get away," Sarah muttered. "Anyway. We got in, grabbed your things, and got out. I also drove your car over here. It's parked in the garage."

"I looked for Corinne's journal," she added quietly. "It was gone. I searched everywhere. It wasn't there."

"Thank you," I said.

Sarah stepped closer. "You don't have to thank me. I'd burn the whole place down if I thought it would help."

Allie held the door. "Come on," she said. "You're home now."

Allie's house smelled like cedar and lemon soap. It was clean, lived-in, and welcoming. The place looked like something out of a magazine, if the magazine catered to overachievers with a Pinterest board for every season.

Wood siding on the outside, dark-stained beams across the ceiling inside. Soft tan walls. Big windows that looked out into the woods behind the house. A stone fireplace sat unused in the corner, and a throw blanket was draped perfectly over the back of the couch, like it had been fluffed just before we arrived.

To the back, a sliding glass door led out to a small deck with a hot tub tucked beneath a pergola. On the left side of the house, half-visible through the kitchen window, I caught a glimpse of Allie's raised garden beds.

I walked inside and eased down onto the couch, careful of my side. The cushions were soft, swallowing me up. Biscuit leapt onto my lap almost immediately. She pressed her body into me, purring like nothing else in the world mattered. I looked down at her, my fingers twitching before finally settling against her fur.

Allie disappeared into the kitchen without a word. I heard the creak of the cabinet doors, the click of the fridge, the soft whirr of something pouring.

Sarah came back first, a steaming mug in her hands.

"It's mostly cream," she said, nudging it into my hands. "Don't yell at me."

"Thanks," I murmured. My voice still felt like gravel.

93

She sat down next to me, close but not touching. Her knees bounced. I wondered if it was for me, or for her.

Allie came back a minute later and sank into the armchair across from us. Not like she was settling in. More like she was preparing. For what, I didn't know.

The silence stretched. No one rushed to fill it.

I could see the trees blowing in the wind outside of the window. Biscuit purred. I took a small sip of the coffee. It was too sweet, but I didn't mind.

I didn't know what to say. Maybe they didn't either.

Then Allie leaned forward, elbows on her knees, hands clasped loosely. "Now that we're alone..." Her voice was quiet but unwavering. "You need to tell us everything."

I looked up slowly.

"No more half-truths," Allie added. "No more 'I don't knows.' We need the real version. All of it."

My throat tightened. "I don't even know where to start," I whispered.

"Just start from the beginning," Sarah said.

So I did.

I told them about the girl in the ER and how something inside me had sparked when I touched her. The dream, the mirror. The strange pull I'd felt toward Corinne's book and some of the things she wrote in it. The letter grandma wrote to Corinne.

I told them about the visit to Corinne, the stone and how the pain in that place felt like it had cracked something open inside me, like I'd been carrying a fuse I didn't know was lit. How the entire building shook.

And then I told them what happened after. How I ran to Michael. How he stabbed me like it was the happiest moment of his life.

Allie didn't speak right away. She stood slowly and disappeared down the hall. When she came back, she was carrying a small stack of old leather-bound journals.

"I found these after Mom and Dad died," she said, settling back into the chair. "They were in a box in the attic. Tucked under some old photo albums."

She handed them to me one at a time. The leather was worn smooth at the edges. Grandma's handwriting peeked through the cracks in the spine.

"They're hers," Allie said. "Grandma's. I read through them a couple years ago."

Her voice was quiet, but sure.

"At first, I thought they were just stories. Fairytales. Her imagination put to paper. You know how she was a little… odd."

She gave a faint smile.

"But they weren't. She was documenting. She writes about magic like it's real. Detailed. Structured. Like… notes from a class."

Allie rested her elbows on her knees again. "According to her, people are born with something called a *mark*—a unique power, tied to their soul. It shows up differently in everyone. Some can heal. Some can feel or manipulate emotions. Others can influence the physical world."

I stared down at the journals in my lap. "So… why me?"

"It's usually passed down," Allie said. "Taught through generations. Grandma must've known what you were, but…"

"She didn't tell me," I interrupted.

"She didn't tell me either," Allie replied. "Hell, I don't even think she told Mom."

"But why now?" I asked. "Why is it only starting now? Why not when I was a kid?"

The room was quiet for a moment.

"Maybe it was dormant," Sarah offered. "Waiting for something to trigger it. Or maybe…" She hesitated. "Maybe someone sealed it. Hid it from you."

Allie didn't answer right away. She just watched me for a long moment before saying, "Lena. Didn't you wonder how I knew to come that day?"

95

I blinked. Of all the chaos, the blood, the sirens, the pain—
I hadn't. I just remembered her face. Her voice saying I was safe. But I'd never asked *why* she was there in the first place.

My mouth parted. "You're right. I didn't."

Allie hesitated, then spoke slowly. "I had a vision."

My brows drew together. "A vision?"

"I was sitting at work," she continued. "Just... charting, nothing unusual. And then it was like I wasn't there anymore. Like I got pulled out of my body."

She paused.

"It was vivid. Like a dream, but sharper. Grandma was there. She looked younger than I remember. And fierce. She grabbed my shoulders and screamed, *'She needs you! Go to her!'*"

Allie's voice cracked. "Then she moved aside. And I saw you on the floor. Pale and bleeding. There was a hole in your stomach and so much blood."

"Then it was gone. I snapped back to real life, back in my chair, hands shaking. But I *knew*. I *knew* it wasn't in my head."

Her hand gripped the edge of her chair. "I grabbed my keys, called 911 from the car, and broke every damn speed limit getting to you. I didn't know what I'd find, but... I knew I had to be there."

I tried to blink back tears. "She sent you," I whispered. "Grandma."

Allie nodded. "I think so."

I stared at Allie. The sister I'd pushed away. The one I hadn't called in too long. And she was the one who saved me.

"You believed it," I said softly. "Before I even told you everything."

Allie gave a small nod. "After that vision? I didn't really have a choice."

I looked down at the journals again. "Does that mean... do you think you have a mark too?"

Allie tilted her head. "I don't know. I've never felt anything like that before. But if I do... maybe it's connected to Grandma. Or maybe it's just... her."

96

"That wasn't just instinct," Sarah said. "That was magic. You saw something none of us could."

"Whatever it was," Allie said, "it brought me to you. That's all that matters."

My throat tightened. I swallowed hard, but it didn't help. "You saved me."

"You're my sister," she said. "You think I'd let you go down without a fight?"

I didn't realize I was crying until Biscuit butted her head against my side and let out a tiny yowl. I wiped my face quickly and whispered, "I missed you."

Allie reached across the space and took my hand. "I missed you, too."

For a moment, we just sat there. There was so much I wanted to say, but none of it came out in the right order in my head.

"What were we even fighting about?" I asked, half-laughing through the tears. "I don't remember."

Allie huffed out a breath, almost a laugh of her own. "I don't remember either. Probably something stupid though."

"So stupid," I echoed.

She squeezed my hand. "We were both stubborn. Both waiting for the other to say it first."

"Well," I said softly, "consider it said."

"Same," she whispered.

Sarah let out a long sigh beside me. "Finally," she muttered. "The two of you could've ended world wars with how long you dragged that out."

We all laughed—tired, emotional, a little cracked around the edges.

The laughter started to fade. I looked down at my lap, at Biscuit curled tight against me, then back at the worn leather of the journal. My fingers traced the edge.

"There's something else," I said quietly.

Both Allie and Sarah looked up.

"When he stabbed me..." I paused, swallowing the memory. "It wasn't just pain. I mean, it hurt—God, it *hurt*—but it was like… something got ripped out of me. Like a part of me was being pulled through the knife."

Allie leaned forward again. "Pulled how?"

"Like… like a string unraveling. From the inside out." I rubbed my arms. "And it didn't stop when I fell. It kept going. Like he was siphoning something off me."

Sarah's eyes were wide now. "Jesus."

"I didn't know what it was at the time. I thought I was dying, and I guess I kind of was, but it wasn't just blood. It was like… something deeper." I looked up slowly. "I think he was taking my power. My mark."

Allie sat back, her jaw tight. "That would explain why you felt it starting to emerge, only for it to vanish again.

"Can someone even do that?" I asked. "Steal a mark?"

"I don't know," Allie admitted.

Sarah was staring at me now like she wasn't sure whether to be terrified or pissed off. "So he didn't just hurt you. He *used* you. Took something that was yours."

I nodded slowly. "It felt… intimate and violent. Like he reached inside and yanked out part of my soul." I paused. "And I let him."

Sarah's eyes snapped to mine. "What? No."

"I let him in," I repeated. "I ran to him. I trusted him. I told him I needed him. And he used that moment to hurt me. To take everything. I didn't even try to stop him. I didn't know I should."

Tears welled again, blurring everything. Shame clawed up my throat like bile.

"I handed it to him," I whispered. "Didn't even realize what I was giving away."

Sarah surged forward, her hand wrapping around mine like a vice. "No. You didn't give him anything. He manipulated you. He's a fucking predator."

Allie's voice was firm. "He didn't win, Lena. He *didn't*. You're here. You're still breathing."

I swallowed, blinking hard. Biscuit curled tighter against me, her purr vibrating through my bones.

Sarah's lips pressed into a line. "I want to kill him."

"Same," Allie said, her voice dark.

I let out a breath. "I don't even know what's left. If I still have any of it."

Allie reached for one of the journals again, flipping it open. "Then that's where we start. We figure out what he took—and what he didn't."

Chapter 11

The next morning, we sat around Allie's kitchen table, picking at breakfast that none of us really seemed to want.

Sarah was stirring her coffee so aggressively it sloshed over the rim every few seconds. Biscuit wove between our feet, occasionally headbutting my leg like she was scolding me for ignoring her.

I pushed the sausage around my plate with my fork. I hadn't taken a single bite. My stomach felt like it had been sewn shut.

Allie watched me from across the table, her eyes sharp behind her mug. She set it down with a quiet, deliberate clink.

"You need to eat something," she said.

I didn't look up. "I'm not hungry."

"I don't care," she said, her voice flat. "You lost a lot of blood. Your body needs fuel to heal."

I stabbed a piece of egg, lifted it halfway to my mouth, then set the fork back down. My fingers felt weak, like they belonged to someone else.

Sarah sighed, dropping her fork with a small clatter. "She'll eat when she's ready, Allie. Jesus."

Allie shot her a look but didn't argue. Instead, she reached across the table and flipped open one of Grandma's journals, already covered in sticky notes and scraps of paper. Her fingers traced a line of cramped handwriting. She cleared her throat.

"I was thinking," she said carefully, "we could try something small today. Just... to see."

I glanced at her, my chest tightening. "See what?"

Allie tapped the open page. "See if there's anything left. Any magic. Any mark still inside you."

I swallowed hard. My throat felt too tight.

Sarah leaned back in her chair, arms crossed, one knee bouncing restlessly. "Maybe we should wait. She's still healing. This feels... I don't know. Rushed."

Allie shook her head, her jaw set. "If he took everything, we need to know. And if he didn't... then she needs to know that too."

"What do I have to do?" I asked, my voice barely above a whisper.

Allie's expression softened. She turned the journal toward me. "It's a simple enchantment," she said gently. "It's meant to call small objects to your hand. Like a key or a coin."

Sarah stood, grabbing my untouched plate and scraped it into the trash. "Fine. Let's do it," she muttered. "Get it over with."

Allie closed the journal slowly, her fingers drumming against the worn leather cover for a moment before she stood.

"Come on," she said quietly. "Let's get set up somewhere more comfortable."

I pushed my chair back, every small movement echoing in my side. Biscuit trotted ahead of us on our way to the living room. Allie placed a quarter in the center of the coffee table like it meant something. Like it could answer the question we were all too afraid to say out loud. Sarah cleared space around it, as if making room would help.

I sat on the couch, knees tucked under me, heart beating harder than it should've. All I had to do was focus. Say the words. Pull the coin to my hand.

I didn't know what I expected—sparks, maybe? A glow? Heat in my hands?

But nothing happened. The coin didn't budge. Not when I closed my eyes and tried to feel it. Not when I whispered the words Grandma had written in looping cursive. Not when Allie told me to "just breathe and focus."

There was nothing. Just me. Empty. Like someone had scooped out the part of me that mattered and left the shell behind.

"I think…" I started, then stopped.

Allie looked up. "What?"

I shook my head. "I think it's gone."

Sarah opened her mouth like she wanted to argue, but I didn't give her the chance.

"I don't feel anything." My voice cracked. "It's just me now. Just… broken."

Silence settled again.

"I know it's dumb," I whispered, "but I keep thinking maybe he'll walk through the door. Say it was a mistake. Say he didn't mean to hurt me." I looked down at my hands—hands that had once held power, maybe. Or maybe I imagined it all.

"I miss him. Not the monster. But the version I thought was real. The one who made me feel safe and loved."

Allie sat still, but her jaw was tight. Sarah didn't move. She just watched me like she was holding her breath.

"How do you stop loving someone who tore you apart?" I asked. "How do you stop needing them?"

No one had an answer. And maybe that was the worst part. We sat like that for a while. Just three women trying to hold something broken between us without cutting our hands.

Later that evening, Sarah disappeared into the kitchen. I barely noticed. I was too busy trying to breathe past the dull, pulsing ache in my side. The stitches pulled every time I moved. Each breath was a reminder of the blade, of his voice, of how close I'd come to dying on the floor of my own house. I adjusted slightly on the couch, wincing. Allie noticed. Her eyes tracked every twitch, every wince, like she was waiting for me to fall apart again.

When Sarah came back, her shoulders were tense and her phone was clutched in her hand.

"I need you guys not to be mad," she said, standing in the doorway.

Allie gave her a look. "What did you do?"

Sarah stepped in, chewing her lip. "I told Abel to come over. He already knew something was wrong when I asked him to help get Lena's stuff. When he texted just now, asking if everything was okay... I told him."

Allie crossed her arms. "Told him what, exactly?"

"I didn't say anything about magic," Sarah said quickly. "Just... that Michael hurt Lena. That we're scared he'll come back. He's... good. And if there's even a chance he can help..."

"You think a cop is going to believe all this?" Allie asked, clearly unconvinced.

I looked down at my hands. "What did he say?"

She hesitated. "He's on his way."

Abel showed up half an hour later.

He was tall, with a solid, balanced build that suggested he could handle himself without needing to prove it. His dark hair, slightly tousled from the rain, framed a face that looked both careful and kind. He wore his police uniform, the badge at his chest catching the hallway light. He stepped into the living room like he was entering a crime scene, gaze sweeping over every detail. He gave Sarah a small nod, then turned toward me.

"Nice to see you again, Lena," he said gently.

"Yeah. You too," I replied.

"And you're Allie?" he asked, looking in her direction.

Allie didn't rise to greet him. She just gave a sharp nod. "So you're the cop."

Abel didn't flinch. "That's me."

His eyes moved back to Sarah for a half-second too long, something unreadable passing between them. Not warmth, exactly. But familiarity. Like he was remembering something neither of them had the right to miss.

We all sat in the living room. I eased back onto the couch slowly, wincing as the stitches pulled against tender skin. Sarah's eyes darted to me, but only for a second—drawn again, almost involuntarily, to Abel as he sank into the armchair across from us.

He glanced around the room like it was evidence. Every detail mattered. But when his eyes found Sarah again, they softened. Just a little.

"Didn't think I'd see you again so soon," he said under his breath.

"Yeah... me either," Sarah murmured.

Allie clocked the exchange but didn't comment. She just raised an eyebrow and waited.

Sarah sat up straighter, clearing her throat like it mattered. "We need to tell you something. And we need you to listen before you start forming opinions."

And Abel did.

He listened while we told him what we could, everything except the magic. Just the truth the world would recognize. Michael. The knife. The hospital. The blood. The police and doctors who didn't listen. The nightmare that hadn't ended.

When we finished, the silence that followed felt like a verdict waiting to fall.

Abel leaned forward, elbows on his knees.

"Okay. I believe you," he said.

Allie's eyes narrowed. "Just like that?"

He looked at her. "Not just like that. But I've seen cases like this before, where the system fails the victim. Where charm covers cruelty. I know the type."

His gaze lingered on Sarah again. "And I trust her judgment."

Sarah's face gave nothing away, but I caught the slight twitch at the corner of her mouth.

Allie folded her arms. "Are you going to report this?"

He shook his head. "Not yet. There's no evidence, and if I push too hard, it'll make things worse. But I can keep an eye out. Quietly and off the record."

He pulled out his phone. "I've got a couple of friends I trust. Ex-military. They'll take shifts keeping watch outside, just in case."

"Why would you do this for us?" I asked. My voice felt too small.

"Because if I'm right about this guy…" He exhaled slowly. "Then I don't want to be the cop who ignored the signs and showed up after the damage was done."

He stood, pulling a worn notepad from his jacket and scribbling something down.

"I'm giving you their numbers too," he said, tearing off the page. "If you can't reach me for any reason, call them. No explanations needed. Just say you're in trouble."

He handed the slip of paper to Allie, then turned to me again.

"I'm going to check the property. Talk to a few people. If he shows up, even breathes in your direction… I'll know."

He looked back at Sarah for a moment. Then he nodded once and slipped out the door.

We were alone again.

Chapter 12

The days passed. Michael didn't come. And I didn't move.

Abel came and went, checking in when he could, but there were no real updates.

The pain in my side dulled to a constant throb, but the pain in my chest stayed sharp. I didn't open the journals. Didn't ask about spells. Didn't try. I didn't want to feel anything. I just wanted to sleep. So I did.

Allie kept a strict schedule with the pain meds. Always on time, always by the book, but I knew what I was doing. I asked for them early. Told her the pain was worse. And maybe it was. But mostly, I just wanted the quiet. The pull. The blur.

There was a follow-up appointment a few days after I got home. Allie drove me. I sat on the exam table in one of her oversized sweatshirts, letting the nurse check my vitals while the doctor glanced at my chart and barely at me.

"You're healing fine," he said, typing something into his laptop.

He didn't ask about the knife. Or the man who held it. Just nodded and said I could come back in another week to have the stitches removed. I didn't make another appointment.

Every time I surfaced, someone was there. Allie or Sarah. They made sure I was never alone.

Allie had taken a leave of absence from work. A decision I knew didn't come lightly. She didn't say much about it, but I caught the tension in her jaw every time a message buzzed on her phone and she ignored it. Whatever responsibilities she had before, they didn't matter now. She was all in—focused on keeping me alive, keeping me safe, even if it meant putting her own life on hold.

Sarah worked remotely, setting up her laptop at the kitchen table. If they had to leave, they did it in shifts. Grocery runs. Coffee refills. Pharmacy. Someone was always here watching. Like I was something breakable. Or something someone was still hunting.

I didn't blame them.

Allie was the one trying to fix me. She read from Grandma's journals in a soft voice like she was telling bedtime stories. She left them on the table beside me, stacked neatly, bookmarks sticking out at angles like makeshift bandages.

I never touched them. But sometimes, I listened.

Tonight was one of those times. Allie sat cross-legged in her armchair, a journal spread open on her lap. I was curled into my usual spot on the couch, blanket pulled to my waist, eyes half-closed but still tracking her voice.

"Some marks resonate more strongly with the body," she read. "Others heighten the mind. But all marks are tied to the soul. They are born there and shaped there. Most people only carry one. But in rare cases, more than one mark can manifest in a single bearer. If that happens, the bearer becomes something rare and coveted. It draws attention and desire. Even danger. Powerful families have killed for less."

Allie looked up. "You think that's what Grandma did? Bound your mark, or maybe marks, to keep you safe? Maybe she knew you were different. That having more than one would make you a target. Maybe she was trying to protect you from being found."

I didn't answer, and she didn't push—just continued reading.

"Magic isn't good or evil. It reflects the soul it's tied to. But some corrupt the bond. Fuel it with fear, greed, or violence until it becomes something else entirely. And when that happens, there's a reckoning. The Severance corrects. Quietly and permanently. You don't seek them out. You cross a line, and they find you."

She glanced up again.

"Severance," she murmured. "She capitalized it. Like it's a title or a group."

"Sounds like magical enforcers," Sarah offered from the other room.

I didn't say anything. But the word stayed with me.

"I really think Grandma knew someone was coming for you," Allie said quietly. "There's a section on how to bind a mark. How to protect it from being sensed. She must've done it when you were little. Before you were old enough to use it."

I didn't look up. "So it's her fault."

Allie slammed the journal closed, the sound sharper than it should've been. "No. She saved you. You just don't see it yet."

She stood, pacing once, then turned on me.

"I know you're hurting. I know this is hell. But you're not even trying, Lena! You sit here every day like you're already gone!" She shook her head, voice rising. "You think I took time off work just to watch you crawl into a hole and stay there? To watch you fade while he's still out there?"

Her voice cracked.

"We *need* you. You're the one this all circles around, whether you like it or not."

I flinched at her tone, then sat up straighter, my heart thudding.

"You think this is easy for me? You're all sitting here trying to fix me like I'm some broken puzzle!"

Allie opened her mouth to respond, but I didn't let her.

"You didn't see him! None of you did! You didn't trust him, love him, sleep beside him and believe—*believe*—he was the safest place on Earth!" My breath caught. "I did!"

Allie's expression faltered. For a second she looked hurt.

"I let him in!" I shouted. "I ran to him! I *begged* him to make it stop. And he smiled when he drove the knife in!" The sound of the blade. The warmth of my own blood. The betrayal in his eyes. It all surged up like bile.

"I don't know what's worse," I said, tears burning now. "That he fooled me... or that part of me still misses the man he pretended to be."

Allie stepped forward, her face softening. "Lena—"

But before she could say more, something inside me lashed out. Not with rage, but with raw, open pain and guilt. Like everything I'd been holding in ripped free all at once.

Allie froze. Her eyes went wide, her breath stuttered like she'd been punched in the chest. Her hand flew to her heart.

"What—what was that?" she said.

I sat there looking at her, my entire body shaking.

"I don't know," I said, my voice barely above a whisper. "It felt like... something gave way. Like I couldn't hold it in anymore."

Allie stared, still holding her chest. Her breathing was uneven. "It was more than emotion. It hit me like a wave. Your grief, your shame, all of it."

"You could feel that?" I said.

She nodded slowly. "It felt like..." She looked at me, stunned. "Like everything you're carrying just hit me all at once."

I looked down at my hands, expecting to see something— light, sparks, *anything.* But there was nothing. Just fingers.

"I didn't mean to," I said quietly.

Allie shook her head. "That wasn't a mistake, Lena. That was power. Real power. You didn't just tell me how you felt. You made me feel it."

Before I could respond, Sarah appeared in the doorway, eyes wide. She looked between us, her voice shaky. "What the hell just happened in here?"

Allie turned to her. "Did you feel it too?"

Sarah nodded. "I was in the kitchen and I suddenly felt like I couldn't breathe. Like... grief. But it wasn't mine." She looked at me, brow furrowed. "It was yours, wasn't it?"

"I think so," I said, my throat tight. "I didn't mean to."

"It slammed into me," Sarah said, rubbing her chest.

Allie nodded. "I read something the other day," she said, glancing down at the journal still in her hand. "About marks tied to emotional projection. Empathy, but not just sensing. It talked about people who could make others feel what they were feeling, or make them feel whatever they wanted. Fear. Love. Anxiety."

I looked at her. "You think that's what this is?"

Allie nodded. "He meant to take everything."

Her eyes met mine.

"But he didn't get all of it. Because you survived. He left something behind. And now we have an idea of what it is."

Allie and Sarah were still staring at me like they'd seen something they weren't supposed to. Something private and bleeding. Not just my magic. My grief. My shame. My guilt. All of it spilled into the space between us like shattered glass.

Sarah's eyes were rimmed with tears. Her mouth opened once, then closed again. She didn't know what to say. Allie looked like she was trying to hold herself together with clenched teeth and tight fists. But her posture had changed. Less sharp. Less angry.

Then Sarah let out a shaky breath and lowered herself onto the couch beside me. "That wasn't just grief," she said quietly. "It was like being in your skin. Like the weight of it all landed in my chest and just... stayed there." She rubbed her sternum like it still ached. "God, Lena."

Allie sat down in the chair across from me. "I felt it too. All of it. And I know I lost my temper earlier, but—" she paused. "I didn't know. Not really."

"I didn't mean to do it," I said again, softer this time. "I didn't even know I could."

"I think that's the point," Allie said. "It was never about control. It came from your *heart*, not your head."

Sarah nodded, her eyes still red. "It wasn't weak, Lena. It was... powerful. And honest."

I looked down at my lap, at my hands. I didn't feel powerful. I felt wrung out. Raw. But also... not as hollow as before. Not completely empty.

Allie leaned forward, voice gentler now. "We should explore this. Figure out what it is. What it can do."

I nodded.

Then a knock came at the door.

Allie stood to answer it, and a moment later, Abel stepped inside. He was dressed down in a soft blue button-down, dark jeans, and a light jacket. I wasn't used to seeing him out of uniform. He almost looked like a completely different person.

He held a small paper tray with three takeaway cups and a crumpled brown bag. "Brought tea," he said. "Chamomile, I think. Heard it helps with, you know… stress."

He gave a half-smile and set it gently on the table. "Also grabbed some pastries. Thought you guys could use something sweet"

Abel's eyes swept the room, quiet and observant. Then he looked at me. "Did I interrupt something?"

Allie shook her head, though her voice was softer than usual. "No. You're fine."

He turned back to me. "How are you holding up?"

I didn't answer right away. I wasn't sure how to. But I gave him a forced smile. It was all I had.

He didn't push. Instead, he stepped forward and offered one of the teas to Sarah. Her fingers brushed his for just a second too long as she took it. "You've been quiet today," she said gently, looking up at him. "Did you find something?"

Abel's expression changed. He sat down in the other recliner, and pulled out his phone. "A few things," he said. "I'm still sorting through some of it, but… Michael's past is a lot more curated than I realized. Some of the info he gave doesn't line up. A few addresses don't exist anymore. One of the companies he claimed to consult for hasn't been active in five years."

Allie raised an eyebrow. "So… what, he built a fake résumé?"

"It's more than that," Abel said. "It's a whole life that's been carefully constructed. Every detail crafted to blend in, to seem normal. You don't do that unless you're hiding something, or trying to get close to someone without raising flags."

Sarah tensed beside me. "You think this was all premeditated?"

"I think he's been laying the groundwork for years," Abel said. "It's not about fraud or identity theft. It's deeper. More personal."

He glanced at me. "Did he ever ask you questions about your family? Anything about your past that he pushed at?"

I shook my head slowly. "No. Not at first. Later he'd ask about my parents, my grandma, but nothing that stood out. It just felt like... like he wanted to get to know me more."

"Did he ever ask for money? Try to isolate you?"

"No," I said. "If anything, he pushed me to reconnect. Said he wanted me to have support."

Abel frowned. "Then it's not about finances or control. Not in the way we usually see."

Allie leaned forward slightly. "Then what is it?"

Abel hesitated. "Obsession, maybe. Or revenge. Could be something else entirely. Whatever it is, it's personal. He didn't just want to be close. He needed to be. For a reason."

I felt my throat tighten, the words sticking like thorns. I knew exactly what the reason was. We all did. But Abel didn't.

So I nodded slowly. Let him think it was about control, possession, or manipulation. That was easier to explain.

"He planned everything," I said quietly. "Every moment."

No one corrected me. I felt something twist in my gut. Not a sharp pain. A slow, unraveling one.

"Everything was a lie," I said, the words dry and distant in my throat. "The places, the jobs, the stories he told me..."

The tea in my hand suddenly felt too hot, like it didn't belong there. Like I didn't belong here.

"He created a whole life," I whispered. "For me to fall into."

Sarah reached for my hand, but I pulled it back. I wasn't angry. I was drowning. Tears burned at the corners of my eyes before I could stop them. I stood too quickly, the tea still in my hand, sloshing slightly over the rim.

No one said anything. I set the cup on the coffee table with shaking hands and walked toward the back door. The air outside was colder than I expected, but I didn't go back in. I just stepped out onto the porch, wrapped my arms around myself, and sat on the top step.

I didn't cry, not really. I just sat there, blinking fast, my jaw clenched against the tremble I couldn't quite swallow. Behind me, the house was quiet. They were giving me space. But a few minutes later, the door creaked open.

Sarah stepped out with a blanket folded in her arms. She didn't say anything. Just draped it over my shoulders and sat beside me, close but not crowding.

The fabric smelled faintly like home. Laundry detergent and something else I couldn't name. I curled into it without thinking. We sat like that for a while, staring out into the woods.

Finally, she spoke. "You didn't deserve any of this, you know."

I didn't answer.

"He didn't break you." She paused. "He wanted to. But you're still here."

I shook my head, voice hoarse. "Barely."

"Barely still counts," she said softly.

The wind rustled the trees. I could hear a coyote somewhere in the distance. Something living. Something unbothered.

I looked down. "It wasn't just the lies. It's knowing... I never really knew him. Not even a little."

Sarah's voice was steady. "That's not your fault."

"Isn't it?" I whispered. "I let him in. I handed him my heart like it was a gift. And he took everything he wanted from it."

She didn't argue. She just bumped her shoulder against mine.

"You're still you," she said. "Even if he tried to erase it."

I swallowed the lump in my throat. "What if what's left isn't enough?"

Sarah turned to me with a fierce look on her face. "Then we duct-tape your soul back together and go hunt down the bastard."

God, I loved her. Not just because she was here, not because she always showed up when it mattered most, but because she never asked me to be okay. She just stood beside me. Like always.

"Where do you think he is?" I asked finally. My voice came out quieter than I meant it to.

Sarah glanced over at me, her expression unreadable. "Abel says he's probably gone underground. Smart predators disappear after the first strike. Wait until you're off guard."

I nodded slowly. "So we just wait?"

"We prepare," she said.

I exhaled slowly. "I don't want you guys getting hurt because of me."

Sarah snorted softly. "Please. We've been through worse."

I gave her a sideways glance.

"Okay," she amended. "Maybe not *this*. But still." She nudged my knee with hers. "I'd take a hundred Michael-level disasters over losing you."

I didn't smile. But something in my chest softened. "What do you think he's planning?"

Sarah's voice was quieter now. "I don't know. But he didn't go through all this trouble to let you walk away. Whatever he wants... he still thinks he can get it."

My eyes stung and before I could stop it, a tear slipped down my cheek.

I leaned into her, my shoulder brushing hers, and the words tumbled out, raw and broken. "I can't believe he did this."

Sarah didn't flinch. She didn't shush me or rush to make it better. She just wrapped an arm around my back, her grip solid.

"I had no idea either," she said. "I mean—God, Lena. He fooled all of us. Not just you."

I sniffed. "But you didn't love him."

"No," she said softly. "But I trusted him. I believed what he showed us. I believed he loved you. So yeah, he fooled me too."

I closed my eyes. "How could he pretend that well?"

"He didn't pretend, Lena. He just showed you the version he needed you to see. Monsters don't lie, they calculate."

Her voice was steady, but there was something underneath. Anger, maybe. Or fear.

I didn't speak. I just let her warmth hold me.

She sighed. "Alright. Back inside before a bear mistakes us for a midnight snack."

That pulled a thin laugh from me. She stood and opened the door. We stepped inside, the warmth of the house wrapping around us.

The lights were low and the living room was quiet. Abel was still in the recliner, phone in hand, the screen casting a faint glow on his face. He looked up as we entered.

"Allie went to bed," he said quietly. "She didn't say much."

Sarah closed the door behind us and kicked off her shoes. "She needed the rest," she said. "We all do."

Abel nodded, slipping his phone into his pocket. "Everything okay?"

I hesitated. Then I nodded. "Better than before."

I crossed the room and sat down on the couch, legs a little wobbly as I lowered myself.

He didn't ask for more. Just leaned forward. "I'm still digging. If Michael leaves even the smallest trail, I'll find it."

"Thank you," I said sincerely.

Sarah dropped onto the couch beside me and yawned. "Can tomorrow come with fewer emotional avalanches? Please?"

Abel chuckled. "No promises."

The conversation drifted after that to low murmurs and tired laughter. The kind that didn't try too hard. No one had the energy to pretend tonight.

After some time, Sarah stood and stretched, her hoodie riding up just enough to show the curve of her hip. Abel glanced at her quickly and then looked away just as fast.

She walked past him, then paused.

"You staying?" she asked.

"If that's alright," Abel replied.

Sarah nodded. "Couch is yours."

She moved further past him and headed for the hallway. He stood as she did. And then, right there in the half-dark, he reached out and caught her wrist. She turned and he leaned in.

The kiss was soft and brief. Nothing showy, but it was real. I didn't mean to see it. But I didn't look away, either. I felt something in my chest. Not pain. Not jealousy. Not even sadness. Just warmth. A pulse of something human and whole. Something that felt like the start of hope.

Sarah deserved this. Love. Safety. A hand that didn't take. And maybe, if the world could still give that to her... it wasn't done with me yet, either.

Chapter 13

The house was quiet when I woke.

For a second, I didn't know where I was. The walls were unfamiliar in the early gray light, the ceiling too high, the blankets too soft. Then I turned my head toward the window and saw the outline of the trees behind Allie's house.

Safety. For now.

I eased out of bed, careful not to wake Biscuit, who had decided sometime in the night that my hip made the perfect pillow. She let out an offended yowl as I moved, then flopped over and went back to sleep. I threw on a light sweater over my tank top and made my way out to the hall.

The kitchen was still dim. I padded barefoot across the tile and reached for the coffee maker, my hands moving on instinct long before my brain caught up.

The coffee pot had just finished brewing when I heard Sarah's door open and close down the hall, followed by footsteps.

Abel walked into the kitchen, rumpled and shirtless, hair pushed up on one side like he'd fallen asleep fighting gravity. His expression froze for half a second when he saw me, like he hadn't expected to run into anyone this early.

I raised an eyebrow, a quick grin tugging at my lips. "Morning."

He cleared his throat. "Morning."

I grabbed a mug from the cabinet, poured a cup, and slid it across the counter toward him.

"No judgment," I said, voice dry with amusement. "Just coffee."

He caught the mug, eyes glancing to mine. "Thanks."

He took a sip, nodding toward the window. "Looks like rain."

I glanced outside. The sky was still pale, but heavy with clouds that were low and unmoving, like they were waiting for permission to break open. "Good," I said. "The trees could use it."

He gave a quiet hum, almost a smile. "Yeah. Everything feels... dusty."

We stood there a moment in awkward silence—him leaning against the counter, me sipping from my mug.

Then I felt a wave of warmth. It wasn't physical. It was deeper than that.

Love.

Not aimed at me, but close enough to feel. It was present and heavy, like steam rising from the mug in my hands. It lingered. And it was coming from Abel.

It radiated off him like a low hum. Not infatuation. Not lust. The real thing. The kind of love that made you stay. The kind that didn't flinch in the dark.

For Sarah. I don't think he even realized he was carrying it.

I looked down into my coffee, blinking hard. I wasn't going to cry over that, but something inside me shimmered just a little. Not from pain but from hope.

He loved her. *Really* loved her.

I heard Sarah's door open again. She stepped into the kitchen, hair tousled and wearing Abel's shirt. It was oversized on her, sleeves swallowing her hands, the hem brushing her thighs.

She saw us and froze for half a second. Then she smiled—wide and unbothered, the most relaxed I'd seen her in weeks.

I didn't say anything. Just looked at her over the rim of my mug.

She looked down, catching herself in the reflection of the microwave, and let out a quiet groan. "Ugh. Of course."

Abel chuckled behind me. "I told you it was early."

Sarah groaned again, dragging a hand through her hair as she shuffled toward the coffee. "I can't believe you two are already upright and talking. It's barely morning."

I took a long sip. "Some of us are built differently."

She shot me a look. "Built annoying, maybe."

I smiled into my mug. "Still your favorite."

Sarah crossed to the fridge, shoving the too-long sleeves up her arms as she opened it. She bent down scanning the shelves and moving a few containers around. "Where's the creamer?" she muttered.

Abel didn't miss a beat. "It's on the top shelf. I'd get it for you, but I'm enjoying the view."

Sarah straightened and glanced over her shoulder, arching a brow. "Pervert."

Abel sipped his coffee, "Allegedly."

Sarah rolled her eyes, but gave a quick smile. She grabbed the creamer, then bumped her shoulder into his as she passed. Abel caught her without missing a beat, one hand brushing the small of her back like it was second nature.

I looked away, suddenly fascinated by the tile grout, or anything that wasn't them. It wasn't jealousy. Not even envy. Just... awe, maybe. Like watching something fragile that had somehow survived the fire.

Sarah turned back toward me with her mug, blowing lightly across the surface. "Allie still asleep?"

"Either that or fighting her way through chapter six of Grandma's crazy journals," I said.

"God help her," Sarah replied.

Abel chuckled and pushed off the counter. "I should get moving." He stretched once, then grabbed his jacket from the hook by the door and shrugged it on over his bare chest.

Sarah raised an eyebrow. "Seriously? No shirt?"

He shot her a grin as he zipped it halfway. "It looks better on you than it ever did on me. And I'll change when I get home."

She rolled her eyes, but the blush creeping up her neck gave her away.

"Still chasing a few threads on Michael," Abel said, more serious now. "One of his old addresses doesn't add up. Thought I'd swing by the courthouse, see what I can dig up."

He paused, gaze glancing between us. "I'll stop back by tonight. Let you know what I find."

"You're working on a Sunday?" Sarah asked.

"Justice doesn't take weekends," he said, mock-serious. "Besides, I've got a guy who owes me a favor. He'll let me in."

Sarah raised her mug. "Bring back something edible, okay? I'm not surviving another round of Allie's kale and bone broth."

Abel chuckled. "Got it. Something with actual flavor."

He turned to me. "Text me if you think of anything else you want me to check."

Then he looked at Sarah again. "Be safe," she said.

"Always," he replied.

And then without hesitating, he leaned in and kissed her like he'd done it a hundred times before. He gave her one last glance, then disappeared, shutting the door behind him.

I let out a slow breath and lowered myself into one of the kitchen chairs, my coffee mug still cradled in my hands.

Sarah stood there for a second, staring at the door like she could still see him on the other side.

I waited. One beat. Two.

Then she turned to me, and I could *see* it bubbling in her. Something between panic and giddy disbelief.

I raised an eyebrow. "You gonna tell me, or should I start guessing?"

She opened her mouth. Closed it. Then dragged a hand through her hair and let out a strangled noise halfway between a sigh and a laugh. "Okay. I wasn't gonna say anything yet, because I didn't want to be an asshole—"

"Sarah."

"But holy *shit*, Lena."

I grinned into my coffee. "There it is."

She crossed the kitchen in three steps, dropped into the chair across from me, and grabbed my hand like she needed it to stay grounded.

"I slept with him," she whispered, loud enough that it wasn't actually a whisper. "Like fully. Shamelessly. Absolutely no regrets kind of slept with him."

"Yeah, I noticed," I said dryly. "You're wearing his shirt."

"I *know*! God." She dropped her forehead to the table for a second, then looked back up, eyes wide. "Lena, he's... *ugh*. I don't even have the words. Like, sexy obviously. But also stupidly kind? And patient? And *gentle*? But also not gentle where it counts?"

She groaned. "God, I forgot how good this feels. Not just the sex. Him. Us."

She paused, then added, quieter, "I didn't think we'd find our way back."

I gave her a look. "You were the one who let him go, remember?"

"I know," she said, almost laughing. "But maybe I was supposed to. Then. So it could be *this* now."

I smiled. "Say one more swoony thing and I swear I'll walk into the woods and let the forest claim me."

She laughed, but there was something softer under it. Something careful.

"I wasn't sure if I should even say anything," she admitted. "After everything. After *him*... it felt wrong to be happy, even for a second."

I set my mug down and looked her in the eye. "Hey. Stop. Don't do that."

"Do what?"

"Try to protect me from something good. Not right now. I need to know that part of the world still exists." My voice cracked a little, but I kept going. "I need this, Sarah. You and him. Something *real*. Something that reminds me people aren't all monsters."

Sarah's face crumpled for half a second, like she was fighting the urge to cry or confess to a felony. "I really, really like him," she said.

"Yeah, well... I have a very strong suspicion he might like you back," I teased.

Biscuit then strolled into the kitchen, her paws silent on the tile. She hopped onto a chair, then onto the table, curled her tail around her feet, and stared directly at Sarah.

Sarah blinked at her. "Is she… judging me?"

I took another sip of coffee. "She judges everyone. But yeah, especially you."

She let out a groan, dramatic and giddy and half-mortified. "I can't deal with this right now. My brain is mush. My legs are sore. I'm wearing a man's shirt that still smells like him and I never want to take it off, and honestly? I am *not okay.*"

I laughed—really laughed—and it felt like shaking loose something tense I didn't know I was still holding.

She leaned across the table and pulled me into a careful hug, squeezing like she was scared I'd break in her arms.

She then got up and wandered to the pantry. After a moment of digging, she pulled out a box of Pop-Tarts, inspected the label, and made a face.

"Strawberry," she muttered. "Of course."

She peeled one from the foil and took a bite anyway then leaned against the island like it was too early for moral decisions.

"So what's the plan today?" she asked around a mouthful. "Anyone doing anything useful?"

I raised my mug. "This is as useful as I'm getting."

Allie snorted as she appeared in the doorway, already dressed, hair pulled back like she'd been up for hours. "Speak for yourself," she said, setting Grandma's journal down on the table. "I need to make a grocery run and check on a few other things in town. Do you two need anything while I'm out?"

Sarah arched an eyebrow. "Anything but more strawberry Pop-Tarts. Get the brown sugar ones next time, please. Or s'mores. Literally anything else."

Allie rolled her eyes but scribbled something on the small notepad she took out from her pocket."

Then she looked over at me. "Lena?"

I shook my head. "I'm good. Thanks."

Allie raised a brow, like she expected me to change my mind, but I just gave a small shrug. She sighed, snapping the notepad closed. "Alright. I'll be back later."

She grabbed her keys off the hook and headed for the door without another word, her footsteps sharp and determined, like she already had ten more tasks queued up in her mind.

Sarah let out a long breath and flopped backward in her chair, arms dangling at her sides. "God, I forgot how exhausting she is in the morning. It's like she's powered by straight espresso and pure spite."

I snorted into my mug. "She's been like that since we were kids. You should've seen her during finals week in high school. I think she survived on Post-it notes and raw determination alone."

Sarah laughed, the sound warm and bright in the quiet kitchen. "Honestly? I'm terrified and impressed."

She stood, stretching her arms above her head until her joints popped, then ambled over to the pantry. She peered inside like it might reveal a hidden treasure.

"God," she muttered. "I forgot what a wasteland this place is. There's nothing but random cans and... one sad bag of rice."

I shrugged. "Allie's not exactly a comfort-food kind of shopper."

Sarah pulled out a half-empty bag of tortilla chips, shook it like it might magically refill, then made a face and set it aside. "Breakfast of champions," she declared, grabbing another Pop-Tart instead.

I pushed up from my chair and wandered to the fridge, rifling through shelves and containers that looked like they hadn't been touched in weeks. I finally found some eggs and a wilted bunch of green onions shoved in the back.

"Eggs?" I offered.

Sarah perked up immediately. "Oh my God, yes. Actual food."

I cracked eggs into a bowl, whisking with the kind of focus that felt almost meditative. Sarah leaned against the counter, munching her Pop-Tart as if it was an appetizer for the real meal to come.

"You know," she said after a moment, crumbs dotting her shirt, "I always forget you can actually cook."

I raised an eyebrow. "I'm a nurse. We survive on breakroom potlucks and questionable leftovers. You learn fast or starve."

She grinned. "Useful life skill. Unlike... whatever this is," she added, waving her half-eaten pastry like a white flag.

A few minutes later, the smell of sizzling eggs filled the kitchen. I tossed in the green onions and a bit of cheese I found, scraping everything together until it looked decent enough.

Sarah snagged two forks from the drawer and we sat down at the small kitchen table, devouring the eggs in comfortable silence.

When we finished, she leaned back, patting her stomach. "Holy shit. I feel like a real person again."

I cracked a small smile. "Don't get used to it. That was pretty much the last edible thing in this house."

She pointed her fork at me. "Worthy sacrifice."

After we finished cleaning up the breakfast mess, we made our way into the living room. Sarah sprawled across one end of the couch, and grabbed the remote to find something to watch. I tucked myself into the other corner, pulling a throw blanket over my knees.

For a while, we just sat there and watched some sad reality TV show.

Sarah's breathing started to even out, like she might drift off any second. Biscuit eventually wandered in, hopping up beside me and curling into a tight ball.

My eyelids grew heavier with each passing minute, my body sinking deeper into the couch. I watched Biscuit's breathing slow, the rise and fall of her small chest soothing in a way I couldn't explain.

Sarah mumbled something half-formed. I didn't answer.

My head tipped back against the cushion. I let my eyes slip shut, just for a second, I told myself. But when I opened them again…I wasn't on the couch.

I stood in a dark, endless space. The kind of darkness that felt heavy, like velvet pressing against my skin. The air was thick, muffled, as if the world had been wrapped in cotton.

Then I saw her.

Another identical version of me, standing just a few feet away in the dim, endless dark. She was completely naked and her skin glowed faintly, like moonlight on water. She looked untouched, unscarred. Her hair fell in soft strawberry blonde waves down her back, her shoulders were loose, and her chin was slightly lifted like she was waiting for someone. She looked… so open. So trusting. So soft.

I tried to call out, but no sound came. My mouth moved, but the air swallowed everything before it could form.

Then Michael appeared. He stepped out of the darkness like he'd always belonged to it, his gaze zeroing in on her with an almost reverent hunger. He was naked too, pale and strong and terrible, his eyes gleaming in the dark.

I tried to run. To move. To scream. But my body stayed rooted, as if invisible chains wrapped around my ankles, my chest, my throat.

Michael moved up behind her, his hands hovering just above her shoulders before slowly sliding down, curling around her waist. He pulled her back against him, her bare spine pressed flush to his chest.

She didn't flinch or struggle. Instead, she leaned into him, her head tipping to the side to bare her throat.

I felt something deep inside me seize and twist, a raw ache spiraling outward from my ribs. Because some horrible, ruined part of me wanted that.

I watched as he bent his head, his lips brushing against her neck slow and deliberate. She shivered under his touch, her eyes fluttering shut in surrender.

His gaze darted up then, meeting mine across the dark.

My breath caught.

He smiled—soft at first, almost loving—as his mouth continued its slow path up the curve of her neck to her jaw. She let out a silent breath, her lips parting as if she might moan.

The ache inside me sharpened. I felt it in my teeth, my fingertips, the hollow space behind my sternum.

I missed it. I missed him.

Even as every rational part of me screamed in horror, some deep, broken place whispered how badly I wanted that warmth again. That touch. That illusion of being seen, chosen, adored.

Michael turned her slowly, so she faced him fully. Their foreheads pressed together, his hands sliding up her arms, fingers grazing her shoulders.

She looked up at him with so much trust, so much love, it made something in me want to break open and scream.

He leaned in, kissing her deeply and tenderly. His hands slid down to her hips, pulling her even closer. Her hands rose to his chest, splaying open like she was trying to climb inside him.

Then his fingers moved higher, curling around her arms, and up her sides.

A glint of metal began to form between them. A dagger. Black and smooth and terrible, born right there in his hands as naturally as breathing.

I fought against the invisible weight holding me still, my body shaking with effort. I needed to stop it. I needed to save her. But I couldn't move. I couldn't even scream.

The other me didn't notice. Her eyes stayed on his face, wide and soft, lips parted in silent devotion.

Then he drove the blade into her stomach.

Her entire body jerked. Her mouth fell open in a soundless gasp, eyes going wide and unfocused.

His expression never changed—only softened, almost sweet, as he leaned forward to press one last kiss to her forehead. Then he took the blade out and stepped back, turning his head just enough to look at me.

That smile. The same smile he wore when he almost killed me. Slow, cruel, and triumphant.

And then he began to fade, dissolving back into the darkness where he came from.

The other me turned and met my eyes. One trembling hand rose to her stomach, her fingers coming away slick and dark. Then a crack appeared. A fine, hairline fracture spread out from the wound in her stomach, delicate and sharp, like a spiderweb etched in glass. It split across her skin in slow, agonizing waves, each line branching and splintering into dozens more.

Another crack formed, then another—faster now, racing up her ribs, curling around her breasts, snaking across her shoulders and down her arms. Each fracture seemed to echo in the silence around us, a brittle, splintering sound that I could almost feel in my own bones.

Her skin wasn't skin anymore. It turned to porcelain, fragile and thin, each new crack revealing the dark void underneath. The breaks fanned down her thighs, around her hips, climbing her neck until she looked ready to shatter with one breath.

Then a shadow slipped out. It slid from one of the deepest cracks in her ribs—a long, sinuous tendril, inky and thick, curling through the air like smoke underwater. It moved slowly at first, testing, tasting, before drifting out into the empty dark around her.

Another shadow followed, spilling from a crack near her stomach, this one twisting and writhing, almost frantic. More began to pour out, each one darker, heavier, moving with a restless hunger that felt almost alive. They coiled around her like mourning veils, wrapping and sliding over each other, reaching outward as if they were searching for something… for someone.

The tendrils didn't lash or snap. They weren't violent. They were grieving. Aching. Each one moved with a painful grace, as though they were fragments of a soul trying to find its way home.

And then beneath all of it, something else began to pulse. A faint glow. It started small, barely there, hidden deep beneath the lattice of cracks that marred her chest. But as I watched, it grew stronger, brighter—a soft, golden light that seemed to breathe in the dark, expanding and contracting like a heartbeat.

The glow spread under her ribs, illuminating the shattered lines from within, spilling upward toward her throat and downward into her belly. It wasn't harsh or blinding. It was gentle and warm. It looked like the last star in a collapsing sky. Like a single flame refusing to die in a storm.

I knew it. Knew it as intimately as my own heartbeat.

Empathy. The last piece of me that refused to die.

She lifted her head then, her cracked lips parting like she might try to speak. Her eyes, dull and gray, locked on mine across the void.

For one split, impossible second, it looked like she might reach for me. Like she might try to step forward, to close the distance, to bridge the void between what I was and what was left.

But her mouth opened… and nothing came out.

The scream inside me roared so loud I thought my chest might rip open, but no sound passed my lips.

The shadows twisted higher, curling above her head like long ghostly arms reaching for the sky. And then everything went black.

I gasped awake, my whole body jerking like I'd been plunged into ice water.

Allie and Sarah were already there. Allie's hands landed on my shoulders. Sarah hovered close, wide-eyed and pale.

"Lena?" Allie's voice was low and careful, like she was talking to something fragile that might bolt. "What happened? You were thrashing."

I tried to speak. Nothing came out but a muffled scream.

Sarah knelt closer. "Lena, talk to us."

130

"I… it felt so real," I finally choked out. My voice sounded shredded, like it had been scraped raw from the inside.

Allie squeezed my arms tighter. "A dream?"

I nodded, shaking. "It wasn't just a dream. It… it felt like I was there. Like I was watching it happen."

Sarah's hand found mine, fingers wrapping tight. "What did you see?"

I told them everything. Every detail. How real it felt and how I was there, trapped, forced to watch. How I knew, the instant I saw that small golden glow, that it was empathy.

"One of my marks survived," I said finally.

Neither of them spoke.

"He didn't take all of it," I said. "He didn't take all of me."

"I thought it might be empathy," Allie said after a long moment. "Back when… you made us feel everything. I wasn't sure."

I nodded. "It was. I saw it. In the dream. Just one ember, under the cracks. But it was there."

Sarah leaned back slightly, eyes wide. "So that thing that happened when it felt like your whole soul hit me in the chest?"

I gave a small nod.

Allie's voice was softer now, careful. "That wasn't just emotion, it was the mark. Empathy doesn't just feel, it shares. Projects. That was your magic speaking for you when you couldn't."

I didn't know what to say to that. It didn't feel like magic. It felt like breaking.

Sarah rubbed her sternum absently. "Well, it nearly knocked me on my ass."

We were quiet for a few beats. No one moved.

Then Sarah spoke again, her voice slow and thoughtful. "If your soul's still reaching for the others… maybe that means they're not completely gone."

Allie looked at her sharply. "What do you mean?"

Sarah glanced at me, then back toward nothing in particular. "I don't know. But if something's missing and your soul knows it... maybe it can find its way back."

Allie didn't respond right away. She was staring at the floor, brows tight with thought.

"Maybe," she said finally. "But I don't think it'll be as simple as finding a lost object. It's not just energy. It's part of her. Part of what was taken."

Allie stood, almost abruptly. She grabbed her laptop from the coffee table.

"I'm going to start digging," she said, already moving toward the recliner. "There has to be something about restoring marks. Or... pulling magic back into alignment."

Sarah watched her go, then looked at me. "You okay?"

I nodded, though it didn't feel entirely true.

"I think I just need a shower," I said. "And maybe a new soul."

She gave me a small, wobbly smile. "We're fresh out of those, but the water pressure's decent."

I managed a huff that almost felt like a laugh. Almost. Then I got up and headed down the hall, leaving them, and the ghost of that dream, behind me. It wasn't a plan. But it was a beginning.

Chapter 14

I stood in the shower longer than I needed to, letting the water stream over the scar carved into my stomach. It had healed into an angry pink line against pale skin. The stitches were more than ready to come out. I could feel it in the way they pulled, tight and unnecessary, like a thread holding together something that was already healed.

It had been just over two weeks.

I stepped out, wrapped myself in a towel, and walked over to the sink. The mirror was still fogged, the air thick with humidity and soap. I wiped the glass clean with the edge of the towel and looked at myself for the first time in days.

Pale. Tired. But not fragile.

Not today. Today felt like the first step forward after getting pushed so far down.

I opened the cabinet and found Allie's stash of supplies, everything organized and labeled in clear plastic bins. I pulled out alcohol, cotton pads, tweezers, and clippers, then laid them out on the counter, one by one. Muscle memory took over. Sterilize. Wash. Be deliberate.

I took a breath, braced myself against the counter, and went to work. The first stitch slid out easier than I expected. The second pinched. By the third, I wasn't breathing through the pain anymore, I was breathing through something else. A strange, quiet defiance.

I could do this. I was doing this. One by one, I removed them all, placing the black threads on a square of toilet paper like they were something sacred. Or maybe something that had overstayed their welcome.

When it was done, I wiped the skin with alcohol again. It stung. I stared at the scar one last time in the mirror, then pulled on clean leggings and a t-shirt. Something comfortable.

Sarah was at the table when I went back into the kitchen, typing something into her laptop with that distracted, half-focused expression she wore when she was toggling between work and worry. She glanced up when she saw me, but didn't say anything. Just gave a small smile, then went back to her screen.

I crossed the kitchen and reached for one of the journals still sitting on the table where Allie had left them.

I hadn't touched them. Not once. But now... I wanted to.

I pulled one from the middle of the stack. The bookmark sticking out looked like it had been there for years. I flipped it open and started to read.

Grandma's loopy handwriting filled the page.

The mark is tied to the soul. It can't be taught or traded. It just is. You don't choose it. You uncover it. And when you do, it feels like remembering something you've always known.

I kept reading.

Some magic is passive. Intuitive. Others are active, meant to shape the world around them. But all marks can be used, even when fractured.

A quiet click pulled my attention. Sarah closed her laptop and looked up. She nodded toward the journal. "Reading or pretending?"

"Reading," I said. "For real this time."

She smiled. "Proud of you, nerd."

I went back to the page. Below the entry, a different passage had been marked with an underline in red ink. It was angrier, less measured.

There was a family north of here, back when I was young. The Torners. Not well known, but old blood. Quiet. Until they weren't. Word spread fast that they'd been using their marks to control people. Kill them for profit and power. That's when The Severance came. One night, they were just... gone. No headlines. No funerals. Just ash and wind and silence where their home used to

be. The Severance doesn't ask questions. They
just correct the imbalance.

I paused. My stomach clenched. Then I turned the journal toward Sarah. "Read this," I said, sliding it across the table.

Sarah skimmed the passage, her brow furrowing.

When she finished, she leaned back slowly, arms folding. "The Severance," she said. "They sound like magical assassins."

"I think they're more than that. They're... balance. And justice."

She leaned back, arms crossed. "Well. Let's hope they're on our side."

Before I could speak again, Allie's voice came from the hallway. "I think they would be."

She stepped into the kitchen, barefoot and holding her coffee like she'd been listening for a while.

Sarah looked up. "Are they even still around? Your grandma wrote about them like it happened forever ago."

Allie shrugged slightly, dropping into the chair across from me. "I'm not sure. But if they're real, they may be the only ones who understand how to fix this. And stop Michael."

I frowned. "You're saying we need to find them?"

"I've been digging," Allie said. "Looking for anything on magical restoration or re-anchoring marks. I've hit nothing but walls. But this..." —she tapped the journal gently— "this is the first thing that makes sense. If there's anyone who understands how this works, it's them."

Sarah glanced between us. "And what if they don't want to be found?"

Allie's expression didn't flinch. "Then we make them want to."

Allie didn't wait for us to respond. She stood, crossed the kitchen and grabbed a notepad and a pack of sticky tabs from the junk drawer and dropped them beside the pile of journals.

"Okay," she said, flipping open the first journal. "Anything that mentions The Severance, mark it. Names, places, anything that even feels connected."

Sarah raised a brow. "So... research party?"

Allie didn't miss a beat. "Call it whatever you need to. We need answers."

She skimmed a few lines and underlined something quickly.

"Start wherever you want. Grandma wasn't linear. Just flag anything that jumps out."

I reached for one of the books, the leather worn soft at the edges. "Do we even know how many of these she wrote?"

Allie glanced up. "There are six here. But who knows if that's all of them. Grandma wasn't exactly organized."

Sarah sighed, pulling her assigned journal toward her. "This better come with snacks."

Allie didn't look up. "Top shelf. Left cabinet."

Sarah muttered something under her breath but got to work anyway. I slid a Post-it free and opened my journal.

Mentions of The Severance were rare and scattered. Usually just a sentence or two. A warning. A name dropped.

"They come when the balance shifts."

"They correct what's been broken."

None of it told us where to find them. But it was enough to know they were real. And that Grandma respected them deeply.

We read for hours.

Eventually, the pages began to blur. Allie rubbed her eyes, muttering something about needing a real desk. Sarah declared she was getting carpal tunnel from flipping through so much "magic cursive." I stood up, stretched, and made grilled cheese with too much butter while they kept reading. By the time I set the plates down, they were both slouched in their chairs like students who'd survived final exams.

We ate at the table, trading theories and half-baked ideas between bites. Then the conversation faded. The fatigue settled in. Not just from the reading, but from the weight of the last few weeks. Of everything.

Later that evening, we migrated outside. The sun had dipped behind the trees, casting the backyard in gold and shadow. The air was warm with just enough bite to promise fall was coming soon. Allie brought out a bottle of wine she insisted we couldn't afford to save, and we didn't argue.

We sat on the back patio, bare feet propped on chairs, glasses in hand, shoulders brushing when someone leaned too far into a joke.

Sarah told a story about a terrible date she once had with a guy who used the phrase "alpha energy" unironically. Allie confessed she once made a guy cry during a couples yoga class because she corrected his form too harshly. I laughed until my stomach hurt.

It felt good. Not like forgetting. Just remembering how to be okay.

Sarah refilled the glasses. Biscuit prowled along the edge of the deck, tail flicking like she was personally supervising our emotional recovery.

Allie was mid-sentence, something about the wine not being as good as she remembered, when a sound reached us.

Tires on gravel. A low, familiar rumble pulling into the driveway. Sarah's head lifted. And then she smiled. A real smile that was wide and open and warm enough to light the whole damn porch.

"Abel's here," she said excitedly. Like he made her entire day just by showing up. Like the night had just gotten better.

Her whole body seemed to lift with it, energy rising to meet the sound. She stood without hesitation, already moving toward the house to meet him at the front door.

A second passed. And then it felt like the world broke open.

BOOM!

The ground shook beneath us... then came the scream. Abel's. A raw, guttural sound that didn't even sound human. It tore through the air, high and broken and full of agony.

Sarah froze mid-step.

"Abel?" she whispered, her voice caught in her throat.

Then she ran.

"ABEL!" she screamed, sprinting in the house to get to the front. Her voice cracked and frenzied. Terrified. "ABEEEEEL!"

Allie jumped to her feet, the wineglass tumbling off the table and shattering on the deck. I was right behind her, legs unsteady, heart hammering.

We scrambled after her through the kitchen, down the hallway, feet pounding on the hardwood. The house blurred past in streaks of light and shadow.

We all reached the front door at the same time and threw it open without thinking.

There were flames.

The truck was on fire, roaring and alive. Fire bled from the hood, the windshield, the cab—black smoke pouring upward in thick, suffocating waves. It curled into the air like a curse, blotting out the stars.

And on the ground beside it—

Abel. Lying crumpled on the gravel, not moving. Burning.

"NO—NO!" Sarah screamed, launching forward. She made it down the front steps before I caught her, arms locking tight around her waist. She fought like hell, twisting, kicking.

"LET GO! LET ME GO! HE'S RIGHT THERE!" Her screams tore through the air like sirens.

I held on. Because I'd seen it. The way he wasn't moving. The way the flames clung to him, alive and ravenous. I knew what she hadn't let herself see yet.

It was too late.

"I HAVE TO GET TO HIM!" she shrieked, sobbing now. "I HAVE TO—"

"Sarah," I yelled, my voice breaking. "You can't."

She collapsed into me, her body shaking, screaming into my shoulder like it could undo what we were seeing.

Behind us, Allie ran back out the front door with a fire extinguisher in her hands. She didn't hesitate. She stormed into the flames like she could fight them with sheer force of will. White foam sprayed as the flames hissed back. Bits of fire gave way, revealing what was left.

Charred skin. Blackened fabric. A hand, outstretched toward the house. Next to him, half-melted and smoking, was a pizza box. He brought us dinner. Just like he said he would.

Sarah let out a sound I'll never forget. Shattered and broken, like something in her had torn in two. Her legs buckled. She crumpled to the ground, hands in her hair, still screaming his name like she could call him back.

And I went with her. I dropped beside her, one arm around her shoulders, the other pressed to my mouth as the sob tore free—loud, ugly, and unstoppable.

He was kind. Good. Real. And now he was gone.

Allie stumbled back from the truck, her hands blackened with soot, her breath uneven. She stared at what was left of him for a heartbeat—just one—and then turned.

She crossed the lawn and dropped beside us, knees hitting the grass. Her arms went around both of us without a word. She didn't speak or cry. She just held us. Because what else was there to do?

Sarah was on the ground, still screaming—loud, shattered sobs that tore through her like something primal. Her fingers dug into the grass, into me, like she needed something solid to keep from falling apart.

And then the hairs on the back of my neck stood up. Something pulled at me. I looked up past the truck and the smoke.

My eyes landed on Michael.

He was standing just inside the treeline, half-shrouded in shadow, but there was no mistaking him. His sleeves were rolled up. His expression was almost… bored.

And in his hand, he tossed something into the air and caught it lazily. Over and over. A ball of flame, small and pulsing like it didn't matter.

He was playing. Smiling faintly, like this was just another evening. Like he hadn't just *ended* someone.

I couldn't breathe.

Allie must've felt me tense. "Lena?"

But I couldn't look away.

She followed my gaze, gasping as her eyes landed on the figure just beyond the smoke. Her voice dropped. "Is that—?"

Michael lifted the fireball again, spinning it lazily in one hand like it was nothing more than a toy.

Allie's arm tightened around me. Her voice, when it came, was ice. "That son of a bitch."

Sarah looked up and saw him. Her eyes widened as the fireball arced lazily through the air, glowing hot against the tree line.

"Michael," she breathed. Then louder, sharper. "*Michael!*"

The fireball vanished midair. Michael tilted his mouth into a cruel half-smile.

That was all it took. Sarah surged to her feet, rage detonating through her like a second explosion. "YOU FUCKING MONSTER!" she screamed, tearing across the yard. "I'LL RIP YOUR GODDAMN HEART OUT!"

"No—Sarah!" Allie shouted, reaching for her too late.

He stood perfectly still as Sarah tore across the yard, like he'd been waiting. Then he lifted one hand.

The magic hit her mid-stride. A burst of unseen force. Sarah slammed into the ground like a doll, skidding across the grass, breath knocked clean from her lungs.

"Sarah!" I cried, already moving.

Allie dropped beside her first, hands hovering, frantic. "Don't move—don't move."

Sarah gasped, rolling to her side. "I'm... fine—" she managed, but her voice was shredded.

His voice then slid into my head like a blade wrapped in silk.

"This is all your fault, darling." It was smooth, almost sweet. *"You should've kept your little friends out of my business."*

I gasped, my hands flying to my ears like I could block it out, like I could keep him out. But the voice was inside my head.

Allie turned sharply. "Lena?"

140

Sarah looked up from the grass, still catching her breath. "What is it? What's wrong?"

I couldn't answer. I was frozen, shaking, the voice cutting through everything else—

"Trust me when I say this… I will take what's left of your life and your soul. Every scrap of power you've managed to cling to.

A pause. Sharp and cruel.

"How many more of your friends have to die before you understand that?"

"I'M GOING TO FUCKING KILL YOU!" I screamed, the words ripping out of me before I could think. "YOU FUCKING COWARD!"

Sarah froze. Allie flinched.

And somewhere deep inside, he laughed. Low and pleased.

"We'll see, my love."

Then he turned and walked into the woods, disappearing.

My hands were still pressed to my ears, even though I knew it wouldn't help. I could feel the echo of him *inside* me— slick and cruel, like oil in water, refusing to wash away.

Sarah was still gasping for air, eyes locked on the place he'd stood. Rage burned behind the pain.

Allie was already moving. "We need to get back inside," she said softly, but firmly. "Come on. Come on, it's not safe out here."

Sarah's gaze stayed fixed on the tree line like he might reappear. Like maybe if she stared long enough, he'd come back and she could kill him with her bare hands.

I felt the same urge. The same burn.

Allie's voice came again. "Lena. We have to go."

My legs felt numb like they weren't mine. But I nodded.

Allie slipped one arm under Sarah's, helping her shakily to her feet. I followed, legs still wooden, heart still racing in a way that had nothing to do with adrenaline and everything to do with fear.

We turned toward the house. But Sarah stopped. Her eyes locked on the body. What was left of him.

Allie tried to steady her, but Sarah shrugged her off. "I have to—" Her voice cracked, nothing but breath. She walked over to him alone.

The flames had mostly gone out. The ground around the truck was blackened and still smoking in places. Abel's body lay crumpled and unmoving. The pizza box still beside him, warped and half-burned, a cruel reminder of what this night should've been.

Sarah dropped to her knees. Her hand hovered just above his chest like she was afraid to touch him. Afraid he might fall apart if she did. She bowed her head, shoulders shaking. Allie and I stood a few steps behind, silent.

There was nothing to say.

Sarah reached for his chest, toward something still intact beneath the scorched fabric. Carefully, she pulled his badge free. It was blackened around the edges. Bent. But still whole.

Then she broke again. Bent forward, clutching the badge like it could stitch her heart back together. Her cries rose unchecked, full of everything she couldn't contain. The kind of grief that doesn't ask permission. That doesn't care who's watching.

I stepped forward moving slowly, like my body didn't trust the ground not to collapse beneath us again. I crouched beside her, said nothing. Just reached for her hand. I wrapped my fingers around hers, guiding them away from the ashes and toward something that might hold her upright. She didn't resist when I helped her stand. Her knees buckled once, and I caught her.

She leaned into me, eyes swollen, mouth trembling. Still crying. Still breaking. I slipped my arm around her shoulders and held her close as we walked back toward the house. The front door was still wide open.

We stepped inside with Allie following behind us. She had her phone in hand as she called 911 with a calmness that didn't match her face.

Sarah was still trembling, clutching Abel's badge like it was the last piece of him she could hold on to. I guided her to the couch, gently, slowly. She didn't fight me. Just sat down like her strings had been cut.

Allie stayed near the front window, pacing in short, stiff lines while she talked to the dispatch. Her voice was measured and clinical. But her hand was pressed so tightly to her forehead, it left red marks.

"I heard the truck pull in," she said. "Then the explosion. We ran to the front and saw the flames."

She left it at that. No mention of Michael. No mention of the fireball. Just the facts that fit into the real world. The safe version. The version that wouldn't land us in a psych eval.

Sirens came next. A distant howl growing louder each second.

Red and blue lights lit up the living room walls in bursts of color. The firetruck pulled into the driveway, followed by an ambulance and a cruiser. I heard the scramble of boots, the slam of doors, the crackle of radio static.

Allie opened the door and stepped out, shoulders back, already in control again. I watched her through the screen speak to the first responders—arms crossing, nodding when appropriate, gesturing toward the truck.

Inside, Sarah hadn't moved. Her hand was still clenched around the badge, her other hand curled into a fist in her lap. Her face was blotchy, tear-streaked, blank in a way that scared me.

Outside, the fire chief said something about a gas leak. Or maybe a misfiring engine. Something about pressure and ignition points. I didn't understand half of it, but Allie nodded along like she did. The word "accident" floated through the door once.

They spent hours out there clearing wreckage and retrieving the body. I didn't watch.

At some point, one of the paramedics stepped inside and asked if we needed medical attention. Allie answered for all of us. No. Just shock. We'd be okay. They didn't press.

143

Sarah didn't look up the whole time.

Eventually, the lights dimmed. The engines quieted. And the house was just a house again.

Sarah's pain was too loud to look away from. It filled the room. Filled *me*.

And the worst part? I could feel it. Every jagged edge. Every sharp, gutted scream stuck behind her ribs. And I still couldn't stop it.

I had this magic, this mark that was supposed to mean something. But all it did was make me feel like I was drowning beside her. I wasn't healing anything. I wasn't helping. I was just bleeding next to her like that counted for something.

God, I would've given anything to take it from her. Just for a minute. But I didn't know how. So I stayed. And I held her. And hated myself for not being enough.

Chapter 15

Morning came, but everything still felt dark.

Sarah was finally asleep. She hadn't said much last night. She just lay there, curled on her side with Abel's badge in her hand, like letting go of it might unravel her completely.

I stayed with her. Held her when she cried, stayed silent when she didn't. There were no right words. No comfort that could hold that kind of pain. So I didn't try. I just stayed.

At some point her breathing became deeper and slower. Her fingers went slack, the badge sliding halfway beneath the pillow. She didn't stir.

I lay there a while longer, just watching her. Her face was blotchy, her lashes stuck together with salt and sleep.

Eventually, I slipped out of bed. Careful and quiet so I wouldn't wake her.

In the kitchen, Allie was already awake but still in her sleep clothes.

The coffee was brewed and a mug sat in front of her, half gone. A second empty mug sat beside the pot, clean and waiting, like she'd set it out without thinking. She was perched on one of the stools, elbows on the counter, staring at nothing. She looked like she hadn't slept at all.

Her eyes moved toward me when I stepped in. No smile. Just that tired kind of acknowledgment you give someone when you've both survived something.

I went over to the pot and poured myself a cup in the awaiting mug. "She passed out," I said softly. "A couple hours ago, maybe."

Allie nodded slowly, her eyes dropping back to the counter. "She cried for hours," she said softly. Not a question. "She loved him," she murmured. "I didn't realize how much until last night."

"She didn't either," I said. "Not really. Not until it was too late."

145

Allie's jaw flexed. She looked like she wanted to fix it. Like she wanted to fix *everything*. But for once, she didn't offer a plan. No journal. No research. Just the quiet admission of helplessness.

I pulled out the stool across from her and sat. "This is my fault," I muttered, shame pressing down on every word.

Allie's head lifted. "Lena—"

"No." My voice cracked. "It is. I let him in. I let him all the way in. I loved him. I trusted him. And now Abel is—" My throat closed. I couldn't finish it.

I pressed the heel of my hand to my eyes. "I should've seen it. I should've known."

Allie pushed her mug aside and leaned forward. "Don't do that. Don't carry this like you asked for it."

"But I did," I whispered. "I asked for him. I chose him. I let him into my life—my heart—and I didn't even hesitate. And now Abel's dead. Sarah is shattered. And he's still out there. Because of me."

"You want to know the truth?" she said. "Even when we weren't talking... even after Mom and Dad... I still checked in. Quietly. Sarah sent me pictures and updates. And every time I saw you with him smiling and laughing, I felt relief."

I looked up, startled.

"I thought, *she's okay.* She's safe. She has someone who loves her. Someone who would die before letting anything happen to her. And I believed that, Lena. I *believed* he was that man."

Tears slipped down her cheeks, but her voice only got stronger.

"I'm your big sister. I'm supposed to protect you. And I didn't. I didn't even see the danger. So don't you dare sit there and carry this like you're the only one who got it wrong."

I wiped at my face, but more tears came. "I don't know what to do."

Allie's hand reached across the counter and wrapped around mine. "Then we figure it out together."

146

My shoulders shook. I dropped my head into my arms, pressing my forehead to the edge of the counter, sobbing in that open way that only happens when there's nothing left to hold in.

Allie stood and moved around the island, pulling a stool next to mine. She sat and put her arm around my shoulders.

"I've got you," she whispered. "You're not alone. We're gonna get through this. And when we do, we're going to burn him down."

Allie didn't let go of me for a long time.

When my tears slowed and my breathing evened out, she gave my shoulder one last squeeze, then stood.

"Coffee's probably old by now," she said. "I'll make a fresh pot."

I wiped my face with the sleeve of my sweatshirt, eyes still burning, voice raw. "You don't have to."

She shot me a look—not annoyed, just tired and full of that older-sister energy that said *of course I do.*

"I'll make eggs," she added, like it wasn't up for debate.

I nodded, even though the thought of food made my stomach twist. I sat at the counter, watching her move around the kitchen. Her shoulders were tight, and her jaw clenched like every motion was holding something at bay. She didn't ask if I wanted anything. She just made it. And that felt like love.

Allie slid the eggs onto two plates. They were scrambled and slightly overcooked, the way she always made them when she wasn't paying attention. She set one in front of me, then leaned against the counter, arms crossed.

Neither of us touched the food.

Then the floor creaked down the hall. We both looked up. Sarah stepped into the kitchen slowly, barefoot, still in the clothes from yesterday—wrinkled and stained. Her hair was a mess, her face pale and blotchy. But her back was straight, like she'd poured every last ounce of strength into posture alone.

Her eyes glanced to the plates. Then to us.

147

Allie spoke first. "I made eggs."

Sarah didn't answer. She moved to the table like she wasn't quite sure what she was doing, pulled out a chair, and sat. Her fingers curled around the edge of the table.

Then barely more than a whisper, "I smelled the coffee."

Allie moved toward the pot, but I was already on my feet. "I got it," I said gently, grabbing a mug and reaching for her favorite creamer, the sweet one she always complained was too expensive but bought anyway.

I poured until it turned the perfect shade of tan, gave it a stir, and set it down in front of her without a word.

Sarah wrapped her hands around it, but she didn't drink. Just held it close and breathed it in, lashes fluttering like she might break all over again.

We sat there for a while. Three women in a kitchen full of grief and eggs no one wanted to eat.

Then, a knock at the door broke through the quiet. Three short raps. Allie stood immediately. Not startled, just alert. She disappeared down the hall, footsteps fading. She returned a moment later, followed by three men.

They filled the room the second they stepped inside. Muscled. Weathered. All wearing jeans and plain t-shirts, but there was no mistaking the way they carried themselves. Military. No question.

One of them looked a little older, maybe mid-fifties, with streaks of gray at his temples and a deep line between his brows. His presence was calm and steady.

The man standing next to him was a little shorter and looked to be about forty. He stood with his arms crossed over a chest that looked carved from stone. Bold tattoos ran down both arms and up his neck. His jaw was dusted with dark stubble, and there was something in his eyes that didn't move. A cold, steady fury.

The third one stood just a little behind them, younger but no less marked by whatever they'd all been through. He looked close to my age, maybe a year or two older. He was tall and leaner than the others, but built like he could hold his own. Brown hair, cropped short on the sides and a little longer on the top, and dark brown eyes that tracked every movement in the room like they didn't quite trust it yet. A line of tattoos ran down one arm, half-hidden beneath the cuff of his sleeve.

They all looked at Sarah. She didn't flinch.

The older one spoke first. His voice was gravel. "Sarah?"

She looked up slowly. "Yeah."

He exhaled, like hearing her name hurt. "Abel never stopped talking about you," he said. "Even before you two… reconnected. Said you were the only woman who ever made him think about staying still."

The youngest one stepped forward, eyes red-rimmed but dry. "He said you were the thing that made him feel like he belonged somewhere."

Sarah's breath caught. Her eyes flooded again.

The shorter one cleared his throat. "We were the ones helping him keep watch on the place."

The older man introduced himself. "Sam Briggs," he said. "I served with Abel overseas."

He gestured toward the others. "This is Dean Tucker"—the shorter one—"and Jack. Jack Harper."

Sarah nodded, eyes still filled with tears.

None of them asked about Michael. Not yet. But I could feel the question sitting in the air.

"Whatever you need," Sam said. "We're here."

Sarah replied, "I—thank you."

They didn't move closer. They just stood there, respectful, heavy with loss. Soldiers who'd just lost a brother.

Then, Sam stepped forward slightly. "We need to know. What happened?"

Sarah opened her mouth, then closed it. Her throat worked like she was trying to speak around a stone.

"He—" Her voice cracked. "He pulled into the driveway. I was going to meet him at the door. And then—"

Her shoulders shook.

All three men turned to me. I felt it then, that line I was standing on. Truth on one side. Consequence on the other.

149

I could tell them what really happened. About Michael. About how the explosion wasn't some freak accident. About the way Abel died because he was trying to protect us. But if I told them the truth, they'd go after him. And they wouldn't survive it.

So I made a choice. "The cops think it was the truck," I said, keeping my voice even. "Something in the fuel line. They think it sparked, and... it went up. Right there in the driveway."

Sam's jaw tightened. "Just... a mechanical failure?"

"That's what they're saying," I replied.

Dean let out a low curse under his breath, pacing behind the chairs. Jack just watched me.

Sam's gaze held steady. "And Michael?"

There it was. I hesitated, just long enough for it to matter. Then I took a breath and said, "Michael hurt me. Badly. We were scared and that's why we called Abel."

I swallowed. "But that was weeks ago. He hasn't come near us since."

Sam didn't blink. "You think he's gone?"

"I think..." My throat tightened. "I think he realized he'd pushed too far. And ran before anyone could push back."

Every word tasted like ash. Dean swore again, sharp and bitter. But Jack hadn't moved. He still hadn't looked away. There was something in his expression now, subtle and sharp. The look of someone putting pieces together in real time. The kind of look that said *he knew I was lying,* even if he didn't know why.

Then Jack spoke. "You're sure?"

That's all he said. Just two words. But they hit harder than all the others combined. Not because of how he said them. But because of the way he looked at me when he did. Like he saw the space between my words and the truth I didn't say. Like he'd already decided this wasn't the end of it.

I held his gaze. And I lied again. "I'm sure."

Jack didn't respond. He just reached into his pocket, tore a small sheet from the back of his notebook, and scribbled something with quiet focus. He slid the paper across the table toward Sarah. "If you need anything," he said, his voice steady, "call me. Day or night."

Sarah looked up, startled by the softness in his tone. Her lips parted like she wanted to say something, but she didn't.

Around us, the other men started to move. Sam turned first, then Dean. Both moving toward the doorway without a word.

Jack turned to follow, but then he paused and looked back at me. "Abusive men don't usually disappear," he said. "They wait. They circle. And then they come back."

I wanted to scream. Tell him he had no idea how right he was. But I didn't. Because if I opened my mouth, the truth would come out like blood.

He met my eyes. "And when he does—because he will— call me."

He didn't wait for an answer. Just turned and walked out, his footsteps fading down the hall. A moment later, we heard the click of the front door, followed by the screen door shutting.

Sarah stared at the paper in front of her, Jack's number written in neat, steady handwriting. She didn't touch it. Just looked at it like it might catch fire.

"I wonder," she said quietly, "about how mad Abel would be if he knew we didn't tell them."

"We didn't lie to betray him," Allie said. "We did it to protect the people he cared about. Abel would've seen that."

Sarah's throat worked like she wanted to argue. But she didn't. I reached for my coffee, even though it had gone cold.

"We did the right thing," I said, but the words didn't feel clean in my mouth. "They don't know what they'd be walking into. Michael's a cold blooded killer with no remorse."

Allie leaned back in her chair, arms crossed. "They're soldiers. They've survived worse."

"Not this," I said. "Not him."

Sarah finally looked up. Her eyes were red, but steady. "We saved their lives," she said. And this time, there was no crack in her voice. No doubt.

151

Allie nodded slowly, like she was convincing herself all over again. "No one else dies for this," she murmured. "Not if we can help it."

I looked at both of them, my sister and my best friend, and felt the truth settle like stone in my chest.

This wasn't the end of something. It was the start of a war. And whether we admitted it or not, we were already counting casualties.

Chapter 16

The day passed in a kind of quiet that didn't feel peaceful.

No one said much. There wasn't anything left to say. The house had already been scrubbed clean, the beds made, the laundry folded. Allie moved through it anyway—dusting surfaces that didn't need it, wiping counters that didn't have a single crumb. She even polished the toaster. She cooked, too. BLT's. Then soup. Then cornbread. No one really touched any of it.

"Pretty sure that counter's going to file a restraining order," I muttered after watching her wipe it down for the third time today.

Allie didn't look up. "Pretty sure you need to take a shower."

I blinked. "Touché."

"I say that with love," she added, wiping the same spot again. "And also because it's true."

I almost smiled.

Sarah barely moved from the couch. She didn't cry often, but when she did it came fast. Sudden and sharp, like a storm cracking open. Then it was gone again, swallowed back down. Most of the time she just stared straight ahead. At the fireplace. At the wall. At nothing. She was wearing one of Abel's hoodies. I didn't ask how she got it.

The funeral was in a couple of days. There'd be a casket and a grave and too many people saying too little. The only thing left to do was wait. And that's what we did.

Mostly I walked the edges of the house. Touched the doorframes. Checked the locks. Sometimes I stood in the hallway and just... listened. For what, I wasn't sure. Footsteps. Breathing. Something.

The silence wasn't empty, it was dense. Like grief pressing down, layered with something else I couldn't name. Grief did that. The way *something else* pressed behind it. Not loud. Not obvious. Just *off*. Like the air before a storm, full of something you couldn't name.

By sunset, Allie had shut herself in her bedroom. The lights were low and the house was spotless. Every surface was wiped down, every dish put away, everything in its place. Except us.

Sarah was sitting on the couch where she'd been all day, curled under the hoodie like it might still hold his warmth.

I made tea. Not because she wanted it. Just to have something to do with my hands. I brought her a cup. She didn't look at it. But she took it anyway. I sat down beside her and wrapped my fingers around my own mug.

Sarah didn't move for a long time.

Then she whispered, "I didn't know one night could hold that much." Her voice didn't tremble, but something underneath it broke. "I fell asleep next to him and everything felt easy. Like we'd never left off. Like the years in between had just... folded into that morning." She blinked slowly, like she was still there. "I didn't get to say any of the big things. But I felt them. I think he did too."

She went quiet again. Then, softer. "I've never wanted a future so badly."

I felt her words land deep. Like they weren't just hers anymore. "I know," I said.

She glanced at me, eyes rimmed with red.

"I felt it," I said. "The morning in the kitchen... it was so strong I could hardly breathe."

Sarah's lips parted, like she wasn't sure if she believed me... or if it hurt too much to believe.

"You don't have to guess how he felt," I said. "I know. I felt it. He loved you fully. No holding back."

Her breath caught.

"I think part of him always did," I added.

She didn't cry. She just looked down at the tea in her hands, like her whole body was too tired to do anything else.

A warmth unfolded in my chest. It was recognizable, but not mine. Not Sarah's, either. It felt like a trace of something left behind. Maybe love doesn't leave all at once. Maybe some part of it stays.

• • •

The morning of the funeral came too fast. None of us said much as we got ready. Sarah sat on the edge of the bed, still in sweats and Abel's hoodie, his badge clutched in both hands. No one told her to get up. No one rushed her.

When she was ready, she moved on her own. She dressed in black. Braided her hair. Slid the badge into the pocket of her jacket like it belonged there. Allie wore a fitted black suit, her hair pulled into a sleek bun that made her look more composed than she felt. I slipped into a simple plain black dress and flats.

The drive was quiet. The clouds pressed low, dulling the light. It was like the world had dimmed itself out of respect.

The cemetery was peaceful and well-kept. Rows of headstones stretched in neat lines, the grass trimmed short and damp from the morning air. A white canopy stood at the center with folding chairs arranged beneath it in perfect symmetry. There were uniformed men standing at attention, flags folded and waiting, movements practiced and restrained. Every detail had the unmistakable sharpness of military order.

We stood off to the side. We didn't know most of the people there, but we weren't alone. I spotted them as soon as we arrived. Sam, Dean, and Jack. Standing in the back, silent and watchful.

They didn't come over or wave. But they saw us, and we saw them. Sam nodded once. Dean did nothing. Jack… just watched. His eyes met mine for a second too long. Not unkind. But not letting go, either.

Then the service began. It was short, clean, and efficient. Like a page being closed. One of the officers stepped forward and knelt in front of an older woman in the front row. Abel's mom. Her shoulders were shaking. She didn't reach for the flag right away. Just stared at it like she couldn't believe it belonged to her now.

When she finally took it, she pulled it to her chest with both hands and let herself fold. Her cries weren't loud, but they carried.

Sarah barely moved. She stood with her hands in her jacket pockets, back straight and chin lifted. Her expression didn't change. But I could feel the aching tension in her.

Allie stood on her other side, arms folded, eyes scanning the crowd like she was expecting trouble.

And me—I kept my focus on Sarah.

The service ended with a slow, quiet closing prayer. A few people bowed their heads. Some just stared at the ground. Then, slowly, the crowd began to move. Murmured condolences. Hands on shoulders. Soft voices sharing memories that didn't feel like enough.

We stayed back. Allie hovered close, a silent wall between us and anyone who might approach. That was when I felt something... wrong.

For a moment, it felt like the air around me pulled in tight—like someone had vacuumed all the emotion out of the space and left a hollow behind. I turned, scanning the space until my eyes caught on the flowers.

A large arrangement stood just apart from the others. It was sleek and elegant. Almost too polished. The ribbon wasn't labeled. The colors were off. It wasn't bright or soft like the others. It was the card that drew me in. It was small, white, and tucked almost out of sight. I pulled it loose with shaking fingers and read it.

With deepest sympathy—

Gone too soon. Hold them close while you can

—M

My chest tightened, breath catching before I could stop it. I curled the card in my palm and slipped it into my coat pocket without looking around.

He was here. Maybe not now, but *recently enough.* Close enough to make sure I'd see it. Touch it. *Feel* him in it. It

156

wasn't just a message, it was a reminder and a warning all in one. He was still watching. Waiting.

Something frenzied inside me. And for a second, I wasn't just feeling my own pain. I felt all of it. The weight of Sarah's loss. Allie's guilt. The quiet despair in a stranger two rows back. A man kneeling by the grave who couldn't stop shaking.

It swarmed in me, pressing down. And then I pushed back. Not on purpose. Not even consciously. It just *happened*. A pulse, low and wide, rippling out from my chest like a shockwave.

People near me staggered. Someone gasped. Sarah blinked hard, clutching the badge in her pocket like a jolt had shot through her hand. A woman nearby started to cry. Not the quiet, polite kind. The *gutting* kind.

I stepped back, shaking. Hands trembling.

Allie's head whipped toward me, eyes narrowing. "Lena?"

I was unraveling. And worse? I was taking everyone with me.

Allie grabbed my arm. "We need to go."

Sarah blinked, dazed, one hand gripping my coat like she wasn't sure how we'd gotten there. No one said anything. We just moved. Fast. Past the rows of chairs. Past the rows of stone and towards the car.

Grief still hung thick around the gathering, but something else clung to it now. Confusion. Fractured emotions. People rubbing their arms like they were cold. A woman whispered to no one, *"Did you feel that?"*

I kept my eyes on the ground. My breath was shallow and my heart was hammering. We were almost to the car. When I looked up, I saw Jack watching us. Standing just beyond the crowd, still as ever. His head tilted slightly, like he was trying to fit a new piece into a puzzle he didn't know he was holding.

Allie yanked the car door open and ushered Sarah in the back. I slid in the passenger seat, slamming the door shut behind me like that could keep the magic in. I kept my hands in my lap, fingers still trembling. The card in my pocket felt like it was burning, but I didn't take it out.

Allie gripped the steering wheel like it had said something insulting. Her knuckles were white, jaw locked. "You okay?" she asked.

"I think so," I replied.

Sarah was curled into the corner of the seat, face turned toward the window, one hand still pressed over the pocket with Abel's badge.

Allie glanced at me again, just for a second. "It happened again, didn't it?"

I nodded. "Yeah."

She didn't ask what. She didn't need to.

"There was an arrangement," I said finally. "Flowers with a plain white card tucked in."

Allie didn't speak, just glanced over briefly. Waiting.

"It was from him," I said. "Michael."

Allie's fingers tightened slightly on the steering wheel.

"There was something about it," I continued. "The moment I touched it... I felt him. Like he left a piece of himself behind. It was cold and controlled. Like—like pride. Like he was watching me touch it and smiling."

Sarah sat up a little straighter in the back.

"I tried to hold it in," I said looking down. "But everything hit me all at once. The grief. The fear. His presence. And then I just... couldn't keep it in."

Allie didn't say anything. She just reached over, touched my knee then went back to the wheel.

"You projected," Sarah said softly. "Again."

I nodded, eyes stinging.

Allie exhaled, slow and shaky. "We've got to find a way to help you control this before it breaks you."

• • •

It's been three weeks.

The grief hasn't disappeared. It just changed shape.

Allie stayed busy over-functioning in silence. Sarah has kept to herself. And me... I feel everything.

158

My empathy mark isn't quiet anymore. It doesn't wait for a panic or a scream or a breakdown. It just *is*. Always humming beneath my skin like a second pulse.

I can tell when Allie's lying about being okay. When Sarah's about to cry. When someone's voice tightens just enough to mean something they don't say.

Some mornings I wake up already exhausted, like I've been carrying the pain of all three of us overnight.

I've tried projecting again. A few controlled attempts.

It mostly fizzles. Either nothing happens, or it hits too wide like throwing a blanket of emotion across the room when all I meant to do was wrap it around one person.

But last week, something different happened. Sarah was sitting on the floor of her room, Abel's hoodie in her lap. She didn't speak or cry. Just sat there, holding it like it was the only part of him she had left.

I knelt beside her, close but not touching. I didn't know what I was doing, just that I needed her to feel something *other* than the ache. Even for a second. So I focused. Found that thread between us. And I pushed. Not hard. Just enough. A quiet pulse of warmth, like a hug she couldn't shake off.

Her shoulders dropped. Her grip on the hoodie softened. She exhaled deep and slow, then leaned back against the bed like something inside her finally loosened.

"That was you, wasn't it?" she whispered.

I nodded.

She leaned forward and wrapped her arms around me like she didn't care what I was turning into. Like I was still me. "Thank you," she said into my shoulder. "God, Lena... thank you."

Since then, I've felt Sarah's emotions more clearly than ever. The grief still spikes sometimes, fast and sharp like it's brand new. But it's not constant anymore. Some days, I can feel her just... breathe. The ache is still there. But it no longer owns her. Like little pieces of who she was before Abel are starting to come back. It's not healing, not yet. But it's something.

Allie's harder. Her emotions stay locked under layers of routine and strategy. I feel the edges—frustration, protectiveness, exhaustion—but she doesn't let much slip. Not even to me.

The more I feel them, the harder it is to feel myself. Most days, it's background noise. But not this morning. This morning hit like a punch. I felt it before I heard it. A spike in Allie's chest. Shock, maybe even fear.

Allie was scrolling her phone in the recliner when she made a sharp and sudden sound. Like a breath dragged in too fast.

I looked up from the floor, where Grandma's journals were spread in a half-circle around me. "What?"

She didn't answer. Her thumb hovered frozen over the screen. Her eyes wide.

"Allie?" Sarah sat up straighter on the couch, the blanket pooling around her waist.

Allie turned the screen toward us. "Look."

The post was already blowing up. A viral video from a Portland news station. The caption was short, punchy, and devastating:

BREAKING: Man Saves Six from Apartment Fire Including Billionaire's Daughter. Hero Identified as Michael Brant.

There was a still frame from the video. A crumbling building with clouds of smoke rising from it.

And Michael. Even frozen, his face was clear. Sweat, ash, and soot streaked just right to look cinematic. He was carrying someone in his arms.

Sarah gripped the edge of the blanket.

Allie whispered, "He's using his real name."

Allie walked over and sat in the middle of the couch, next to Sarah. I got up and sat on her other side. Then I pressed play. The footage was filmed from across the street and it was chaotic. Flames roared from the top floor, sirens wailed in the distance and people were screaming.

Then Michael emerged from the smoke calm and focused like the hero in a disaster movie. He carried a young unconscious woman toward the waiting EMTs. He set her down carefully, then looked directly at the camera.

The video cut and another started playing immediately. This time it was clear and clean. A press conference.

Michael stood behind a podium in a charcoal-gray shirt with his sleeves rolled. He had ash on his temple like a trophy. Behind him was Ellis Ryker, the billionaire tech mogul. His face looked both wrecked and grateful.

Michael spoke first. "My name is Michael Brant," he said, voice smooth and rehearsed. "I was walking by when I saw the flames. I didn't think, I just acted." He smiled. Just enough.

Ryker stepped forward, voice thick. "This man saved my daughter. You can't put a price on that... but we tried."

Laughter from the press.

Then the anchor's voice came over the top, "Sources confirm Ryker has donated ten million dollars to Brant, who has already pledged to donate a portion to charity..."

Cut again. Back to Michael, front and center. "I'll be giving part of it to a psychiatric facility here in the city," he said. "It's a cause close to my heart."

The words hit like a slap.

Sarah covered her mouth. "He didn't—"

"He did," Allie said.

I just stared at the screen. The image of him standing there in perfect lighting with ash on his cheek like stage makeup was burned into my mind. I felt the surge before I understood it. Not my emotions, but theirs. Allie's fury. Sarah's betrayal. My own rising nausea.

The air tightened in my chest. My mark pulsed. The world was clapping for him. Laughing at his jokes. Handing him money. Calling him a hero. The man who stabbed me. The man who murdered Abel. The man who stripped pieces of my soul like they were his to take.

161

And now here he was. Framed by soft lighting. Flanked by power. Smiling into cameras like he didn't have blood on his hands. No one saw the monster. They saw a savior.

And he knew it.

God, he knew it. That's why he gave the donation to a psychiatric facility, of all things. Because he wanted me to hear it. He wanted to remind the world I'm the "unstable one." He's not hiding anymore. He's erasing me.

How are we supposed to fight that? He has the money. The charm. The eyes of the world. He could turn everyone against us with a single press conference. And if we try to expose him? They'll call us crazy, angry and delusional. We're not just outnumbered. We're outplayed.

Sarah spoke, her voice shaking. "He's not even trying to hide." She stared at the screen like it had personally betrayed her. "He murdered Abel. And now he gets headlines? Applause? A fucking spotlight?"

Her head shook slowly. Not in disbelief. In bitter recognition. "They'll never believe us," she added. "Not unless he hurts someone in public. Not unless they can *see it*."

Allie hadn't taken her eyes off the screen. "He's not just lying low anymore," she said. "He's building something. A brand, a reputation. Once he's labeled a hero, anything we say becomes noise."

I swallowed. "Do you think he started that fire?"

Allie didn't blink. "Yes. And I think he picked that building for a reason."

She looked up, jaw tight. "He knew Ryker's daughter was there. He wanted an audience and a reward. A *headline*."

Sarah exhaled like she'd been punched. "He *orchestrated* it."

Allie nodded once. "Of course he did. That's what he does."

"So what do we do?" I whispered.

Allie finally looked at me. "We survive. We learn. And we prepare."

"Prepare for what?" I asked.

"For when he comes back," she replied.

"Then what?" Sarah asked, voice raw. "What do we do when he shows up again? Call the cops? The same cops who thought *you* stabbed yourself?" she said, pointing at me.

Allie's silence said everything.

"We can't fight him like this," I said. "He has power. And not just magic. The kind that makes the world listen."

Allie's jaw clenched. "Then we take it from him." That landed like a thrown knife. "We can't beat him by staying quiet," she continued. "We need allies. People who know what he really is. People who know what *you* are. People who can fight him on his level."

She didn't move. Just stared down at her phone, her thumb hovering like she was already searching for something. Allie's voice sharpened. "We need to find The Severance."

Sarah let out a quiet, tired laugh—more exhale than sound. "We've read every journal Margot left behind. Multiple times. Every note. Every cryptic line. And we're still no closer."

We weren't just lost. We were losing.

I nodded, my fingers tightening around the pillow by my side. "They could be anywhere. Anyone. For all we know, they're dead."

Allie didn't look up. "Then we keep looking," she said. "Because if we don't... we already lost."

Allie stood, still clutching her phone, and walked into the kitchen without another word. Sarah and I stayed on the couch.

After a few seconds, Sarah muttered, "I don't know what she's expecting." Her arms were crossed tight over her chest, eyes fixed on the empty space where Allie had been. "If The Severance were still out there, I think they would've shown up by now. I mean, after everything?" She shook her head. "It feels like we're chasing a ghost."

I didn't answer. My thoughts were still back at that press conference. His face. His voice. His smile. The fucking ash on his cheek.

I reached for my phone, not sure why. Maybe I thought I could make it make sense. The news app was already open. Michael's photo was plastered across the screen. He was clean-cut and heroic looking with just enough shadow under his eyes to look noble.

I scrolled.

The headline:

"Portland Fire Hero Speaks Out: 'Anyone Would Have Done the Same'"

And beneath it, the comments.

This man is incredible.

True alpha energy. I'd run into a fire if he was waiting on the other side.

Please tell me he's single.

That SMILE.

My stomach twisted.

I scrolled faster.

What a man.

We need more like him.

He's not just hot, he's brave. A real hero.

I locked the screen. I couldn't read another word. He was everywhere. His lies were viral. And the world had already decided how they'd remember him. Not as a murderer. Not as a manipulator. Not as the monster who burned everything he touched. But as a man worth praising. A man worth *loving.*

"Was it bad?" Sarah asked.

I nodded.

She leaned in, resting her head lightly on my shoulder.

Just then Sarah's phone buzzed and lit up. She glanced at it, then turned the screen toward me.

Jack: *Looks like he didn't run after all.*

Another message followed seconds later.

Jack: *I won't be far. If you need me, don't hesitate.*

"At least he's not buying the bullshit," Sarah said.

But it didn't matter. One person believing me wouldn't change the rest of the world. And right now, the rest of the world was winning.

Chapter 17

It's been ten days since the fire. Ten days of unanswered questions, dead ends, and watching the world fall in love with a lie.

We kept digging, kept searching, always coming up empty-handed.

This morning, Allie stood in the kitchen, phone in hand, eyes glassy like she hadn't slept.

"I've been thinking," she said.

"Uh-oh," Sarah murmured.

Allie didn't even crack a smile. "We have one lead left."

I looked at her. "What?"

"Corinne," she replied.

My stomach dipped. "Allie, she has dementia."

"I know," she said quickly. "But she's the only person Grandma trusted who's still alive. And we've hit every other wall we can."

"What do you think she's going to tell us?" Sarah asked. "She doesn't even know where she is. Or who she is"

"Maybe not with words," Allie said. "But she was a part of this. She might remember something. Or react to something. I don't know. But I can't just sit here and wait for him to strike. I can't."

She didn't sound cold. Or frantic. She sounded scared. And that scared me more than anything.

Allie didn't move from the doorway. "We should go today."

Sarah tilted her head. "Today?"

Allie nodded. "I can call the facility. Just say we are family and see if we can visit. Maybe something will spark when she sees the journals. They were close and if there's anything still in her… maybe this will bring it out."

Sarah looked uncertain, but not opposed. "It's worth a shot," she said finally. "It's not like we have any better ideas."

Allie's eyes softened, just a little. "I don't like waiting," she said. "I don't like feeling helpless. I've never met a problem I couldn't fix. And right now... I feel like I'm failing both of you."

"You're not," I said immediately.

"I know," she said. "But it still feels like it."

• • •

We left within the hour.

The facility hadn't changed. Same beige walls. Same peeling sign near the door. Same waiting room that smelled like lemon cleaner and stale air. But I had.

The second I stepped inside, I braced myself. The wave of grief, loneliness, and confusion came fast. All of it swirling like fog around my ribs. But this time, I was prepared and I held it back. I breathed through it. Slow and steady.

Allie checked in at the front desk. The same nurse from before greeted us, all smiles.

"She's had a quiet morning," she chirped.

We followed her down the hall. I kept my eyes on the floor. My hands clenched tight around Grandma's journal.

Corinne's room was exactly the same. She sat by the window, swaying gently in her chair. She didn't look up when we entered. Her hair was pulled into a loose bun, strands falling free at the temples. Her lips moved constantly, but the words were soft nonsense.

The nurse stepped back. "I'll give you some time."

Allie walked forward. "Hi, Corinne."

No response. Sarah stood beside me, hands in her pockets. We all waited. Ten seconds. Then twenty. Nothing.

Corinne kept humming.

Allie tried again. "We brought one of Margot's journals. Do you remember her?" Allie took the journal from my hand and laid it in front of Corinne. Still nothing.

I stepped closer. My heart kicked once, hard, when I saw the split stone. It was still clutched in her hand, like she hadn't let go of it since the day it woke something inside me.

168

I knelt slowly. "Corinne? It's me. Lena."

Her lips kept moving. The words meant nothing. Just a slurry of nonsense and broken fragments.

I swallowed and reached toward the stone, slowly and carefully like I might startle her. My fingers brushed the edge of it. Corinne snapped her hand back with surprising speed, curling her body away from me like I'd tried to steal something sacred.

Her eyes flashed sharpness. Not recognition. Just... warning. Then she turned back toward the window and resumed humming. That was it.

I looked at Allie. Her mouth was pressed in a thin line and her brows were pulled together in a tight knot.

Sarah exhaled hard through her nose. "Well. That was worth the drive."

I picked the journal back up. Corinne didn't even glance at it. She never looked at us again.

We walked back to the car feeling defeated. Allie unlocked the doors and slid into the driver's seat. Sarah climbed into the back. I took the passenger seat and slammed the door harder than I meant to. For a moment, the car was still. Then Allie let out a growl and slammed both fists against the steering wheel.

Once. Twice. And a third time. The sound cracked through the air. "Goddammit!" she screamed. Her voice ripped out of her throat, raw and unrestrained. She hit the wheel again, harder, the horn blaring for half a second before cutting off. "Fuck!"

Sarah flinched behind me.

Allie shoved her hands through her hair, yanking hard, like if she pulled hard enough, she could rip the frustration out of her skull.

"I thought she'd say something!" she shouted. "I thought there'd be a sign.. a spell.. *Anything!*" Her hands hit the steering wheel again. "I'm so fucking sick of guessing! Of chasing shadows! Of feeling like I'm the only one even trying to hold us together!"

Sarah leaned forward, voice careful. "Allie—"

"Don't," Allie snapped. "Don't tell me it's okay. It's *not* okay. None of this is okay!" She was breathing fast now, chest heaving like her rage was the only thing keeping her upright. "I don't know what I'm doing," she spat. "And I'm terrified. You want the truth? There it is. I don't have a plan. I don't have a clue. And I feel like I'm fucking drowning."

She collapsed forward, her forehead hitting the steering wheel. Her voice dropped, hoarse and brittle. "I just... I don't know what else to do."

"Neither do we," I said. "And maybe that's okay for five fucking minutes."

Allie blinked like I'd slapped her. But I didn't take it back.

A beat passed. Then Sarah leaned forward between the seats and muttered, "Cool. So we're officially out of ideas. Anybody wanna try sacrificing a goat or...?"

Allie let out something between a snort and a laugh, wiping her eyes with the heel of her hand.

Sarah shrugged. "Hey. Desperate times."

I laughed, too.

Even Sarah cracked a smile. And somehow, for just a moment, things felt lighter. Still broken. Still messy. But lighter.

Allie cleared her throat, eyes a little puffy, but steady. Then she turned the key in the ignition, put the car in gear, and pulled out of the lot without a word.

About ten minutes later, she turned onto a side road and pulled into the cracked lot of a run-down ice cream shop that looked like it hadn't been renovated since the '90s.

The sign out front was sun-faded and crooked, the giant plastic cone on top leaning at a questionable angle. The building itself was a squat, flat-roofed thing with chipped pink paint and a neon "OPEN" sign that flashed weakly like it was debating its own truth.

Sarah leaned forward. "Are we seriously getting ice cream right now?"

Allie rolled down her window. "Listen, I just emotionally combusted in a parking lot. I've earned a cone."

Sarah huffed a laugh. "Fair."

When we pulled up to the speaker, Allie didn't even look at the menu. "Three peanut butter swirl cones. No sprinkles. We're in mourning."

The teenager's voice crackled through the speaker. "Uh… okay. Drive up."

Allie glanced at me, deadpan. "I swear, if they mess this up, I'll burn this place down with my mind."

I smiled.

She passed out the cones like she was dealing drugs. We just sat in the car, parked beneath a buzzing light, eating soft-serve in a sad little lot that somehow felt like neutral ground. And for a few minutes, nothing hurt.

Allie finished the last bite of her cone and wiped her hand on a napkin. "We're out of coffee," she said. "And bread. And a few other things. There's a store a couple blocks up. Let's just get it over with."

I didn't argue.

The grocery store was small and slightly fluorescent. It had linoleum floors scuffed to hell, rows of dusty boxes stacked too high, and a squeaky cart wheel that screamed every few seconds like clockwork.

For once, my empathy didn't feel like a curse. Ever since it surfaced, I've been surrounded by grief—hospital walls, funeral homes, and the quiet collapse of people I couldn't save. But this? This was something else.

In aisle three, a little girl dropped a pack of gummy bears into the cart, grinning up at her mom like she'd won the lottery. I felt the spark of her bright, sticky sweet joy.

Down near the dairy section, an older couple debated between two kinds of yogurt. His hand brushed hers, and the love that passed between them was so soft, I nearly cried. Not because it hurt, but because it *didn't.*

It felt like warmth. Like memories. Like hope. Is this what it was supposed to feel like? Empathy without suffering. Emotion without collapse.

I wasn't drowning in their feelings. I was floating in them. Drifting in something human and whole. I actually smiled. The kind that sneaks up on you.

We turned into aisle eight. There was a woman who looked to be in her mid-forties. She had a neat ponytail and was wearing a business suit. She had a jar of tomato basil sauce in one hand, and her cart was half full. She looked up and her eyes locked on me. Then stayed there. She gave me a smug smile.

"You're her," she said. "Michael's ex, right?"

The words landed like a dropped glass. Allie tensed beside me. Sarah's shoulders pulled back, spine straightening like she was preparing for a fight.

The woman tilted her head, her voice dipping into something low and sweet, laced with venom. "Some people don't know how lucky they are until it's gone," she continued. "Though I guess he's doing just fine now."

Then she gave me a once-over. Top to bottom. Like she was doing the math on what he'd lost. She didn't wait for a response. She just turned her cart and walked away like she'd just done a public service.

"You should really get all the facts before you worship a murderer," Sarah called after her.

The woman didn't turn.

"Keep cheering him on," Allie added, her voice low and cold. "You'll regret it."

That made the woman hesitate for half a second. Then she pushed her cart faster, disappearing around the corner without a word.

The happiness in my chest vanished. The sweetness, the warmth, the fleeting normalcy was gone. Michael wasn't even here. And somehow, he still managed to ruin everything.

Allie turned to me, her eyes still burning. "How the hell does she even know who you are?"

I shook my head. "I have no idea."

Allie didn't say anything as we made our way to the checkout, but I saw it in her eyes. The way she scanned every face. Every cart. Every casual glance. She was watching for more of them. The look in her eyes had anyone daring to confront me.

We loaded the groceries into the trunk. Allie scanned the lot again before getting in, like she expected another person to come out of nowhere with a verbal knife.

I slid into the front seat and shut the door. My phone was already in my hand. Maybe someone's posted something. Anything to explain how that woman knew who I was. I opened Facebook. I didn't even have to scroll. The second the app opened, I knew.

His face was everywhere.

A video auto-played at the top of my feed. An influencer stared back at me, all pouty lips and perfect angles, framed by the front seat of a luxury SUV. Her lashes were thick enough to cast shadows, her pastel hoodie slightly off-shoulder like it had just *happened* to slip that way. In the corner of the video, a smaller box played a clip on loop: Michael, stepping out of a burning building, soot-smudged and glowing in golden smoke like a goddamn movie hero.

Allie glanced over.

Sarah leaned forward from the back. "Is that—?"

"Yeah," I said.

The woman on screen smiled wide, her voice was smooth and fast. It was the kind that made people think she was just stating facts when she was really lighting matches.

"Okay, so let's talk about Michael Brant, who just saved a billionaire's daughter from a literal inferno and still managed to look good doing it."

She laughed softly. "I mean... heroic *and* hot? Yes, please."

The video cut to a screenshot of my profile pic. A photo of me and Michael, laughing like idiots. Shit. I haven't even touched my profile since this all happened.

Maybe because part of me didn't want to erase what we used to be. Because it hurt to admit it was never real.

The woman's voice dipped, soft and syrupy, soaked in weaponized compassion.

"Now, I did some digging because obviously the world wants to know if he's single, and what I found is... honestly, upsetting. Apparently, he was in a relationship. With this woman whose name is Lena Merrow."

The image of me lingered on screen.

"So yeah, they were dating. But get this, she tried to frame him. Like, full-on psycho. She stabbed herself and tried to make everyone think it was Michael. The nerve, right? He stayed with her, supported her through her mental health issues, tried to get her help... and *this* is how she repays him? Let that sink in. This man saves people from burning buildings and *still* has the patience to deal with this kind of toxic drama."

"Michael, if you see this. *We see you.*" And then a slow, reverent zoom on his perfect, lying face.

Sarah sat back hard against her seat. "Guess we know how she knew who you were."

Allie exhaled. "They used your name. Your face. And twisted the whole damn story."

My mouth was dry. My hands were shaking. Psycho. Mental health issues. Toxic drama. They made me the villain. And him the savior.

Sarah's voice was sharper now. "They just... used your life like it was content."

Allie swore under her breath. "Unbelievable."

"They're eating it up," Sarah added, disgust in every syllable. "They want him to be a hero so bad, they'll rewrite reality."

"Are you okay?" Allie asked me, her voice softer now.

I wanted to say yes. I wanted to lie and move on. But instead I just whispered, "I don't know."

I opened the settings on the app, and deleted my account. But it didn't matter. His image still burned behind every screen. And mine? Mine was a smear on the glass.

Chapter 18

The sun was warm on our backs as we pulled weeds from the garden bed. Michael sat beside me in the grass, sleeves pushed up, dirt streaked across his forearm. There was a smudge on his cheek, and I reached over to wipe it away with my thumb. He caught my wrist and grinned.

"Admit it," he said. "You're terrible at this."

I scoffed. "You're literally planting the same weed you just pulled."

He leaned back on one hand and held the other to his chest, mock offended. "I'm giving it a second chance."

I rolled my eyes, grabbed a handful of dirt, and tossed it at him.

His eyes went wide. "Oh, you're dead."

He lunged.

I squealed as he tackled me back into the grass, laughter spilling between us. The scent of sun-warmed soil and crushed clover filled the air. He hovered above me, elbows braced, that crooked smile softening into something quieter.

"I hate you," I whispered.

He brushed a piece of hair from my face. "No, you don't."

My heart swelled. I was full and sure and safe. He leaned down and kissed me. Slow and gentle. Like he had all the time in the world.

And when he pulled back, his voice was just a breath against my skin. "You have no idea what you mean to me."

I smiled.

And woke up. For a second, everything was still. The room was cool, the blanket warm, and my body was curled toward the right side of the bed—toward where he should be.

My hand reached out, fingers brushing against nothing but wrinkled sheets. Then reality came crashing in, loud and brutal and merciless. The air vanished from my lungs like it had been ripped out. The dream clung to me. It was too vivid. Too real. My stomach turned. My chest seized.

I sat up. Not with a jolt. Not with a scream. Just the slow, suffocating realization that the only place he would ever hold me again was in a nightmare.

My lungs locked. The walls pressed in. I needed air. I didn't think. I didn't grab shoes. Still in nothing but sweatpants and a thin tank top, I moved like I was being hunted. I ran through the hall and out the back door barefoot. The night met me like a slap, cold and unforgiving.

But I didn't stop. I ran into the trees, past the place where light reached. My breathing was labored and my feet stung against the earth, but I didn't care. The dream was still inside me, crawling under my skin.

I didn't stop until I stumbled into a small clearing and dropped hard to my knees. I pressed my palms into the dirt, needing the feel of it—something raw and solid beneath me to keep from slipping away.

"Did you like that dream, love?"

I looked up. Michael stood a few feet away, leaning casually against a tree, a cruel smile plastered on his face.

"One of the new tricks you so graciously gave me," he said, tapping his temple. "Took a little practice. But for you?" He winked. "Worth it."

I was frozen. He stepped forward like we were just two old friends reuniting in the woods.

"Had to get you out of that house somehow," he said. "Could've killed all three of you, but... reputation's important. Can't have anyone getting suspicious, can we?"

My voice scraped out, brittle and breathless. "Why are you doing this? You already took everything. I have nothing left."

Michael tilted his head, eyes gleaming. "Ah, but you do. There's still a piece of you left. And you know it."

He crouched in front of me, lifting my chin with two fingers, forcing me to look at him. Forcing me to meet his eyes. The second our gazes locked, something inside me seized.

"Follow me," he said.

And I did. My body moved without permission. Step by step. Into the trees. Into the dark.

No. No. Please, no.

I screamed inside my head. Begged my legs to stop. But they didn't listen. They listened to *him*.

Michael didn't even glance back.

The ground was cold and rough beneath my bare feet. Each step brought sharp jabs from sticks and rocks, cutting into my skin, leaving bruises. Still, I didn't stop.

"I need to stop," I choked out. "Please—I can't—STOP!"

He laughed. "That's not how persuasion works, Lena. You feel it, don't you?" he said, glancing over his shoulder with a gleam in his eye. "The command. That low, humming thing under your skin. You're fighting it, but your body already knows who's in control. That's one thing I didn't get from you. Persuasion. It's not one of your marks."

He kept walking like we were on some lazy stroll through the woods. Like he hadn't just hijacked my entire body.

"That one... I perfected on my own. Years of watching. Studying. Learning every hesitation, every weakness. Perfecting the pitch, the pause, the lie. Until people bent without ever realizing why."

He glanced back again, smiling like it was a private joke.

God. A man like that with the power to control anyone. What chance did I ever have?

"Where are we going?" I managed, my voice barely holding together.

He smiled like it was a secret he'd been waiting to share. "Fenwick Cliff," he said, light and easy. Like we were on our way to brunch. "You know it, right? Not far from your sister's place." His voice softened with delight.

"Everyone will just think you jumped," he said. "Poor, broken Lena Merrow. Traumatized and unstable. A tragic end to a tragic story." He grinned wider, all teeth. "It'll be the perfect headline."

I tried to stop. Tried to dig my heels into the earth. But my body... my body obeyed *him*.

179

"Why me?" I asked.

He sighed, like he'd been waiting for the question. "I was born into a powerful magical family," he said. "Powerful bloodlines older than most countries. "But me? Nothing. No mark. Just a stain on their perfect little world."

He kept walking, each step slow, deliberate.

"They treated me like I didn't exist. Like a memory they were trying to erase. So I studied. I learned about things they whispered about and locked away. I searched for alternatives."

His fingers brushed a branch as he passed, snapping it in half without looking.

"And I found it. An old dagger that was hungrier than any spell. It was designed to siphon magic directly from another."

My heart pounded against my ribs.

A cruel amusement spread across his face.

"My parents were first. They begged at the end. That's the part no one tells you. The mighty always beg when they bleed."

My stomach twisted.

"But it wasn't enough," he said, his voice tightening. "The magic came... and it went. A few weeks, maybe a month. Then it fizzled. Like it had never been mine at all."

His hands flexed, remembering. "So I tried again." He turned his head slightly and his gaze darkened. "My brother was twelve. My sister, ten."

My feet faltered, but the magic dragged me forward.

"They cried," he said softly, almost nostalgic. "They clung to me. Called me 'Mikey' between sobs." He tilted his head. "And I killed them anyway."

He inhaled deeply, as if savoring the memory, then let out a low laugh. "And that's when I noticed it," he murmured, tapping his temple lightly. "With every mark I stole... something else came alive. Persuasion. At first, it was just a hint. A nudge here, a suggestion there. But it grew stronger."

His lips twisted into something like wonder. "I think... I think that was meant to be my mark," he said, almost like a confession to himself. "If I'd been born with one at all. The power to bend anyone until they break."

I tasted blood where I'd bitten my own tongue.

"My sibling's magic lasted a little longer," he continued. "It felt... heavier and stronger." He smiled again—a slow, rotting thing. "But it still faded. Like everything else."

I wanted to vomit.

He shrugged. "So I hunted. I killed. Again and again. Took what I could. And still, it faded. Every time. Until one day, someone I was about to gut offered me a trade. A name. A girl hidden by blood and binding. Power unlike anything seen in centuries."

He smiled at me like we shared a private joke. "You."

I wanted to scream.

"I was intrigued," he said. "But frustrated. Power that fades is worthless. And that's when he told me... there was another way. A way to take a mark and make it mine for good."

Michael's voice dropped lower, hypnotic. "Not through force. But through *trust*. Through *love*."

His lips curled. "If I could make you love me—*really* love me—your marks would become mine. Forever."

"I killed him anyway. And I made the plan. I found you and found your hospital. I staged the accident using what little I had to persuade a stranger into traffic so I could play the hero." He shrugged. "Had to kill her, of course. Loose ends."

My vision spun. We kept walking. Wind whispered through the trees. Fenwick Cliff was close.

"I used persuasion on the hospital staff too," he said casually. "Doctors. Nurses. Cops. They all believed you tried to kill yourself. I even tried it on your sister and Sarah," he said, sounding almost amused. "Allie stared at me like I was made of knives. Sarah almost hit me."

Allie. Sarah. Always in my corner. A tear slipped down my cheek.

He shook his head, laughing softly. "It's always the ones you don't expect who ruin the plan."

181

Then he stopped. So did I. His eyes burned as he turned.

"Your mother," he said. "She knew. Not everything, but enough. She had a whisper of magic in her blood. Just enough to feel what you couldn't yet."

He smiled, cruel and slow. "She didn't trust me. She tried to warn you, didn't she? Little comments and hesitations. That prickle at the back of her neck every time I smiled."

My throat burned. I couldn't breathe.

"I couldn't persuade her," he said, almost amused. "Not fully. I wasn't strong enough with the little bit I had. And that little bit of magic made her slippery and resistant."

His gaze slid over me, lazy and cold. "But your father?" Michael shrugged. "Easy." His voice dropped to a near-whisper. "One little nudge before he got behind the wheel." He leaned in closer, his breath brushing my skin. "That's all it took to kill them."

The trees blurred. The earth spun. The air clawed at my lungs like fire.

He killed them.

He killed them.

He killed them.

My mother's hand on my hair—gone.

My father's laugh in the garage—gone.

All the nights I cried and cursed the stars, blaming fate... I should have blamed him. Tears streamed down my face, but I barely felt them. Somewhere, deep in the hollow place he'd carved inside me, a voice whispered.

They died because Mom tried to warn you. And you gave yourself to him anyway.

The shame hit harder than the grief. It wrapped around my ribs like barbed wire, squeezing until I couldn't breathe. I thought I had nothing left to lose. I was wrong.

Michael smiled, watching me break like he was savoring it.

Something inside me twisted at seeing his smile. He stole everything. My family. My future. Innocent lives. Abel. *Me.*

182

For the first time, I fought back. "STOP!" The word ripped from my throat. It was wild and raw. The invisible chain between us strained... and then snapped. The pressure inside me shattered like glass. My body was mine again. I staggered back a step, gasping

Michael's smile faltered. Just for a second. A crack in his perfect control. And then he laughed, low and cruel. He took a step toward me, slow and sure, eating up the space between us. "Oh, sweet Lena..." he murmured. He circled me like a wolf scenting blood. "You still don't get it, do you?"

His voice wrapped around me, sticky and poisonous. "This isn't a fight." He leaned in close, his breath hot against my ear. "You already lost."

His gaze roamed down my body, slow and invasive, like he was tasting every inch with his eyes.

I stayed still.

"You know," he said, voice curling into a mockery of tenderness, "out of everything I faked..." He smiled, slow and sick. "...fucking you was the one part I actually enjoyed."

My stomach heaved. But I stayed standing.

He touched me with the back of his fingers, gliding from my jaw to my throat like I belonged to him. Gentle, but soaked in something foul.

My skin recoiled, even if I didn't.

"That mouth," he murmured, almost fond. "So soft when you weren't crying."

His hand slid lower, skimming my hip and my thigh. His fingers pressed just hard enough to leave shame behind. "All that power," he whispered against my ear, "and you still opened up for me like you were made for it." He dragged his fingers up my side, slow and claiming, his breath curling against my skin. "All that fight in you," he continued, his voice a low growl, "and I still fucked you soft."

Tears blurred my vision. My skin crawled.

He leaned back slightly, admiring his own cruelty like an artist admiring a painting. "And after I'm done squeezing the last bit out of you..." he said, voice casual, "maybe I'll see if your sister moans just as sweet."

Something in me snapped. There was no thought. No plan. Just white-hot fury. I lunged at him—teeth bared, hands clawing, a scream ripping from my throat.

"DON'T YOU TOUCH HER!"

Michael's eyes went wide with shock. Real, human shock. Like he hadn't truly believed I could still fight. My hands hit his chest and for a heartbeat, he actually staggered back. And then he snarled.

The air between us shuddered. A ripple of power came bursting from his hand. The same sickening, invisible force he'd used against Sarah.

It slammed into me, lifting me off my feet and hurling me across the woods like a ragdoll. I hit the ground hard, skidding across the dirt and dead leaves. A sickening crack split the air and pain exploded up my arm. I screamed, clutching my right arm instinctively, but the damage was already done. It was broken. The stars spun above me and the world tilted.

Michael stood where I'd left him. He was brushing imaginary dust off his jacket while his smile twisted into something crueler. "Tsk, tsk, Lena," he said, voice dripping with mockery. "You were always so dramatic."

He pulled the dagger from inside his jacket, the black blade catching the moonlight. Strange symbols were carved along its edge. They were thin, angular markings that looked almost burned into the metal.

He strolled toward me, casual and cruel with the dagger loose in his hand. "I was planning to finish this at the cliff," he said. "Let the ocean clean up the mess." He tilted his head, his smile sharpening. "But since you want to be a bitch about it... I guess I'll just kill you right here."

Michael twirled the dagger lazily in his hand, stepping closer until he loomed over me, all teeth and triumph. "You should've stayed quiet," he said, almost fondly. "Would've been quicker."

He raised the dagger—

—and the world tore open.

A flash of motion emerged from the trees. A shadow stepping into existence, already midair, sword raised high. The man moved faster than thought. A war cry tore from his throat as he drove the sword straight into Michael's chest, driving it clean through. The tip burst from his back, slick with blood.

The impact knocked Michael off balance. A sharp, wet gasp tore free from his mouth. He staggered, clutching at the blade, stunned.

The stranger didn't wait. He dropped down, boots hitting the earth, and crossed the space between us in two strides. Strong arms swept me up, cradling me like I was weightless.

"Got you," he said. His voice was low and rough... one I'd never heard before.

Before I could even scream, the shadows coiled around us. Then came a rush of cold and pressure that stole the breath from my lungs. When the darkness peeled away, we were in another part of the woods. Another step and the shadows took us again.

A heartbeat later, we were standing outside of the house. I gasped, struggling weakly against him, my broken arm screaming in protest.

"Easy," the stranger said, setting me down carefully. "You're hurt."

I scrambled back a step, heart pounding, every muscle screaming to run. I had no idea who he was or why he had saved me. But before I could decide whether to fight or bolt, the back door of the house slammed open.

Sarah and Allie came rushing out. They were barefoot, wild-eyed, and still in sleep-clothes.

Allie was clutching a cardigan half-on, the sleeves twisted around her elbows as she sprinted across the yard, her bare feet thudding against the dirt. Sarah was right beside her, swallowed up by an oversized hoodie and loose pink sweats, her toes kicking up dust as she ran.

"Lena!" they screamed.

185

Allie's eyes found me first. They dropped to my broken, bloodied arm, then moved to the man standing protectively at my side. Her face drained of color. Sarah skidded to a stop beside her, chest heaving, tears already blurring her eyes.

And behind them, there were others. Men and women, maybe five or six total, spilling out of the house and fanning across the yard. They wore black combat gear, just like the stranger beside me. All of them were armed. Some with swords and knives, others with guns. Something thrummed in the air like a static charge. Magic. I wasn't sure how I knew, but I could tell.

A man and a woman approached the stranger, their weapons still drawn.

"He won't stay down long," the stranger said. "We have to move. Now."

He glanced toward the front, where two black jeeps sat idling, engines rumbling low.

Allie stepped instinctively in front of me, one arm raised like a shield.

"Hold on," she said sharply. "Where the hell are you taking us?"

The stranger didn't flinch. "Somewhere safe," he said.

"That's not an answer," Allie snapped, her voice cutting through the night.

The woman in front of us spoke before he could. She looked to be a few years older than me, taller too, with a lean, athletic frame. She had tan skin and long black hair that was braided tight down her back. Her dark, sharp eyes scanned us with cool precision. She carried herself like she'd been forged in fire and didn't mind the burn.

"We're The Severance," she said. "We protect people from monsters like him. That's all you need to know right now."

Allie's hand twitched, like she was weighing whether or not to punch someone. Sarah edged closer to me, one hand lightly brushing my uninjured arm.

186

The Severance. The ones we'd read about. Searched for. Begged the universe to send. And now they were here. Real, alive, and armed.

"But... you stabbed him," I rasped, turning toward the stranger. "He's dead. Right?"

For a heartbeat, no one answered. Then the woman with sharp eyes looked at me with a hard, almost furious expression on her face.

"He can heal," she said coldly. "Thanks to you."

My eyes dropped to the ground, shame burning through me, hot and fast.

"Lena," Sarah whispered. "What do you want to do?"

I swallowed hard, my broken body barely holding together. I didn't know if I could trust them. But I knew one thing for sure. If we stayed here, he would come back.

I met Sarah's eyes, then Allie's. Better the unknown than the monster I already knew. "Let's go," I rasped.

The stranger nodded once and the group moved as one. They rushed toward the jeeps, boots pounding the dirt.

Allie cursed under her breath but moved fast, grabbing Sarah's arm. Sarah reached for me without hesitation, gripping my good hand tight. Together, we ran—half-dragging each other toward the nearest jeep.

"I need my stuff," Sarah panted. "My phone, my bag—"

"There's no time," the sharp-eyed woman snapped, shoving open the back door of the jeep. "Move!"

Sarah hesitated for a split second, torn—then obeyed, diving into the backseat, Allie following right after. I was right behind them, but I stopped short, chest heaving.

"Biscuit!" I gasped. "My cat. I can't leave her. I have to—" I turned, stumbling toward the house, broken arm clutched tight against my chest. Before I could take two steps, a strong hand caught my good shoulder.

"Go," the stranger said, voice rough but steady. "Get in the jeep."

I shook my head, breath hitching. "You don't understand—"

"I'll get her," he said firmly. "I promise."

His eyes locked with mine, bright green and burning in the dark. There was no lie there. No hesitation.

"I swear, Lena," he said. "I'll bring her to you."

I flinched. He knew my name. For a heartbeat, I wanted to fight him. I wanted to tear free and run into that house, broken arm and all. But something solid in his voice made me freeze. I gave a shaky nod, a sob catching in my throat as he gently turned me toward the jeep. He waited just long enough to make sure I was moving, then turned toward the house. The shadows near the jeep stirred, rippling like disturbed water. He stepped into them and vanished.

I stumbled up to the jeep, heart hammering, lungs burning. Sarah was already inside, crammed against the far side by the door, her hands clenched white in her lap. Allie sat next to her in the middle seat, tense and braced, one hand gripping the back of the front seat like she was ready to lunge forward if she had to. I climbed in beside Allie, slamming the door shut behind me, my broken arm cradled against my chest.

The sharp-eyed woman threw herself into the driver's seat, the engine rumbling low and steady. A man with broad shoulders and a scarred face jumped into the passenger seat, gun already drawn, scanning the shadows.

Weapons. Eyes. Movement. They were ready to fight. Ready to kill at the first sign of threat.

And then I saw a ripple at the edge of the trees. The stranger stepped out with Biscuit cradled carefully in his arms. She was curled against his chest, tiny paws kneading at his jacket, her head nudging up under his chin like she'd known him forever. A wave of relief swept through me.

He didn't waste a second. He hauled open the back hatch, crawled inside, and yanked it shut behind him. The space was too small for him. His shoulders pressed against the side, his knees bent awkwardly, but he didn't complain. He just curled around Biscuit like she was the only thing that mattered.

I twisted in my seat, heart still hammering, and really looked at him for the first time. He was big, easily six-two, maybe taller, even folded awkwardly in the back hatch. Broad through the chest and shoulders, solid like someone built to fight and win. His skin was sun-bronzed and he looked to be about thirty years old.

His dark hair was longer than I expected, unruly waves falling across his forehead like the world's chaos didn't faze him. It wasn't styled. Just wild, windswept, like he didn't care about rules. His jaw was sharp and rough with stubble. He had a faint scar near his left temple disappearing into the mess of his hair. He looked like someone who'd bled and healed more times than he could count.

But it was his eyes that held me. They were bright green, too light to feel real, almost glowing in the dark. He caught me staring, but he didn't look away. Just resettled Biscuit gently in his arms and gave the smallest smile.

A second later, the jeep shot forward spitting gravel, tires grinding against the dirt. I gasped at the jolt, my body slamming back into the seat. Pain flared through my arm, and I winced. But I couldn't stop looking at him.

He didn't even flinch. Still folded in the hatch, one arm curved protectively around Biscuit, the other braced against the side panel—he just smiled at me.

Not wide or cocky. Just enough to say, *You're okay. We made it.*

His voice was kind when he finally spoke.

"My name's Cade," he said. "Cade Mercer."

I swallowed thickly, tasting blood and dust.

"My name's Lena," I said, my voice barely louder than a whisper.

Cade moved slightly in the back, the sound of Biscuit's soft purring filling the space around him. "I know," he said simply.

Allie turned toward me, her eyes wide, brimming with a thousand unspoken demands for answers she wasn't ready to receive yet.

189

Sarah sat rigid in her seat, still staring ahead. Then, slowly, almost like her body was moving without her, she reached into the front pocket of her hoodie. Her fingers fumbled for a second before pulling out Abel's badge. The silver caught the passing headlights, flashing once before disappearing into her trembling hands.

My chest caved inward, pain sharper than any broken bone. I curled tighter into my seat, my broken arm throbbing with every bump in the road.

And somewhere behind us, in the blood-soaked dark, Michael was getting back up.

Chapter 19

The jeep rumbled over back roads and highways, the world outside blurring. Up front, The Severance team exchanged a few clipped words.

For a few minutes, Allie, Sarah, and I stayed silent, the shock of the night sitting between us. But it couldn't last.

Allie twisted toward me, her cardigan still half-hanging off one shoulder, her face pale and raw. "Lena," she rasped. "Why were you outside? What the hell happened?"

Sarah leaned forward to look at me, her eyes wide and desperate. "What did he do to you?"

I swallowed hard, the words scraping up my throat. I forced the words out. "He lured me out of the house. It's hard to explain." My voice dropped. "He tried to kill me... again."

Allie made a wounded sound, half growl, but said nothing. Sarah's hands tightened on the badge.

"I'll explain everything," I whispered. "Just... not here. Not now."

I couldn't destroy Allie with the truth about our parents while armed strangers sat two feet away. She deserved a quiet place. A moment without an audience. Somewhere she could fall apart safely.

The rest of the drive was spent in silence. Every so often, I glanced toward the back and saw Cade folded awkwardly into the cramped space with Biscuit resting on his chest. He didn't speak. Just kept his eyes fixed on the darkness beyond the window.

We drove for over an hour before the jeep finally slowed. The trees began to thin, and a building emerged from the shadows. It wasn't what I expected. Just a long, low building, its frame blending into the shadows of the trees behind it. The driveway wound up to the entrance, gravel crunching under the tires as we climbed. The place didn't scream magic or power. It didn't scream anything at all. A place built to be overlooked by anyone who didn't know better.

The jeep rumbled to a stop near the entrance. For a second, none of us moved. Then, someone cracked open their door up front, the sound jarring in the stillness. Cade moved first, uncurling from the back hatch with Biscuit still tucked carefully against his chest. He slipped out with a grace that didn't match his size, landing lightly on the gravel. Allie twisted in her seat toward me, hovering like she wanted to help but didn't know how.

Sarah fumbled with her door handle and slid out, hissing when her bare feet hit the gravel. I reached for my own door with my good hand, gritting my teeth against the fresh spike of pain. I opened my door slowly, pain blooming in my arm as I moved.

Then Cade was there, reaching back through the door, one steady hand beneath my good elbow, his other arm acting like a bench for Biscuit. "Easy," he said.

I gave a shaky nod and let him help me down. The gravel tore at my soles. I winced, but didn't complain. Allie and Sarah were already moving, sticking close, their bodies tense and alert. Cade kept one hand light against my back as we crossed the space toward the building.

Up close, the place looked even plainer. Weathered siding. Reinforced wooden door. A chimney that rose near the front. No signs. No names. Nothing to hint at the magic. Cade leaned in and punched a code into a small keypad by the door. The lock disengaged, and he pushed it open.

Inside was not what I expected. Warm light spilled over gleaming hardwood floors and thick woven rugs. Leather couches framed a massive stone fireplace, where a fire crackled low. Bookshelves lined the walls between windows. An enormous wooden table occupied the far side of the room, papers, laptops, and weapons spread across it. Hallways branched off in three directions—left, right, and straight back.

It didn't feel like a bunker. It felt...expensive. Immaculate.

And we weren't alone. Several people sat by the fire, relaxed but ready. Others hovered around the table, scanning maps and murmuring over glowing screens. Every head turned when we entered. Their conversations died mid-sentence.

Allie and Sarah inched closer, arms brushing mine. Not scared. Just bracing.

A man stepped away from the group at the table. Tall, pale, mid-to-late thirties by the look of him, with short blond hair and a neatly kept red beard that didn't quite match but somehow worked.

His smile was easy, but his blue eyes were watchful, taking in every detail. "Hey," he said, voice steady and warm. His gaze landed on my arm, then my face. "I'm Nick."

He didn't offer his hand. Maybe he knew I couldn't take it anyway.

"I'm the healer here," he said. "You look like you could use some help."

Allie's arm moved in front of me slightly, a barrier I hadn't even seen her raise. "Healer?" she said sharply. "What do you mean healer?"

Nick didn't seem offended. If anything, his smile turned a little more patient, like he was used to people not trusting him right away. "My mark," he said simply. "Mine's healing. Broken bones. Cuts. Internal injuries. If it's a physical injury, I can fix it."

His eyes moved to my arm again, still cradled tight against my chest. "You don't have to let me," he added, softer. "It's your choice. Just... it'll hurt less if you do."

Allie glanced at me, jaw tight. Protective. Silent. Sarah was quiet too, hugging Abel's badge close to her hoodie.

The fire crackled behind Nick, throwing soft light against his blond hair and that strange red beard. There was something in the steady way he stood there that didn't feel like a stranger at all. It felt more like a brother reaching for a sibling who needed help.

"Okay," I rasped.

He gently reached and straightened my arm. His fingers barely brushed my skin before I felt something. It was thick. Like honey pouring through my veins. It didn't erase the pain. It wove through it. Like stitching a torn seam from the inside out.

Tears pricked behind my eyes. Not from pain, but from the strange weight of it easing.

Nick didn't speak. He just worked quietly. His thumb brushed lightly against the break, and the fractured bones knit back together with a soft, almost imperceptible twinge inside me.

When he finally pulled his hands away, the pain was gone. I flexed my fingers carefully, half-afraid it would still hurt if I moved. It didn't.

Nick gave a small nod, almost to himself, and stepped back. Around us, the others watched in silence. Not unfriendly, but not inviting either.

And then, a woman stepped forward. She had bronzed skin, wild dark curls, and wore a flowing bohemian dress that swayed around her ankles. She looked to be in her mid-thirties, with the kind of ageless beauty that made it hard to tell for sure. She stopped a few feet from us, her hands loose at her sides.

"I'm Lorelei," she said, her voice a low current that seemed to cut through everything else. "And you have a lot of questions." Lorelei's gaze swept over me. "Would you like to get cleaned up first?" she asked.

It took me a moment to realize what she meant. Then I looked down. My tank top was streaked with dirt and blood. My sweatpants were ripped at the knees. My arms were smudged with dried mud, twigs still tangled in my hair. I looked like something dragged out of a grave.

I hadn't even noticed. I opened my mouth, but before I could speak, Allie stepped forward.

"Wait," she said. "Can we... just talk first? Please." Allie's eyes moved between Lorelei and the others. "We've been trying to find you for weeks. You're the only ones who might actually know what the hell is happening and why it's happening to her."

She wasn't demanding. But she wasn't backing down, either.

Lorelei nodded. "Of course," she said. "Let's sit. You deserve answers."

She led us to the sitting area with couches and deep chairs arranged in a loose circle around the hearth. The fire burned low, the light catching on the smooth curve of stone and worn leather.

Cade was already there, leaning against the stone fireplace. Biscuit was curled in his arms, fast asleep, her small body rising and falling with each quiet breath. He didn't say a word, just met my eyes for a second before turning towards Lorelei.

I sank into one of the couches, body aching in places I hadn't realized were sore. Allie sat beside me, her arms folded tight across her chest. Sarah sat on my other side, still clutching Abel's badge in one hand like it might break if she let go.

Lorelei didn't sit. She stood in front of us, hands loosely clasped, her presence calm but undeniable. Around us, the others started gathering in the room. Nick near the edge of the firelight, the woman with dark braided hair posted quietly by the hallway entrance. Watching.

Lorelei's gaze settled on me. "You've been through more than most people survive," she said gently. "And I imagine it feels like every answer has been just out of reach."

I didn't respond. I wasn't sure I could. My throat was dry. My mind a churn of pain, fatigue, and disbelief.

Lorelei turned slightly, speaking not just to me, but to all of us. "There's no easy place to begin. So I'll start with what you are."

My stomach twisted. Allie's hand found mine.

"There are people," Lorelei said, "born with magic. It's not like the stories. We don't use wands or fly on broomsticks. Not usually." A private smile passed briefly across her face.

"We call it a mark. It's not something you choose. It's more like a signature, woven into your soul the moment you're born."

She moved slightly, hands still clasped loosely in front of her and continued. "Most people are born with only one mark. A single ability that reflects who they are. For some, it's fire. Others, healing. Some can influence memory or move objects with their minds. There are even those who can walk through shadows." Her gaze glanced at Cade.

She paused, her eyes returning to mine. "A mark isn't just a power," she said. "It's your essence. Your soul's true signature. Someone with fire can only create and control fire. Someone with healing can only heal. There are no shortcuts. You can't trade for another, learn new tricks, or cast spells to mimic someone else's gift."

Her voice dropped slightly. "Except for the mark we call alchemy," she continued. "Those born with it can create runes, potions, and enchantments. But even then, these creations are temporary. Most runes fade within a day or two. Potions lose their strength and must be recharged by the alchemist who made them. And for a rune or potion to work at all, the alchemist themselves must create it. No one else can simply copy the pattern and expect it to work."

Lorelei's expression changed, something like reverence passing through her features. "Your grandmother was an alchemist, and a powerful one. What she did—binding all your marks so completely—was beyond anything most alchemists could imagine. It was ancient, sacred work, meant to protect you until you were ready."

She hesitated, her voice lowering. "And Michael's dagger... that too is something far beyond ordinary alchemy. Both speak to knowledge and power that most of us have never seen, or even believed possible."

Allie looked up and turned toward me. "That explains why you couldn't do that spell from Grandma's journal," she said, her voice tight with sudden understanding. "It wasn't about trying harder. You literally couldn't. You're not an alchemist."

I swallowed hard, my mouth dry.

Lorelei nodded, eyes steady on me. Her voice lowered just a fraction. "Even one mark can make someone powerful. But you weren't born with one, Lena. You were born with many."

I felt the words like a punch to my chest.

"People like you…" she hesitated, just for a breath, "they don't come around often. Maybe once in a century. Sometimes longer. You aren't just powerful. You're… catalytic. You change the rules, just by being alive."

Something twitched in her expression. Reverence, maybe. Or fear. "That's why it was bound and why no one told you. That much magic in a child, even before it manifests completely? It could level a house in a tantrum. And the kind of people who would want to *use* that magic? They've existed for generations."

Allie leaned forward, her voice low but steady. "And what about you?" she asked. "The Severance. Who exactly are you in all of this?"

Lorelei nodded, like she'd been expecting the question. "We're what happens when magic is abused," she said simply. "When people with marks decided the world should kneel to them."

She stepped slightly closer to the firelight, her voice calm but steady. "A long time ago, people with marks believed they were above the rest. Some formed secret circles, bloodlines that believed the unmarked existed to serve them. They used their gifts to control, manipulate, and destroy… whatever kept them in power."

"But not everyone agreed. A small group of marked individuals stood up. They severed ties with the others and left behind wealth, legacy, and bloodlines. They gave up everything to keep magic from destroying more than it healed. That's how we started. That's why we're called The Severance."

Lorelei's gaze swept across the room, briefly meeting the eyes of the others—the woman by the hallway, Nick near the

197

hearth. Cade, still silent by the fire, holding Biscuit, who was sleeping contently in his arms.

She paused, her hands still loosely clasped in front of her. "Our purpose has always been to protect the balance. Not to rule or punish. But to stop those who would twist magic into something it was never meant to be."

Then Lorelei turned slightly, glancing behind her. "And sometimes... protecting balance means seeing what others can't."

A woman stepped forward from the shadows. She looked like she'd stepped out of another time. Her dark skin was glowing in the firelight, her long silver-white braids trailing down her back like strands of starlight. Her eyes were pale, almost translucent, and yet somehow filled with knowing.

She didn't speak right away. Just looked at me, her head tilting slightly like she already knew what I was going to say.

"My name is Evangeline," she said quietly. "I have the mark of premonition. I see pieces of what's coming. Not all of it and not always clearly, but enough."

I didn't move. Neither did Sarah or Allie.

Evangeline took one more step forward. "Nearly fifteen years ago," she said, "I saw you."

Something inside me lurched.

"You were about the age you are now," she went on. "And you were burning. Not actual flames, but something deeper like a heat under your skin. Your marks... pleural. Your fury. It poured out of you like wildfire."

She paused, her voice lowering. "I didn't just see it. I *felt* it. The rage. The devastation. The power." She looked down, then met my eyes again, gaze unreadable. "It wasn't just raw... it was *limitless*. And that terrified me."

Her next words came quieter, edged with fear. "No one person should hold that much magic. You weren't just powerful, you were a storm waiting to break. A ticking bomb. And if it went off, we didn't know what would be left standing."

She exhaled, slow and tight. "At the time, I thought *you* were the danger. That we had to stop you. So we started looking, tracing and following the threads of what I saw."

Her gaze met mine again, not unkind, but heavy with something else. Regret, maybe. Or guilt. "We found your grandmother," she said. "We knew she had power, but she wasn't using it recklessly." She paused, fingers brushing the edge of a carved pendant around her neck.

"Eventually, we found you too. But you showed no signs of magic. You had no mark that we could sense. At first, we thought we were wrong. That it couldn't be you. But we kept watching. And then we realized she'd done something we'd never seen before. She bound your magic. She tied it to your soul in a way only someone who loved you deeply could've done. It was a protective spell. Old, sacred, and nearly impossible to undo without her presence."

Evangeline's voice dropped slightly. "She wasn't trying to suppress you. She was trying to shield you from the dangers that came with your powers. She wanted to wait until you were older and stronger. Until your soul was ready to carry the weight of it. Margot never meant to leave you unprepared," Evangeline said. "Even when she knew she was dying, she had a plan. She arranged for someone to guide you once she was gone. Someone she trusted."

She didn't say the name right away. But I already knew. "Corinne," I whispered.

Evangeline gave a slow nod. "Yes. Corinne was meant to be your tether. The one who'd help awaken your power gently, safely. She'd agreed to take on the responsibility. She knew it all—what you carried, what you might become, and what you needed in order to stay whole."

I felt Sarah move beside me. Allie's fingers tightened around mine.

"But something happened," I said slowly. "Grandma didn't plan on Corinne getting dementia."

Evangeline didn't answer.

Then another voice spoke. It was so soft, I almost missed it. "It was me."

A woman stepped forward from the edge of the room. She looked to be in her forties. Shoulder-length brown hair tucked behind her ears, clothes plain and unassuming. She looked... tired. Not in the way of someone who needed sleep, but in the way of someone who'd carried guilt too long.

"I'm Vallerie," she said. "My mark is memory work. I can manipulate memories... plant them, alter them, erase them."

I felt Allie tense beside me.

Vallerie's hands twisted together at her waist. "I intervened with Corinne." She didn't look at any of us. "We thought we were doing the right thing. We thought... if Corinne didn't remember what Margot told her about the marks, the binding, then Lena's powers would stay dormant. Locked away, where they couldn't hurt her or anyone else."

The room went still.

Sarah opened her mouth, then closed it again.

Vallerie finally looked up, her eyes rimmed red. "You have to understand. We weren't trying to destroy her. We just wanted to stop what we believed was coming. The vision... it terrified us. We thought if Lena never knew who she was, none of it would unfold."

"And Corinne?" I asked.

"She fought back," Vallerie said, her voice cracking. "I tried to take only the memories Margot gave her. But she was strong. She resisted. And I... I pushed too hard."

Her next words dropped like stones. "She didn't forget. She fractured... she doesn't have dementia. Her mind is broken by what I did."

My heart kicked hard against my ribs. They hadn't just stolen Corinne's memories. They stole her mind. And they did it because of me. A slow, sick feeling twisted in my gut. Guilt surged first. It was sharp and suffocating. But underneath the guilt, something else simmered. Anger. They broke her. To stop a version of me that hadn't even existed yet.

Tears slid down Vallerie's cheeks. "I visit her sometimes. I told the staff I'm her niece. We pay for her care. But nothing fixes it. Nothing makes it right." She looked down again, voice barely above a whisper. "I'm so sorry. I never meant to hurt her."

I stared at her, heat rising in my throat. "You're sorry?" I said, my voice tight, the words gritted out like they burned. "She doesn't even remember her own name, and you think *sorry* covers that?"

Allie went rigid beside me, tense, but I barely noticed.

"She was Grandma's best friend," I said, still seated but leaning forward now, elbows braced on my knees, fists clenched. "She knew me. She loved me. And you... you just took that from her."

Vallerie didn't move. Her head stayed bowed, shoulders drawn inward like she was trying to make herself smaller.

I waited for her to defend herself. To explain or fight back. But she didn't.

And then it hit me—hard and quiet, like a drop of ink in water spreading outward before I could stop it. Grief and shame. A crushing sorrow so thick I couldn't breathe around it. It wasn't mine. It was hers.

Vallerie stood completely still, but the emotions coming off her rolled like a tide. Quiet and suffocating.

I pressed a hand to my chest, trying to block it out, trying to stay angry. But all I could feel was her regret. Her sorrow. The way she carried it like an old injury, long past bleeding but never healed.

I sank further down into the couch, my voice lower now. Strained. "She forgot me. She forgot who she is. And Grandma. And you... you're the reason."

Vallerie finally looked up. Her eyes were glassy, lashes clumped with tears. "I know," she whispered. "I live with it every day."

I believed her. I could feel it. I didn't forgive her, but I believed her.

Sarah's voice broke the silence. "But... if Corinne never helped her," she said slowly, "why did Lena's powers start to come back at all?"

Lorelei glanced at her, then looked to Evangeline.

"We don't know," Evangeline said. "Something began to trigger them. Possibly emotional, possibly magical."

"But the timing was... strange. Too perfect," Lorelei added.

Sarah's brow furrowed. "Could it have been Michael?"

A beat of silence followed.

"We've considered it," Lorelei admitted. "There are rituals alchemists can do that can interfere with enchantments. If Michael found someone with that mark, or even commissioned the work without understanding it, they might have weakened the seal just enough. You wouldn't have known it was happening."

I felt a chill run through me. Of course it was Michael. He needed my marks unbound so he could take them. Take me.

Allie cleared her throat, her voice quiet but steady. "Can I ask something?"

Lorelei turned to her. "Of course."

"Some things have happened over the last couple of months," she said. "Things we haven't been able to explain."

Lorelei turned her attention toward her. Listening.

Allie glanced at me, then continued. "Lena had a dream with Corinne. In the dream, Corinne told her that he was almost ready. We didn't know what that meant at the time, but now..."

She let that hang for a moment before going on.

"She also saw Grandma. Not in person, just... her reflection. In a mirror. And then there's me." Her lips tightened. "I don't think I have a mark, but I had a vision. The only time anything remotely magical has ever happened to me. Grandma was there. She told me Lena needed me. And then I saw her bleeding on the floor. Her stomach was spilling so much blood... God, it was everywhere."

202

Allie's voice cracked for the first time. "That vision is the only reason she's alive." She turned her gaze on Lorelei, something close to desperation lurking under the surface. "So tell me. Was that Grandma? Was it one of Lena's marks? What was that?"

Lorelei's expression changed. "It was Margot," she said quietly. "She was trying to help by leaving you what pieces she could. They weren't just fragments. They were her way of guiding you."

I stood without realizing I was going to. My voice came out hollow. "She gave me *clues*," I said. "That's what you're saying?"

Lorelei didn't speak.

"While I was falling in love with a fucking psychopath, while he was bleeding me dry, my grandma was leaving me cryptic little horror movie moments?"

Silence.

"She whispered my name through a mirror. Sent me a dream about a woman who couldn't even talk. Do you know what that dream did? It made me think I was losing my mind. It made me run straight to *him*. To the person who nearly killed me."

My hands were trembling now. I clenched them into fists.

"She could've warned me," I snapped. "She could've said, 'Hey sweetheart, your boyfriend's a lying, power-hungry murderer. Maybe don't let him sleep next to you.'"

Still, no one interrupted.

I let out a bitter laugh. "But no. That would've been *too easy*. Better to drop puzzle pieces and hope I somehow put them together before he drives a knife into my gut."

I turned away from them, blinking back hot, furious tears.

"She was supposed to protect me," I said through gritted teeth. "Instead, she played ghost charades while everything I had burned to the ground."

"She did what she could," Lorelei said. "Crossing the veil to interfere with the living... it's forbidden and dangerous. We don't know what it cost her to do even that much."

I blinked, stunned silent.

"It may have taken everything she had left," Lorelei continued. "Her essence. Her peace. Her chance to rest. We don't know."

The words hit me like a slap. I instantly regretted the words I'd said. What did she mean, *her chance to rest*? Her *peace*?

The anger drained from me all at once, leaving a hollow, aching space in its place. I suddenly wanted to sink into the couch and never surface. She'd crossed some sacred boundary, risked whatever remained of her soul or essence, just to try and warn me. And I mocked her. Raged at the scraps she left behind, like they were some kind of cruel joke.

I'd accused her of doing too little. But maybe she gave me everything she had left. My legs gave in before the rest of me did. I eased back into the cushions, too full of regret to hold myself upright.

Allie blinked quickly beside me, then pressed her fingers beneath her eyes.

I looked down at my hands. Dirt still lined my palms. A smear of dried blood curved along my wrist. All of this was part of something she saw coming. Something she tried to stop.

Allie's voice was quiet. "You've known about Michael for a long time, haven't you?"

Cade straightened slightly, arms still wrapped around Biscuit. His voice, when it came, was quiet but iron-edged. "We've known who he was for a long time," he said. "He's my cousin."

My head jerked up to look at Cade. Cade didn't look at me. Just stared at the fire like it might burn through everything he couldn't say fast enough.

"He came from power. Our family line's old and the magic runs deep. But Michael was born without a mark."

He looked down for a moment, like the firelight was too much to meet.

"I think part of him always hated us for it. Hated being looked at like a mistake. When he was 17, he snapped. He killed his parents, my aunt and uncle. He used the cursed dagger and siphoned their magic."

"Oh my god," Allie whispered.

Cade's fingers brushed once down Biscuit's back. She blinked slowly in his arms, oblivious to the storm unfolding around her.

"It didn't work," Cade said. "At least, not the way he wanted. He got power for a short time before it faded. But he didn't stop. My parents took in his younger siblings. They were just kids. I left determined to find him. I thought I could stop him before he did anything worse."

His jaw clenched. "I was wrong. Michael went back to my home while I was gone and killed them all. The kids. My parents."

My throat tightened, air catching behind it like a scream I couldn't make.

He looked up then, straight at Lorelei.

"I've been hunting him ever since," Cade said. "I joined The Severance because I wanted justice. Or revenge. I don't even know the difference anymore."

Lorelei's voice came in gently, like a tether pulling us all back. "That's when we started tracking him. He was smart. He changed names and location often. He knew just how to disappear."

"He was born Michael Underwood," Cade said quietly. "But he left that name behind a long time ago. By the time he found you, he was going by Michael Brant."

Evangeline stepped in again, her silver-white braids catching the firelight like strands of frost. "One of our best field trackers, Ben, got close. Too close."

"He wasn't just a tracker," Cade added. "He was my friend."

"He found Michael," Lorelei said. "We didn't know how close until it was too late. We think... Ben confronted him. Or maybe Michael found him first. Either way, Ben never came back."

"He died trying to stop him," Cade said. "But we think, before he did, he gave Michael something."

Lorelei looked at me. "Your name."

I felt every muscle in my body go still.

"That's how he found you," Cade said. "He didn't just stumble into your life. He *planned* it. Researched it and waited."

Sarah inhaled sharply.

"And then," Lorelei said softly, "he stopped hiding. When he showed up on the news pulling survivors out of a burning building unscathed, we knew. He had power. Real power. Too much of it. And that could only mean one thing."

"He'd found a way to steal it," Cade said. "And he wasn't afraid anymore."

"So we sent in a freelancer," Lorelei continued. "Someone with a detection mark who can read what lives inside a person. What kind of marks they carry."

Her gaze met mine again. "He confirmed what we feared. Michael had multiple marks. Six to be exact."

Allie's head turned sharply. Sarah's eyes widened. The three of us exchanged a stunned look. Six. He'd taken six pieces of me.

Lorelei's voice stayed steady. "The first mark is fire. It's destructive, raw, and elemental. It's one of the most aggressive of your marks, and the one he's flaunting most often. That fire on the news wasn't an accident."

"The second mark is telekinesis. He can move and manipulate anything in his environment. He's using it with more control than most people who are born with it."

I swallowed hard remembering how it felt to be thrown across the clearing.

Lorelei continued. "The third mark is healing. It allows the person to mend physical injuries almost instantly. Broken bones, deep wounds, even organ damage. It works like time rewinding inside the body."

I glanced toward Nick without meaning to. He stood near the edge of the room, and when our eyes met, he gave me a reassuring smile.

"The fourth mark is mind weaving. He can enter a person's thoughts or dreams, distort perception, and twist reality from the inside."

"The fifth mark is a shield. When triggered, it creates an invisible barrier that deflects most physical attacks, magical force, and even mental intrusion. It's fast and almost impossible to break through once it's up."

"And the sixth," Lorelei said, her voice darkening. "Oblivion. A death mark. It doesn't require touch. He can end a life with a look, a breath, a thought. Most people who carry it never use it. But in his hands…" She trailed off. She didn't need to finish.

The room felt still, but my thoughts were racing.

Evangeline's voice cut through, calm but cold. "After we found out about the marks, we traced his last known movements," she said. "Found his aliases. One led to a small town in Maine. Ashmore. That's when we put it all together."

"You," Cade said, eyes locked on mine. "He took them from you."

Lorelei's voice was steady. "He took something sacred from you," she said. "But he didn't take all of it. If he had, you wouldn't be sitting here."

My body felt like it had been hollowed out and stitched back together with thread I didn't recognize.

Lorelei looked at me carefully. "Do you know which mark remains?"

I let out a breath that didn't feel like relief. "Empathy," I said, the word sharp in my mouth. "Lucky me, right?" I gave a bitter little laugh. "He got fire and death and I got feelings."

Cade's bright green eyes held mine. And for just a moment, I forgot how to breathe. "Empathy," he said, "can make a grown man fall to his knees in agony. It can break people without touching them. Don't underestimate it." He wasn't trying to comfort me. He was stating a fact.

Lorelei nodded. "And if you're willing… we'll help you find the rest. And put a stop to Michael for good."

Vallerie was watching me with a kind of solemn understanding. Nick was silent but steady in the corner, like his presence alone was meant to say *you're not alone anymore.*

I didn't trust myself to answer. I didn't know what I was anymore. A victim. A weapon. A mistake…

My hands were shaking again, and not from cold. My mind kept spinning back to Corinne, to Grandma, to the marks he took like trophies.

I wasn't ready to fight. I wasn't even sure I was still whole. I could feel their eyes on me.

I wanted them all to go away.

I wanted someone to hold me.

I wanted to scream until the walls cracked.

But I did none of those things. I just sat there, hurting in places no healing mark could reach, and wondered how much more I could lose before I stopped being me at all.

Chapter 20

Lorelei's gaze lingered on me a moment longer before she stepped back. "You've all been through enough for one night," she said gently. "There's time for decisions tomorrow. Tonight, you need rest."

She turned slightly toward Cade. "Would you show them to their rooms?"

He adjusted his grip on Biscuit and said, "Sure. If she allows it," nodding toward the cat like she was calling the shots. A faint smile tugged at his mouth.

"We want to stay together," Allie said quickly, glancing between Sarah and me. "Same room, if that's okay."

"Of course," Lorelei said. "There's a room big enough for all three of you at the end of the hall."

She paused, eyes sweeping over us once more. "I'm the head of The Severance," she added, like she'd just realized she hadn't said it outright. "This place, the people in it… they answer to me. But that doesn't mean I make decisions alone."

Her gaze settled on me again. "When you're ready, we'll talk more. Until then, rest."

Cade didn't say much as he led us out of the main room. His footsteps were soft and steady, his silhouette cutting a calm path through the low, golden light of the corridor.

The hallway was simple but warm. The walls were lined with old wood and narrow sconces casting soft golden light. It didn't feel like a compound. It felt like a place built by people who'd seen too much and wanted at least one hallway to feel like peace.

Cade paused in front of a wide door at the end of the hall. "This one's yours," he said, pushing it open.

The room was modest, but cozy. One queen-sized bed was tucked along the far wall, a soft couch against the other. A small dresser sat beside a floor lamp, and heavy curtains framed the window. In the corner, a narrow door stood slightly ajar, revealing a small attached bathroom.

Sarah glanced around and gave a nod. "This'll be fine."

Allie added, "It's more than enough. Thank you."

Cade looked around the room. "I'll grab some extra pillows and blankets. And maybe a few things for her," he said, glancing down at Biscuit, still nestled like royalty in his arms.

He stepped forward and carefully transferred her to my arms. Biscuit gave a sharp meow, just loud enough to voice her irritation, then curled into my chest with a low, steady purr. I hadn't realized how much I needed that weight, that warmth. I sat down on the edge of the bed, trying not to jostle her.

Cade watched for a moment, then gave a faint half-smile, so quick I almost missed it. "I'll be back in a few," he said, then turned and walked back into the hall.

Once the door closed behind Cade and we were finally alone, they both turned to me at once. Allie's eyes were sharp and searching. Sarah's were wide and shining with unshed tears.

"So, what happened in the woods tonight?" Allie asked.

I looked at her, then at Sarah, who stood close by, her eyes wide and unblinking, waiting. And I told them. About the dream that wasn't a dream, the way he called me out into the dark, the fight. His threats, his sick confessions. My anger. My fear. How close it had come to ending right there in the dirt. How Cade jumped from the shadows just in time.

I told them everything, except the part about our parents. I don't know why I didn't say it. Maybe because Allie already looked like she was holding herself together by a thread. Maybe because I didn't know how to speak it without breaking apart myself.

Sarah dropped onto the couch with a long, slow exhale, then leaned her head back and closed her eyes. "Jesus Christ. Is this what your life is now?"

Allie gave her a half-hearted glare and tossed one of the throw pillows at her.

Sarah caught it without opening her eyes. "Rude."

Allie walked to the bed and sat down heavily beside me.

Sarah cracked one eye open. "So... you're some kind of nuclear magic prodigy, Allie had a psychic breakdown, and the people funding Corinne's care are part of a magical rebellion?"

"Basically," I said. My voice came out hoarse. "With a little murder sprinkled in."

Sarah let out a noise somewhere between a snort and a groan. "I'm gonna need therapy. And tequila."

I glanced over at her. Her face was pale and drawn, but she was trying. I could see it in the dry humor, the forced smile. She was grieving Abel. But she was still trying to make *me* smile. Trying to hold things together, even when hers had fallen apart.

"We'll make tea," Allie said dryly. "Less destructive than tequila."

Despite everything, I smiled. Just barely. But it was real.

Allie reached down and picked at a loose thread on the blanket. "Do you think we can trust them?" she asked quietly.

I thought about that for a long second.

"I don't know," I said honestly. "But right now... I think they're the only ones who actually know what's happening."

Allie nodded. "I hate this."

"Me too," Sarah agreed.

"I need a shower" I said, looking down at myself.

"We'll be here when you get out," Allie said.

I got up and went into the attached bathroom. It was small but clean, with white tiles and a faint scent of eucalyptus clinging to the air like it had been scrubbed recently. I stood there for a minute, staring at my reflection in the mirror.

There was dried blood on my wrist. Dirt beneath my nails. My face was pale, my eyes dark-rimmed and exhausted. I didn't look powerful.

I turned on the shower. The sound of running water filled the small space, and steam began to rise, curling around the edges of the mirror.

I stripped off the clothes I'd been wearing. The fabric was stiff with sweat and dirt, clinging in all the wrong places. I stepped into the water, and for the first few seconds, I didn't move. I just let it fall over me, hot and steady.

I didn't cry. I thought I might. But the tears never came. Maybe I was too wrung out or exhausted. Or maybe whatever part of me used to break that way had finally snapped for good.

A soft knock interrupted the quiet hum of the water.

"Hey," Sarah's voice called through the door. "Cade came back. He brought a bunch of stuff. Some blankets, clothes, cat accessories." There was the sound of something being set on the counter. "I'm leaving you some clean clothes, okay? They're not hospital scrubs, so I'm calling that a win."

I heard her linger for a second, then her footsteps padded back across the room.

I finished my shower in silence. My skin was raw from scrubbing. I wasn't sure I'd ever feel fully clean, but it helped. At least a little.

When I stepped out and wrapped a warm towel around me, I saw the clothes she'd left—a soft black t-shirt and gray joggers. Nothing fancy, but they were clean. I changed and walked barefoot back into the bedroom.

The lights were dimmed. Allie was already curled up on one side of the bed, her back to me, breathing slow and even. Sarah sat cross-legged on the bed beside her. She looked up and gave me a half smile.

I saw that a neat stack of blankets and pillows had been left at the foot of the couch, along with a set of folded clothes that looked just about my size. And beside the dresser sat a litter box, a small bowl of food, and a matching bowl filled with water. Biscuit was already curled up beside them.

"I'm so tired I think my bones are melting," Sarah muttered. "Do you want the bed or the couch?"

I glanced at the bed, where Allie was already asleep, then at the neatly arranged blankets waiting on the couch.

"I'll take the couch," I said, lowering myself onto the cushions. "I don't trust myself not to kick someone in my sleep."

"Then the couch is yours," she said, grabbing a blanket. "But I'll be close if you need anything."

A few seconds passed before I said it. "I'm sorry, Sarah. For dragging you into this. For all of it."

She turned toward me, eyebrows lifting slightly. "You think you dragged me?"

I shrugged. "You could've stayed out. You didn't have to follow me into... whatever this is."

She scoffed. "Please. If you think I'm letting some magical psychopath take you down without me, you're dumber than you look."

I let out a quiet laugh, but she wasn't done.

"We're soulmates," she said, completely serious. "You're stuck with me. Unfortunately, we're also cursed to like dick, so the romance is off the table. But emotionally? Ride or die, bitch."

I laughed harder than I expected. It came out choked and sharp, but real.

"God, I love you," I said, wiping at my eyes even though I wasn't crying.

"I know," she said. "Now sleep. I've got you."

The room fell into a hush again. Biscuit leapt onto the bed with a soft thump, padded over to Sarah, and curled up beside her, pressing into her leg like she'd chosen her comfort for the night. Sarah let out a slow breath and rested a hand gently on Biscuit's back, her fingers moving in slow, absentminded strokes.

I pulled the blanket around me and laid down, the couch creaking just slightly beneath me. Michael's face flashed behind my eyelids—the way he stood in the clearing, so calm, so sure, like none of this meant anything. Like I was just another check mark on his to-do-list. A stepping stone on his way to something bigger.

He killed my parents. He killed *his* parents. His siblings. Children. And tonight, he nearly killed me... again.

And I loved him. I gave myself to him completely. Trusted him with every part of me—my body, my heart, my future. I let him hold my pain. I let him *touch my soul.*

He was never a man. He was a monster wearing a beautiful face. How did it come to this? How was I so easily fooled?

I turned onto my side and stared into the dark, my chest aching. The shame settled in first. Then something sharper beneath it. Something that burned low and hot, just out of reach.

I should've seen it. I should've known. Maybe I *did* know. I just didn't want to believe it. He made me feel wanted. Safe. Seen. It was all a lie.

I thought maybe sleep wouldn't come. That my mind would stay there, trapped in that clearing with him, replaying every second like a punishment. But it didn't. I was too exhausted to keep bleeding for him. The only thought left as my eyes began to close was small, and bitter, and steady as a heartbeat.

I loved a monster.

• • •

I woke up stiff. My neck ached. My back ached. Even my hips were mad at me. Nick may have healed my broken arm, but the after effects of being thrown across the clearing last night stayed.

The light coming through the window was bright. It was midmorning at least. Maybe later. I sat up slowly, rubbing at the knot in my shoulder, the blanket sliding to the floor.

Allie and Sarah were already awake. Both of them were sitting on the edge of the bed, dressed in clean clothes—black leggings and long sleeves, hair damp like they'd showered not long ago. They were talking in low voices, but stopped when they saw me stir.

214

"Look who finally decided to wake up," Sarah said, stretching her arms overhead.

I yawned. "You say that like it was an easy decision."

Allie stood and crossed the room, grabbing a hair tie from the dresser. "Well, rise and shine. We need to venture out and find coffee before Sarah starts getting weird."

Sarah yawned dramatically. "Too late. I've already accepted death."

"Dramatic," I muttered, then dragged myself off the couch with a grunt. The clean clothes Cade had left the night before were folded on the corner of the dresser. Black leggings and a plain blue long-sleeved shirt, similar to what Allie and Sarah were wearing. Did The Severance have a uniform policy, or was this just the official outfit of magical trauma recovery?

Either way, I grabbed them and made my way to the bathroom without another word. The cabinets beneath the sink were stocked with deodorant, a clean toothbrush still in its wrapper, toothpaste, and a brush. Everything I needed, already waiting.

I tied my hair up into a high ponytail, changed into the clean clothes, and took a few minutes to make myself presentable. Washed my face, brushed my teeth, put deodorant on. Nothing fancy, but enough to feel like a person again.

Today, I was supposed to figure out what came next. But first—coffee.

When I stepped back into the room, Allie and Sarah were already putting on shoes—basic black slip-on tennis shoes that looked like The Severance had stocked them in bulk. A matching pair sat near the dresser for me.

"Ready?" Allie asked.

"As I'll ever be," I muttered.

The three of us ventured out together, slipping into the hallway and falling into a quiet, familiar rhythm. The lighting was soft and warm, casting long shadows that felt more intentional than eerie. Voices carried from the common room.

As we entered, a few heads turned, but no one stared. Vallerie was the first to approach. She stood from where she'd been sitting at the edge of a table, brushing her hands on the thighs of her jeans.

"Morning," she said with a small, cautious smile. "You're up just in time. Come on. I'll show you the kitchen."

She led us down the hallway straight ahead. It opened into a large, open-concept kitchen that looked like it had been designed by someone with a caffeine addiction and a Pinterest board. The centerpiece was the most high-tech coffee setup I'd ever seen—chrome machines, stacked syrups, a grinder the size of a toddler, and what looked suspiciously like a built-in milk frother.

I stopped short.

Sarah let out a whistle. "Jesus. I think Lena's drooling."

"I am not," I said automatically, even though I probably was.

"This thing could fuel a whole city," Allie muttered.

Vallerie chuckled. "We take coffee very seriously around here. Comes with the job. You want something fancy, I can help. Otherwise, that one's the regular drip." She gestured to the side where a standard coffee pot sat, steaming patiently.

"I want the fancy one," Sarah said immediately, stepping forward like a kid let loose in a candy store.

I looked over the options, glancing at all the labeled syrups and flavor shots, then pointed. "Vanilla latte. Extra shot of espresso."

"Regular coffee," Allie said looking over the selection, a little overwhelmed. "Do you have creamer?"

Vallerie raised a brow, her voice teasing. "Allie, we've got more options than Starbucks. I could make your coffee taste like a birthday cake if you wanted."

Sarah gasped. "Can you really?"

Vallerie winked. "Don't tempt me."

Sarah, naturally, dove straight into chaos. "Okay then— mocha caramel swirl, whipped cream, extra drizzle, and I

216

want sprinkles. If I'm going to be traumatized, I'm going to do it in style."

Vallerie laughed and turned to the machine, clearly at home behind it. "I like you guys already," she said over her shoulder.

She was trying. I could see it now, in the way she smiled a little too brightly, kept her hands busy, and offered comfort like she owed it.

Maybe she did. I'd felt her guilt last night—raw and suffocating, poured straight into me through that mark I barely understood. And I'd been cruel. Not unfair, but sharp and unforgiving.

Now, standing here in a bright kitchen, surrounded by syrup bottles and milk frothers and Sarah demanding whipped cream, it was harder to hold onto the heat of that moment.

I stepped forward, just enough for her to notice.

"Thanks," I said softly.

Vallerie looked up.

I offered a small, genuine smile. Not an invitation. Just... acknowledgment.

She gave a nod. Nothing more. But something in her shoulders eased.

Once we all had our drinks—Sarah's with whipped cream towering like a monument to excess—we sat at a small table tucked into the corner of the kitchen. It was quiet here. No one staring. No looming revelations or magical breakdowns. Just four girls and a very expensive espresso machine.

Sarah sipped hers, sighed with dramatic bliss, and immediately turned to Vallerie. "So. The Severance." She lifted an eyebrow. "What's the deal? Secret government agency? Magical Avengers? Underground cult?"

It was nice hearing her sound like herself again. The quick wit. The raised brow. Like we were back in my kitchen, not sitting in the nerve center of a magical rebellion. But I knew better. I could still see the grief in her eyes, quiet and sharp beneath the surface. She hadn't healed. Not really. But she was trying.

Vallerie laughed into her coffee. "Depends on who you ask."

Sarah leaned in, wide-eyed. "I'm asking you."

"We're... a network," Vallerie said after a moment. "We operate outside normal channels. Our job is to keep magic in balance, stop threats before they become disasters. We're not perfect, but we try to keep people safe."

"Safe from people like Michael," I said quietly.

Vallerie nodded, her expression sobering.

I took a long sip of my latte and glanced around the room. There were a few other people drifting through the far hallway, none of them paying much attention to us. It felt weirdly peaceful.

But curiosity still gnawed at me.

"There was a woman last night," I said. "Sharp eyes, long dark hair, looked like she wanted to murder everyone. Who is she?"

Vallerie gave a knowing sigh. "Kaylen."

"Friendliest one of the bunch," Sarah muttered.

"She's... intense," Vallerie admitted. "But she's good. Loyal and tough as hell. She's one of our best fighters—her mark lets her summon weapons on command. She could probably take out a small army with nothing but a glare and a dagger."

Sarah raised an eyebrow. "Wait. Like, *any* weapon? Could she summon some futuristic alien blaster and vaporize a building?"

Vallerie cracked a faint smile. "Not quite. Her mark isn't imagination-based. She can only conjure weapons that exist in the real world. Things she's seen or studied. Knives, guns, swords, tactical gear. She's deadly with all of it, but no plasma cannons."

"Shame," Sarah said. "I was really counting on the alien tech."

Allie snorted, then asked, "What's her deal?"

218

"Her brother," Vallerie said softly. "He was one of ours. Michael killed him during a recon mission a few years back. She's never forgiven herself for not being there."

That landed hard.

"She's not mean," Vallerie added. "Not really. Just... doesn't waste time on people she hasn't decided are worth it yet."

"So, basically... she hates everyone until proven otherwise," Sarah said.

"Exactly," Vallerie replied.

"How many people has Michael killed?", I asked.

The question left my mouth before I could stop it.

Vallerie's smile faded. She set her cup down with a soft clink and leaned back in her chair.

"We don't know the exact number," she said. "Some... we couldn't confirm. Others, we didn't even know about until years later. But confirmed? At least twenty. Possibly more."

Sarah's mouth opened, but no words came out.

"He doesn't always leave a trace," Vallerie went on. "And most of the ones we've been able to track—he killed for power. They were all marked."

"And the others?" I asked, even though I wasn't sure I wanted the answer.

"Collateral. Or just... loose ends."

My thoughts snagged on those words—*collateral. Loose ends.* My parents hadn't been marked. They were just in the way. And I was going to have to tell Allie that.

Allie's hands tightened around her mug. "And no one's been able to stop him?"

"We've tried," Vallerie said. "We've lost people trying."

Sarah sat back in her chair, stunned. Allie looked like she was trying to hold in a thousand questions.

I met Vallerie's eyes. "How? I mean... how has no one stopped him? You said you've been after him for years."

Vallerie's expression tightened. "Because he's not reckless. He's calculated. Every move he makes is planned, including his escape. He studies his targets, but he also studies the surroundings—timelines, exits, cover stories. By the time we find the body, he's already gone."

I swallowed. God.

"And with each mark he's stolen," she continued, "he's only gotten harder to track. He uses their powers to disappear, manipulate, and cover his trail."

Vallerie leaned forward now, both hands around her coffee cup.

"He's left a string of bodies and not a single mistake big enough to bring him down. It's one of The Severance's greatest failures. We've hunted some of the worst magical offenders in history, but him? He's like a ghost that always slips through."

Allie took a slow sip of her coffee, then leaned forward with that look she always got when her brain kicked into overdrive.

"Okay, so... logistics. How are you funded? Do you guys have government ties? Or is it just you?"

Vallerie smiled like she'd been waiting for that question. "We're independent. Completely off-grid. We don't answer to any government, magical or otherwise."

Allie's brow furrowed. "So where does the money come from?"

"Gage," Vallerie said, like that explained everything.

"Who?" Allie replied.

"Our finance and logistics guy," she said. "He's in his late twenties. Shaggy hair. Glasses. Looks like he lives off cold brew and sarcasm. But his mark is intuition. Basically, supercharged gut instincts. He's never wrong when it comes to investments, hacking, strategy. Give him a stock portfolio and a twenty-minute window, and he'll triple it before lunch."

Sarah let out a low whistle. "Can he teach me how to never overdraft again?"

"No," Vallerie said without missing a beat. "But he could probably erase your debt."

"I'm listening," Sarah said, leaning forward dramatically.

Allie grinned, but kept going. "So he runs your finances?"

"And our tech. He's usually in the control room. Likes to stay behind the scenes, but don't let that fool you. He's always watching. Always a step ahead."

Allie tilted her head, clearly not done yet. "How many of you are there? I mean… is this it? Just this compound?"

Vallerie shook her head. "No, this is just one base. There are Severance chapters all over the world. Each group oversees a region, kind of like a magical jurisdiction. But it's not rigid, we cross over when needed. Share intel. Back each other up. If something's too big for one chapter, we handle it together."

Sarah raised an eyebrow. "So… magical international task force?"

"Something like that," Vallerie said with a grin. "Some groups are bigger, some smaller. Ours is one of the older ones. Most of us have been working together for years."

"And you all do this… voluntarily?" Allie asked.

Vallerie nodded. "We protect people. That's the point. Magic isn't good or bad on its own, it's what people do with it. And when someone like Michael starts tipping the balance, we step in."

She paused, then added, "But we're not saints. While we're active, we're provided everything we need—housing, food, gear, protection—and a small monthly allowance for personal use. And when someone decides they're done… they leave with a generous pension and full support."

Allie's eyebrows lifted slightly. "So it's not a lifetime sentence?"

"Only if you want it to be," Vallerie said.

"If the world needs that many Severance teams… how bad are most marked people?" I asked.

Vallerie didn't flinch, but her gaze sharpened slightly.

"They're not all bad," she said. "Just like anyone else. Marked people are still human. Some are kind, generous, use their powers to help. Others…" She paused, swirling her drink. "Others are reckless. Dangerous. And some… some are monsters."

"Can't the police handle them?" I asked, realizing too late that it was a stupid question.

Vallerie gave a small, humorless smile. "Not when someone can melt a gun in your hand. Or walk through walls. Or convince you to turn the weapon on yourself."

A quiet chill crept through the table.

"That's why we exist. Because the regular systems don't work on people like that. Most governments don't even know what to do with magic. Hell, half of them don't even believe in it."

"So you're the unofficial cleanup crew," Allie said.

"Exactly. We keep things from spiraling. Quietly and carefully."

Before I could ask more, the sound of heavy footsteps and bickering echoed from the hall. A moment later, three people stumbled in, red-faced and drenched in sweat, smelling faintly of smoke.

The guy was tall and lean, with straight, long, dark blond hair tucked under a black bandana and a towel slung over his shoulder. His grin was quick and unbothered, like life was one big inside joke. Behind him came two women who had to be identical twins. They were both athletic, blonde, and flushed from exertion. One had her braid half undone, soot streaked across one cheek. The other looked only slightly more composed, twisting her hair back into a neater knot as she walked. Their eyes moved quickly, like they hadn't quite shaken off the adrenaline from whatever they'd just been doing.

"Breakfast or death," the guy announced dramatically. "And I'm not picky."

Vallerie didn't even look up. "Logan," she said, then gestured to each twin in turn. "Mariah. Nicole."

The girl with ash on her cheek, Mariah, pointed at her sister. "She cheated. Used wind to knock me off my feet."

Nicole didn't even look up as she grabbed a glass of water. "It's called *strategy*, pyromaniac."

222

"Oh, I'm sorry, I didn't realize *cheating* and *strategy* were synonyms now," Mariah shot back.

"Girls," Logan said, dramatically placing a hand over his heart, "please. You're scaring the newcomers."

He glanced toward us with a grin. "Don't mind them, they've been trying to kill each other since the womb."

Vallerie waved a hand toward us. "These are our guests—Lena, Allie, and Sarah."

Logan offered a friendly smile. "Nice to meet you. Hope the coffee's doing its job."

Sarah raised her cup. "So far, so good."

He grinned. "Then we're off to a strong start."

Mariah gave a short nod, brushing sweat from her forehead. "Hey."

Nicole offered a quieter, "Morning," as she headed for the fridge.

Vallerie added, "They're siblings. Logan's the oldest."

"Only technically," Logan said, flashing a grin. "I wouldn't say I'm the most mature."

Nicole shot back without looking. "No one would."

Mariah grabbed a banana from the counter. "We just finished morning training. Didn't mean to crash anything."

"You're good," Allie said. "It's nice to meet more of you."

Logan leaned back against the counter. "We're not all as intense as Kaylen, promise."

Vallerie leaned against the table, arms folded. "They're some of our best frontline fighters. Mariah can summon and manipulate fire, Nicole controls wind, and Logan here..." She gave him a look. "Well, he breaks things with sound."

"Vibration manipulation," Logan said, sounding far too pleased. "But yeah, basically I'm a walking subwoofer."

Nicole rolled her eyes.

They each grabbed something quick—fruit, coffee, bars—and began heading back toward the hallway.

Logan gave us one last nod. "We'll be around. Don't let Gage talk you to death."

223

Then they were gone, the soft echo of their voices trailing off as they disappeared through the open doorway.

I sipped my latte and glanced at Vallerie. "They seem...intense."

Vallerie gave a soft laugh, leaning back in her chair. "That's one way to put it."

Allie nudged her mug toward the center of the table. "They're so young. They have to be in their early twenties. How did they end up here?"

Vallerie hesitated for just a moment, then said, "A man with a mark had taken an interest in their mother. She was powerful. Her mark was fire, like Mariah's, but more than that, she was kind. And beautiful. He wanted her. Claimed it was fate, but she turned him down."

I felt a sick twist in my stomach.

"He didn't take the rejection well. One night, he found them. Broke in and killed her right in front of the kids."

"Oh my god," Sarah whispered.

"They were just young teenagers," Vallerie continued. "None of their marks had fully manifested yet. But trauma has a way of snapping things loose. The man wasn't prepared for how powerful their response would be. Mariah and Nicole snapped. Think fire tornado. Logan followed with a concussive blast that leveled the house."

Allie blinked. "So they killed him."

"In one of the most gruesome cases I've ever seen," Vallerie said quietly. "We tracked them down after that. They weren't hiding, just...running. The Severance gave them a choice. Disappear into normal life, or train and help protect others like them."

"They chose this," I said softly.

"They chose each other," Vallerie corrected. "And the chance to never feel that powerless again."

I glanced toward the door, thinking of the twins' sharp banter and Logan's easy grin. No wonder they were so tightly wound. Every laugh, every jab was a thread holding something heavier in place.

A moment later, a tall guy stepped through the open doorway holding a steaming mug that read *I'm not arguing, I'm just explaining why I'm right.* He wore a zip-up hoodie over a faded graphic tee, dark shaggy hair curling slightly at the ends, and glasses that slid down his nose as he took a sip.

"Morning," he said, voice low and even. His gaze swept over us. "You must be Lena, Allie, and Sarah."

"That's us," I said cautiously.

"Gage," he replied with a small nod. "I handle tech, logistics, and communication around here."

Vallerie added, "And funding. Security. Half the systems in this place wouldn't run without him."

"I keep things stable," Gage said simply. "Lorelei wants to talk to everyone. As soon as you're done with breakfast." Then, to us, "No rush. She's terrifying, but polite."

He took another sip from his mug, eyes flicking briefly toward the hallway. "I'll let her know you're awake," he added, then disappeared without another word.

Vallerie glanced toward the hallway where Gage had left, then looked back at us with a faint smile.

"You guys want breakfast?" she asked. "We've got more than just coffee. I can throw something together."

Allie gave a small nod. "That would be great."

"Nothing fancy," Vallerie said, already moving toward the fridge. "Toast and eggs okay?"

"That sounds perfect," I said, quieter than I meant to.

The kitchen filled with soft sounds—the rustle of a paper towel, the low click of the stove igniting, the gentle sizzle of butter hitting the pan. The smell of warm food curled into the air, settling into the edges of the room like comfort.

When Vallerie set the plates down—eggs, toast, and a small dish of sliced fruit—I barely remembered saying thank you before I was eating.

I hadn't realized how hungry I was. I ate fast, almost too fast, like my body had been waiting for permission to refuel. It wasn't elegant. But it was good. When I looked up, my plate was empty.

Allie was finishing hers, slower and more methodical. Sarah was picking at the last piece of toast, quiet, her thoughts clearly elsewhere.

Vallerie leaned back against the counter, drying her hands on a towel. "Lorelei's ready when you are."

We pushed our chairs back without a word, plates left neatly behind. Then we followed her out. The hallway outside the kitchen was quieter than before. The hum of conversation and movement from earlier had faded.

Vallerie led us through a narrow corridor, then down a short, steep stairwell. The air changed as we descended— cooler, drier. Stone replaced wood, and the lighting dimmed to a low golden glow cast by inset sconces. The space felt different down here. Older. Like it had existed long before the world above even noticed.

No one spoke as we moved.

Halfway down the hallway at the base of the stairs, we passed a set of massive reinforced doors with dark metal framed in stone. There was a narrow window set into the door, just enough to see through.

The room beyond was enormous. A wide open floor stretched across the space, lined with chalk markings and scarred with years of use. Weapons hung along the far wall— swords, staffs, and training gear that looked both ancient and practical. Padding covered parts of the floor. One far corner bore the blackened residue of fire damage.

And Cade was there. Alone. He moved with calm precision, striking a thick training dummy in a rhythm that felt more methodical than aggressive. Step, strike. Pivot, strike. A swift combination that ended with a sharp elbow cracking through the air. He moved like someone who didn't waste energy. Who hit only what needed hitting, and only as hard as required.

Something pulled tight in my chest. Not fear. Not awe.

Want. I wanted that steadiness. That control. That refusal to flinch. I lingered a second longer before pulling myself away and falling back in step with the others.

At the end of the corridor, Vallerie stopped at a matte black door and knocked.

A quiet voice from the other side answered, "Come in."

Vallerie opened it, stepping aside so we could enter.

The door opened into a long, spare room with stone walls, a heavy wooden table at the center, and maps pinned along one side like evidence of a war that never ended. High above, a stained-glass window cast fractured light across the floor.

Lorelei stood at the far end of the table. She didn't move when we entered. Just watched us with a calm expression.

Vallerie gave a small nod and stepped aside. "I'll give you some space." Then, without waiting for a response, she slipped back into the hall and pulled the door quietly shut behind her.

The sound of it closing echoed just enough to make the silence that followed feel heavier.

Lorelei didn't move at first. Just watched us for a breath or two, then straightened slightly and gestured to the chairs surrounding the table. "Please, sit."

We took our seats, the scrape of wood on stone sounding louder than it should have. I ended up across from her, close enough to see the faint circles beneath her eyes, the wear in her expression that no amount of poise could fully hide.

"How did you sleep?" she asked. "I know it's not home, but I hope it was enough for one night."

"I slept," I said quietly. "Better than I thought I would."

"Same," Allie added. "The room was perfect."

Sarah nodded. "And the coffee helped."

Lorelei offered the barest smile. "We have Gage to thank for that. He once threatened to reroute power from the security grid if we didn't upgrade the espresso machine."

Sarah blinked. "Wait, seriously?"

Lorelei gave a subtle shrug. "Let's just say… no one's tested him on it."

"Is there anything you need?" she asked. "Clothes, supplies, personal things?"

Sarah leaned forward a little. "Actually... we were wondering. Is it possible for us to go back to Allie's house? Just for a little while? We left everything there—clothes, phones, laptops, even my prescription. I don't mean all together. Just one of us, maybe."

Lorelei's expression softened, but her answer came without hesitation. "I'm sorry. It's too risky."

Sarah's brows knit. "Because of Michael?"

"Yes," Lorelei said. "We believe he may still be watching the house, or at the very least, expecting you to return. And I won't send you into a trap, not even briefly."

She held Sarah's gaze. "But if you make a list, I'll send a team. They can retrieve anything you need."

Sarah didn't argue, but I saw the hint of frustration in her eyes. Still, she gave a small nod. "Okay. That makes sense."

"We'll be discreet," Lorelei added. "Nothing will be touched or left out of place."

Allie glanced over at me, then down at the table. Her fingers tapped a restless rhythm against the edge, like she was holding back the urge to move. Or speak. Or just *do* something.

Lorelei must've seen it too. Her expression changed, the warmth giving way to something steadier. Sharper. The kind of focus that said the small talk was over.

Then she looked at me. "You know why he stopped hiding," she said. Not a question.

I nodded. "Because he got what he wanted."

"More than that," Lorelei said. "He got what he'd been chasing for years. Real power. Power that wouldn't fade."

She paused, then added gently, "Because you gave it to him."

The words landed like a blow I knew I deserved.

Allie stiffened beside me. Sarah stayed quiet, eyes fixed on a crack in the table.

"I'm not saying that to make you feel guilty," Lorelei went on. "But to make something clear. What Michael took from you—your marks, your magic—they weren't just energy.

228

They were tied to trust. To love. To *you*. That's why he's stronger now than he's ever been."

I swallowed. "And that's why you want me here."

"It's why we need you here." Lorelei's voice didn't rise, but it felt tighter somehow, like a truth being lowered onto the table between us. "You're the only person who's ever given him lasting power. And that connection? As dangerous as it is, it also makes you the only person who might be able to *disrupt* it."

I felt Allie glance at me, but I didn't look away from Lorelei.

"I can't promise you answers. Or revenge. But if you stay, we'll train you. Help you understand what's left of your magic. Help you rebuild." Lorelei let the silence stretch before stepping around the table and taking a seat beside me, her posture steady but no longer guarded.

"You're not powerless, Lena. Not even close," she said. "Michael took your marks, yes, but not all of you. What he has is only part of what you were. The rest is still here. Buried and waiting."

She rested her hands on the table. "You still have your empathy. But even more important than that, you still have your connection to the power he stole. You're the only person alive who shares that bond."

"What does that mean?" Allie asked quietly.

"It means she's not just a victim," Lorelei said. "She's a *link*. That bond works both ways. He took something from her, but because it was given willingly, part of *him* is open to her now."

I frowned. "I don't feel anything."

"You will," Lorelei said gently. "As your empathy strengthens, as you train, emotionally and magically, you'll be able to *feel* your marks again. The ones he stole. Not because you can take them back with force, but because you may be able to unravel the hold he has on them."

"Like... destabilize him?" Sarah asked.

Lorelei nodded. "Exactly. He's holding magic that was never meant to be his. And he's built his new identity on the illusion that it belongs to him. But it doesn't. It belongs to Lena."

I sat with that for a moment. I didn't speak. Because something inside me was breaking wide open—not with pain, but with memory. The floor of the clearing. The cold air. His voice. That moment of realization, not that I was dying, but that he wanted me to.

And before that, the hospital. His hands on me. His eyes. The knife. His smile. The sound of my own cries as he pulled something *out* of me.

I blinked hard, my hands curling into fists in my lap. "I want to learn," I said quietly.

Lorelei inclined her head. "We'll start tomorrow."

But I wasn't done. "Not just magic."

She straightened.

"I want to fight," I said. "With my hands. My body. I want to know how to throw someone off me. I want to know how to hurt them if I have to."

Allie drew in a breath, but she didn't stop me.

"He stabbed me," I continued. "He threw me across a field like I was weightless. I couldn't stop him. I couldn't *do* anything."

My voice wavered, but I didn't look away. "I don't ever want to feel that powerless again."

For a beat, no one said anything. Then, from the doorway, a quiet voice said, "Then you'll train with me."

I turned. Cade stood there, calm and unreadable, his arms crossed loosely over his chest. He must've entered quietly and unnoticed, but he wasn't hiding now.

"If you're serious," he said, "I'll work with you. Hand-to-hand, weapons, whatever you can handle. But I won't go easy on you."

"I don't want easy," I said.

He gave a single nod. "Then we start tomorrow."

I sat there, suddenly aware of how sore my body still was. How heavy everything felt. My soul throbbed. And now I was apparently gearing up for combat training with a guy who could probably throw me through a wall.

What the actual fuck did I just sign up for?

Chapter 21

I didn't remember much of what was said right after. Not because it wasn't important, but because my brain had decided to stop processing anything besides *holy shit, what did I just agree to* on repeat.

Cade had left as quietly as he'd come. Lorelei gave me a nod that might've been approval—or pity—and told us we had the rest of the day to get settled.

Sarah walked ahead of us as we stepped back into the hallway, her arms crossed.

"So... that happened," she said.

"Mm," Allie said.

I didn't say anything.

Vallerie was waiting at the end of the hall. She looked up from a tablet as we approached, then gave us a smile that landed somewhere between calm and *you poor traumatized idiots.*

"Well?" she asked. "Still breathing?"

"Technically," I muttered.

"Good," she replied. "You want the grand tour?"

Sarah snorted. "Is there a gift shop?"

"No, but there's a greenhouse, a weapons vault, and a woman named Helen who will absolutely gut you if you leave dishes in the sink. So... close."

Allie smiled faintly. "We'd love the tour."

We followed her down the hallway and passed the gym on the left. I glanced through the window, half-expecting to see Cade still inside, but it was empty now—just a few scattered mats.

"The compound's split between two floors," Vallerie explained as we walked. "The top level is where most of us live and work—kitchen, common room, private rooms, war room, a couple of lounges. Downstairs is where we train, treat injuries, and store things that don't like being stored."

She glanced back. "Don't open any locked doors down here unless you're ready to meet something that bites."

"Noted," Sarah said.

I couldn't tell if she was joking... and I really didn't want to find out the hard way.

"We all have private rooms," Vallerie went on. "No bunking up. We rotate chores—cleaning, laundry, kitchen help—but we've also got someone full-time who keeps the place running. Helen. She's Logan and the twin's aunt. No magic, but she cooks, manages supplies, patches up the kitchen when someone blows a cabinet off the wall. And she doesn't take shit from anyone."

"She sounds like a menace," Sarah said.

"She's the reason we haven't all starved or strangled each other," Vallerie replied. "So try not to piss her off."

We turned a corner, and Vallerie stopped in front of a thick wooden door.

"This is the medical ward," she said. "Nick's usually down here or nearby. If he's not, there are basic supplies inside—bandages, splints, antiseptics. Enough to get you stable until he can help."

She pushed the door open, revealing a surprisingly bright room. The overhead lights were soft but steady, reflecting off clean counters and rows of labeled cabinets. A small fridge hummed quietly in the corner. There were two beds against the wall, each made with crisp, pale sheets. A metal cart stood between them, stacked with gauze, gloves, and a few packaged surgical instruments.

Sarah ran her fingers along the edge of the nearest bed. "It's cleaner than most hospitals."

Vallerie gestured back toward the hall. "Come on. I want to show you the control room next."

We followed her out and down another hallway. Monitors buzzed quietly from a small room ahead. A glass panel framed the doorway, and inside, we saw Gage seated in front of three glowing screens, a headset around his neck and the same coffee mug from earlier balanced on a stack of manuals.

He looked up as we entered and gave a small nod. "Hello again."

"Everything you see in here," Vallerie said, motioning around the room, "Gage either built, rewired, or hacked into place. If something's happening—anywhere—you can bet he knows about it."

Gage lifted his mug in mock salute. "And people say I don't have a social life."

Vallerie turned to us again. "This is where most of our eyes and ears live. If anything breaches the perimeter, Gage will be the first to know. And the last person you want on your bad side."

"I thought that was Helen," Sarah said.

"Different kind of scary," Vallerie said, deadpan.

Sarah grinned, but Vallerie was already stepping back into the hallway.

"Come on," she said. "Let's head outside. Most of the real training happens there."

We followed her around another corner, up a flight of stairs and past a set of wide double doors. One was propped open, letting in a spill of bright sunlight and the sharp scent of pine.

"Indoor sparring rooms are fine," she added, "but when magic gets involved, it's safer to keep things out in the open. Fewer walls to rebuild."

As we stepped outside, I noticed a large open field stretched ahead, dotted with wooden dummies, stone markers, and a few raised platforms. Beyond that, I could already see movement. And sparks.

The grass was trampled in places, the earth scarred from whatever strikes had come before us. A row of worn weapons leaned against a rack near the edge of the field—swords, staffs, things I didn't recognize.

Vallerie stopped just short of the main clearing and gestured ahead. "Welcome to the yard."

235

It wasn't exactly welcoming. Several Severance members were already in motion, their bodies cutting through the air in smooth, practiced rhythms. We followed Vallerie to the edge of the field, where a few benches marked the viewing line.

Sarah squinted at the action. "Wait, didn't they already train this morning? I swear Logan was dripping sweat when he came in for breakfast."

Vallerie gave a small shrug. "They don't like to sit still. Especially that crew."

Logan was the first I spotted too. He stood at the far edge of the field, hands loose at his sides. His long hair was pulled back into a bun, bandana still wrapped around his head. With a grin that didn't belong on someone about to demolish something, he cracked his knuckles and stomped once—hard. The ground vibrated beneath us.

I watched as Logan spun midair, his boot landing against the dirt with a concussive *crack*. A training dummy forty feet away exploded into splinters.

"Holy shit," Sarah whispered.

Next came Mariah. She was all motion—fluid, fast, fire. Literally. Flames spun in coils around her arms as she danced between the scattered obstacles, tossing bursts toward metal targets without slowing. Her clothes—form-fitting black gear—were clearly custom-made, designed to withstand the heat.

"They went through a lot of outfits before someone thought of fireproof fabric," Vallerie said wryly.

Nicole, followed seconds later, less flair, more precision. Wind wrapped around her like a second skin, lashing out in sharp arcs that knocked over wooden barriers and kicked up whirlwinds strong enough to lift a grown man.

Together, the sisters moved like they shared a brain, fire and wind crashing forward in harmony. Mariah launched a flaming strike upward. Nicole curved the wind to arc it sideways, catching two dummies behind cover.

Then Kaylen stepped into the field. She wore tight, black tactical gear, her dark braid swinging behind her like a blade.

She raised a hand, and a blade appeared. One second empty-palmed, the next, a gleaming dagger rested against her thigh. Then another. Then a sword. Weapon after weapon materialized in and out of reality, until she was armed like an ancient god of war.

"All physical," Vallerie said. "Steel, wood, silver, even obsidian if she's really pissed. She can only hold so many at a time, but she makes them count."

Kaylen launched forward. Her blades didn't slow her, they moved with her. A spin. A throw. Another draw mid-motion. She struck dummies with bone-snapping accuracy, then tossed a dagger that embedded with a *thunk* inches from where Logan had just been. He gave her a thumbs-up.

Then Cade stepped forward. He wore black pants and a fitted charcoal t-shirt, a dark tattoo peeking out from under one sleeve. One second he was just standing there, and the next, he *wasn't*. A blur of movement as he shadow-stepped across the field, appearing behind one of the dummies and taking it down in a single, brutal motion. Another flash, and he was on the opposite side, dodging fire and slicing through falling debris with nothing but his bare hands. There was something terrifyingly calm about it, like violence had become instinct.

Farther across the field, more Severance members trained in smaller groups. A stocky woman with thick arms and a buzzed head sprinted toward a line of dummies, each one bursting into shards the moment she touched them. "That's Emma. She has kinetic touch," Vallerie murmured. "She only needs a fingertip."

A wiry man with copper-colored hair stood with arms slightly raised, veins glowing faintly gold. With each flick of his fingers, bursts of light pulsed forward—like focused beams of sunlight—cutting clean through thick targets. Light-based projection, maybe. Precise and deadly.

Another young woman stood barefoot in the dirt. She was short, but striking. Her skin was a deep, warm brown that caught the sunlight like polished bronze. Slate-gray eyes stayed locked on the targets ahead, calm and unblinking. Curls of dark hair framed her face and spilled around her shoulders, moving gently in the breeze. She looked almost ethereal at first glance, like she belonged somewhere quieter than a battlefield.

Then she exhaled. The air in front of her shimmered and cracked, as if reality itself had hiccupped. Her opponents lurched in mid-movement, suddenly slowed—caught in invisible resistance, their momentum strangled mid-strike.

"Alice. She manipulates inertia," Vallerie explained softly. "Objects, people, force… she's like gravity's temper tantrum."

The whole field buzzed with energy and purpose. My heart pounded. How could I ever keep up with this?

My eyes darted between the whirling flames, the gusts of wind, the shockwaves, the glinting blades, and Cade's impossible movements. Every person on that field knew who they were. What they could do. And me? I was barely holding myself together.

I couldn't breathe. My chest felt too tight, like the air had thickened into something unbreathable. I pressed a hand against my ribs like that might hold everything inside.

They wanted me to fight Michael. To *defeat* him. How? With what? My feelings? He can literally kill anyone just with a look. I'm no match for him.

My fingers trembled. I tried to steady them, but the panic bloomed faster than I could stop it. I wasn't enough. I'd never be enough. It was too much.

Suddenly, it was too much. My breath hitched. My hands trembled. A wave of heat rushed up my neck. Something inside me buckled… and then snapped outward.

Shit. Not again. The impact was immediate.

Mariah startled mid-throw, her fire bolt veering wildly and nearly striking a nearby member, who dove out of the way with a yelp. Logan stumbled back, blinking hard. Nicole flinched, wind faltering. A few other members froze, staring in our direction with wide eyes.

238

Allie was at my side in an instant, her voice low but steady. "Lena, you're okay. We've got you."

Sarah reached for me too, jaw tight, eyes locked on mine. "Just breathe."

They knew what this was. We all did.

Kaylen stormed over, her tone sharp. "You need to fucking control that before someone gets hurt!"

Sarah moved between us without hesitation, planting herself squarely in Kaylen's path. "Back off, Discount GI Jane. She's had her mark for, what, a couple of months? Not her whole damn life like you."

A pause. Then Kaylen snapped back. "Your loyalty's cute. But it'll probably get you killed."

Sarah's mouth opened like she was one second away from throwing hands, but Nick appeared beside me like he'd been summoned before she could make her move.

"Breathe," he said gently. "In through the nose."

I did.

"And out through the mouth."

My hands had stopped shaking. My mind hadn't.

"I didn't mean to project. I didn't even do anything," I whispered.

"Yes, you did," he said. "You felt. Hard."

That made no sense.

"I'm not a weapon," I said.

"Empathy can be one," Nick replied. "You projected. Unintentionally, but still. Your magic is responding before you know what you're asking of it. That's not failure. That's potential."

I looked at him.

He smiled. Not the kind you give a patient. The kind you give a person.

"You're not broken," he said. "You're just waking up."

The sound of the compound's back doors creaking open broke the moment.

Gage stepped out, blinking against the sunlight, tablet in one hand and urgency radiating off him like heat. Lorelei emerged behind him, brow furrowed as she followed.

"Uh, hey," Gage called, waving the tablet. "Sorry to crash the bonding session, but you guys need to see this."

Cade and several other members made their way toward us, catching the change in mood.

Vallerie turned to Gage. "Now?"

"Now-now," he said, already walking toward us. "I was poking through recent high-dollar real estate transfers, don't ask why, my brain just said look, and boom." He flipped the tablet around. "Guess who bought a goddamn mansion outside of Portland?"

"You were looking at real estate?" Sarah asked, incredulous.

Gage shrugged. "My gut told me to. You know how it is."

Nicole let out a dry snort. "Duh. He has the mark of intuition. It's literally what he does."

He gave a quick grin. "This was recorded three days ago. Pulled it from a private drone network I have access to. Don't ask."

An aerial shot of a massive estate filled the screen. It was sprawling and tucked deep in the woods. Forests stretched in all directions around it. Miles of land. Completely secluded.

Gage tapped the screen again and the footage switched to a closer angle. The estate's gates opened, and several people passed through.

Some wore street clothes—hoodies, jeans, coats with deep pockets—while others were dressed for combat in tactical vests and utility belts. One of the first was a tall woman in combat boots and a dark, sleeveless vest. Her arms were covered in faded tattoos, and her shaved head gleamed under the floodlights. She moved like someone who didn't hesitate, like someone who never had.

Behind her came a man in a long coat, broad-shouldered, his hands gloved, his face unreadable. He scanned the perimeter with the slow, practiced gaze of someone who had done this before too many times.

Then another woman, younger, walked past the gates. A bold tattoo slashed across her neck and disappeared into the collar of her jacket. She chewed gum as she walked, casual, like none of this mattered. There was no fear in any of them. No glancing back. Just precision. Purpose.

And there Michael was. Standing tall on the front steps, arms crossed, face tilted toward the sun like he was basking in his own empire. The camera panned slightly, revealing a tall, dark-skinned man beside him.

Allie leaned in. "Who's the guy next to Michael?"

"That's Chad," Gage said grimly. "Chad Greesley. West Coast Severance went after him a few years back. He got away before they could pin anything solid. Something involving children. Really bad shit."

"It looks like he's recruiting," Sarah said.

Lorelei folded her arms. "Gage, I want full reports on everyone in those photos. Names, known marks, affiliations... whatever you can dig up."

Gage nodded, all business now. "I'm on it."

He turned and jogged back toward the compound, already tapping commands into the tablet.

Nicole muttered, "Guess training just got a hell of a lot more real."

No one disagreed.

Lorelei spoke, her tone settling into command. "I want everyone to meet later this evening. Once we have more information, we'll decide our next steps."

She looked to me, Allie, and Sarah. "You three as well. You're part of this now."

We all nodded.

Then her gaze moved to Sarah. "Do you have the list of personal items you need from Allie's house?"

Sarah shook her head. "I can get it ready soon."

"Good." Lorelei turned to the short woman who had manipulated inertia earlier. "Alice, you and your team will handle retrieval."

Alice gave us a warm, friendly smile. "No problem. We've got it covered."

People began to disperse. Some drifted back toward the field, shaking off the tension like dust, while others filtered into the compound's rear entrance, voices low and cautious. The buzz of conversation picked up again, but it didn't quite return to normal.

Vallerie gave us a lingering glance, her expression unreadable but heavy with thought. "I'm going to see if there's anything I can do to help Gage piece together more intel," she said. "You're free to explore more if you'd like, just don't go wandering into anyone's private quarters."

"Noted," Sarah said, tipping her head.

With a faint nod, Vallerie turned and followed the others toward the compound. The three of us were left standing there, the field behind us slowly returning to motion.

Allie exhaled hard. "Well. That was...a lot."

"No kidding," Sarah said, her voice still edged with adrenaline. "Discount GI Jane looked like she was ready to skin me."

I let out a shaky laugh. "You kinda earned it."

"She deserved it," Sarah muttered, arms crossed. "You didn't do anything wrong, Lena."

"I lost control again," I said.

"You'll learn to control it," Allie said gently.

Sarah nudged me with her shoulder. "Come on. Let's go snoop around this place."

I smiled, but the nerves still lingered in my stomach like smoke after a fire.

We made our way back into the compound, wandering the halls for a bit without much direction. We passed a few people who barely glanced up as we moved by. Most doors were closed, but we did pass one open room that looked like a lounge. A couple of worn couches circled a low coffee table scattered with empty mugs and a half-eaten bag of chips. A pool table took up the far end of the room, its surface covered with a paused game. Someone had left a cue stick propped against the wall.

We didn't linger.

We made our way toward the familiar warmth of the common room. The fire wasn't lit this time, but the smell of food was strong—rich, earthy, comforting. A few people were already inside, chatting in low voices or flipping through worn books.

A woman with steel-gray hair that was twisted into a bun stood at the far end, clearing a stack of papers off the table.

When she noticed us, she didn't miss a beat. "Lunch in twenty. Sit yourselves down."

"Thank you," I said, though my stomach twisted at the thought of food. "I'm not really hungry."

The woman gave me a look. The kind that could silence a storm. Her brow rose. "You'll eat a proper meal while I'm here," she said firmly. "That's not a suggestion."

Sarah held back a grin. Allie gave me a look like *don't argue with her.*

"Yes, ma'am," I said quickly.

"Helen," she corrected.

We made our way to the long table and sat down. The wood was scarred and scratched but clean. It smelled faintly of lemon oil.

A few other members wandered in, nodding politely but not sitting too close. One of them, a young woman with short blue hair and copper bracelets, offered us a cautious smile. Another, the man with glowing veins from the training field, gave a small wave before grabbing a glass of water and disappearing down the hallway.

"I feel like the new kid at school," Sarah muttered under her breath.

"You are," Allie whispered back.

I leaned on the table, arms folded. My body was still buzzing from everything—my projection, the surveillance footage, the growing threat just miles away.

Sarah looked around, then flagged down a man walking past. "Hey, do you have a pen and some paper?"

He nodded, disappearing through a side door and returning moments later with a notebook and pen. Sarah offered a quick thanks, then flipped it open and started scribbling.

"What are you doing?" I asked.

"Writing down everything we need from the house," she said without looking up.

Allie leaned in. "Get Grandma's journals. And some clothes. And my phone and laptop."

Sarah nodded, writing fast. "Lena?"

I hesitated. "Just... my phone. And some clothes. Whatever's easy."

Sarah didn't ask twice. She finished the list, tore the page free

Alice entered the room a few minutes later, wiping her hands on a towel tucked into her waistband.

Sarah stood and handed her the list. "Here, it's everything we could think of."

Alice scanned it quickly, then nodded. "Perfect. We were just about to head out. We should be back in a few hours."

"Thank you," Sarah said, her voice sincere.

Alice gave a small smile, tucked the paper into her jacket, and turned to leave.

Sarah sat down and leaned back in her chair. "Do you think we should check on Biscuit?"

"I left her in our room," I said. "With the door closed. I didn't want her getting into anything, or disappearing into a wall vent or something."

Allie gave a faint smile. "She's probably curled up on someone's pillow like she owns the place."

"She *does* own the place," Sarah said. "We're just the help."

We fell quiet again. A few more people filtered into the room.

Ten—maybe fifteen—minutes later, Helen reappeared, pushing a cart laden with mismatched plates and heavy ceramic bowls. The scent of beef stew and homemade bread cut through the air. My stomach twisted again, still not ready to cooperate.

Without a word, she set three steaming bowls in front of us, then returned to the cart and began distributing more down the table.

"Smells amazing," Allie murmured politely.

I tried to focus on the texture of the wood under my fingers, the hum of low conversation behind us, the clink of a spoon in a nearby bowl. Anything but the storm in my chest.

Then the lights flickered. Not the casual, old-building kind of flicker, but a pulse. A sharp dip in power followed by a subtle vibration in the air.

Allie stiffened. "Did you feel that?"

I opened my mouth to answer, but a low chime cut through the room. Two quick tones, sharp and deliberate. The kind of sound that doesn't just grab your attention but *hooks* into you. Chairs scraped against the floor as every member of The Severance in the room suddenly stood at once.

Gage's voice came over a speaker none of us had noticed until now, strained and hurried. "This is not a drill. Repeat. Perimeter breach. Multiple signatures incoming. All hands to positions. Team One and Two to the field. Team Three hold the line."

Helen dropped the serving spoon and turned sharply toward us.

"Get under the table. *Now!*" she snapped.

Allie's chair flew backward. Sarah grabbed my arm, and the three of us ducked just as something *hit*—a deep, vibrating *boom* that made the walls shudder.

Dust rained from the ceiling.

Helen reached into a hidden drawer under the cart and pulled out a wicked-looking dagger. Her stance transformed

245

immediately—no longer grandmotherly, no-nonsense Helen, but something lean and dangerous.

Two members sprinted past the doorway, one carrying a long staff crackling with pale lightning, the other tossing conjured orbs that exploded in bursts of blinding light. A third figure—smaller, barely more than a blur—darted after them, blades glinting.

The girl with the blue hair backed toward the exit, whispering something rapid and foreign under her breath. A soft glow began to pulse from her hands.

The man with glowing veins burst back into the room, already mid-transformation. His skin shimmered with pulsing lines of golden light, his eyes lit like embers. "They're inside," he said breathlessly. "Coming from the north wall. They blasted through."

Another *boom*, this one closer. The floor pitched slightly, and we heard shouting.

Helen turned to the blue-haired girl. "Get them out. The east hallway. Take the service passage. Now."

"But—," the girl started to reply.

Helen cut her off with a look. "Now!"

Just then, the wall by the front door *exploded* inward.

Not crumbled—*exploded*.

A shockwave slammed into us with impossible force. Wood, plaster, stone, and fire erupted in every direction. The air turned white-hot. The impact hurled us backward like rag dolls.

I hit the floor hard, the back of my head cracking against it with a sickening thud. My vision went blank. My ears rang—a high, piercing tone that drowned everything else. Smoke and dust choked the air. I coughed, blinking through the haze, and sat up fast—too fast.

"Allie?" I rasped. "Sarah?"

A low groan answered me. I turned to see Allie sprawled on her side, cradling her arm but conscious, blinking at me through ash.

"I'm okay," she said, voice tight with pain. "Where's—"

"Sarah?" I shouted.

"I'm here!" Sarah coughed, crawling out from under a broken beam. She was covered in soot, and had a thin cut bleeding above her brow, but she was alive.

Relief hit me like another blast.

Then I saw Helen.

Her body was twisted near the edge of the blast zone, blood blooming dark and fast across her chest. Her face was pale… and still.

I crawled to her, every limb screaming, instincts kicking in as the nurse in me surged forward.

"No, no, no—" I murmured, pressing both hands to her wound. Hot blood soaked through my fingers.

I searched for a pulse. Nothing.

"Come on, Helen, come on," I whispered, leaning down, checking again, desperate.

"Where the hell is Nick?" Allie's voice broke behind me, high with panic. "We need him *now*!"

A hand grabbed my shoulder and yanked me back.

"Lena!" Cade's voice cut through the ringing.

I wanted to scream. To go back. To fix it. But I couldn't fix anything.

"She's gone," he said, firm and raw. "We have to move. Now."

Somewhere down the hall, I heard Logan's voice roar, followed by a bone-rattling *boom*. A sonic blast. The walls shook. Someone screamed in agony.

Just then, the wall groaned and then splintered further as boots crunched through the rubble. Figures began moving through the hole in the wall, emerging from the smoke and debris. I couldn't see how many. All armed and all marked. But I recognized the man in front. I'd seen him in the surveillance footage—the same sharp build, the same way he moved like nothing could touch him.

Michael's people.

"Shit," Cade muttered.

He snatched a small, crackling device from his belt and barked into it. "Common room breached. Need backup. *Now.*"

Without hesitation, he shoved me, Allie, and Sarah behind a half-toppled table, crouching low with us as another fireball lit up the far wall. The heat was sharp and immediate, like opening an oven with your face too close.

"Stay down," he growled, then vanished. His body slipped into shadow like smoke sucked into a vent.

I barely had time to process before a scream cut through the haze. One of Michael's people burst through the jagged hole in the wall, flames curling from his hands and shoulders like living things. He barely had time to look around before Cade appeared behind him, blade flashing like a streak of night. The sword cut clean through his side, just below the ribs. Blood sprayed in a wide arc across the floor, catching the light like shards of red glass. The man choked, a gurgling rasp clawing from his throat as he collapsed in a heap.

Another followed. This one faster, his short sword crackling with dark energy that pulsed up his arm. Cade stepped through the shadow again, reappearing at the man's flank. The first strike sliced through the tendon at the back of the man's knee, dropping him instantly. The second plunged deep into the space between his shoulder and neck.

"Holy shit," Sarah whispered beside me.

I could see other fighters clashing down the hallway. A man with a shimmering energy shield deflecting a barrage of knives, a woman sending wave after wave of greenish energy that rippled like heat through the air. The hall was a storm of movement, magic, and screams.

Another intruder stumbled through the hole in the wall, eyes scanning. She spotted us crouched behind the overturned table. "There!" she shouted, raising a jagged, cruel-looking weapon I didn't recognize.

My heart stopped. Allie moved instinctively, pulling me closer, shielding my body with hers. Sarah had her hands on a nearby chair, like she meant to use it as a weapon.

But before the woman could move, a blast of light hit her like a battering ram, slamming her into the far wall with bone-shattering force.

The blue-haired girl stood nearby, breathing hard, one side of her head matted with blood. Her bracelets glowed faintly. She must've just regained consciousness. But her hands were steady now, crackling with magic.

Kaylen burst in next, vaulting over debris like it wasn't even there. Her blades shimmered with silver heat as she took down another invader trying to circle behind the wounded girl.

The man with the glowing veins stormed forward, lines of gold pulsing across his arms like lightning trapped in skin. He flung a surge of energy that split a chair—and the man hiding behind it—in two.

Screams. Magic. Shouts in every direction.

And then the others came.

Logan, eyes burning with focus. He let out a roar that shook the room, followed by a sonic blast that shattered the remaining windows and sent two of Michael's people crumpling to the floor.

Mariah and Nicole surged in behind him, fire and wind dancing between them like twin storms. Nicole lifted her arms and a cyclone formed in the center of the room, sucking another attacker upward, limbs flailing. Flames roared as Mariah scorched a path through two more intruders, shielding Kaylen as she regrouped.

We had them. We were winning. The last few of Michael's people began to hesitate, some backing toward the hole they'd come through.

For a moment, it was a standstill. An eerie pause. Smoke curled in the air. Bodies—both moving and still—littered the ruined common room. Mariah stood with flames crackling in her palms, Nicole's winds howling low around her feet. Cade stood by us, blade at the ready.

Then Michael stepped through the jagged hole in the wall with the calm arrogance of someone who already knew how it would end. His coat drifted behind him, untouched by soot or flame, as if the fire itself didn't dare touch him. His smile wasn't just lazy, it was cruel. Patient. Like he was waiting for someone to scream.

Kaylen didn't hesitate. She lunged, blades aimed for his throat. Michael barely moved. A flick of his fingers and she was yanked mid-air by an invisible force, slammed into the ceiling, then hurled back down with a sickening thud. She didn't rise.

Mariah screamed and launched a fireball at him. Nicole followed, swirling the flames into a vortex with her wind, sharpening it like a flaming spear.

It struck—or should have. The fire collided with something unseen, just inches from Michael's body. A ripple shimmered through the air—like heat waves on pavement—before vanishing entirely. Not a single flame touched him.

He stepped through the dying embers, unscathed. Smiling. "Oh, come on," he said. "This isn't even a fight. Why are you still trying?"

That's when Cade moved. He shadow-stepped directly behind Michael, sword aimed for his spine. It was fast, almost too fast to see.

But Michael spun at the last second, catching Cade mid-lunge with a telekinetic blast that hit like a wrecking ball. Cade was thrown across the room, crashing through an overturned table and hitting the wall with a heavy crack. He didn't rise immediately.

The blue-haired girl rose behind him. She let out a war cry, glowing bracelets flaring with desperate magic.

Michael didn't even look at her. He lifted one hand and closed his fist. She choked as she was lifted off the ground, limbs flailing. Her scream cut off mid-breath. He twisted his wrist, and her neck snapped with a hollow crack. Her body crumpled like paper.

"No!" someone shouted. Logan, maybe.

The man with glowing veins charged, fury lighting his skin like a supernova.

250

Michael turned toward him, eyes flat. He raised his palm and the man stopped. Blinked. Then dropped to his knees, clutching his head. His glow trembled—then died, veins going dark. Blood leaked from his ears. Then his eyes. He fell forward, still.

"Really?" Michael said. "This is the great Severance?"

He stepped further into the room, surveying the others like he was bored.

"This is embarrassing," he said. "Honestly. You all train, fight, guard your little compound, and for what?"

From across the room, I saw Cade move. He pushed himself to his knees, blood trailing down the side of his face. His hand braced against the wreckage as he stood, just barely steady. But when Michael's eyes landed on me, Cade moved faster.

I rose instinctively, heart pounding. Allie stepped up beside me, then moved half a step in front, like she could shield me with her body. Sarah reached out and caught my arm, fingers tight with unspoken fear.

Michael's gaze slid over me, slow and deliberate. "There you are," he said softly, like it was some romantic reunion. "I've missed that look on your face. The mix of hate and heartbreak."

Cade stepped between us without a word, shielding me with his body.

Michael raised an eyebrow. "Ah. And here we are." His smile darkened as his eyes landed on Cade. "Family reunion."

Cade didn't flinch. "You're not my family."

Michael let out a low, humorless laugh. "Come on, cousin. Don't be like that. We played in the same dirt, remember? You just never outgrew it."

"You murdered my family," Cade said coldly. "You lost the right to call anyone family."

Michael shrugged. "They were weak. Just like your little collection here."

Around us, the remaining defenders staggered to regroup, some dragging the wounded to safety, others forming a shaky line against the remaining invaders.

Then Michael looked back at me, leaning slightly to peer around Cade.

"Tell me, cousin... have you fucked her yet?" A pause. He grinned when Cade didn't answer. "No? Pity. She's incredible. Especially that mouth."

I flinched. My stomach twisted. Shame, fury, and something far more dangerous surged up my throat. My empathy mark flared like a scream, and for one impossible second, I *felt* Michael. The cold rot. The hunger. His soul was curdled with cruelty, and it recoiled from mine like it had been burned.

Cade stepped forward immediately, blade drawn, his body tense with rage. "Talk about her again, and I'll carve the words out of your throat."

Michael stepped closer, voice smooth and venomous. "There it is. The famous Cade temper. Always so dramatic. You couldn't protect your own blood, what makes you think you can protect hers?"

Cade moved. He vanished and then appeared right beside Michael, sword already slicing toward his spine. But the blade struck something unseen. It rebounded with a harsh clang, ricocheting from his shimmering shield and flying from Cade's grip.

Cade didn't pause. Before the sword had even hit the ground, he drew a smaller blade from his side and thrust upward, fast and brutal.

This time, there was no barrier. Michael must have dropped the shield after the first failed attack. Steel punched into Michael's throat, a deep, clean, and perfect strike.

Michael jerked, choking. Blood surged down his neck. He staggered a half-step, gurgling, but then reached up and pulled the blade out slowly, like it was an inconvenience.

Blood spattered against the floor before the wound sealed itself with horrifying ease.

He looked at the blade in his hand, then at Cade.

"Ouch." He grinned. He rolled his shoulder, trying to play it off, but his eyes flicked warily toward Cade. He wasn't laughing anymore.

Cade didn't wait. He surged forward again, but Michael's gaze locked on him, and in the blink of an eye, Cade dropped. His knees slammed into the ground with a sickening crack, his body rigid, trembling against the invisible force. Michael didn't move a muscle. He just stared at him with quiet, focused cruelty.

But even as pain contorted his face, Cade's glare never wavered. His teeth were clenched, his jaw tight, but his eyes were locked on Michael with pure murder—like he was already imagining ripping his spine out through his throat.

"I'm getting bored of this," Michael snapped, turning away from Cade like he was no longer a threat. A fireball sparked to life in his palm, glowing hotter by the second. He aimed it toward a Severance member who'd just staggered in— Vallerie, covered in blood but standing tall.

He pulled back his arm—

"Michael!" Gage screamed.

He burst into the room, bleeding from his arm, limping but wild-eyed. In his hand, a battered tablet pulsed faintly with light.

"I've got it all," Gage shouted, raising it like a weapon. "Fifteen years of evidence. Security footage, witness accounts, forensic trails. Every lie. Every kill."

Michael froze, just a split second, but it was there. A flare in his eyes. Not fear, but calculation.

I saw Cade stand, his face no longer twisted in pain—the hold broken, but the hatred still burning.

Gage's voice shook with fury. "I'll show them everything. You want the world's love? Then let them see who you *really* are."

Michael's fireball hovered in his palm. "You think they'll believe you?" he said. "You think they *want* to?"

"They won't have a choice," Gage snapped. "I'll flood every screen. Every feed. Every damn device. I'll rip your mask off in front of the world."

"You'd really risk that?" Michael retorted. "Expose us all? The Marked ones? You think the world will spare *you* once they know what you are?"

Gage didn't flinch. His voice was iron. "Try me."

It felt like everyone in the room was holding their breath.

"Kill me, and it still uploads," Gage added, lifting the tablet higher. "It's already set. One heartbeat after mine stops, it hits every major news outlet in the world."

Cade stepped forward slowly. "You care about your image? Then walk away. You're not done, but neither are we."

For the first time, I saw what Michael feared most. Not death. Not even defeat. But exposure. A world that no longer adored him. That was what made him pause.

Michael's gaze slid from Gage to Cade, then to me. For a heartbeat, he looked like he might strike anyway. Burn the entire room down out of spite.

But then his jaw tightened.

He exhaled sharply, the fire in his hand flared, then vanished.

"Next time," he said, and that familiar, venomous smile returned. "But when I come back... I won't leave anyone breathing."

He turned slightly, just enough to catch the eye of one of his men. The same one from the drone footage. Tall, dark-skinned, with a hard stare that didn't waver. Chad. Michael gave a sharp nod. Chad raised both palms, fingers splayed. A pulse of energy swept outward, and then the air cracked. In an instant, they all vanished.

But the damage was still here. And the echo of what he promised next.

Chapter 22

Silence fell like ash.

Michael and his men were gone, but the wreckage they left behind remained. The bodies of his followers lay scattered among our own, blood pooling on shattered floors. Broken walls groaned around us, the scorched scent of magic still thick in the air. For a moment, no one moved.

Then came the sound that split everything wide open.

A scream.

Logan.

He dropped to his knees beside Helen's body, his shoulders shaking as Mariah and Nicole stumbled behind him, their faces twisted in disbelief. The three of them clung to her, to each other, as if refusing to believe she was really gone.

People came running in from the hallway. Lorelei strode in like a storm, her clothes torn, bloody, and streaked with ash. Nick followed close behind, sleeves rolled, his shirt singed along the collar. Neither of them looked hurt. Nick must have already healed whatever damage they took.

Nick scanned the room like a soldier surveying a battlefield. "Who needs me?" he called, voice loud and sharp.

Vallerie was crouched beside Kaylen, who lay half-conscious, blood seeping beneath her. Her voice cut sharply through the chaos. "Over here!"

Nick was already moving. He dropped to his knees beside her, his hands outstretched as he reached for Kaylen's side.

Lorelei stepped further into the room, surveying the wreckage with a cold, unreadable stare. "Report."

Vallerie looked up, her face tight. "Three dead. Michael's gone, but I don't know for how long."

Lorelei's expression didn't change. "Anyone who can stand, get to the perimeter. I want eyes on every approach,

255

armed and ready. If he comes back, I want to know before he's through the damn wall."

Chairs scraped. Boots pounded. Voices shouted over one another as people grabbed weapons. A woman sprinted past with a bloodied towel pressed to her side. Two more shoved overturned furniture out of the doorway to clear the exit.

A loud grunt came from near the collapsed wall. One of Michael's men had landed on top of the blue-haired girl—his body sprawled across hers like a final insult. Her head was twisted at an unnatural angle, bracelets dark, her lifeless eyes fixed on nothing.

A Severance member struggled to roll the body off, gritting his teeth as he tried to move the dead weight. Allie and Sarah didn't hesitate. They rushed over, bending beside him to help. Together, they dragged the body away and threw it on the floor like garbage.

The chaos didn't let up. Footsteps pounded past. Somewhere, someone was crying. Shouts layered over one another until it was just noise.

Too much noise. Too much movement. Too much *everything.* I was drowning in fear, pain, and grief. My chest tightened. My hands trembled.

No, no, no. *Not now. Not here. Don't do this again—*

My eyes darted wildly around the room. Every injury, every scream, every single *feeling* pressed in like barbed wire wrapping tighter and tighter.

Fuck, Lena. This is not the fucking time. No. No no no no—

A strangled breath caught in my throat. My vision narrowed. I was going to explode. Then, there were arms around me and I felt the world tilt. The next second, I was in the woods. But I barely registered the trees or the quiet or the cool press of wind against my skin.

I collapsed to my knees, hands clutching at my head as the flood surged through me. It was still there. All of it. Pressing. Screaming. Shredding. A sob tore from my throat as the energy burst outward. Cade stumbled beside me with a grunt, one hand clutching his chest as if I'd knocked the wind from him.

Time slipped sideways. I don't know how long I knelt there, shaking. A minute? Five?

Eventually, the wave passed. Cade's boots crunched the leaves as he stepped closer. Blood was smeared across his shirt, his hands, even up his arms—drying in thick patches that didn't seem to bother him at all. He moved like someone used to carrying other people's blood, like it barely registered anymore. He crouched, gently helping me to my feet, then guided me over to a fallen tree. I didn't resist. I sank onto the rough bark, and he sat beside me, close but not too close.

Only then did I look around. We were tucked in a patch of woods outside the compound. I could still see it, broken and half-lit through the trees, maybe a quarter mile away. We sat in silence for a while. The wind rustled through the trees like a hush, like the world was giving us space to breathe.

Cade didn't look at me. He stared ahead, elbows resting on his knees, letting me come back to myself without pressure. I was grateful for that.

Finally, my voice scraped out, raw and quiet. "Are you okay?"

His head tilted slightly, a half-shrug. "I've had worse."

I turned toward him. "You looked like I knocked the wind out of you."

"You did," he said, then gave me the barest grin. "Didn't say I minded."

I huffed, the smallest, broken laugh slipping free. "I'm sorry."

"Don't be." His tone softened. "Most people would've broken under that kind of weight. You're still standing."

I stared down at my hands. They were trembling and still smudged with Helen's blood. "Why are you so nice to me?" I asked before I could stop myself. "You don't even know me."

He paused. "True," he said slowly, "I don't know you, not really. But I've seen enough to get a good idea."

That made me look up.

257

He continued. "When your name came up after the news report, when we realized who Michael had been with, Gage started digging up information on you. I helped. We found employee files, old news pieces, social media, school records, phone records. Everything legal... and some things that weren't."

I made a face. "That's not creepy at all."

He smiled. "It wasn't personal. It was about protecting people. But I'll admit... once I started reading about you, it *felt* personal."

I looked at him, puzzled.

He regarded me with a thoughtful, almost amused look. "You fought for your patients. You got written up for it more than once, by the way," he added with a small smirk. "But you didn't stop. You donated to GoFundMes you couldn't afford. Protested when your hospital tried to cut funding to the psych unit. There's even a photo of you in the paper, drenched in rain, holding a hand-painted sign and looking like you'd fight the hospital board with your bare hands."

A small, almost knowing smile touched his lips. "And all those messages with Sarah... checking on each other after long days, sending each other memes to survive the hard days, reminding each other to eat or sleep or just breathe. You two looked out for each other like it was second nature. No questions, no keeping score. Just loyalty."

He paused, softer now. "You searched late at night for how to help people through panic attacks and grief. You read fantasy books about quiet women who become dangerous. Your playlists were half heartbreak, half battle cry. And you send toys to the local animal shelter every month, with no name attached."

He hesitated, then added, "And there was this message... someone from your work. She reached out a couple months after quitting and said she was in a bad place. You didn't ignore her. You stayed on the phone with her all night."

I looked down at my hands, picking at the edge of a cracked nail. "Doesn't feel like that person exists anymore."

258

"She does," he said quietly. "She's sitting right beside me. A little bruised. A little lost. But still here."

There was a pause, and then his voice dropped lower and rougher. "The more I learned, the angrier I got. Seeing what Michael did to you... what he took from you. How he manipulated you. It made me furious, Lena. You didn't deserve that. No one does."

I blinked hard, heart twisting. "Well... I feel like I owe you. You saved my life last night. Put yourself between me and Michael today. Hell, you even saved my cat."

I lurched upright. "Biscuit! Oh my God—" My breath hitched. Panic flared like a fresh wound. "I left her in the room—"

"Hey," Cade said gently, his voice steady as a hand on my spine. "Breathe."

I looked at him, wild-eyed.

"She's okay," he said firmly. "That side of the compound wasn't touched. I promise. She's fine."

My heart thudded hard against my ribs, like it hadn't decided whether to believe him. But his calm was so absolute, so sure, it began to pull the panic out of me like a thread being unraveled.

"She's probably curled up in a pile of clothes," I muttered, half to myself. "Annoyed no one's fed her. Or plotting revenge."

Cade gave a soft chuckle. "Yeah. She struck me as the vengeful type."

I glanced over at him. The tension in my chest had eased, but my mind was still buzzing. Everything that had just happened. Everything he'd just said.

"I'm... I'm so sorry about your family," I said quietly. The words felt small, too thin to hold the weight they needed to.

Cade's gaze dropped to the ground. "Thank you," he said after a moment. "It doesn't really get easier. You just... learn to live around the hole it leaves."

I hesitated, chewing at the inside of my cheek. "Do you think he ever... I don't know. Regrets any of it?"

His jaw worked, like he was biting back something sharp. "No. Regret requires a soul." He met my eyes, and for a moment there was a fire there, cold and bright. "He doesn't feel sorry. He never did. And that's what makes him so dangerous."

I swallowed hard, struggling to speak. "Michael killed my parents."

His head turned toward me slowly. He didn't speak, just listened.

"My mom," I went on. "She apparently had a whisper of magic. Nothing strong, but enough. She knew something was off about him. She kept trying to warn me... and I didn't listen." My throat tightened. "He got rid of her because she saw through him."

"And my dad..." I swallowed. "He was just collateral."

Cade was quiet for a moment. Then softly, "You couldn't have known, Lena. You loved him. That doesn't make you blind. It makes you human."

He looked at me, steady and calm. "What happened to them... that's on him. Not you."

I stared down at my hands again, picking at the dirt under my nails, trying to keep my voice steady. "You must think I'm pathetic. Falling for someone like that. Letting him take everything."

Cade's brows pulled together, his voice suddenly sharper. "No. Don't ever say that. You were loyal. You loved him the way you love Sarah. The way you fight for your patients, your friends, even strangers. That loyalty isn't weakness. It's the best part of you. He just... twisted it."

I met his eyes, my heart thudding unevenly.

"You still have that loyalty," he said, softer now. "You just have to decide who deserves it."

For a moment, I didn't know what to say. The forest felt impossibly still around us. Then, almost without thinking, I let out a shaky breath. "So... how does it work? The shadow stepping?"

Cade let out a small breath, some of the tension easing from his face like he was relieved for the subject change. "It's... not as flashy as some of the others. But it's useful. I can step through one shadow and come out through another. Kind of like folding space, but with rules."

"What kind of rules?" I asked.

He gave a short breath of amusement. "The annoying kind. I have to be able to see the shadow I want to step out of. Or, at least have a crystal-clear memory of it. Otherwise, I could end up literally anywhere."

I blinked. "Anywhere?"

"Let's just say I once ended up in the wrong country trying to skip out on algebra finals," he said, rubbing his jaw as a grin formed. "My dad had to fly to Scotland and pick me up. I was thirteen. Mortifying."

I let out a surprised snort. "Wait—seriously?"

"Oh yeah. And I didn't even make it back in time for the makeup test."

He shook his head, clearly amused by the memory, then added, "When I was sixteen, I tried to step out of gym class and ended up locked inside a Costco storage closet three states over."

I stared at him. "That's incredible."

"True story," he said with a laugh. "Sat between a crate of pool noodles and a 72-pack of toilet paper for six hours until someone unlocked the door. I was too scared to shadow step out of there. Who knows where I might have ended up."

He gave a small shrug, the corner of his mouth tipping up. "At least I could see in the dark. It comes with the mark—perfect night vision. My dad wasn't even mad. He just sighed and told me next time to at least land somewhere with snacks."

I let out a short laugh—quiet, but real. It startled me more than anything else had today. "Your poor dad," I said, shaking my head. "Sounds like he got used to rescuing you."

Cade's mouth lifted in a sad smile. "Yeah. He did. My mom too, when she was still alive. She used to joke that

261

shadow stepping would either make me a superhero or a cautionary tale."

He huffed a soft breath. "She wasn't wrong."

I exhaled slowly and rose to my feet, brushing the dirt from my hands. "We should head back," I said. "Sarah and Allie are probably freaking out."

Cade rose with me. Without a word, he stepped closer and gently pulled me into his arms. He looked down at me, and for a split second, I forgot what we were doing. God, those eyes. Green and fierce and impossibly kind, locked onto mine. He really was a beautiful man.

Then he looked past me, toward the compound.

And in the next instant, the woods vanished.

We were standing just outside the shattered break in the compound wall, smoke curling through the air. The compound looked quieter now, but in a hollow, exhausted way. I could see figures moving inside—some carrying supplies, others moving debris into piles. A few stood as lookouts at the remaining walls, tense and alert.

Cade guided me forward, his hand hovering near my back without touching—protective but giving me space. As we stepped through the broken wall, I saw Allie and Sarah standing just inside the common room. The moment they saw me, they started moving.

Sarah reached me first, throwing her arms around me so tightly I felt my ribs strain. Allie wrapped around both of us from the side, burying her face into my hair. We just stayed like that—breathing, shaking, silent. No one tried to speak. There was nothing to say that wouldn't shatter us.

Eventually, Allie pulled back, her hand brushing my hair behind my ear with trembling fingers. When we all finally stepped apart, I turned and took in the room.

The bodies of The Severance members were gone. I didn't know where they'd moved them. Across the far side of the space, a few members were dragging the bodies of Michael's men roughly toward the exit, like they couldn't get them out fast enough. Some of the larger debris had been pushed to the sides, leaving uneven paths through the wreckage. Splintered beams were piled along the walls, and dark stains still marked the places where people had fallen.

Logan, Mariah, and Nicole were gone. I didn't see Lorelei either. Cade hovered behind me, his presence solid and steady, but he didn't speak. Neither did Allie or Sarah. We just stood there, breathing the same dusty, scorched air, bracing ourselves for whatever came next.

That's when Nick appeared, moving toward us from across the room. He looked... drained. Like he'd poured every last drop of himself into holding everyone else together. His gaze landed on me first, sharp and searching. "Are you hurt?" he asked, already lifting a hand toward my face.

"No, I—" I started, but Cade's voice cut in from behind me.

"Yes," Cade said, stepping closer. "She was flung across the room. She hit her head."

Nick's eyes turned to Cade, then back to me. I opened my mouth to protest again, but he didn't wait. He pressed his fingers lightly to my temple. A rush of warmth filled me, so clean and bright it felt like sunlight breaking through fog. The low, pounding ache in my skull evaporated so fast it made me sway. I hadn't even realized how badly it hurt until it was gone.

Nick's hand dropped away. "Better?" he asked softly.

I nodded, giving him a small smile. "Thank you."

His eyes darted back to Cade, scanning the cut at his hairline and the way he still favored one side.

"And you?" Nick asked.

Cade shook his head. "I'm fine. Save it for the others."

Nick frowned, a tired, exasperated look that said they'd had this argument before. "You're a pain in my ass," he muttered, but he let it go. Even I could see the tremor in Nick's hands, the bone-deep fatigue beneath his skin.

To the left, Lorelei entered followed by Gage, his tablet clutched to his chest, dark circles under his eyes. Conversations dropped off as they entered. Lorelei's sharp gaze swept over us, pausing briefly on each face. I could see the tension in her shoulders, the exhaustion dragging at her edges—but her spine stayed straight, her chin high.

"We've contacted the New York chapter," she said, her voice carrying even though she didn't raise it. "They've been fully briefed. Reinforcements are on their way now. They'll arrive tonight."

A few murmurs rippled through the room. Lorelei continued, her tone softening. "When they arrive, I want everyone to gather. We will meet together to plan and decide what comes next."

She paused then, her eyes drifting toward the empty spaces where bodies had been. "Before that," she went on, her voice dipping lower, rougher around the edges, "we need to honor the people we lost today."

"Helen," she began, her voice unwavering. "She was the backbone of this compound. The first to rise, the last to sleep. She taught half of you to hold a dagger, and she made sure we never forgot why we fight."

She swallowed, her eyes flicking upward like she could blink the tears back into place.

"Talia," she continued, softer now. "Wild-hearted, always too quick for her own good. She laughed louder than anyone in the training yard. She never hesitated to stand between danger and someone she loved."

A tremor slipped into her voice as she said the last name. "Jalen," she breathed. "Quiet, patient, always listening before he spoke. Strong in ways that didn't need to be loud."

Lorelei paused, her shoulders rising and falling once, slowly. "They gave everything," she said. "And if we are here now, if we get another sunrise, it is because of them. We don't move forward today out of vengeance alone. We move forward because they believed we were worth dying for."

Her gaze swept over each of us, steady and fierce.

"A moment of silence," she finished, her voice softer but no less resolute. "For them. For what they gave. And for what we have left to do."

Heads bowed. The room stilled into something deeper than quiet—a collective breath held for the ones who could no longer take one.

After a few minutes, people settled back to what they'd been doing before—clearing debris, sorting supplies, moving bodies. There was a new tone in the room, a shared understanding of what they'd lost and what still had to be done.

Allie, Sarah, and I joined in. Someone handed me a broom. Allie and Sarah began gathering splintered wood and pushing it into neat piles against the wall. It felt mechanical at first, but with each movement, something in my chest loosened.

While we worked, Cade appeared in the doorway. His hair was messy and pushed back from his forehead, a fresh shirt thrown on hastily, and the blood had been washed off. In his arms, squirming and glaring at the world, was Biscuit.

Relief punched through me so fast I almost dropped the broom.

Cade crossed the room and set her gently in my arms. She immediately pressed her face against my neck, purring. When I finally set her down, she blinked once at me, then trotted straight to Cade. She circled his legs twice before settling at his feet.

I let out a small, broken laugh. Even now, she chose exactly where she wanted to be.

At some point, someone suggested putting together a meal. It sounded almost absurd, dinner after everything, but no one argued. We needed warmth, something to fill the aching quiet inside us.

"We'll do it," Sarah said before anyone else could move. Her voice was steady, and she gave Allie and me a quick look that said she wasn't asking.

Allie nodded immediately. "Yeah. We've got it."

I didn't argue.

We headed for the kitchen and started rummaging through cabinets and drawers. Sarah pulled out a massive box of spaghetti, the kind you'd see in a restaurant kitchen.

"Spaghetti," she announced, holding it up like a small victory. "Garlic bread and veggies if we've got them. Simple."

Allie nodded again, already reaching for a pot. "Perfect."

We moved around each other without much talking— chopping, stirring, sliding garlic bread onto battered trays. Every motion felt like stitching a torn seam, small but necessary. The smell of toasting bread and simmering tomato sauce slowly pushed back the acrid tang of smoke that still clung to everything.

When it was finally done, we called for everyone to come grab a plate. The big table in the common room was shattered beyond saving, so people just lined up in the kitchen. One by one, they took their portions, murmuring soft thanks.

Logan, Mariah, and Nicole moved through the line together, silent. Logan's jaw was clenched, his shoulders set like stone. Mariah's eyes looked swollen, as if she'd been crying somewhere private, and Nicole kept her head low, barely glancing at anyone. They took their plates without a word, drifting to a corner where they sat close together on the floor. None of them spoke. They just ate in small, slow bites, like they were trying to remember how.

Some stood with their plates, leaning against counters or walls. Others found an unbroken chair, or sank onto the floor with their backs against each other, knees tucked up.

There wasn't much talking. A few people exchanged quiet words—reminders to eat, to drink water, to rest later. Someone offered a slice of bread to a friend who hesitated at the end of the line.

Once or twice, I caught a low, strained laugh—the kind that sounded like it might turn into a sob if it went on too long.

"Eat," Vallerie murmured as she passed, pressing a hand to someone's shoulder. "We need you strong."

Cade stood near the doorway, plate in one hand, Biscuit sprawled at his feet like she'd declared him her personal fortress. He didn't say much, just watched the room with those unflinching eyes.

I found a spot on the floor next to Allie and Sarah. We didn't say anything at first, just leaned into each other, eating mechanically. Each bite felt heavy, like it had to fight its way down.

After a few minutes, Allie let out a shaky breath. "Feels wrong," she murmured, staring at her half-empty plate. "Eating. After... all of it."

Sarah nudged her knee gently. "We have to."

Allie didn't answer, but she took another small bite.

I didn't say it out loud, but I agreed. It felt wrong. But it was also the only thing that felt remotely human.

By the time the last plates were scraped clean, the sky outside had turned deep blue, the kind of color that settles in just before full dark. Overhead lights buzzed softly, a few darkened or blown out from the damage left behind.

People strolled back toward the kitchen to drop off plates, murmuring quiet thanks or simply nodding. No one lingered long. Most just returned to their tasks—patching walls, organizing supplies, checking weapons. A few sat with their backs to the walls, heads tipped forward, eyes closed.

I gathered the empty pots, stacking them near the sink. My movements felt distant, like my body was following instructions from miles away. That's when I heard the low rumble of approaching vehicles outside. Engines cutting off, doors slamming. Boots on gravel.

I set down the last pot and wiped my hands on my pants without thinking, then trudged to the common room, drawn with everyone else toward the sound.

Lorelei was already there, flanked by Logan and Gage. Her expression was sharp, but beneath it was something steadier. A sense of forward motion, like a current pulling us all along.

"They're here," she announced simply.

As if on cue, figures began filing in from the hole in the wall. They moved in that unmistakable way soldiers do—alert, measured, taking in every angle of the room as they stepped inside.

At the front was a tall man with dark hair grown out just enough to look unruly, pushed back from his forehead with one careless swipe. His beard was long and rough, streaked with gray in places. His eyes moved over the crowd, quick and assessing, before landing on Lorelei.

"David," Lorelei said, her voice dipping with a note of respect I hadn't heard before. "Welcome."

He nodded. "You kept it standing." His voice was rough, but there was something undeniably solid in it.

A few more followed him in, each carrying gear or weapons slung over their backs. One of them, a tall Hispanic man with close-cropped hair, set down a heavy pack and began surveying the broken walls with a craftsman's eye.

"That's Mateo," Lorelei said quietly to someone near her. "Restoration mark. He'll start repairs tonight."

David scanned the space again, his eyes lingering on the broken beams and charred scars across the floor. Then he looked at Lorelei, his expression firm. "We need to discuss the next steps."

I glanced at Allie and Sarah. They both looked pale and worn, but when they caught my eye, they each nodded. Ready.

Beside me, Cade stood a little taller, his jaw tight. Biscuit pressed against his leg, tail curled close, as if she understood something big was coming.

I swallowed hard, tension tightening in my chest. *Here we go again.*

Chapter 23

We all gathered in the training field since it was big enough to hold us all. Floodlights buzzed overhead, throwing bright white pools across the packed dirt. The night air carried that crisp edge that always came with fall—not quite cold, but sharp enough to prickle at my skin and make me wish for a jacket.

People stood in loose clusters, talking in low voices or not at all. Weapons hung at their sides or rested across their backs, but no one looked actively wounded anymore. Nick had seen to that. Instead, there was just an exhausted stillness.

Allie stood close enough that our shoulders brushed, her hand occasionally drifting toward mine before pulling back. Sarah hovered on my other side, her eyes scanning every movement across the field.

Cade stood a little behind us, his focus locked on the front. Biscuit wove in and out between our feet, occasionally pressing against Cade's leg before circling back to me.

At the front, Lorelei and David stood side by side. Lorelei's posture was rigid, chin high, but the tension in her jaw betrayed the exhaustion simmering beneath. David looked carved from stone, eyes scanning the crowd with unhurried precision.

David stepped forward, the slight crunch of dirt under his boots the only sound for a moment. His gaze moved slowly across the group, pausing briefly here and there, measuring. When he finally spoke, his voice was low but carried easily, each word landing like a quiet command.

"You've survived something tonight that most wouldn't," he began. "You held this ground against a threat that should have leveled you completely. That speaks to your preparation and to your resolve."

He paused, eyes sweeping the edges of the field again before settling on Lorelei at his side. "But resolve isn't enough if we keep playing defense," he continued. "Michael knows where you are now. He'll keep coming. Over and over because that's what predators do."

He turned slightly, his eyes landing on me for the first time. "Which one of you is Lena?"

My stomach dropped. I felt Allie tense beside me. Slowly, I raised my hand halfway, my fingers trembling despite my best effort.

David continued, unflinching. "You are the reason Michael came here. The reason he'll keep coming. If you stay, you don't just put yourself at risk. You put every single person here in his line of fire."

He glanced at Lorelei, then back to the crowd. "The only way to protect the most people is to separate our highest-value target from the rest. You—" he nodded to me again "— will leave tonight for a safehouse up north. It's remote and hard to track. A skeleton team will go with you. The rest will stay here and rebuild, preparing for what's next." He paused, eyes moving across the group as if already calculating pieces on a board.

But before he could continue, Lorelei stepped forward. "Cade will go," she called. " And Kaylen, Vallerie, and Alice." Then she stepped back, her shoulders stiff but steady.

David stepped forward again, his dark eyes scanning the chosen group before turning to the rest of his team. "I have two who will join them," David said, his voice low but certain.

He stepped aside slightly and motioned to the pair behind him. The first was a tall, young Asian man with sharp cheekbones, neatly cropped black hair, and a presence that felt both calm and alert—like he could hear the thoughts you didn't say aloud.

"This is Hiro," David said with a nod. "Sensory link mark."

Beside him stood a Latina woman who looked like she'd stepped out of a myth. She looked to be in her early forties, though something about her presence made age feel irrelevant. She was shorter than Hiro, but power radiated from her in quiet waves. Her rich bronze skin was inked with swirling, runic tattoos from her shoulders to her wrists, glowing faintly when the light hit them just right. Her thick dark hair spilled down her back, and her full lips curved slightly like she knew every secret worth keeping.

"And this is Marcela," David continued. "Alchemy mark."

Alchemy. The same mark as grandma. It made sense. Marcela carried herself with the same quiet confidence, like she understood the patterns beneath the chaos.

Sarah leaned toward me with a low whistle. "I'm not even into women, but... damn."

I snorted quietly.

Lorelei took a slow breath, then turned her gaze toward the chosen group.

"Pack what you need," she said. "You leave tonight."

A hushed tension moved through the field. Allie squeezed my hand once before letting go, her face pale but resolute.

Not long after, the sound of vehicles rolled up near the main entrance. Doors slammed, heavy footsteps echoed across the dirt. I turned just as Alice climbed out first, her hair pulled back tight, eyes clear despite the exhaustion etched across her face. She and her small team stepped out, some of them carrying bags and looking a little rough.

Lorelei strode forward, brows knitting. "What happened?"

Alice dropped her pack with a heavy thud. "Ran into a couple of Michael's men at Allie's house," she said, voice clipped but steady. "They were waiting, probably in case Lena came back. "We handled it, but it took some time to clean up.

She paused, glancing toward Lorelei. "Evangeline called while we were wrapping up. She filled me in on what happened here." Tears pooled in her eyes then, and she looked down quickly. "I'm sorry I wasn't here."

Lorelei touched Alice's arm lightly. "We're just glad you made it back."

Alice's gaze moved toward us, softening slightly. "We got everything you asked for."

"Thank you," Allie said first, her voice tender.

"Really… thank you," I added.

A few of Alice's team members nodded back, some with small, weary smiles. Alice gave a short, almost relieved dip of her head, her eyes lingering on each of us for a beat.

"Gather what you need," Lorelei said. "You leave within the hour."

The team finished setting the bags down, then Alice and Lorelei turned and started walking off toward David, their voices low as they moved away.

Allie grabbed her bag first, rifling through it. I reached for mine next. Sarah picked up her bag last. She unzipped it, pulled out her phone, and froze.

"Shit," she muttered, staring at the screen. Her thumb hovered as she scrolled. "A bunch of missed calls from my mom… and some texts." Her voice dropped lower. "And a few from Jack."

Allie leaned closer, her brow furrowing. "What do they say?"

Sarah's throat bobbed as she swallowed. "My mom's just… checking in. Worried because I didn't respond to her text this morning. She thinks I'm avoiding her." Her fingers tightened around the phone. "And Jack… he was just checking in. Then—" she paused, her voice catching, "—'Please answer. I'm worried.'"

Her eyes lifted, wide and raw, like she didn't know whether to laugh or break down completely.

Allie watched her for a second, then said, "we should head back to the room. Grab Biscuit's things. We don't really have anything else to pack."

"OK," I said, my fingers curling tighter around the strap of my bag.

We gathered the few things from our room—Biscuit's bowls, her litter box, the borrowed clothes we'd been given— and made our way back to the front entrance. I held Biscuit close against my chest, her purr a low, steady hum that kept my hands from shaking too badly.

272

Sarah had stepped aside to call her mom, telling her that her phone wouldn't charge, and that was why she hadn't answered. I heard her voice soften, something almost like relief washing across her face when she hung up.

Before we knew it, two jeeps rumbled up to the front, headlights cutting wide curves across the yard. Kaylen climbed out of one, tossing her hair over her shoulder, while Alice slid from the other, already scanning the group like she was checking for holes.

The other members going with us arrived moments later, moving with steady focus as they dropped bags into the back and checked their weapons. Just as we finished loading the last bag, Lorelei appeared beside the jeeps. Her gaze settled on me first. For a moment, she just studied me, as if searching for something beneath the surface.

"You need to train," she said finally. "You have more power than you realize, more than any of us can afford for you to waste." She didn't wait for me to answer. "Vallerie will work with you," Lorelei went on, nodding toward her. "Her mark, memory weaving, isn't the same as your empathy, but it touches the same depths. Both require entering into someone else's inner world. She can help you learn to set boundaries inside yourself. To protect your mind as much as your heart."

She glanced toward Kaylen and Cade. "Kaylen and Cade will handle your physical training. Strength, endurance, combat. Your magic is powerful, but your body needs to be able to carry it. To withstand it."

Lorelei stepped closer, close enough that her voice dropped to something almost intimate. "You don't just survive this by hiding. You survive by becoming someone he can't touch. Someone he can't even approach without paying a price."

I opened my mouth, but nothing came out.

Lorelei's eyes softened, just for a moment. She reached out and laid a hand gently on my arm. "We'll be with you every step. But you have to choose to fight." She paused, eyes

273

moving to Allie and Sarah before returning to mine. "All of you do."

I nodded once, a sharp, instinctive movement. Allie echoed it beside me, her jaw set. Sarah squeezed my wrist lightly, her silent way of agreeing.

Gage stepped forward then, holding out a small box. "Here," he said. "Untraceable phones. They look normal, but they're clean. No trackers, no way for Michael to find you through them."

He glanced at us, his expression serious but kind. "You can't keep your own phones. It's too risky. He could track them to the safehouse, even if they're turned off. You can still call or text your family if you need to. Just... keep it short. And don't share your location or mention the safehouse. We can't risk it."

Sarah reached for one, turning it over in her hand. "I need to write down some numbers first," she said, her voice tight. "My mom would lose her mind if I just disappeared."

Gage nodded, his voice softer. "Of course."

One by one, we handed over our old phones. Sarah had scribbled a few numbers onto a scrap of paper, her fingers trembling. Allie hesitated, her thumb brushing the screen one last time before passing it to Gage. I didn't bother to write anything down. Everyone I cared about was right here with me.

We then piled into the jeeps without much ceremony. Allie, Sarah, and I climbed into the back of the one Kaylen would drive. Cade settled into the passenger seat, his frame tense but focused. The others loaded into Alice's jeep, doors slamming shut in quick succession.

The engines roared softly as the compound began to slip away behind us. Cade sat silently in the passenger seat, eyes scanning the treeline like he expected an attack at any moment. The road stretched on, headlights slicing through the dark, trees flashing past in quick, steady rhythm. Biscuit purred in my lap, her fur warm against my hands.

Allie leaned forward slightly. "How long until we get there?"

Kaylen didn't even look back. "Long enough for me to regret agreeing to this babysitting gig."

Allie stiffened beside me, but before she could respond, Sarah leaned forward, her voice sharp. "Wow. Do you practice that attitude in the mirror, or are you just naturally insufferable?"

From the front seat, Cade let out a low, surprised breath, almost a laugh, and a small, approving smile tugged at the corner of his mouth. Then he glanced back, his gaze moving to each of us before landing on Allie. "We'll be there in a couple of hours," he said.

I lowered my gaze to Biscuit, who had already started to curl into a small ball in my lap. I stroked her fur slowly, focusing on the warmth seeping into my hands. The steady drone of the engine and the gentle sway of the jeep pulled at my focus, dragging me toward sleep. My eyes slipped closed, the darkness behind my lids surprisingly quiet for once.

I don't know how long I dozed. There were no dreams, just a blank stretch that felt like floating. When I blinked awake again, the jeep was rolling to a stop, gravel popping under the tires. I pushed up straighter and peered outside.

A large log cabin stood nestled among the trees. Its wood siding glowed warmly in the headlights, and soft golden light shone through a few windows. A porch wrapped around the front, and a tall stone chimney reached into the sky.

Kaylen shut off the engine, and Cade was already stepping out, moving around to open the back door before we could react.

"Come on," he said. "We'll figure out rooms inside."

I gathered Biscuit, who squirmed once before settling, her small head pressing under my chin. Allie and Sarah climbed out beside me, stretching and glancing around. The second jeep pulled in behind us, headlights cutting briefly across the drive before flicking off.

For a moment, we all stood facing the cabin, the smell of pine drifting faintly around us. Then, we all grabbed our bags and moved forward toward the door.

We stepped inside, and the warmth hit me immediately. The cabin had thick wooden beams that stretched across the high ceiling, a wide stone fireplace dominated one wall, and plush couches and chairs crowded around it in a half-circle. The scent of cedar curled through the air, and warm light spilled from lantern-style fixtures, pushing the night firmly out.

Beyond the living area, the space opened seamlessly into a large kitchen. A long counter divided the two spaces, lined with sturdy wooden bar stools that looked handmade. The kitchen itself was all warm wood and matte black fixtures, with a massive farmhouse sink and a wide stove that looked ready to feed a small army. A long, rustic dining table sat nearby, flanked by mismatched chairs that somehow all belonged together, ready for shared meals and late-night conversations.

Cade shut the door behind us, his boots thudding softly on the hardwood. He surveyed the space, then turned toward us.

"There are only five bedrooms," he said. "Some of you will need to bunk up, but there are enough beds for you each to have your own. I'll take the couch. It's easier to keep watch from here."

Allie glanced at me and Sarah, and without hesitation, she said, "We'll stay together."

Sarah echoed her with a quick, quiet, "Obviously."

Vallerie stepped forward next, her hand brushing lightly against Kaylen's arm. "I'll share with Kaylen," she said simply.

Alice looked around, pushing a strand of hair behind her ear. "I can bunk with whoever," she offered, her voice practical, already moving forward to set her bag down.

Marcela stepped forward, her dark eyes steady. "With me," she said, her tone leaving no room for argument. Alice gave her a small, grateful nod.

Hiro stood at the edge of the group, watching the rest of us quietly. Finally, he gave a single short shrug and headed down a hallway toward one of the rooms, claiming it without a word.

That left one spare room, but Cade only shook his head, resolute.

"I'll stay out here," he said again, softer this time. "Close to the door. Just in case. The biggest bedroom is upstairs and to the right. It has three beds," he said, jerking his chin toward the narrow staircase that hugged the wall. "Should be plenty of space for the three of you."

Allie stepped forward and hefted her bag. Sarah followed, rubbing a thumb over her phone's new case like a nervous tic. I adjusted Biscuit in my arms and grabbed my own bag. Without another word, we climbed the stairs together and turned down the short hall, the wooden floor creaking softly beneath our feet.

At the end, we found the room. It felt more like a small, cozy loft than a standard bedroom. Warm wood paneling covered the walls, and an angled ceiling made the space feel tucked away, almost secret. A small door opened up to an attached bathroom and a thick rug covered most of the floor, worn but soft beneath our feet.

Instead of one big bed, there were three twin beds arranged in an L-shape against the far walls. Simple, sturdy wooden frames, each piled with mismatched quilts and extra blankets folded at the foot. A small dresser stood in the corner with an old mirror propped on top, and a narrow window looked out into the trees.

Allie dropped her bag by the bed closest to the window and let out a quiet sigh. Sarah set hers down next to the middle bed, her fingers hesitating on the zipper before she finally pulled it open. She rummaged for a second, then pulled out Abel's badge. Her shoulders tensed as she looked at it, her thumb brushing over the worn metal. Then she leaned forward and carefully slid it under her pillow. She sat there for a moment longer, staring at the bed as if gathering herself.

277

I moved to the last bed, gently setting Biscuit down on the quilt. She immediately started kneading the fabric. I dropped my bag beside the bed and unzipped it, pulling out Biscuit's bowls and the small bag of litter I'd managed to bring. I found a spot in the corner near the dresser, poured water into one bowl and kibble into the other, then set up the litter box.

Biscuit watched me from the bed, her ears twitching, as if judging my setup. When I finished, she hopped down, sniffed each bowl, then turned back toward the bed as if to say *acceptable* before curling up.

Allie let out a quiet, strained laugh and shook her head. "I can't believe she still acts like she owns the place no matter where we go."

Sarah leaned against her bedpost, arms crossed, her expression softening for the first time in what felt like days. "She does. We're all just guests in her empire."

I glanced at them, feeling that rare warmth spark in my chest. "She's the real boss here. We all know it."

Allie sank onto her bed, running a hand through her hair. "God, I don't even know how to sleep after tonight."

Sarah dropped onto her mattress, bouncing slightly, and rolled her eyes. "I think it's like riding a bike. You just… do it."

Allie snorted, a small sound that almost passed for a laugh. Then she glanced down at her dirt-streaked arms and wrinkled shirt, her nose wrinkling. "But first… showers. I smell like smoke."

Sarah made a face. "Agreed. You go first. Just don't use all the hot water or I swear to God…"

Allie pushed up from the bed with a groan. "No promises." She grabbed fresh clothes from her bag and disappeared into the attached bathroom. The distant sound of running water started almost immediately.

Sarah flopped backward on her bed, staring at the ceiling. "I know I joked about riding a bike, but honestly… I don't think I've been this tired since… ever."

I dropped onto my own bed, stretching my legs out, the quilt soft beneath me. "We'll sleep. Even if it takes a while, our bodies will force us to."

Sarah rolled onto her side to face me, her eyes softer now. After a second, she reached under her pillow, fingers brushing something unseen, as if to check that it was still there. She didn't say anything, but her shoulders seemed to ease just a fraction.

The bathroom door finally opened, steam billowing out as Allie stepped into the room, her hair damp and twisted up messily, her skin flushed from the heat. She looked slightly more human, a little less haunted. She tossed her dirty clothes toward her bag and gave a tired half-smile. "Your turn."

I nodded, pushing up and gathering my own clean clothes. I stepped into the small bathroom, shutting the door behind me. The mirror was still fogged from Allie's shower, and for a moment I just stood there, watching my blurred reflection.

Then I stripped off my clothes and stepped under the hot spray. The water felt like it was washing away more than just sweat and dirt. It felt like a small, fragile piece of myself coming back.

By the time I emerged, hair damp and skin warm, Allie was already lying down. Sarah sat up as I entered, grabbing her own clothes with a grunt.

"Last one in," she muttered, rolling her eyes as she slipped past me into the bathroom.

I settled onto my bed, reaching out to stroke Biscuit's fur. She stood, head butting against my hand before laying back down and curling into a little ball.

"I need to tell you something," I said softly to Allie.

Allie turned, just enough to glance back at me over her shoulder.

"It's about Mom and Dad."

Her gaze sharpened. She turned fully then, propping herself up on one elbow.

279

"They didn't die by accident," I said. "Michael killed them."

Allie stilled. Her face didn't move, but something in her eyes cracked.

I kept going. "I guess Mom had a hint of magic. Just enough to *sense* something was wrong with him. She tried to warn me more than once... but I didn't listen."

Allie's brow furrowed. "I remember her saying she didn't like him. That he gave her a bad feeling. I thought she was just being paranoid."

"She wasn't. He knew she'd get in the way," I said, unable to stop the tears from falling.

Allie's lips parted, but no sound came out.

"He used persuasion on Dad. Right before they got in the car," I continued. "He made Dad crash the car."

Allie's face crumpled for just a second before she clenched her jaw, blinking hard.

"He murdered them," she said, her voice like gravel.

I nodded. "I'm sorry I didn't tell you sooner. I didn't want to—"

"Don't." She shook her head, sharp and fierce. "Don't protect me from this. I needed to know."

"I'm sorry," I choked out. "I didn't know. I let him in and I'm so goddamn sorry—"

My voice broke. "I should've seen it. I should've known."

Allie was already moving. She crossed the room in two steps and dropped beside my bed, wrapping her arms around me so tightly it knocked the breath from my lungs.

I buried my face in her shoulder, and we just held on—trembling, sobbing, breaking.

"This wasn't you," she whispered fiercely. "You didn't do this. *He* did."

I couldn't stop crying. "But I loved him. God, Allie, I *loved* him—"

"I know," she said, holding me tighter. "And he used that against you. That's what monsters do."

We stayed like that, two broken pieces clinging together, letting the grief out in heaving breaths and quiet apologies.

The hot water still ran behind the bathroom door, hiding our pain in the steam.

Sarah eventually stepped out, towel in hand, her hair dripping and skin flushed from the heat. She stopped mid-step, eyes darting between us—me sitting rigid on the edge of the bed, tears still fresh, and Allie, curled beside me, eyes red.

Her voice softened immediately. "What happened?"

Neither of us answered right away. I swiped at my face and looked down, unable to form the words.

"Michael killed our parents," Allie said quietly.

Sarah's mouth dropped. "What?"

Allie nodded. "He... used persuasion on our dad and that's what caused the crash. Our mom had a touch of magic. She sensed something was off about him and tried to warn Lena."

Sarah sat down hard on the edge of her bed, towel forgotten. "Jesus."

I looked at her, guilt flooding my chest. "She did try. I just... I didn't want to believe her."

Allie reached over, squeezing my hand again. "That's not on you. He's the one who did it. Not you."

I swallowed hard. "I'm so sorry."

"I know," Allie whispered. "Me too."

Sarah leaned forward, pressing her elbows to her knees. "God, I hate him."

None of us spoke for a long moment. The room settled into quiet again—thick with grief, but not alone.

I wiped at my face, the tears still coming in quiet waves. "If Mom saw me now..." My voice cracked. "If she knew what I let happen, what I brought into our lives, do you think she'd still look at me the same?"

Allie turned to face me fully, her eyes already glassy again. "Don't you dare ask that. She was Mom," Allie said, like it was a fact that could break stone. "You could've torched the whole goddamn neighborhood and she'd still hold your face in her hands and ask if you were okay."

I let out a shaky breath.

"She loved us," Allie continued, softer now. "In this wild, stubborn, unstoppable way. And if she were here? She'd be holding you right now. She'd tell you this wasn't your fault. That loving the wrong person doesn't make you bad. That you were good. Still are."

My throat burned. I nodded, but it didn't stop the tears. "I just miss her," I whispered. "I miss them both."

"I know," Allie said, brushing my hand with hers. "So do I."

She sat there a minute longer, then sniffed hard and wiped at her face with the back of her arm like she was mad at the tears for still being there.

Finally, Allie stood. "We should try to sleep."

We all moved slowly, like our bodies weighed more now. Allie curled beneath her blanket, her back to the wall. Sarah lay facing the ceiling, eyes unfocused. I stretched out on my bed beside Biscuit, who tucked herself against my legs.

I laid still, eyes open, the ceiling above me blurred. I saw my parents in flashes—Mom laughing at something Dad said, Dad pulling me into a hug after a hard day. They were good people. And I let a monster into our lives.

I turned my face into the pillow, heart cracking all over again. Sleep came slow and cruel. And even in my dream, I couldn't stop hearing the crash.

Chapter 24

I didn't know what time it was when I woke up. My body felt heavy, my head thick, but I forced myself up anyway.

Allie and Sarah were still asleep. Allie's arm was thrown over her eyes, her hair a tangled mess on the pillow. Sarah had curled up on her side, one hand tucked beneath her cheek, Abel's badge hidden under her pillow.

I moved slowly, careful not to wake them, and slipped out of bed. Biscuit lifted her head to watch me but didn't bother to move.

When I made it downstairs, Vallerie was standing by the back door drinking a cup of coffee. She was dressed in simple jeans and a sweater with her brown hair pulled back in a bun. She tilted her head slightly. "Sleep okay?"

I shrugged, rubbing my neck. "As well as I could."

A small understanding smile touched the edge of her mouth. "Good enough." She looked me over again, assessing but not unkind.

"Get something to eat and then get dressed," she said. "I want to start working with you and your mark. We'll go outside when you're ready."

"Why outside?" I asked, clearing my throat.

Vallerie shrugged, utterly matter-of-fact. "Fresh air helps. And fewer walls to absorb whatever you might throw at me."

My stomach twisted at the thought, but I nodded.

"Take your time," she added, already turning to look out through the glass door at the trees beyond. "But not too much time. We've got a lot of work to do."

I glanced toward the kitchen, the faint smell of coffee drifting out in a quiet invitation. For a moment, I almost felt normal, like it was just another morning in a house full of people who weren't preparing to fight a monster.

But that feeling was gone as quickly as it came.

I poured myself a mug of coffee, found a breakfast bar on the counter—something quick, easy, no real taste but enough to quiet the hollow ache in my stomach.

Afterward, I slipped back upstairs. Allie and Sarah were still asleep, so I quietly pulled on a clean crew neck sweater and leggings, brushed my hair until it looked halfway human again, and took a moment to wash my face and brush my teeth.

When I finally stepped out onto the back patio, the mug still clutched in my hands, Vallerie was waiting.

"You ready?" she asked.

I nodded, even though my hands were still shaking slightly.

She studied me for a moment, then added, "Before we start, I wanted you to know. I spoke with Lorelei. We're moving Corinne to a different facility."

My heart skipped. "Why? Is something wrong?"

"No," she said quickly. "But we can't risk Michael using her to get to you. The new place will have stricter security protocols, and we're admitting her under a false name. He won't be able to find her."

My chest filled with dread at the thought of him finding her. "She won't understand what's happening."

"She won't be hurt," Vallerie promised. "She'll be confused, maybe unsettled, but safe. That has to come first."

A wave of guilt rolled through me, sharp and sudden, gone just as quickly.

Vallerie turned to face me fully, tucking a loose strand of hair behind her ear.

"Our marks might seem nothing alike," she continued, "but in the end, they're both deeply tied to connection. Mine is memory work. Yours is empathy. Both force us to open ourselves to other people, to feel what they carry, even when we don't want to."

She paused, glancing away as though looking for the right words. "When my mark first manifested, it was chaos," she said. "I'd be talking to someone, and pieces of their memories would slip through. Sometimes I wouldn't even realize I was changing them until it was too late. I didn't have control."

She turned her gaze back to me. "I had to learn to focus. To reach for what I needed instead of letting it crash through me. To feel without getting lost inside someone else's mind."

She stepped a little closer. "Have you ever been able to control your empathy?"

I hesitated. My fingers fumbled at the hem of my shirt. "There was one time," I said. "A few weeks after Abel died. Sarah was falling apart, and I... I don't know how, but I pushed this feeling of calm into her and it worked. She felt peace for a little bit."

Vallerie's eyes softened slightly. "And the rest of the time?"

"It just happens," I admitted. "Sometimes I don't feel anything. Other times I feel everything. And when I can't hold it anymore, it explodes out."

Vallerie gave a slow nod. "That's what we're going to change," she said. "The mark doesn't own you. You decide what to hold and what to let go. You decide who gets to feel you and who you get to feel."

Vallerie motioned for me to follow her to a pair of weathered wooden chairs set a little ways back. She sat in one and gestured for me to take the other.

I sank into the chair slowly, my coffee still warm in my hands, and set it down on the small table between us.

She leaned forward slightly, her voice lowering. "Close your eyes."

I hesitated but obeyed, pressing my palms to my knees to keep them from shaking.

"Breathe," she murmured. "In... and out. Find that place inside you where the mark lives. The place where you keep it caged."

I inhaled slowly, feeling the tangle of raw edges inside me. The grief. The fear. The flash of rage I barely understood.

"Good," Vallerie said softly. "Now... instead of pushing it away, let it come forward. Just a little."

My chest tightened. My fingers curled into the fabric of my leggings.

"Steady," she coached. "Feel it... but don't drown in it. You decide how deep to go."

A tremor rolled through me. The emotions flooded closer, heat rising under my skin like a tide creeping in. My throat ached. I tried to hold them, like Vallerie said. But the second I thought I had them contained, something inside me lurched. A sharp heat burst in my chest and rushed outward before I could stop it.

Vallerie sucked in a sudden breath, her eyes going wide. Her hand flew to her heart, her shoulders curling forward. "Lena—" she gasped.

I shot up from my chair, panic tearing through me. "I'm sorry—God, I didn't mean—"

Vallerie lifted a hand shakily, stopping me. She took a few uneven breaths, her fingers trembling. Slowly, her posture straightened, and she let out a long, shaky exhale.

"It's all right," she managed, her voice thin but steady. "You didn't hurt me. But you did project."

I stood frozen, my pulse pounding in my throat.

Vallerie's gaze softened as she looked up at me. "That... was strong," she said, almost to herself. She took another slow breath, her fingers still flexing lightly. "I think... you even *amplified* the emotions. That's part of your mark. The ability not just to share or project, but to magnify feelings inside someone else."

She paused, studying my face. "With control, you'll be able to choose which emotion you want someone to feel and decide exactly how strongly they feel it. Comfort, calm, fear... even rage. All of it. At any degree you choose."

I swallowed, my mouth suddenly dry. The idea of that much power, to build someone up or break them entirely, felt like holding a live wire in my hands.

"I feel like... it's going to take forever for me to be able to control it," I said, my voice low.

Vallerie gave a small, understanding smile. "It might feel that way now. But, with help, you'll get there faster than you think.

Vallerie studied me a moment longer, then straightened, her expression thoughtful. "Okay," she said finally, her voice firmer now. "Let's try something different."

She leaned forward slightly, her eyes steady on mine. "I want you to dig deep and feel all of your emotions. You don't have to let them overwhelm you, just *feel* them. Try to separate them out, like pulling apart tangled threads."

She paused, waiting to make sure I was following. "Then," she continued, "I want you to assign a color to each one. Any color you choose. Don't overthink it. Just let it happen."

My brows drew together, but I nodded slowly.

Vallerie gave me an encouraging look. "Once you have them separated and colored, I want you to focus on just one. Pick a single color, a single emotion. Then try to project only *that* one to me. Make me feel it and nothing else."

I closed my eyes again, trying to follow her instructions. I pictured my emotions laid out in front of me, each one its own bright knot.

Rage came first—hot and sharp, pulsing like an open wound. Red.

Anxiety hovered behind it—restless, electric. Blue.

Grief sat heavy in my chest—deep, aching. Gray.

Guilt coiled tight around my ribs—dark green, thick and thorny.

Fear curled low in my gut—deep purple.

But somewhere underneath all of it, was something softer. The tiniest ember of happiness that hadn't fully died out.

Yellow.

I focused on that yellow. Let it glow a little brighter, just enough to make the other colors fade into a quiet background hum.

When I felt it steady, a small warmth sparking behind my ribs, I opened my eyes. Vallerie's gaze met mine, patient but alert.

287

I pictured the yellow in my mind, bright and warm, and imagined it flowing from me to her, like a thin stream of golden light stretching across the space between us.

For a moment, nothing happened. Then I saw her shoulders ease, the tension in her jaw softening. A slow, gentle smile spread across her face—not forced or polite, but genuine.

She exhaled, her eyes brightening as she looked at me. "That's it," she said softly. "You did it."

"I did?" I asked, my voice thin, like I might shatter it just by speaking.

Vallerie nodded, her smile lingering. "You did. You made me feel... a real, gentle happiness. Clear as day."

I blinked hard, my hands curling slightly in my lap. A tiny laugh slipped out and I pressed a hand to my chest, almost like I was checking if my heart was still there.

A flush of warmth spread through me, mixing with the faint echo of that yellow light I'd conjured.

"I didn't think it would actually work," I said.

"It did," Vallerie replied. "Because you trusted it. You trusted yourself, even for just a moment."

I looked down at my palms, trying to steady my breathing. Maybe I wasn't as broken as I thought. Maybe there was a version of me under all the wreckage who could still do this, who could still fight back.

A new thread of confidence wound through my ribs, fragile but real. I looked back up at Vallerie. "Can we try again?"

We kept going. Over and over. Vallerie guided me through each emotion like a patient conductor—pushing me to separate them, to shape them, to trust them.

Somewhere along the way, others started gathering outside. Cade leaned against the railing with his arms crossed, his bright green eyes tracking every movement in me. Kaylen watched from a few steps back, her expression unreadable but her focus unmistakable. Even Hiro appeared briefly, a mug of something steaming in his hand, his gaze moving between us before he quietly settled against the wall.

At one point around lunch time, Allie marched outside with a plate in each hand and insisted we take a break. She pushed a sandwich into my hands and sat nearby with Sarah, watching like a pair of worried parents at a school recital.

By midafternoon, my mind felt like a frayed wire—buzzing, tender, but alive. I had managed to project different emotions at different strengths. A ripple of calm, a sharp pulse of frustration, a comforting warmth that left Vallerie blinking hard for a moment before she collected herself.

Vallerie finally stepped back, exhaling deeply. "That's enough for today," she said. "You need to rest your mind before it burns out. Besides…" Her gaze turned toward Cade, still leaning against the railing. "I think you have another teacher waiting."

The thought of training with Cade sent a ripple through my chest—part nerves, part curiosity, maybe even a tiny edge of excitement. I didn't know what to expect. But after this morning, a part of me wanted to see what else I was capable of.

Cade walked over to me and said, "Get some water. Grab a quick snack if you need. Meet me back here in ten."

I headed to the kitchen and grabbed a bottle of water and a handful of trail mix from a bowl someone had set out. My hands felt clumsy, my mind buzzing with everything Vallerie had pushed me to feel.

A moment later, Sarah slipped in behind me. She leaned against the counter, arms crossed loosely over her hoodie. "You good?"

I hesitated, hand hovering over a granola bar. "I think so," I said. "It's… a lot. I didn't realize how much control this would take."

Sarah snorted. "Yeah, no shit. You're basically learning to be a magical emotional sniper. Not exactly a weekend hobby."

A short laugh slipped out of me. I grabbed the granola bar and ripped it open, taking a small bite.

Sarah watched me, her expression softening. "You're doing better than you think," she said. "I mean, I wouldn't want to be on the other end of your rage when you figure it all out."

I raised an eyebrow at her, chewing. "Comforting."

She pushed off the counter and bumped her shoulder lightly into mine on her way past. "Go kick his ass," she said over her shoulder. "But like... in a sexy, empowering way."

I rolled my eyes, another laugh threatening, but it stayed lodged in my chest as I watched her slip out toward the patio. I finished the bar quickly, took another long sip of water, then made my way to the backyard.

Cade was already there, standing in the center of the yard beyond the patio. He wasn't stretching or showing off. He was just standing, hands loose at his sides, watching the treeline as if listening to something only he could hear. He wore dark pants and a charcoal-gray shirt, both loose enough to move in, but snug enough to show every muscle trying to press through. His boots were worn, his stance relaxed but alert, like he was always halfway to action.

The others were scattered across the patio. Allie leaned against a post, arms crossed tight, her jaw set in a firm line. Sarah sat on the top step, her gaze darting between Cade and me, eyes bright with anticipation. Kaylen stood near the railing, long dark hair pulled back, arms folded and expression unreadable. Vallerie, composed as ever, stood with one hand resting lightly on the back of a chair that Marcela sat in. Alice, short but solid, crouched casually near the edge, her elbows on her knees. Hiro watched from the shadows near the house, tall and still, his dark eyes tracking every movement without a word.

Cade finally turned as I approached, his gaze sweeping over me once, quick and assessing.

"You hanging in there?" he asked.

"Yep," I said, adjusting my stance slightly.

He didn't reply, just stepped closer and tapped the side of my ankle with his boot. "Square your stance. Ground first. Always."

290

I moved my feet, feeling suddenly aware of every awkward angle, every breath. He moved around me once, correcting small things—a touch to my elbow, a gentle push at my shoulder to straighten it out. His hands were firm but careful, and each small contact sent a sharp, electric awareness through my skin.

He didn't flirt. He didn't tease. But the closeness—the way he stepped into my space without hesitation, like he belonged there—sparked something low in my chest I couldn't quite name.

Once he seemed satisfied, Cade stepped back a few paces. His gaze locked on mine, steady and unreadable.

"First lesson," he said. "Balance isn't just physical. It's in your head too. You lose it here—" he tapped his temple lightly, "—you lose it everywhere."

I looked at him, trying to keep my breathing even.

He lifted a hand and beckoned me forward. "Come at me. Try to move me."

I hesitated. "Move you how?"

"Any way you can," he said. "Push me. Try to throw me off balance. Doesn't matter how. Just try."

For a second, I stood frozen, my mind stuttering. Then I lunged forward, aiming a push at his chest.

He didn't budge.

"Again," he said, voice calm.

I pushed harder. He caught my wrists easily, turning them just enough to redirect my force so I stumbled sideways.

Heat rose up my neck.

"Again," he repeated.

I tried again and again, each time with more force, more frustration threading through my movements. Cade's hands were always there—redirecting, catching, guiding. Each touch lit a spark under my skin.

"Stop fighting like you're asking permission," he finally snapped, his voice cutting through my rising panic. "You're not here to play nice. You're not here to hold back. Move me."

Something in me snapped at that. My pulse roared in my ears. I lunged forward again, my whole weight behind the shove.

This time, he let me push him back a step. Just one.

My chest heaved, my hands trembling where they rested against him.

When I looked up, his mouth was curved into the barest hint of a smile, proud and edged with something fierce.

"Good," he murmured. "That's it."

For a heartbeat, neither of us moved. The distance between us felt electric. I felt every inch of him—the strength under my hands, the steadiness in his breath.

Then he stepped back, rolling his shoulders out. "Again," he said, but there was a softer note threaded through now. Encouragement.

Out of the corner of my eye, I saw Allie's arms slowly lower, her posture loosening. Sarah leaned forward on the steps, her eyes bright, her mouth parted like she wanted to cheer but was holding back.

I lunged again, this time aiming low, trying to catch him off guard at the waist. He moved easily, stepping aside and letting me move past him.

"Better," he said, turning smoothly to face me again. "But you're still hesitating. You think too much."

I turned back, breathing hard. My heart pounded in my throat, my palms damp.

"How do I *not* think?" I snapped, frustration bleeding into my voice.

His eyes locked on mine. "You stop asking for permission. You trust your body. You let go of the fear of failing."

I swallowed, that spark in my chest stuttering, then flaring hotter.

Without warning, Cade stepped forward, closing the space between us fast. He hooked his arm lightly around mine and pushed, sending me sprawling backward onto the dirt.

A gasp tore from my throat as I landed, the impact jarring but not painful.

He didn't move to help me up immediately. He just stood there, watching.

"Get up," he demanded.

I pushed up, my arms shaking, and stood. Dirt clung to my palms, my hair falling loose around my face.

Again, he advanced, fast and sharp. This time, I braced and ducked, instinct flaring. I shoved upward with everything I had.

He staggered back a step, surprise flashing across his face.

A rush of exhilaration shot through me, so strong it nearly took my breath.

Cade's mouth twitched. "Good," he said, breathless now too. "Again."

I didn't wait this time. I moved first, driving toward him with all my weight. He met me, his hands locking around my arms to redirect, but I twisted and broke free, forcing him to pivot sharply to keep his balance.

A cheer broke out behind me—Sarah's voice, bright and sharp.

Cade's grip tightened on my arm, and before I could react, he swept my leg out, dropping me back onto the ground.

I landed with a grunt, my back hitting the earth.

He stood over me, his chest heaving, a faint flush on his neck. For a moment, we both just stared at each other.

God, those eyes.

Then, slowly, he offered his hand.

I took it, my fingers closing around his. His hand was rough and warm and impossibly steady.

He pulled me up in one strong, fluid motion.

For a second, we didn't let go. My heart slammed against my ribs, every nerve humming.

We kept going. Cade didn't let up, and I didn't want him to. We practiced dodging, learning when to hold my ground and when to move. He corrected my stance a hundred times, each small adjustment making me feel more solid, more rooted.

We went over blocking, how to use my arms and shoulders to deflect blows without wasting energy. He showed me where to center my weight, how to stay balanced even when it felt impossible.

At one point, he knocked me down three times in a row, and each time, I got up faster. Dirt caked my palms and knees, sweat ran down my spine, and my breath came in tattered gasps. But under the exhaustion, there was a quiet thrill. A sense of power creeping back in.

Through it all, Cade stayed focused. Encouraging, patient, but unyielding. Every once in a while, I'd catch a glimmer of approval in his eyes—a small, hard-won spark that pushed me to keep going.

When we finally paused, my arms hung heavy at my sides, my legs trembling with fatigue. I leaned forward, hands on my thighs, trying to catch my breath.

Cade watched me for a long moment. "Good work," he said. "That's enough for today."

Behind us, Sarah whooped, and Allie let out a low, incredulous laugh. The others were still watching from the patio, some with cautious smiles, some with quiet respect.

I straightened slowly, wiping the sweat from my forehead, and met Cade's gaze. Then I let myself smile.

Cade stepped closer, his expression softer now that the intensity had drained away.

"You did good," he said, his voice low enough that only I could hear. "Really good."

I let out a shaky laugh. "Thanks. I feel like I got hit by a truck, but... in a good way."

He smiled. "That's the idea."

For a moment, we just stood there. Close enough that I could feel the warmth of him, see the tiny scratches on his forearms, the sweat darkening the edge of his hair.

I swallowed, glancing at the patio where the others were still gathered. "Should we... head in?" I asked.

He nodded, stepping back just enough to give me room. "Yeah," he said. "Whenever you're ready."

I nodded, drawing in one last deep breath before turning toward the house. The others began to move too, the quiet hum of conversation starting up again as we all went inside.

Upstairs, I peeled off my clothes and caught a glimpse of myself in the mirror. Darkening bruises mapped their way across my ribs and hips, thin scratches ribboned over my arms and shoulders.

I let the hot water run longer than necessary, scrubbing away the dirt and sweat from the day. When I finally stepped out and toweled off, I felt like I'd shed a layer I didn't know I'd been carrying.

By the time I made it downstairs, the smell of food hit me like a wave—garlic, herbs, something rich and savory. I turned the corner and saw Marcela moving through the kitchen like she owned it, her dark curls swinging behind her as she stirred a steaming pot on the stove with one hand and slid a tray of golden, bubbling rolls into the oven with the other. Her skin glowed in the amber light, sleeves rolled to her elbows, cheeks slightly flushed from the heat.

I glanced at the clock above the fireplace. Eight o'clock. I hadn't even realized how late it had gotten. I slipped into a seat at the counter, my hair still damp against the back of my neck.

Marcela glanced over her shoulder when she heard me enter. "I hope you like chicken and noodles and dinner rolls," she said, nodding toward the stove. "It's not fancy, but it'll fill you up."

"Sounds perfect," I said. Someone must have made a grocery run while I was outside training.

People started floating in, pulled by the smell. Allie and Sarah took seats at the counter next to me. Vallerie and Kaylen claimed spots at the big table, their heads ducked close in quiet conversation. Hiro lingered at the edge, leaning against the wall with that silent, observant presence he carried everywhere.

Alice slipped in next, moving quietly but with an ease that said she was always half-ready for a fight. She dropped into a chair beside Kaylen, stretching her arms above her head before leaning forward on her elbows.

Cade entered a moment later, sliding onto a stool at the far end of the counter. His hair was still damp from his own shower, and he gave me a small smile when our eyes met.

Marcela finally turned off the stove and started plating. "Help yourselves," she said. "Eat before it gets cold."

It didn't take long before the sound of forks on bowls and quiet sighs of relief filled the kitchen.

I hadn't realized just how hungry I was until I tasted the first bite. The chicken was tender and perfectly seasoned, the noodles silky and lightly coated in a rich, savory sauce. The dinner roll was warm and soft, the butter melting into every crevice.

Sarah let out a low groan of approval. "God, I think I might marry you, Marcela."

Marcela snorted without looking up. "You'd have to survive my training first."

Alice let out a small, genuine laugh, shaking her head. "I don't think she'd make it past the first morning drills."

Sarah smirked. "Hey, I've got stamina."

Alice raised an eyebrow. "Do you, though?"

Before Sarah could fire back, she glanced around at the others and grinned. "Okay but seriously, do people date in The Severance? Or is it like... vow of celibacy meets secret magical monk cult?"

A few people chuckled. Even Hiro cracked the faintest hint of a smile.

Vallerie looked up from her bowl, amused. "No vows of celibacy, I promise. People date. Some even marry."

"Really?" Sarah asked, eyebrows raised. "I figured you all just communed with ancient trees and repressed your feelings."

"Seriously," Vallerie added, setting down her fork, "Lorelei and Nick have been married for over ten years."

I swallowed a bite of food. "Lorelei and Nick? Really? I would've never guessed."

"They tend to keep things professional when dealing with situations," Vallerie said with a shrug. "But yes, they're very much married."

Allie leaned forward, glancing around the room. "What about here? Anyone here married?"

For a second, everyone glanced at each other.

"Nope," Alice and Vallerie said at the exact same time.

Kaylen shook her head. "Definitely not."

Marcela shrugged. "No. Came close once though."

Even Hiro gave a small shake of his head, silent but clear.

I glanced at Cade before I could stop myself, heart ticking up for no good reason. He didn't look at me, just quietly said, "No."

My chest did something stupid, like it was trying to remember how to breathe all over again.

Sarah raised an eyebrow at me but said nothing. "So," she said, recovering, "do marked people only date other marked people?"

Vallerie shook her head. "No. We date whoever we want. Marked, unmarked, it doesn't matter. Though, honestly? Sometimes unmarked people don't handle the truth very well. I've had to intervene more than a few times."

Alice grinned. "You mean wipe memories."

Vallerie nodded with a sigh. "Especially with Logan. He thinks he's found the love of his life every other week. I've had to erase so many girlfriends' memories it's honestly embarrassing."

Kaylen snorted. "Didn't one start a TikTok account called 'Dating a Warlock'?"

Vallerie huffed. "We had to shut it down after she got half a million followers."

Laughter echoed through the kitchen, easy and warm. Even Cade laughed, his eyes looking up just long enough to meet mine before returning to his plate.

Somewhere near the end of the meal, Cade's phone buzzed against the counter. He glanced at the screen, his expression tightening just slightly.

"It's Gage," he said, already standing as he answered. "Yeah. You're close? ... Got it. See you soon." He ended the call and looked around at the rest of us. "Gage will be here in about ten minutes. He wants to check the security system, make a few updates. Tech stuff."

A few nods moved around the room, forks paused midair.

By the time I pushed my plate away, my eyelids felt heavy, my muscles sluggish and sore in that satisfying way that only came after real work.

A few minutes later, headlights swept across the windows. Cade stood first, glancing toward the door.

Biscuit trotted ahead of him, tail high, and stopped right in front of the door like she intended to screen whoever was on the other side.

Cade paused, then bent down and scooped her up with one arm. "Not your job, sweetheart," he murmured, scratching behind her ear as she blinked lazily. He opened the door with his free hand, and Gage stepped inside, already shrugging off a light jacket.

"Smells like I missed a good meal," Gage said, offering a faint, tired smile as he stepped fully into the room.

Marcela snorted from where she leaned against the counter. "If you're lucky, there might be a roll left."

Gage lifted a hand in a half-salute of surrender. "I'll live."

He set down a small duffel bag by the door and glanced around the room, eyes moving quickly over each of us before settling on Cade. "I'll check the security system first. Then update the perimeter protocols and do a full scan of communications."

As he turned to go, I pushed myself up, the question burning at the back of my throat before I could stop it. "Gage... do you have any new information about Michael?"

The room went still for a moment, everyone's attention on Gage.

Gage looked at me, his expression unreadable for a beat. Then he shook his head, his jaw tightening slightly. "It's been quiet," he said. "Too quiet."

He paused, glancing briefly at Cade before looking back at me. "We've been watching his estate. A few of his men have come and gone, but no sign of Michael himself. No confirmed sightings anywhere else either. We don't even know if he's still in Maine."

Cade spoke up. "He could be laying low because of the threat. If he thinks Gage might go public, that's enough to make him pause."

Gage gave a small nod. "It's possible. The threat of going public might've rattled him more than we expected."

A heavy knot formed low in my stomach. The thought of him simply... gone, moving freely, felt somehow worse than knowing exactly where he was.

Gage's eyes softened, just a fraction. "We're keeping eyes on everything we can. If anything changes, you'll know as soon as we do."

Gage started to turn towards the door when I stopped him. "Wait ... is Corinne safe? Has she been moved?"

He paused, then looked at me with a nod of reassurance. "She's secure. We got her relocated early this morning. The new facility's private, unlisted, and her name's not attached to anything. No paper trail. No access from outside."

A quiet breath of relief slipped out of me. "So he can't find her?"

"No," Gage said firmly. "She's untraceable. He'd have to be a goddamn psychic, and even then he'd hit a dozen dead ends first."

My chest loosened, the knot there unwinding just a little.

"Thank you," I said softly.

"Of course," he replied as he headed out with Cade to check the security system and perimeter.

Marcela and Vallerie started clearing dishes in the kitchen. Sarah offered to help, but they declined and said she could do dinner tomorrow night.

Allie's eyes scanned the kitchen before landing on a dusty bottle of red wine on a high shelf. She raised her brows at me and Sarah.

"Back patio?" she suggested.

I didn't even hesitate. "Yes."

Sarah grabbed three mismatched glasses from a cabinet, and we slipped outside into the evening air. It was cooler now, a light breeze carrying the scent of pine. Allie popped the cork, managing not to spill, and poured each of us a generous glass. We sank into the patio chairs, the quiet around us feeling almost too big after everything.

Sarah's burner phone buzzed and she pulled it out, tapping quickly. Allie squinted at her. "Who are you texting?"

Sarah hesitated, her thumb hovering over the screen. "Jack," she admitted finally.

Allie's eyebrows shot up. "Oh?"

Sarah let out a breath, her shoulders slumping. "He's worried. I told him we're staying with friends, but... he isn't buying it. He knows something's off."

Allie studied her for a moment. "He sounds like he really cares about you."

Sarah looked away, her fingers tightening around her glass. "Yeah... maybe. But after Abel... I don't know if I can even think about that. Not now." She paused, then forced a small, crooked smile. "But you," she said, gesturing to me. I saw the way you looked at Cade today."

I let out a short, sharp laugh. "Oh, no. Don't start."

Sarah raised her eyebrows, ignoring me. "There were sparks. Admit it."

I shook my head, swallowing hard. "The last man I had sparks with put a hole in my stomach and tried to throw me off a cliff. As far as I'm concerned, I'm going to be single for the rest of my damn life."

Sarah let out a soft, surprised laugh, her eyes shining a little. Allie snorted into her wine.

"Well," Allie said, lifting her glass toward me. "To being single and alive, then."

I clinked my glass against hers, then against Sarah's. "Single and alive."

We drank, and I let the cheap wine burn its way down. Sparks, men, magic—all of it could wait. Tonight, I had wine, my girls, and a porch that wasn't on fire. Good enough.

Chapter 25

I woke up the next morning to a dull, persistent ache running through every inch of my body.

I turned my head, squinting toward the small digital clock on the dresser. 5:07 a.m. Of course. My body apparently decided sleep was optional now.

I grabbed a sweatshirt from the chair and slipped quietly into the hallway, easing the door shut behind me.

The cabin was silent as I padded downstairs, each step an awkward negotiation with my aching legs.

When I stepped into the open living room, I stopped short.

Cade was sprawled on the couch, one arm slung over his chest, and there, curled up like a tiny queen on a throne, was Biscuit, sound asleep right on top of him.

"Traitor," I murmured.

I slipped into the kitchen and rummaged through cabinets until I finally found a small first aid kit. Inside, thank God, a bottle of ibuprofen. I popped the cap and shook four into my palm, swallowing them dry.

Behind me, there was a soft grunt and the creak of the couch.

I turned to see Cade pushing himself up, scrubbing a hand over his face. He wore dark sweatpants and a plain tee clinging to him just enough to make it rude. Biscuit jumped down from his chest and trotted over to me without a second glance back, her tail flicking smugly.

"Sorry," I said quickly. "I didn't mean to wake you. I really needed some ibuprofen. Every single muscle hurts. I feel like I've been hit by a truck... then thrown off a cliff for good measure.

Cade looked at me, then let out a low, rough laugh, still half asleep. "You're fine. And... it'll get easier. Eventually."

I let out a dry laugh, shaking my head. "Eventually? That's the most unhelpful motivational speech I've ever heard."

His eyes softened with amusement as he pushed a hand through his hair. "I'll work on my delivery."

I turned to the counter. "Coffee?"

His eyes lit up instantly. "Please."

I started the pot, moving carefully. Cade got up and sat on one of the bar stools, leaning forward on his elbows to watch me.

"You did good yesterday," he said.

I glanced at him over my shoulder. "Good? I fell on my ass like a hundred times."

"And you got back up a hundred times," he said simply. "Most people wouldn't."

I focused on the coffee instead of the way my stomach flipped at his words. When it was done brewing, I poured two mugs and slid one over to him.

Just then, footsteps thudded on the stairs. A second later, Sarah appeared, hair sticking up in every possible direction, hoodie half-zipped and eyes barely open.

She squinted at us like she was trying to remember how to speak. "Jesus Christ. Who in their right mind is awake at this hour? Did the world end again?"

I snorted and reached for another mug. "Good morning to you too, sunshine."

Sarah dragged herself to the counter, leaning heavily against it like she might fall asleep standing.

I handed her the coffee, and she wrapped her hands around it like it was the last source of warmth in the universe. "Bless you," she mumbled, taking a cautious sip.

Cade pushed off the stool, stretching his arms overhead. "Think I'll go for a run," he said, almost to himself.

Sarah cracked an eye open. "You mean willingly? Before the sun is even up? You're what's wrong with society."

Cade let out a low laugh, shaking his head as he moved toward the door. He grabbed a pair of worn tennis shoes from beside it and sat on the bench to lace them up. As the door clicked shut behind Cade, I glanced over at Sarah.

304

"Why are you up so damn early?" I asked, trying to sound light, but it came out softer than I meant.

Sarah's eyes dropped to her mug. She shrugged, but the motion was too tight, too practiced.

"Had a dream," she murmured. "About Abel."

My chest tightened. I opened my mouth, but no words came.

Sarah kept staring into her coffee like it might hold an answer. "He was just... there. Making breakfast. Laughing at something stupid I said. And for a second, I forgot." She let out a shaky breath. "When I woke up... I couldn't go back to sleep after that."

I reached out, hesitating before resting my hand lightly on her arm. "I'm so sorry," I said.

She blinked hard, then gave a small, hollow laugh. "Don't apologize. You didn't do it. You didn't take him away."

A beat passed between us, heavy and tender all at once.

"I miss him," she finally said, her voice breaking around the words.

"I know," I said, my own throat tight. "I know."

For a moment, we just stood there in the kitchen, holding onto the warmth of our mugs and the ache of everything we'd lost.

Then Sarah drew in a slow, unsteady breath and squared her shoulders. "God, I need like... ten more cups of this before I even think about facing today."

A thin, fragile smile slipped across my face. "I'll make a second pot."

• • •

Later that morning, after everyone had gathered downstairs, Vallerie found me near the kitchen.

"Ready to work?" she asked, her expression patient but expectant.

I nodded, rolling my shoulders despite the dull ache still lingering there. "As ready as I'll ever be."

305

We stepped outside onto the back patio. The boards were still damp with morning dew, the air cold enough to nip at the edges of my sleeves. A breeze moved through the trees, sharp and brisk, cutting across my skin and reminding me just how sore I really was.

Vallerie crossed the space with smooth, purposeful steps, settling into one of the weathered chairs and motioning for me to do the same.

"Same techniques as yesterday," she said, folding her hands loosely in her lap. "Feel. Separate. Project. And control."

I took a seat, the wood cold against my thighs through my leggings.

"Close your eyes," she said gently. "Breathe."

I obeyed, drawing in a slow inhale through my nose and exhaling through parted lips.

"Good," she murmured. "Now go inward. Find the core. The mark. You know what it feels like now, where it lives."

I searched for it—the dense, shimmering pulse that lived somewhere between bone and soul. It always felt like it was just out of reach until I stopped chasing it.

"There," I whispered.

"Colors," she said. "Separate the emotions. Name them."

My jaw clenched. The swirl was already building—grief, rage, fear, guilt. They rose like heat behind my eyes, each one sticky and loud.

"Red," I murmured. "For the anger."

"What shade?"

"...Bright. Hot."

"Good. Next."

I worked through them one by one. Purple for fear. Gray for grief. Blue for anxiety. Green for guilt. Yellow for happiness. The colors glistened through me like light glancing off water, beautiful and blinding.

"Now pull one forward," Vallerie said. "Only one."

I reached for the yellow, but the red flared instead. Too fast. Too strong.

"Lena," Vallerie said calmly, sensing the shift. "Pull back. Choose."

"I'm trying," I breathed, fingers tightening into fists. "It won't stay—"

The red surged forward, dragging others with it. Grief blurred into rage, guilt fused to fear. The colors collided. My skin felt too tight. The world around me shimmered at the edges like heat off pavement.

"I can't—"

"You can," Vallerie said, her tone sharpened now. "You're in control. You are not a vessel. You are a gate. You open it. You shut it."

I squeezed my eyes tighter, willing myself to find the gate she spoke of. Somewhere in the chaos, I imagined a door. Rusted. Iron. Locked from the inside. I slammed it shut. The emotions recoiled like a snapped rubber band. The weight eased and my chest loosened.

When I opened my eyes, Vallerie was watching me with a kind of solemn approval. Her knuckles were white where they gripped the arm of her chair.

"You almost lost it," she said. "But you didn't."

"I didn't mean to—"

She cut me off with a small shake of her head. "I'm not here to protect your feelings. You did what needed to be done. That's what matters."

I nodded, still catching my breath.

"Let's try again," she said, smoothing her hands over her knees and leaning forward slightly.

"But this time, don't just hold the emotion. Shape it. Choose what it becomes before it reaches me."

I exhaled once, then closed my eyes again.

This time, I was ready.

By afternoon, it was Cade's turn. He waited in the yard with that same quiet focus, and as soon as I joined him, we started right in. My body already felt like one big bruise, and each movement dragged at me like lead. But he never let me stop. Never let me quit.

We worked on stances, dodges, footwork—small corrections and sharp reminders. My muscles screamed, my breath burned, but somehow, I kept moving.

And so it went. The rest of the week blurred into a pattern. Mornings with Vallerie on the patio, afternoons with Cade in the yard. Each day I felt a little stronger. A little more like I was reclaiming my body, my mind, my magic—piece by unsteady piece.

Then, the routine changed. Hiro stepped in next. He didn't announce himself or ask if I was ready. He simply appeared beside me after one of Cade's sessions, tall and silent, with a stillness that somehow made the air feel heavier. He gave a small nod, then turned and walked toward the shaded edge of the yard. I followed without a word.

"Your mark is empathy," he said. "But it's tied to your physical state. If your body is reactive, your magic will be too."

I nodded, unsure if he expected an answer.

"My mark is called sensory link," he continued. "While we train, I'll experience your physical senses in real time. What you see, hear, and feel. Not emotions, just the body. I'll know when you're tense, off balance, or holding your breath before you do."

I blinked. "So you're... already connected?"

"I have been since you walked out here."

The hairs on my arms stood on end.

We began simple—stance work, projection drills, slow emotional builds. But nothing stayed simple with Hiro. He didn't correct with words at first. He would pause, tilt his head slightly, and say something like, "You're favoring your right leg." Or, "Your breath stopped just before you reached for the emotion."

Every time, he was right. It was unsettling, being mirrored like that. It felt like training beside a shadow that knew me better than I knew myself.

"You flinch before you reach for anything volatile," he said as we worked. "You don't trust your own control yet."

"Should I?" I asked, frustrated.

"You should start." Hiro's tone was never harsh, never condescending, but it carried weight. Like he wasn't guessing. Like he already knew where I'd fail before I did.

We circled each other in slow projection drills, where I had to send out a controlled pulse of emotion while maintaining balance and breath. Whenever I slipped, I didn't even have to say it. He already knew.

"Your hands are twitching again. That's fear, not power."

"I'm not afraid," I snapped, even though I was.

Hiro just looked at me, unreadable. "Fear isn't the enemy. Denial is."

I ground my teeth, exhaled through my nose, and tried again. This time, I caught the panic just before it broke through. My spine stayed straight. My breath stayed even. The projection landed, small but clean.

"Better," he said simply.

With each session, the connection became less invasive. I started noticing things before he did. I became aware of my own micro-reactions—the tightening of my jaw, the way I lifted my toes slightly when anxious, how shallow my breathing got when I reached too far.

By the end of our last session, I was drenched in sweat and shaking with fatigue. But I felt more present in my body than I had in weeks.

"You're getting quieter," Hiro said as we finished. "That's a good thing."

Marcela's lessons came next. She met me just after breakfast one day, already outside, her dark curls twisted into a braid and her sleeves rolled up to her elbows, showing all of her elaborate runic tattoos. I swear some of them glowed when the light hit them just right.

A small wooden table had been set up at the edge of the yard, cluttered with vials, herbs, small metal tools, and a ceramic bowl that shimmered faintly with some kind of powder.

"Alchemy is transformation," she said as I approached. "Of the body, the spirit, and the world around you. It's not

309

flashy magic. It's quiet. Intentional. And if you don't respect it..." She lifted a vial delicately between two fingers, "...it will bite."

I stood across from her, watching as she poured a pinch of something violet into the bowl and stirred it gently with the back of a spoon. The scent that rose was sharp and citrusy, laced with something faintly floral.

"What's that for?" I asked.

"A muscle salve," she said. "You're going to need it after Kaylen gets a hold of you."

That pulled a small laugh from me. "Noted."

Marcela gave me a warm smile, then gestured for me to sit on the small bench beside the table. "Your mark isn't alchemy," she said, "but it runs in your blood. Sometimes legacy gives us fragments. Learning the rhythm of this kind of magic can still help you."

I watched her work, movements smooth and methodical. Every ingredient was measured with care, every stir and word deliberate.

She paused and tapped the ceramic bowl with a small iron tool. "Alchemy is part science, part magic, all intention. I can draw runes on weapons, the body, even fabric and infuse them with temporary power. But the magic doesn't last. It fades."

She hesitated. "At least... it's supposed to." A faint crease formed between her brows. "Michael's dagger and your binding spell don't follow the normal rules... ."

"How fast do they fade?" I asked.

"Depends. Some last a few hours. Others, a few days if they're stable enough. Potions work the same way. Most need to be used within a window or they lose potency."

She uncorked a small bottle and handed it to me. The liquid inside shimmered faintly gold. "But I can recharge them. Every couple of days, I pour fresh energy into the symbols or brews and they're good as new."

I held the bottle carefully. "So... anyone can use them after you make them?"

Marcela nodded. "Sure. But only an alchemist can create them. If someone else draws one of my runes, it won't do anything. Looks pretty. No power."

I glanced at tattoos on her arms. My curiosity got the better of me. "Are those runes?"

She smiled. "Runic tattoos. Bound to me. They stay charged because I'm always connected to them. Living circuits."

"What do they do?"

She chuckled. "Depends on the rune. Some help me focus. Others give me a split-second warning when something dangerous is nearby, like a magical sixth sense. Useful in a fight."

"Like a spider-sense?" I said smiling.

Marcela blinked, then grinned. "Exactly like a spider-sense."

I snorted. "That's awesome."

"I can do spells and enchantments too," she added, brushing a curl from her face. "But I don't rely on them during a fight. During battles, seconds matter. You don't always have time to stop and whisper your intentions to the universe."

She tapped one of the runes on her arm. "Potions and runes are faster. I prep them ahead of time and trust the work I've already done. No guesswork or delays."

She poured the finished salve into a small ceramic jar and pressed it into my hand. "For the bruises," she said. "Physical and otherwise."

I hesitated, then said, "We have some journals from my grandma, Margot. Would you... want to see them?"

Marcela's entire expression lifted. Her posture straightened, her eyes lit with something close to awe.

"Did you know her?" I asked.

Marcela shook her head. "Not personally. But I knew of her. Most of us did. An alchemist of her caliber? She was respected. Feared, sometimes. She wasn't just talented, she was wise. She wrote things some of us study. She made breakthroughs no one else has duplicated."

I swallowed, emotion creeping up unexpectedly. "To me, she was just... my quirky grandma with too many jars and too many cats."

"That tracks," Marcela said with a smile. "The best ones are always a little strange."

I laughed quietly. "I think she wanted me to find the journals. Like she left them behind on purpose."

Marcela's voice softened. "Then she probably knew exactly what you'd become."

We spent the rest of the lesson learning about different potions and runes. Marcela explained each one with care, showing me how specific ingredients paired with symbols to direct intent. Partway through, she drew a small rune on my forearm—a swirling design anchored by sharp lines. It glowed briefly when she finished, and a faint tingle ran up my arm, like the magic was testing me too.

"It's just a focus rune," she said. "It should help you sort through the emotions more clearly."

I looked at the mark, unsure what to expect, but as I reached for my emotions, everything felt... quieter. Like someone had turned down the background noise.

"That's wild," I muttered.

Marcela smirked. "Enjoy it, but don't get used to it. You need to learn to control your mark on your own. This is just training wheels, not a crutch."

I nodded, still staring at the rune as if it might start glowing again. Part of me wished I could keep it forever. But the other part, the part that was finally waking up, knew she was right.

After Marcela's lesson, I barely had time to catch my breath before Alice waved me toward the far side of the yard.

"Come on," she said with a small grin. "Your brain's warmed up. Let's see what your body can do."

I followed, still rubbing the faint rune Marcela had drawn on my arm, the edges already beginning to tingle and fade. Alice moved with easy confidence, a spring in her step that didn't match how deadly I knew she could be. We stopped in the middle of the yard, where she crouched and picked up a smooth stone.

"My mark's inertia," she said, turning the stone over in her palm. "It lets me mess with momentum. I can slow things down, freeze them for a second or two, even change direction mid-movement. Think of it like… gravity's glitch."

Before I could ask what she meant, she tossed the stone in the air and waved her fingers. The rock stopped mid-fall. Just hovered there like it was trapped in honey.

I stared with my mouth open.

A beat later, it dropped naturally to the ground.

"In a fight, that moment can change everything," she said, straightening up. "Buy yourself time. Catch your opponent off guard. Regain balance."

I nodded slowly, impressed. "That's… kind of badass."

Alice grinned. "I know."

The lesson started light—just walking, changing direction, trying to sense the subtle tug when she altered the way my body moved. Then came faster things. She threw a soft ball at me and I had to notice when it slowed unnaturally or when it dropped early. Next, she altered *me*, making me stumble forward when she accelerated my momentum, or freeze in place with a sudden stop.

"Trust your instincts," she coached. "Let your body adjust. Don't think too hard."

That was easier said than done. I was still sore from all the prior lessons, and my brain was swimming with runes and potions from Marcela's teachings. Still, Alice's encouragement never faltered.

"You're adapting fast," she said, after one particularly clean dodge. "Most people trip over themselves for days."

I offered a wry smile. "I have plenty of experience falling on my face."

She laughed. "Yeah, well… if you can learn to fall *right*, you're already ahead."

By the end of the session, I was winded and flushed, but lighter somehow.

Alice tossed me a water bottle. "You're getting stronger. Even if it doesn't feel like it yet."

It didn't. But maybe that didn't mean it wasn't true.

A few days later came Kaylen. Kaylen didn't teach. She pushed. She demanded we spar, really spar, in the backyard while the others watched from the patio or leaned against the railing. From the start, she didn't hold back. Her strikes were fast and sharp, her footwork precise and merciless. Luckily though, she only conjured wooden weapons. If she used real weapons... I'd be dead.

It wasn't like training with Cade. With him, there was patience. With her, there was none. I stumbled more than once, landing hard enough to knock the air from my lungs. I scrambled back up, only to be knocked down again. The ache in my arms and legs flared like fire, my breath coming in ragged gasps.

At one point, I snapped, words tearing out of me before I could stop them. "Goddammit, Kaylen! You don't have to kill me to make a point!"

Kaylen didn't even blink. She stepped forward, eyes sharp and cold, her voice cutting through the yard like a blade. "Do you think Michael or any of his men will go easy on you?" she spat. "This isn't some training montage in a movie. This is real life. You don't get to tap out. We don't have time to coddle you."

I stood there, chest heaving, every muscle screaming in protest, but I didn't move. I didn't look away. And slowly, the anger that burned behind my ribs twisted. Hardened into something sharper.

Kaylen saw it. Her mouth twitched—not a smile exactly, but close.

"You want to survive? Then act like it," she said, stepping back into position.

I sucked in a breath, tasting iron at the back of my throat. The urge to yell at her again coiled tight in my gut, but I swallowed it down.

Instead, I planted my feet. When she lunged this time, I didn't flinch. I moved, just half a step, but it was enough. Her hand grazed my arm instead of slamming into my ribs.

Kaylen paused. Her gaze looking over me, and something unreadable flashed in her eyes. "Better," she muttered. Then she came at me again.

We kept going. Over and over. Until my arms shook so badly I thought they might stop working altogether. But every time I hit the dirt, I got back up.

When Kaylen finally dropped her stance and stepped back, my chest was heaving so hard it felt like I might split open. She nodded short and sharp. Then she turned and walked toward the patio without another word.

I stood there a moment longer, fighting to catch my breath, the world tilting around me. And despite the exhaustion, a small, fierce grin formed at the corner of my mouth.

I didn't win. But I survived.

Cade stepped out onto the field. He scanned me over—the dirt on my arms, the rawness in my breathing, the wild glint still lingering in my eyes. A low, approving sound rumbled from his chest. "Nice work," he said.

I tried to snort a laugh, but it came out closer to a wheeze. "Define 'nice.'"

"She didn't go easy on you," he said, glancing over his shoulder toward where Kaylen had disappeared.

"Understatement of the year," I muttered.

Cade stepped closer, his gaze steady on mine. "But you held your ground. You're ready for the next step."

I tilted my head. "Next step?"

He smiled. "Weapons training."

A strange rush went through me—part dread, part excitement.

"Okay," I said. "Bring it on… tomorrow. I'm done for today."

"Deal," Cade chuckled.

The next morning came too fast. My muscles were still raw from Kaylen's brutal sparring, but I refused to let the ache stop me.

Cade met me in the backyard just after breakfast. This time, instead of open-hand drills, he had a small array of weapons laid out on a weathered blanket. A short sword, a long, slim staff, a set of throwing knives, and a single, dagger with a dark leather-wrapped hilt.

He looked up at me, his expression unreadable. "Pick one."

I stepped forward, my gaze sweeping over each weapon. My fingers hovered over the short sword, hesitated at the staff, but when I reached the dagger, something in me stilled. I picked it up. It settled into my palm like it had always belonged there. The balance felt right, the curve of the blade familiar in a way I couldn't explain.

Cade watched me closely, then gave a slow, approving nod. "Good choice."

Cade crouched briefly and picked up a worn leather strap with a buckle from the edge of the blanket, clearly made for holding a blade.

"You'll need this," he said, rising.

I glanced down at my leggings. "Not really working with a belt here."

He didn't respond, just stepped closer.

"May I?" he asked.

My pulse jumped. "Sure," I said, trying to sound casual.

He knelt beside me with slow precision, wrapped the strap around my upper thigh, fitting it snug over the outside of my leggings. His fingers brushed my skin through the fabric as he adjusted the buckle.

A breath caught low in my throat. The warmth of his hands. The focus in his expression. The faint pressure of the leather tightening. By the time he stood again, the dagger felt heavier in my grip, and heat bloomed low in my stomach, pooling in places I didn't want to think about.

I turned the dagger over in my hand, my thumb tracing the smooth leather hilt. "Feels… right," I murmured.

"It should," he replied. "A weapon isn't just about killing. It's an extension of you. Your focus, your intent. It should feel like part of your own body."

I nodded, the blade suddenly heavier with meaning.

"Show me your stance," he said.

I moved automatically, squaring my feet as he'd taught me before. The dagger's tip wavered slightly, betraying my unease. Cade reached out, steadying my wrist with a firm but gentle grip. His fingers slid along my arm, correcting my angle. Every touch sent tiny sparks up my spine.

He stepped back, eyes meeting mine. "Good."

We moved through basic drills. My muscles burned with every repetition, but somewhere in the ache, I felt something new take root.

Determination.

By the time Cade finally called a halt, sweat was dripping from my hairline and my fingers were cramped around the hilt.

He stepped closer, his hand coming to rest lightly on my shoulder. "You're stronger than you think," he said, low enough that only I could hear.

I met his gaze, my heart pounding from the training, from his closeness, from everything I couldn't yet name.

Cade squeezed my shoulder once more, then stepped back. "That's enough for today," he said, though his eyes stayed locked on mine a moment longer.

I nodded, lowering the dagger slowly. My arm felt like it weighed a thousand pounds, but I didn't loosen my grip until he gave a small nod of approval. As we walked back toward the cabin, the others fell in step around us, quiet but present. For once, I didn't feel like they were watching to judge me.

I slipped the dagger into my thigh holster as we reached the porch, a strange, almost fierce comfort settling in my chest. I might still be broken in places, but each day, I felt less like prey and more like a weapon.

Chapter 26

The weeks passed in a blur of sweat, bruises, and relentless practice.

There had been no word on Michael. No surprise attacks. No cryptic threats whispered in the back of my mind. The silence felt unnatural.

Every morning started the same, mark training with Vallerie, Marcela, and Hiro. I had moved past simply projecting my own emotions and had started learning to single people out, to feel the pulse of their feelings beneath the surface, to track them like threads in a dark room.

It was harder than I ever imagined. My own emotions were loud and messy, but at least they were mine. Other people's feelings clung to me like wet clothes, heavy and suffocating. Sometimes it felt like drowning.

When I tuned into someone's fear, my hands shook as if I were the one facing a nightmare. When I touched their grief, it hollowed me out from the inside, leaving me raw and brittle. Even joy wasn't simple. It flooded through me so sharply it almost hurt, lighting every nerve until I thought I might burst from the inside.

There were days I left those sessions shaking so badly I could barely hold a glass of water. Days when I hid in the bathroom afterward, gripping the sink until my knuckles turned white, just trying to remember which feelings were mine and which weren't. But every morning, I went back.

Some days, Hiro caught me before I could spiral. "You're holding it in your throat again," he'd say quietly, reminding me to breathe through it. One morning, the feedback hit him so hard he stumbled, and we both ended up on the ground laughing, breathless and dizzy. "Guess you weren't ready for that burst of teenage angst," I muttered, and he actually smiled.

By the afternoons, I was back outside. It was getting colder, which made every hit sting that much more. Cade pushed me harder with each session, my dagger becoming an extension of my own hands. It still felt like it was made for me, the hilt molding to my grip in a way that made my pulse quicken.

Kaylen joined in often, never once holding back. Her conjured weapons changed by the day—daggers, staffs, even a pair of nunchucks once. She was fierce, her strikes brutal and unyielding, but I learned to move with them. Slowly, I started recognizing the flick of her wrist before a strike or the switch in her weight before she lunged. The moment I blocked one of her attacks cleanly, she simply nodded and conjured something heavier. A faint scar now marked my left shoulder, a reminder of the day Kaylen had switched from wooden weapons to the real thing. She hadn't warned me, and the edge had cut clean. Afterward, Cade had cleaned the wound in silence, his touch gentle in a way that made my throat ache.

Alice's training was almost just as brutal. She was smaller, but no less lethal. One minute I was standing, and the next I was flat on my back, breath knocked clean from my lungs. She grinned, helped me up, and said, "ready for round two?"

Mornings with Marcela were different. Less violent, but just as intense. She drew runes across my arms with ink that shimmered faintly, showing me how each one served a different purpose. We spent hours cataloging rune types and their effects. I learned more about my grandmother in those sessions than I ever expected to. Marcela spoke of her with reverence.

My body changed faster than I expected. The softness in my arms gave way to lean muscle. Even my movements became more precise. Less like someone trying to survive, and more like someone preparing to fight.

Allie and Sarah remained constants—always present, always near. I noticed how easily they fit into life at the cabin despite being unmarked. Allie helped Marcela in the kitchen and often organized supply runs. Sarah flitted through the compound like she'd lived there forever, sharing jokes, helping Alice with training gear, bringing Hiro tea without being asked. They had each found a place here.

Biscuit made herself at home, too. She had developed an annoying habit of following Cade silently through the cabin like a tiny, entitled shadow. I pretended to be annoyed. But truthfully, it made me feel better knowing she had picked someone strong to follow.

Every day, I got back up. Every day, I learned a little more about what I could endure. At night, I collapsed into bed so tired I barely remembered laying my head on the pillow. I was exhausted. I was sore.

When I finally dragged myself inside after another grueling evening session, sweat sticking my hair to my forehead, I found Allie at the big table, hunched over her burner phone. Her shoulders were tight, her fingers white-knuckled around the device.

I slowed when I saw her expression. "What's up?" I asked, wiping my forehead with the back of my hand.

Allie looked up sharply, eyes flashing. "Gage called your phone," she said, her voice clipped. "I answered." She held up the phone and then tossed it onto the table with a dull clatter. "He wanted you to know Michael's been popping up in the news again. A lot."

I stepped closer, hesitating before I reached for the phone. The screen was still lit, headline after headline blurring past. Michael at a children's cancer ward, crouched down and hugging a small, bald child. Michael standing beside a mayor, cutting a ribbon at the grand opening of a mental health center. Another story about a massive donation to a women's shelter.

Allie's voice trembled as she spoke again. "It's like he's buying their love. And it's working. Look at the comments. People think he's a fucking saint." She stood up abruptly and started pacing. "I don't understand how he's doing this. Even

321

with Ryker's money, that only goes so far. He's spending millions like it's nothing."

I stayed quiet, staring at the images. The warmth in his eyes. The easy, practiced smile. I felt the familiar burn of shame and rage crawling up my throat. After a long pause, I forced the words out. "I don't know. Maybe... maybe he's found a way to get more money with the marks he has now." My voice felt small, tight. "With everything he took."

Allie froze mid-step, turning toward me. Her expression softened just for a breath, then hardened again. "This is sick. He's fooling them all the same way he fooled you."

I swallowed, my jaw clenching. I thought of his hands on me, his voice in my ear, the knife in my stomach.

Finally, I looked up at her. "It won't last forever. We'll stop him."

Allie's shoulders sagged, her breath leaving her in a shaky rush.

Then, Cade cleared his throat from behind me. "You two good?" he asked, his voice gentle.

Allie snorted, shaking her head. "Define good."

"Did you see this?" I asked, holding it out to him.

Cade stepped closer and took the phone, his eyes scanning quickly over the images before he handed it back. "Yeah," he said. "Gage called me too."

Allie let out a rough exhale and started pacing again, her fingers flexing at her sides.

Just then, Sarah pushed through the doorway. She paused when she saw us, her eyes moving between our tense faces. "What's going on?" she asked, her voice edged with concern.

Allie turned toward her, her jaw working. "It's Michael. He's—"

But I didn't hear the rest. My focus snapped back to the phone in my hand. The screen glowed up at me, headline after headline smearing together in a blur. Images, videos, comments—all of it clawing at the raw edges inside me.

My heart pounded so hard it drowned everything else out. My breath stuck in my throat, rage spiraling through me in sharp, blinding flashes. I didn't hear Sarah's gasp, didn't see Allie's hands gesturing wildly as she tried to explain. I only saw him.

That night, I barely slept. I lay on my bed with the burner phone clutched in my hand, the pale glow slicing through the dark. My eyes scanned headline after headline, fingers trembling as I scrolled. Michael's face was everywhere— smiling that familiar, practiced smile I'd once thought was meant only for me.

The comments clawed at me more than the images ever could.

A true savior.

Proof there are good men left in the world.

I'd trust him with my life.

I felt the rage build in my chest, thick and hot, until it pressed against my ribs like something trying to claw its way out. My pulse pounded behind my eyes, my breath coming in sharp, broken pulls.

At some point, the phone slipped from my grip and thudded to the floor. I didn't bother to pick it up.

By dawn, I was shaking.

When Vallerie called me out to train that morning, I could barely look at her. My head felt like it was filled with smoke and fire. We started with the usual grounding exercises. I tried to focus on the steady rise and fall of my breath, on the feel of the ground beneath my feet, but my thoughts kept fracturing.

Every time I closed my eyes, I saw him. Smiling. Laughing. Holding me like I was the only thing that mattered. Then the flash of the knife, the warmth of my blood, the look in his eyes as he ripped everything away. How he took my parents from me. And now, the headlines. The praise. The adoration spilling toward him like he deserved it. Like the world was kneeling at his feet, blind to the monster underneath.

The rage crept up, coiling tight in my chest. Then I felt it amplify and burst out of me.

Shit.

Vallerie flinched first, her breath catching as she stumbled back a step, her hand flying to her temple like she'd been struck. Her eyes went wide, whipping from me to the others in alarm.

Alice snarled and spun on Hiro. "Back the fuck up!" she snapped, shoving him hard in the chest. He stumbled, arms flailing slightly before catching his balance.

"What the hell is wrong with you?" Hiro shouted, already closing the distance between them. His calm shattered, replaced with a storm of fury. His fists clenched, his chest heaving like he wanted to throw the next punch.

Marcela growled something low and vicious and lunged toward Kaylen. "I'm not afraid of you, you smug bitch!"

Kaylen didn't back down. She stepped forward, nose to nose with Marcela, the air between them crackling like a lit fuse. "Try me," she hissed. "Fucking try me."

Marcela's hand twitched like she was ready to slap her across the mouth.

Even Allie, who had been sitting on the steps, shot to her feet so fast she nearly tripped. Her eyes blazed, her fists trembling at her sides. She looked like she might lunge straight into the fray without a second thought.

"Lena," Vallerie called, her voice strained, cracking under the force of it. "You need to stop projecting!"

I tried—God, I tried—but it felt like trying to shove a wildfire back into a matchbox. My heart thundered against my ribs, the rage boiling up, flooding the space around me like thick smoke.

Kaylen's voice finally sliced through the chaos like a blade. "Get her the fuck out of here before I lose it and someone gets seriously hurt!"

I stood there, gasping, sweat slicking down my back, my hands trembling.

Cade stepped forward then, his expression unreadable. Calm, but hard like stone. "With me," he growled, his voice leaving no space for questions.

I followed him into the woods, my feet crunching over twigs and leaves. Each step felt like it might break me open.

He didn't speak. Neither did I. We pushed deeper until the cabin disappeared entirely, replaced by tall pines and a hush that felt almost sacred.

In a small clearing, Cade finally stopped. He let out a slow breath, his broad shoulders rising and falling before he crouched and set a bag on the ground. He unzipped it, revealing a few weapons. He looked up at me, his eyes steady but distant.

He didn't offer comfort. Didn't ask if I was okay. Instead, he reached in and picked up one of the daggers, rolling it once between his fingers before slipping it into his belt. His gaze moved down to my thigh, where my own dagger rested, the handle now starting to wear from hours of training.

He stood, brushing dirt from his hands, and met my eyes. "Again," he said.

The word snapped through me like a wire pulled tight. I lunged at him, my dagger slicing the air between us. He deflected easily, his movements fluid as water, twisting my wrist and sending me stumbling back.

I caught my breath, teeth bared, and charged again. Every failed attempt made the fire inside me roar higher. I could see Michael behind every move.

Jab—*his lips on my neck, whispering lies.*

Pivot—*his laughter echoing in my head, that easy, careless charm.*

Stab—*the moment he pressed the blade into me, stealing everything.*

Again. And again.

Cade moved around me with ease, catching my arm, disarming me, tossing me to the ground. Each time, I scrambled back up, dirt clinging to my skin, my hair sticking to my damp forehead.

I felt the tears on my face before I knew I was crying. "Again," I spat, my voice raw and shredded.

I lunged, wild and reckless. This time, something was different. Maybe it was the angle, maybe it was the force, maybe it was the rage finally boiling over. I caught him off-balance, my shoulder slamming into his chest. We crashed to the ground in a tangle of limbs, and before I knew it, I was straddling his hips, the dagger pressed against the strong line of his throat.

We both froze. Our labored breathing filled the small clearing.

Cade's green eyes locked on mine, searching. His chest rose beneath me, heat radiating between us.

I hovered over him, trembling, the dagger clenched tight in my fist. Rage still burned under my skin, but something else pulsed beneath it. Something darker. A dangerous hunger, coiled so tight it ached.

His piercing eyes didn't flinch, didn't plead. They just held me steady in a way that made my head spin even more violently.

I should have moved. I should have pulled back. But every part of me felt like it was vibrating like fire roaring under my skin.

I repositioned my weight just a little bit, the press of my hips against him sudden and electric. His breath hitched. Only slightly, but I felt it like a shock.

"Lena," he murmured, his voice somewhere between a warning and a plea.

The sound of my name snapped something inside me. Without thinking, I leaned down and crashed my mouth fiercely onto his. The dagger slipped from my fingers, landing with a muffled sound beside us, forgotten.

His surprise lasted only a second before he responded, his mouth opening under mine.

Then his hand rose slowly, his fingers brushing gently against my cheek. His touch was soft, caressing.

I froze, every muscle going taut, panic surging through me like venom in my bloodstream. No. Not gentle. Not soft. Softness is dangerous. Softness lies.

My eyes flashed as I grabbed his wrist sharply, slamming it into the grass beside his head. My other hand caught his second wrist, pinning him hard.

Our gazes locked.

For a moment, he just looked at me—not resisting, not pushing me off—just waiting. Then something clicked in his eyes.

Understanding.

He surged upward, his mouth colliding with mine again, answering my violence with a deep, hungry heat. I felt his hands straining beneath my grip, but I didn't let go.

I pushed my hips, grinding down against him. A raw sound came tearing from his throat that vibrated my bones.

I didn't want gentle. I didn't want comfort. I wanted the violence of it. The way my blood screamed under my skin, the way my body felt like it would tear itself apart if I didn't do something, *anything*, to release it.

I broke the kiss just long enough to suck in a stuttering breath, my chest heaving. Cade's eyes burned into mine, his pupils blown wide, his jaw clenched tight like he was barely holding himself together.

I released his wrists to tear at the waistband of my leggings, shoving them down past my hips in a frantic, stumbling motion. My fingers caught briefly on the thigh holster still strapped to my leg. I fumbled with the buckle, cursing, then yanked it loose and tossed it aside. My shoes caught next, and I kicked them off so hard they thudded into the underbrush. The leggings and underwear went with them, ripped off and flung aside without a second thought.

Cade's hand shot up, his fingers digging into my hip so hard it bordered on pain. His other hand tangled in my hair, yanking my mouth back down to his.

I rocked against him, a desperate, raw friction that had me gasping into his mouth. My fingers fumbled with his belt, the metal buckle clinking sharply in the quiet clearing.

"Now," I snarled against his lips. "I need you—*now.*"

His answering groan was low and savage. He shoved up, tearing at his belt and jeans, shoving them down his hips in one rough, impatient motion. His boots kicked against the dirt as he pushed everything away, leaving him bare beneath me.

I barely gave him time to breathe. My fingers wrapped around his already hard cock, guiding him to me without hesitation, my nails scraping his skin as I lined us up.

Jesus.

He was thick, hot, heavy in my hand—almost too much. A flash of wicked anticipation curled low in my belly.

Perfect.

Then I slammed down onto him in one brutal, unstoppable motion.

A strangled cry tore from both of us. His head snapped back, mine falling forward onto his shoulder.

God, the stretch burned. My body clenched around him, struggling to take all of him in. I didn't think I'd ever been this full. The pressure made my thighs shake, my breath catch. It was too much, and yet nowhere near enough.

He filled me so deeply I swore I could feel him everywhere—splitting me apart, dragging me open in the most delicious, devastating way.

I didn't wait. I set a punishing rhythm immediately, grinding down hard, again and again, each thrust a fierce, wild release of everything he'd awoken inside me. The pressure of his pelvis against my clit sent sparks shooting through me, every grind lighting me up in ways that felt violent and holy.

"You feel even better than I imagined," he groaned, voice thick with hunger. "So fucking tight around me."

My skin was slick with sweat, thighs sticking where they met his. The friction only drove me harder, desperate for the next hit of pleasure, the next jolt of something sharp enough to drown out the noise in my head.

His hands clawed at my hips, fingers digging in hard, dragging me against him like he needed to bury himself so deep I'd never be able to pull away. I could feel the tremble in his arms, the restrained violence in his grip, the ragged sound of his breathing.

I rode him like I was trying to destroy something inside myself... and maybe I was.

"Show me," he growled through clenched teeth. "Show me what that rage looks like when it's dripping down my cock."

My body jerked at his words, a sharp pulse of pleasure and fury slamming through me like a punch.

His hands shot up, yanking at the front of my shirt. With a sharp, guttural growl, he *ripped* it open, seams splitting and fabric tearing loud enough to echo. The sleeves caught around my arms for half a second before he shoved them down, rough and impatient. My bra followed, snapped open with one rough tug, the straps sliding down.

Cold air rushed against my skin. Goosebumps rose in an instant, but it wasn't the chill that made me shiver. It was the way his gaze dragged over every inch of exposed skin like a second touch.

My nails dug into his chest, as I used him for leverage, riding him harder, faster. I was dripping, the wet heat between my legs coating him with every grind. My thighs shook from the effort, from the strain of holding on while my body demanded more, more, more.

His hands roamed up my now-bare torso, fingers bruising, thumbs brushing over my nipples in a rough, almost punishing pass that made me jolt and curse. I didn't care about modesty, didn't care about the torn scraps of my shirt falling away. I wanted him to see every inch of me. Every piece of rage and ruin he'd uncovered.

I leaned forward, my teeth catching his lower lip in a savage bite that drew a hiss from him. He answered with a violent thrust upward that almost knocked the breath from my lungs. My spine bowed, muscles locking. The burn inside me twisted tighter.

I didn't stop. I couldn't. I felt like I might shatter into pieces if I didn't burn this all out of me. If I didn't break something open and let it pour out.

He surged up beneath me, and in one brutal movement, flipped me onto my back. The cold dirt and rough sticks dug into my skin, poking sharply at my sides and hips—but I didn't care. I welcomed the sting. It kept me grounded, kept me real. Kept me present in this moment of pure, feral need.

He stayed buried inside me, not missing a beat, hips slamming into mine with a force that knocked a strangled cry from my throat.

I clawed at his sides, then reached up, yanking at his shirt. He lifted just enough for me to rip it up and over his head, tossing it aside.

For the first time, I paused.

His chest rose and fell above me, every ridge of muscle etched like it had been carved by firelight and fury. Veins threaded down his arms, pulsing beneath skin dusted with dirt and sweat. The sight alone made my walls flutter around him.

But it was the tattoo that caught my breath. Black ink curved across his ribs, winding over his shoulder and down his bicep like smoke made solid. An intricate shadow shaped into something ancient and haunting. I couldn't tell if it was a dragon or a demon, or some forgotten thing that only he knew the name of. It wrapped him like armor, dark and violent and beautiful.

God. He was the sexiest man I'd ever laid eyes on. Raw. Unrelenting. Ruined in all the right ways.

Then he moved, his eyes locking on mine again, and the moment shattered. He crashed down again, his mouth on mine. He didn't kiss to comfort. He devoured. His lips dragged down my jaw to my throat, where he sank his teeth deep enough to make my whole body arch. I gasped, pleasure surging hot and fast under my skin.

I bucked beneath him, nails digging into his back, dragging down hard enough to leave welts.

"Mark me all you want," he snarled, teeth still against my skin. "I want to feel you tomorrow."

My fingers clenched harder, clawing him like I wanted to carve that permission into his flesh. I wrapped my legs around his waist, heels digging into him, urging him deeper, harder. I could feel the drag of him inside me, every thick inch scraping against my tight grip.

The ground tore at my skin, sticks snapping beneath me, dirt smearing up my back and into my hair.

I didn't care. I wanted more.

He pulled back for a split second, eyes blazing down at me, chest heaving. My hands shot up to his hair, dragging him back down.

"Don't you fucking stop," I snarled, voice shredded with need.

His mouth twisted into something feral. "I wasn't planning to." He leaned down, lips brushing my ear as his voice dropped to a growl. "Not until you're screaming."

He pinned my wrists above my head with one massive hand, the other gripping my hip so hard it felt like he might leave bruises for days. Every thrust was punishing, his cock dragging against a spot inside me that made my toes curl and my vision blur. I was slick and swollen, my body pulsing around him with each brutal drive of his hips.

I couldn't tell where my rage ended and my need began—they tangled together into something feral and unstoppable.

Without warning, he pulled out and yanked me up, flipping me onto my stomach. My face slammed into the dirt, the earth cold and rough against my cheek. More twigs jabbed into my ribs, sharp pebbles pressing into my knees, scratching across already tender skin. Before I could even catch my breath, his hand fisted in my hair, pulling my head back just enough for me to gasp.

Then he slammed back into me from behind—so hard I nearly sobbed, my fingers clawing at the ground, the brutal stretch lighting my nerves on fire.

He filled me to the hilt, deeper in this position, the new angle forcing a gasping whimper from my throat. I felt every inch of him dragging against the hypersensitive walls inside me, making my legs tremble violently.

His other hand slid around to my throat, gripping it firmly, not quite cutting off my air but letting me feel the threat of it— the promise.

I moaned, my body arching into him, desperate for more, for everything.

"Is this what you wanted? To be wrecked like this?" he snarled, low and merciless, every word vibrating through my bones like a warning.

I couldn't even form words—just a strangled, wild sound that tore from my throat.

He pounded into me again, harder, deeper, his grip on my throat tightening just enough to make the edges of my vision shimmer. I pushed back into him, meeting every brutal snap of his hips, lost in the haze of pain and pleasure, rage and release.

I felt the burn of the sticks and stones digging into my knees, the sting only fueling the frenzy climbing higher and higher inside me.

My body trembled, shaking under him, every nerve set on fire, and I knew I was close—so dangerously close I thought I might shatter. But something inside me snapped—a vicious, hungry spark demanding that *I* finish this on my terms.

I slammed my hips back against him once more, then pushed up, twisting beneath his weight. Before he could react, I shoved him back, forcing him upright into a sitting position against the cold ground.

I climbed into his lap, straddling him, my knees digging into the earth on either side of his hips.

His eyes flared wide, wild and dark, but he didn't resist. He just gripped my waist as I sank down onto him again in one fierce, claiming thrust. I felt everything. Every vein, every twitch. He filled me completely, the pressure building until my breath came in shallow pants.

I rocked my hips hard, grinding down, taking every inch like I was starving for it. His head tipped forward, his forehead brushing mine, panting like he was fighting to stay in control. I tipped my head back, spine arched, every thrust hitting the spot that made my vision white out. My clit rubbed against his pelvis with every grind, building a crescendo I couldn't hold back.

His mouth crashed against my throat again. His teeth sank in—deep, possessive, like he wanted to leave proof of this moment etched into my skin. Pain and pleasure collided in a blinding, electric shock that ripped through me.

I lost it. A scream tore from my throat as my entire body locked up, the climax detonating so sharp it bordered on pain. My walls clamped down on him in rhythmic waves, milking every inch, pulsing with a need so fierce it stole my breath.

"That's it," he groaned, voice feral. "Let me feel it. Fucking fall apart for me."

I was unraveling, not just physically but soul-deep, every wave crashing through me like a scream I couldn't voice.

He slammed up into me one last time, his own snarl muffled against my skin as he followed me over the edge. His hips stuttered, his cock twitching inside me as he emptied himself with a broken sound that barely reached my ears. I felt the heat of it spill deep, a savage, messy claim that sent another ripple of aftershocks through me.

I was shaking, slick, stretched, and completely undone. I stayed straddling him, my chest heaving, forehead pressed against his as our shuddering breaths tangled. My fingers slipped from his back, leaving faint streaks of blood and raw skin behind.

His hands slid up my sides, rough and possessive, calloused fingertips grazing over bruises he'd helped put there. One hand lingered at the swell of my ribs, the other traced slowly up my spine, like he couldn't stop touching me.

For one long, burning moment, there was nothing but the two of us—feral and unmoored, bound by the violence of our release.

I swallowed hard, the air thick with earth and sweat and something primal that refused to let go. Slowly, I eased off him, every inch a drag of sensation that left me shivering, overstimulated and aching.

Cade sat up more, pushing his hair back, his chest rising and falling in sharp waves. He glanced at me, then reached for his shirt. Without a word, he handed it to me.

I took it, fingers brushing his for a split second, that same flash of heat sparking in the contact. I pulled the shirt on quickly, swallowing the strange new vulnerability that threatened to edge in.

Cade stood, fastening his pants with rough movements. He slipped on his boots, not bothering to tie them. He then crouched to grab my dagger and holster, putting it in the bag with the other weapons.

I reached for my leggings, which had ended up bunched and tangled up with my shoes nearby. I yanked them back on with clumsy, shaking hands, wincing at the dirt and twigs sticking to my scraped knees. Then I grabbed my shoes, shoving them on without bothering to re-tie them properly.

For a moment, we just stood there, neither of us saying anything.

Finally, he broke the silence. "Feel better?"

I huffed out a breath, somewhere between a laugh and a scoff. "Yeah… for now."

His mouth twitched. "You, uh… might want to avoid mirrors for a while."

I snorted, shaking my head as I wiped sweat and dirt from my cheek. "I have no idea how we're going to explain this."

Cade slung the bag over his shoulder, giving me a long, slow once-over. "We don't," he said, a hint of dry amusement in his voice. "We let them make up their own stories. Saves us the trouble."

I let out a sharp laugh despite myself. The sound echoed through the trees, oddly freeing.

He started walking back toward the cabin, and I fell into step beside him, tugging at the hem of his shirt.

He glanced sideways at me, and for one fleeting moment, something warm—almost soft—edged in at the corners of the rage still burning in my veins.

We didn't say anything else as the cabin came into view through the trees, both of us marked and disheveled, carrying more than just the weapons in that bag.

As we climbed the back steps, I silently prayed everyone would be off training or hiding in their rooms—anywhere but right here.

But the universe, of course, had other plans.

The moment we stepped into the open kitchen, I froze.

Everyone was there. Allie, Sarah, Vallerie, Kaylen, Marcela, Hiro, Alice—all crowded around the big table and kitchen counter, plates in front of them. Half-eaten sandwiches, chips, and fruit.

All eyes snapped to us at once. Forks froze mid-air. Someone actually dropped a piece of bread.

It was dead silent for half a beat. Then:

"Oh my *God*," Sarah blurted, nearly choking on her drink. She set her cup down, eyes darting between my tangled hair, Cade's bloody scratches, and his missing shirt—now hanging off my shoulders like a makeshift dress.

Allie's jaw dropped. "Are you—Is that—" She pointed at Cade's shirt, words failing her entirely.

Vallerie had been mid-sip of tea. She froze, eyes wide above the rim. Slowly, she set the mug down with exaggerated care, then looked at us, blinked once, and said in a perfectly dry voice, "Well. I suppose that's one way to clear blocked energy."

Marcela laughed so hard she actually slapped the table. "Holy shit. You two look like you got in a bar fight and then—" *snort* "—decided to reconcile immediately after."

Kaylen leaned back, arms crossing over her chest, an unbothered smirk spreading across her face. "Finally," she drawled. "I was getting bored watching you two make googly eyes every day."

Alice just gave a single, slow clap. "Guess you found a new way to burn off that aggression."

Hiro cleared his throat, trying—and failing—to hide his grin behind his hand. "I, uh... assume training went... productively?"

My face burned so hot it felt like I might spontaneously combust. Cade looked almost sheepish as he stepped past me to drop the weapons bag by the counter.

"Really?" I hissed under my breath to him. "This is worse than any injury you've given me."

He snorted, tossing me a quick, teasing look over his shoulder. "You'll live."

Mortified, I ducked behind him, gripping the edges of his—my—borrowed shirt tighter.

Cade cleared his throat, trying and failing to look serious. "We... worked some things out."

Sarah laughed so hard she nearly choked. "Oh, you *worked* something out all right."

Allie just put her head down on the table, muttering, "I'm going to need bleach for my brain."

I peeked out from behind Cade, glaring halfheartedly at them all. "You're all terrible."

Sarah wiped tears from her eyes, breathless. "We love you too, baby. Now please, for the love of god, shower before you traumatize us further."

Cade chuckled, reaching to pluck a leaf from my hair before stepping away. I spun on my heel, heat still flooding every inch of me, and fled towards the stairs, their laughter echoing after me like a chorus of very loud, very annoying birds.

I nearly sprinted up the steps, ducking into the bedroom and closing the door so quickly it rattled in the frame. My heart hammered in my chest, part embarrassment, part leftover adrenaline.

I peeled Cade's shirt off and let it drop to the floor. When I turned to the mirror above the dresser, I froze.

My reflection stared back at me—wild hair, flushed skin, lips still swollen from his teeth and tongue. Bite marks bloomed dark along my neck and collarbone, a few trailing lower. Finger-shaped bruises wrapped around my hips, stark against the pale skin. Scratches marked my ribs and thighs like chaotic little trophies.

I lifted a hand, tracing one of the bite marks lightly. A shiver ran through me. *Shit.* A crooked, private smile pulled at my lips. Heat curled low in my belly, unexpected and dangerous.

He could become addictive, I thought, and the realization slammed into me almost as hard as his body had.

I forced myself to turn away, stepping into the bathroom and twisting the shower knob. Steam billowed out, fogging the mirror, swallowing the evidence of my reckless grin. I stepped under the hot spray, wincing as the water stung over the raw patches of skin. But the pain felt good, proof of something real, something that wasn't Michael.

I braced my hands on the tiled wall, water cascading over my shoulders, my forehead pressed against the cool surface. Memories of Cade's hands, his mouth, the low, broken sounds he made against my skin…

For a split second, Michael's face cut through—the laugh, the lies, the knife. My stomach twisted. I squeezed my eyes shut, forcing the thought away. *No. Not here.*

I stayed under the spray until the heat began to fade, until my muscles felt loose and heavy. When I finally stepped out, I wrapped myself in a towel and looked at my reflection again. Still marked. Still mine.

For the first time in what felt like forever, a small, dangerous spark curled low in my chest. I wasn't just surviving. I was starting to feel alive again.

When I stepped out of the bathroom, steam billowing around me, I nearly jumped. Sarah was sprawled across my bed, propped up on her elbows like she'd been waiting there forever. Her eyes were wide and gleaming, practically vibrating with curiosity.

"Finally," she hissed, her voice sharp and urgent. "Tell me *everything.*"

I gaped at her, towel still clutched to my chest. "Sarah—"

She sat up straighter, waving both hands. "Don't you *Sarah* me. I want details. How was it? How big? How long did it last? Was he as intense as he looks? Spill."

I let out a strangled laugh, dropping my towel and reaching for my clothes. "God, you're a menace."

She grinned, unabashed. "And you love me. Now *talk.*"

I pulled on my hoodie and slid into jeans, trying—and failing—to hide my smile. "Fine. You want a play-by-play?"

Sarah practically bounced. "Yes. Preferably with sound effects."

I rolled my eyes, but the old, playful Lena slipped back in.

"Well..." I flopped onto the bed beside her, lowering my voice conspiratorially. "Let's just say... he's big. Like... *really* big."

Sarah slapped a hand over her mouth, her eyes going huge. "Oh my God."

"And strong," I continued, warming to it now. "I think I've got bruises in places I didn't even know I had skin. And those scratches on his back? Yeah. All me."

Sarah cackled, grabbing a pillow and hugging it to her chest. "Holy *shit*, Lena!"

"And the stamina? Jesus," I added, throwing an arm over my eyes dramatically. "I think I might still be vibrating."

Sarah squealed, nearly falling off the bed. "Stop. No, don't stop. Oh my *God.*"

I peeked at her from under my arm, grinning like an idiot. "He literally ripped my shirt. Like, actually ripped it in pieces."

Her mouth dropped open. "Jesus. That's the hottest red flag I've ever heard. Who is he, fucking Wolverine?"

338

I laughed, my cheeks aching. "I don't think I've ever wanted someone that badly. It was... animal. I don't even know how to describe it."

Sarah's eyes went dreamy, her fingers curling around the edge of the pillow. "Tell me there was biting. Tell me there was hair pulling. Please."

I snorted. "Oh, there was biting. My neck is going to look like a war zone. And I think I still have twigs in my hair from... everything."

She shrieked again, pressing the pillow to her face to muffle the sound. "Jesus Christ, Lena, I am so proud of you."

I laughed so hard I had to clutch my stomach, tears welling in my eyes.

Sarah finally caught her breath, wiping tears from her eyes. She went quiet for a moment, studying me, her expression switching from gleeful to thoughtful.

"Wait, are you still on birth control? Or are we about to get a tiny shadow-stepping rage baby in nine months?"

I snorted, flopping back dramatically. "Relax. I still have my IUD. Doesn't expire for another three years."

Sarah let out a relieved gasp. "Thank God. The world is not ready for little Cade juniors. They'd come out kicking down walls."

"Right?" I laughed, shaking my head.

She smiled, then hesitated, her fingers fiddling with the edge of the pillow. "So..." she said more quietly, "what does this mean? You and Cade?"

The question hit me like a sudden gust of cold air. My smile faltered. I sank back onto the edge of the bed, my fingers twisting in the hem of my hoodie.

"I... I don't know," I admitted, my voice small. "It doesn't have to mean anything. It was just... sex. That's all."

Sarah's eyebrows shot up. "Just sex?"

I swallowed, my throat tight. "Yeah. Just... a release. I needed it. He needed it. We're both adults."

She tilted her head, her gaze sharp but gentle. "You don't sound like you believe that."

I looked away, focusing on a faint scratch on my forearm. "I don't want it to be more. I can't... I can't do more. The last time I fell for someone, he destroyed everything."

The words came out in a rush, my fingers digging into my knees.

Sarah's face softened. She scooted closer, resting her hand over mine. "Hey. I get it. You don't owe anyone anything. Not even Cade. But... you also don't have to shut yourself off forever."

I forced a laugh, brittle and low. "I don't think I even know how to let someone in again. And I don't think I want to."

Sarah squeezed my hand once more, then let go. "Then don't. Just... be honest with yourself. That's all I'm saying."

I took a shaky breath, my shoulders rising and falling as I steadied myself. "Yeah," I said finally, my voice barely above a whisper. "Yeah."

Then I lifted my eyes to hers. "You know... you should be honest with yourself too," I said, my voice a little stronger now. "I know you still miss Abel. But you don't have to just shut yourself off forever."

Sarah's eyes went wide for a second, her lips parting in surprise.

"And Jack..." I pressed, tilting my head slightly. "He texts you every day, doesn't he?"

Sarah let out a rough breath, her gaze dropping to her hands. "Yeah," she admitted softly. "Every day. Just checking in. Making sure I'm okay." She hesitated, then added, "He's been asking to see me, just to make sure I'm really okay. He knows something is off."

I nodded, studying her carefully. "He cares about you, Sarah. Maybe more than you realize."

She hesitated, her fingers twisting into the blanket beside her. "I know. I just... I'm not ready. I don't know if I'll ever be ready. After Abel... it's like there's this wall I can't get past."

I reached out, nudging her shoulder lightly. "That's okay. Just... don't pretend the wall isn't there. And don't pretend it doesn't matter."

There was a long pause. Then, like she knew we needed to break the heaviness, Sarah gave me a little nudge. "Now, you need to go raid the kitchen and rehydrate before you pass out. Sex queen duties require electrolytes."

I snorted. "Bossy."

She shot back. "And you love me."

I stood, moving toward the door, pausing just once to look back at her. "Yeah," I said softly. "I really do."

Chapter 27

I made my way downstairs, my body still humming in that odd, shaky way that came after pushing it too far—or maybe just after Cade. I paused at the bottom step, my fingers brushing the railing as I glanced into the kitchen.

Cade was already there. Freshly showered, damp hair pushed back from his forehead, a dark t-shirt clinging to his shoulders. He stood at the counter, quietly making a sandwich. For a second, I considered turning around and retreating upstairs. But before I could, he looked up and saw me.

He didn't say anything at first. Just gave me a small, almost shy smile that tugged something low in my stomach. Without a word, he turned back to the counter and reached for another slice of bread.

I stepped into the kitchen, suddenly aware of every tiny bruise, every mark hidden beneath my clothes. I settled into one of the chairs at the big table, watching him work. He finished quickly, set a sandwich on a plate in front of me and a glass of water, then slid into the chair across the table with his own.

For a while, we just ate. Every now and then, our eyes would meet, and I'd look away too fast, heat crawling up my neck. At some point, I realized I was absentmindedly rubbing the side of my throat. One of the bite marks. Cade's eyes tracked the movement. He swallowed, then set his sandwich down, his gaze steady on me.

"Does it hurt?" He asked.

I startled a little, my hand dropping back to the table. "No," I said, then hesitated, a small, crooked laugh escaping. "No... not really. Just... reminds me."

Cade's jaw tightened, his gaze dipping to my neck and then back to my eyes.

343

And then, without meaning to, I felt it. A slow, coiling heat rising from him. Want. Hunger. Arousal. It hit me like a spark catching dry tinder, making my breath catch in my throat. I forced my eyes down to my plate, but my mind spun.

Color, I thought wildly, trying to ground myself. Assign it a color. Molten gold. Bright, heavy, almost liquid. Warmth and hunger all tangled together. It wrapped around me, molten and unstoppable, searing through every nerve.

I swallowed hard, pressing my palm flat against the table to steady myself. The edge of that heat brushed against my skin from across the wood, invisible but undeniable. I almost laughed—or maybe moaned—at the ridiculousness of it. We were sitting here, quietly eating sandwiches, and he was practically radiating that low, smoldering want.

I dared a quick glance up. His hands were resting on either side of his plate, fingers curled slightly, knuckles pale. His chest rose and fell a fraction too quickly. My own pulse thudded in my ears, my throat suddenly dry. I dragged in a breath and pushed my plate back a few inches, leaning back in the chair.

"Looks like it might snow," I blurted, gesturing vaguely toward the window.

His lips twitched faintly, like he knew I was deflecting. Cade followed my gaze to the window. "Yeah. Supposed to start tonight."

Another quiet stretch settled between us. But it wasn't tense. It felt... okay. Eventually, I stood, picked up my empty plate and carried it to the sink. Cade's eyes followed me the whole way, warm and watchful. "Thanks," I said as I rinsed the plate.

"Anytime," he replied, and something in the way he said it made me pause, my fingers tightening around the edge of the sink. I turned to glance at him over my shoulder. For a beat, we just looked at each other. Then I gave a small smile and started toward the stairs.

Halfway up, I paused at the window on the landing. Outside, small white flakes started drifting down, catching in the branches, dusting the ground. I stood there at the window longer than I meant to, watching the snow gather.

But my mind was still in the clearing. Still with Cade.

• • •

Over the next few days, the snow kept falling, and over the next month, winter truly arrived. Snow piled along the edges of the clearing and blanketed the trees so thickly it muffled every sound. The cabin's training yard turned into an icy arena, cleared daily by Kaylen and Hiro with the four-wheeler plow.

We wore lighter jackets to keep our movements free, relying on motion and adrenaline to keep warm. I started wearing fleece-lined leggings, grateful for every bit of insulation I could get.

Inside, the fire burned constantly. Coffee steamed on the counter every morning. Quiet conversations, clinking mugs, the occasional bark of laughter—it should have felt cozy and safe. But beneath it all pulsed an uneasy rhythm.

Michael still haunted the news. A hospital wing he funded. A children's shelter he visited. Another massive donation with his name attached. Sometimes the reports came with videos. Michael, stepping off a private jet, shaking hands like a celebrity, wearing that soft, calculated smile like a mask he never had to take off.

The Severance was keeping tabs. Gage called in updates every few days, reporting Michael's movements. He was traveling constantly, across states and even out of the country. But no one knew why.

Cade tracked each report. Sometimes he'd stay up late, alone in the living room, quiet and brooding, the glow of his burner phone painting harsh lines across his face. Biscuit had made a habit of curling up beside him, as if she'd taken it upon herself to keep him company through whatever late-night plotting he was doing.

One small comfort came in the form of Corinne. Lorelei kept me updated. Corinne was safe, hidden away in a secure location.

Meanwhile, I trained. Cade suggested mock battles using our marks about a week into the new year to prepare for what we'd face against Michael and his followers. These weren't just sparring matches, they were full simulated skirmishes where we used our marks like we would in a real fight.

Sometimes, I would catch Cade watching me. Not just in a teacher's way, but with that deep, steady heat that curled low in my stomach every time I met his eyes. But neither of us acted on it. We skirted each other in quiet, electric silence. I caught him watching me in the kitchen. In the yard. Across the table when we ate. Sometimes, I would catch my reflection in the window and see a flush creeping up my neck just from the memory of his hands.

Allie and Sarah became my reluctant cheerleaders. Allie would hover at the edge of the yard, arms crossed, calling out pointers in her stubborn, no-nonsense way. Sarah would slip me energy drinks or little candies, claiming they were "focus fuel."

When it was one-on-one, I excelled. I could easily sense my opponent's emotions and use them against them—amplifying their anxiety until their hands shook, flooding them with fear until they hesitated, or pushing a sharp wave of hopelessness that made them drop their guard entirely. In those moments, I felt powerful, precise, almost unstoppable.

But the moment it turned into a group battle, I unraveled. Instead of wielding my mark like a weapon, I became a vessel for everyone else's chaos. Kaylen's explosive aggression, Cade's burning focus, Hiro's darting instincts, Alice's coiled momentum…it was too loud. Too much.

It wasn't just the numbers. It was the noise. One mind, I could dismantle. But many? They dismantled me. I stumbled more than I struck, nearly tripping over my own feet. My focus shattered, my dagger felt like dead weight in my hand. Sometimes I froze completely, wide-eyed, breath locked in my chest as the swirl of everyone's emotions crashed over me like a tidal wave.

No one yelled at me. That almost made it worse.

Kaylen didn't snarl or snap. Instead, she stood off to the side afterward, arms crossed, her expression unreadable. Not disappointed, but watchful, as though she were trying to decide if I would sink or claw my way up.

Cade stayed steady. Supportive. He never pushed too far, but he didn't coddle me either. His quiet belief felt like a silent pressure against my ribs, both comforting and suffocating.

Sarah and Allie watched each match, calling encouragement, trying to keep my spirits up. But inside, the failures piled up like bruises.

Every night, I went to bed with my muscles screaming and my head pounding. Every morning, I woke up with the cold dread of failure clinging to my skin.

Allie would try to tell me it was just a learning curve. Sarah would squeeze my hand and tell me I was stronger than I thought. But each failure dug deeper, making that raw edge inside me sharper, angrier.

After about a month of doing the mock battles, one session finally broke me. It started like the others—a snowy yard, teams split up. Me and Kaylen against Cade and Hiro. I tried to steady my breathing, to stay in the moment. But as soon as they moved, the flood hit.

I stumbled again, hitting the frozen ground so hard that the breath whooshed out of me. I tried to scramble up, but my knees buckled. I pressed my palms to the snow, gasping.

"Get up!" Kaylen barked from somewhere behind me.

But I couldn't. I couldn't even breathe. My head was a swirling storm of other people's emotions—fear, frustration, anger, impatience—all clawing at me, burying me alive.

"I can't do this!" I screamed, my voice ripping out of me so sharp it echoed across the yard. I slammed my fists into the ground, over and over. "I can't! I can't fucking do this!"

Hot tears burned down my cheeks, freezing in the cold air. "I'm not strong enough!" I sobbed. "I can't control it, I can't

347

even control myself! I don't know what the fuck I'm doing out here. I'm not a fighter! I'm not some chosen hero! I'm nothing!"

My breath tore in and out of me in labored, uneven bursts. The snow around my hands was streaked with red from my scraped knuckles. I lifted my head, vision blurring. "I'm never going to be ready! Michael will kill me—he'll kill all of us—because I can't do it!"

I heard footsteps crunch toward me, but I didn't look up. My whole body shook, a deep, wild tremor that started in my chest and spread outward like a shattering window.

Then a shadow fell over me. I didn't even have to look up to know it was Cade. He didn't speak. Didn't demand I get up. Didn't tell me to stop. Instead, he crouched down beside me, his big hand settling gently on the back of my neck. For a second, I almost flinched away. But his touch was warm and comforting.

I let out a strangled sob, my forehead dropping to the ground again. Cade didn't move. He stayed right there, his hand firm and steady. After a long moment, he leaned in closer, his breath curling against my ear. "Get up," he said quietly. Not an order. An invitation.

I shook my head, my fingers digging into the snow. "I can't," I whispered, my voice hoarse. "I don't know how."

Cade's thumb pressed lightly into my neck, almost like a pulse point. "Yes, you do," he murmured. "You've gotten up every single time life has knocked you down."

My shoulders trembled.

"You don't have to do it alone," he said. "But you have to stand."

I stayed there, panting, my heartbeat roaring in my ears. Finally I slowly pushed up onto my hands. Then my knees. Cade didn't rush me. He rose to his feet as I did, moving in close when I wobbled. My breath stuttered out of me, but I looked up. Met his eyes. His gaze was fierce and unwavering, but there was something else there too. Something soft, something only for me.

348

Without a word, he reached down and hooked his arm around my waist. Then, with that same unshakable calm, he stepped us both into the shadows.

When we landed, we were deeper in the woods—trees crowding around us, snow clinging to the low branches. Cade didn't pause. Another step. Shadows rolled up and over us again. When we reappeared, it was in the familiar clearing—the same one that had burned itself into my memory with the taste of his mouth and the scrape of his hands.

Cade didn't let me go. His hand fisted in the back of my jacket, his other arm banding around my waist like iron. Our breaths steamed in the cold air, mingling between us.

Then his fingers found my chin, tilting my face up to his. "You don't get to say that," he rasped, his voice vibrating through me. "You don't get to give up. Not here. Not now. You hear me?"

I tried to turn my face away, but he tightened his grip, forcing me to meet his eyes.

"Say it again," he demanded, his tone a dangerous low growl. "Say you're nothing. I fucking dare you."

I swallowed hard, my throat raw. The words tangled there, refusing to come out.

He shook his head, fierce and close. "You're not nothing. You're everything. You're more than any of us. You just haven't seen it yet."

My pulse thundered between us, my body strung so tight it felt like I might shatter.

Then, with a single, violent haul, he dragged me even closer. "Now," he snarled, his breath hot against my lips. "Show me you're still here."

My hands shot up, grabbing at his hair and yanking him down to my mouth. The kiss was need, pure and desperate. My fingers twisted in his hair as I opened to him, my breath catching when he groaned low in his chest.

Cade didn't hesitate. His hands were already at my hips, yanking my leggings and underwear down in a rough, hungry motion. I kicked them off, boots vanishing somewhere in the

349

snow, not that I cared. The cold slapped against my thighs, but it only fed the fire roaring inside me.

I reached for his belt, fingers fumbling, shaking with adrenaline and heat, but he growled and knocked my hands away, tearing it open and shoving his pants down with a sound that was more beast than man.

We were a mess of limbs, gasps, desperate touches. His hands found my hips again, gripping the exact spots he'd bruised before, his fingers digging deep like he wanted to feel the imprint later.

Before I could draw another breath, he spun me, pushing me forward until my palms slammed against a snow-covered tree.

"Don't move," he growled, his voice feral. "Stay just like that. I want you to feel every inch of what you do to me."

My forehead dropped to the bark. My breath fogged in front of me, chest heaving, heart galloping.

Then he was there—his cock thick and hot and hard as steel, lining up at my entrance. One brutal thrust and he was inside me, buried to the hilt.

I cried out, body arching back against him as the shock of it tore through me. He filled me so completely, it bordered on bliss. The pressure was perfect. Overwhelming. Maddening.

I clung to the bark, my legs trembling, barely able to hold myself up as he set a vicious pace, every thrust pounding into me like he was trying to push me through the tree itself. The length of him dragged against every swollen nerve, the head of his cock hitting that spot so deep I saw stars.

His hand slid around my front and wrapped around my throat, yanking me upright so my spine arched against him. "Feel me," his voice pure gravel, teeth scraping along my neck. "Right here. Right fucking now."

I could only gasp, my voice breaking into low, choked moans as he drove into me again and again.

He bit down on my neck, and I screamed, the sound raw and wild. His hand clamped down on my waist, holding me

350

steady as he pounded into me, harder, deeper, ruthless with every thrust.

"Is this what you need, baby?" he growled, voice hot against my ear. "You need me to fuck the fear out of you? The doubt? Every last excuse?"

The word *baby* slammed into me like another thrust. I felt myself unraveling—tight, white-hot, every nerve raw. His rhythm was relentless, punishing, perfect. My cries turned feral.

Then his mouth was at my neck again, his teeth dragging over my skin as his grip on my throat tightened, just enough to make the world tilt.

I shattered.

My scream ripped through the trees, sharp and wild, my body clenching around him as the orgasm tore through me, violent and uncontrollable.

"Fuck, that's it," he rasped against my neck. "Look at you. Coming so fucking hard on my cock. Proving you're still here."

My knees gave out but he held me up, grinding deeper as I broke apart in his hands.

He paused only long enough to pull back—and I turned, wild-eyed, grabbing at him as I jumped. My legs wrapped around his waist, my back hitting the tree so hard snow rained down in glittering flurries.

He caught me without faltering, one hand locking under my ass, the other fisting in my hair. I was already grinding against him, already guiding him back inside, dragging my teeth across his jaw.

His head dropped forward, his breath frantic against my mouth. "Lena—fuck—you feel like goddamn heaven."

I rolled my hips hard and fast, making us both moan as I tightened around him. "Give it to me," I hissed, biting his bottom lip until I tasted blood. "Fill me."

He let out a strangled sound, fucking up into me with brutal force, his fingers digging into my skin like he didn't trust I was real. I clenched hard around him and he shattered, slamming into me with three final, desperate thrusts. His head tipped back as he came with a cry that sounded like my name and something darker, deeper.

His release flooded into me, hot and pulsing, and the feeling of it—of *him*—triggered mine all over again. My body locked down, muscles seizing, thighs trembling around his waist as I came hard, lips parting on a broken, breathless moan that didn't sound human.

We clung to each other, bodies shuddering, breath catching, sweat already cooling too fast in the sharp winter air. I could feel every twitch of him still buried inside me. Every aftershock, every staggered breath.

When the last wave finally ebbed, Cade sagged forward, pressing his forehead to my shoulder, his breathing labored.

After a long, panting moment, I eased back. His cock slipped free with a slow, wet drag that made both of us shudder. I slid down his front until my feet hit the snow, my legs shaky, barely holding me up.

I felt the warmth dripping down my thigh. A slick, messy trail of both of us, already cooling against the frozen air. I felt raw. Stretched. Claimed in every way but name.

His arms stayed around me, steady and warm even as the cold bit at our bare skin. I leaned into him, pressing my lips to his jaw, my fingers tracing the fresh red lines I'd left on his neck.

For a long, breathless moment, we didn't move. We just held each other—a wild, broken, perfect mess in the snowy clearing. Then his eyes met mine, raw and unguarded, shining with something I didn't dare name. Before I could look away, he leaned in and pressed his lips to mine.

But this kiss... it wasn't violent. It wasn't sharp or punishing. It was slow, warm and achingly gentle. I froze at first, caught off guard by the tenderness. My fingers hovered uncertainly at his shoulders, my lips barely moving under his.

But he didn't push. He just stayed there, kissing me like I was something treasured.

A shaky breath escaped my chest, and my hands finally slid up, curling around his neck. I kissed him back, hesitant at first... then deeper. A delicate sound slipped from my throat, and I hated how much I needed it, how much I craved that softness, that warmth.

His hand rose to cradle my cheek, thumb brushing beneath my eye, his mouth moving against mine like he had all the time in the world. I melted into it, into him, letting that slow, gentle heat replace the rage, the sharp edges, the fear.

When we finally broke apart, my forehead rested against his, our noses brushing lightly. There were no words. Just a soft, fragile hush that felt more intimate than anything else we'd done.

Reluctantly, I moved out of his arms and reached for my leggings, the cold biting hard now that the fire between us had quieted. My fingers fumbled at the waistband as I shivered, trying to pull them up with some dignity.

Cade was moving too, fumbling to get dressed.

"Are you just going to whisk me away every time I lose my shit?" I asked, breathless and half-laughing, even as my fingers shook from the cold.

He glanced up at me, mischief glinting in his eyes. "Maybe," he said, straightening up. "It works, doesn't it?"

I rolled my eyes as I struggled to get my second boot on. "I guess I'll just have to start throwing fits more often."

Cade stepped closer, his eyes softened just slightly as they held mine. "Don't tempt me," he murmured, voice low enough that it shivered right through me.

I opened my mouth to fire back some witty retort, but the words died in my throat when I saw the faint curve at the edge of his lips. I huffed out a shaky laugh instead. "Come on," I muttered, turning toward the path. "Before I freeze to death out here."

A low huff of amusement rumbled in his chest. Without another word, he wrapped his arms around me, and the world slipped sideways in that familiar rush of cold shadow.

When the ground steadied beneath me again, we were standing at the edge of the yard behind the cabin. When we got inside, I glanced around. The main area was warm and quiet, the scent of cedar and faint traces of dinner still lingering.

Vallerie sat at the counter with a book in one hand and a half-drunk mug of tea in the other. She looked up as we entered, one brow arching just slightly.

"You better now?" she asked, voice even but laced with meaning.

"Yes," I said, cheeks already flushing.

Marcela and Kaylen were at the table playing cards. Marcela looked up and smirked. "Well, that didn't take long."

Kaylen didn't even glance up. "At least you're both fully clothed this time."

Cade walked past them without comment, and I followed, cheeks burning.

Allie sat on the couch by the fireplace, her legs tucked under her, reading something on her burner phone.

I looked around the room. "Where is everyone?"

Allie looked up. "Oh. Sarah, Hiro, and Alice ran to the store. Sarah insisted on going. Not sure why."

I blinked, puzzled, but before I could ask more, the front door swung open. Sarah practically stomped inside followed by Hiro and Alice. Sarah's arms were loaded with grocery bags. She made a beeline for the kitchen island, dropping the bags with a loud thud. Allie arched an eyebrow, and I walked over, curiosity burning through my cold-numbed limbs.

Sarah started pulling things out. Boxes of cake mix, bags of powdered sugar, cartons of eggs, bottles of oil, food coloring... and finally, with a dramatic flourish, she hauled out a giant bottle of vodka and set it down with a heavy clunk.

My eyes went wide, then I laughed. It burst out sharp and surprised, curling through my chest like a sudden spark.

Sarah shot me a wicked grin. "You didn't think I'd let you keep spiraling, did you?" She gestured broadly at the supplies. "Drunk baking. Tonight."

I nearly doubled over. "Sarah... Oh my God."

Vallerie stepped closer, eyeing the pile like it might explode. "What in the world is drunk baking?"

354

Sarah spun on her heel to face her, looking downright delighted. "It's exactly what it sounds like. You get drunk, you try to bake something pretty, and you fail spectacularly. Think *Nailed It* but with more swearing and a serious lack of coordination. Lena and I used to do this all the time. It's been way too long."

Marcela's eyes gleamed with interest. "Isn't that dangerous?"

"Extremely," Sarah said, deadpan. "Which is half the fun."

Kaylen scoffed from her spot at the table. "You seriously think now's the time for this kind of bullshit?"

Sarah didn't even blink. She turned, looked Kaylen straight in the eye, and said calmly, "I may not have a mark, but I'm not an idiot. I know Lena. And I know when she's about two steps from burning out. So here's the deal, she's taking tonight and tomorrow off. No sparring, no mock battles, no mark training. You can have her back the day after."

Kaylen's lips parted like she had something to say, but she caught herself and stormed out of the room instead.

Sarah turned back to the group, hands on her hips. "Anyone else got a problem with it?"

A beat of silence.

Marcela shrugged. "Hell, I'll taste-test whatever chaos comes out of that oven."

Alice smiled. "Better than another strategy meeting. I'm in."

Vallerie sighed, but a tiny smile tugged at the corner of her mouth. "Just... try not to burn the kitchen down."

Sarah winked. "No promises."

I looked at her, warmth blooming under my skin, so fierce it nearly knocked me off balance.

"Thank you," I said, my voice barely above a whisper.

She softened instantly, stepping forward to pull me into a quick, fierce hug. "Always."

It didn't take long before the kitchen looked like a war zone. Sarah immediately claimed DJ duties, blasting a chaotic mix of pop, old-school rock, and random dance

355

anthems loud enough to rattle the cabinet doors. She bopped around with a mixing spoon like a microphone, shrieking lyrics between swigs of vodka.

Allie had cake mix in her hair within five minutes. Later, she tried to measure out oil with shaky hands, only for Sarah to "help," jostling her elbow and sending half the bottle splashing straight into the mixing bowl.

"Jesus Christ!" Allie yelled, flinging her hands up.

"It's fine!" Sarah shouted back, tears of laughter streaming down her face. "Extra moisture makes it fluffy!"

Biscuit paced along the edge of the kitchen like a tiny, judgmental overseer. Every time someone dropped something, she darted over to sniff it, only to recoil dramatically and skitter back under the table like it had personally offended her.

Vallerie and Marcela hovered near the island, pretending to be horrified, but I saw the way Marcela was hiding her giggles behind her fingers. Even Vallerie cracked a reluctant smile.

Kaylen reappeared eventually, arms crossed and eyes narrowed like she was watching a dangerous experiment. But when Sarah passed her a shot, she took it without blinking and then slammed it back like a challenge.

"Holy shit," Sarah gasped, clutching her chest. "She lives!"

Cade leaned against the counter, an amused expression on his face as he watched me drunkenly swirl blue frosting that was supposed to be "sky blue" but looked more like alien sludge.

"I think I nailed it," I announced proudly, brandishing the frosting knife like a sword.

"Lena, babe," Allie called, squinting at my lumpy cake, "what exactly is it supposed to be?"

I looked at it. Really looked. Then I burst into giggles so hard I nearly fell over. "A fucking masterpiece!"

Sarah doubled over laughing, her head nearly hitting the counter. Marcela was crying. Even Kaylen snorted, shaking her head as she took another sip of vodka.

At one point, I tried to pipe "Eat your heart out" across the top of a cake, only to realize halfway through I'd run out of room and had to awkwardly squish the last few letters in a crooked line down the side.

I stepped back to admire my creation, arms flimsy, chest heaving from laughter. My face was red, my stomach hurt, and my head felt light and blissful.

I yanked off my hoodie, too warm from the alcohol and chaos. I stood there in just a tank top and sweats, hair messy, cheeks flushed, and not caring one bit. Across the kitchen, I caught Cade watching me, his gaze hungrier than it had any right to be.

Everything was messy, loud, and absolutely ridiculous. But for the first time in so long, I felt... free. No panic clawing at my ribs. No pressure. Just sugar, alcohol, and the people who had somehow become my whole world.

Sarah stumbled over, arm slinging around my shoulders, eyes bright and glassy. "You good?" she slurred.

I looked at her and nodded, a wobbly grin spreading across my face. "Yeah," I breathed. "I think I actually am."

The night wound down, but no one seemed ready to leave the table just yet. Empty bottles and half-eaten cake slices cluttered every surface, powdered sugar dusted across the counter like a snowdrift.

Most of us were drunk—blissfully, ridiculously drunk. Allie was slumped forward with her cheek pressed against her arm, giggling at something Vallerie was muttering under her breath. Marcela was perched on the edge of her chair, cheeks flushed, laughing at Hiro, who had his head tipped back, nearly falling off his seat when Alice swatted at him with a frosting-coated spoon. Even Kaylen, who had been the last holdout, was snickering softly, her chin propped on her palm.

Cade, of course, sat at the far end of the table, nursing a glass of water. His arms were crossed over his chest, and every so often he'd shake his head, amusement tugging at the corners of his mouth.

"You know," I slurred, pointing my fork at him from across the table. "You'd be so much hotter if you joined us."

Cade raised an eyebrow, clearly fighting a smile. "I think I'll survive," he said dryly. "One of us has to stay upright in case someone decides to set the kitchen on fire."

Sarah snorted so hard she nearly spit out her drink. "We already told you, Cade, we're *professional* drunk bakers. Nothing to worry about."

"Professional," he echoed, a hint of a laugh slipping through. "Right."

Allie suddenly lifted her head, squinting blearily around the room. "Wait... did we even turn the oven off?"

Everyone froze.

Then, as one chaotic, tipsy mass, half the table bolted up and stumbled toward the kitchen.

I cackled so hard I almost fell out of my chair, tears blurring my vision. Cade sighed and finally stood, following us into the kitchen with that resigned patience of someone who knew they were entirely outnumbered.

When he passed me, he paused just long enough to lean in close, his voice low enough for only me to hear. "You," he murmured, eyes flicking to my lips. "Are going to feel this in the morning."

A shiver slid down my spine, cutting through the haze of alcohol, and for a moment the noise of the room faded entirely.

Then he straightened, stepping past me to rescue what was left of the kitchen.

Maybe an hour later, people started wandering toward their rooms in slow, clumsy waves. Alice, Vallerie, and Marcela disappeared first, giggling and leaning on each other for balance. Kaylen wandered off next, muttering something about "never doing this again"—though the smile on her face suggested otherwise. Hiro was still at the table, slumped forward with his head on his folded arms, snoring lightly.

Allie and Sarah finally pushed back from the table, weaving toward the stairs in a crooked line. "Lena!" Sarah called, her voice pitching high with tipsy glee. "Come on! Bedtime!"

"I'm coming!" I called after them, pushing up from my chair a little too fast. The room spun and I teetered forward.

I slowly made my way to the staircase and when I tried to go up, my foot caught on the first step. I went down in a graceless heap.

"Shit!" I gasped, but before I could scramble up, I heard Sarah's shriek of laughter from the landing above. She dropped to her knees, cackling so hard tears streamed down her face. Allie leaned against the railing, her face bright red with giggles.

I started laughing too, breathless and snorting, unable to stop. Sarah finally flopped down completely, clutching her stomach.

Cade appeared at my side, sighing. He shook his head, scooping me up into his arms like I weighed nothing.

"Oh my god," I wheezed, arms looping around his neck. "I swear I had that step under control."

"Mm-hm," he hummed, carrying me easily up the stairs.

When we reached the bedroom, he laid me down gently on my bed. Allie had already face-planted onto her mattress, her shoes still on. Sarah barely made it to hers before collapsing in a pile.

I looked up at Cade, a dopey, lopsided grin on my face. Without thinking, I reached up, curling my fingers into his shirt, trying to tug him down. "Stay," I mumbled, leaning in to kiss him.

He paused, eyes searching mine for a moment that stretched and softened. Then he gave a quiet chuckle, slipping a hand to my cheek. He pressed a kiss to my forehead instead, warm and lingering.

"Get some rest," he murmured, gently untangling my hand from his shirt and tucking the blanket around me.

I cracked one eye open, lips quirking. "I only let men tell me what to do when they're fucking me."

359

Cade grinned, brushing his thumb along my lips. "Then lucky for me... I'm the one doing both."

A lazy smile tugged at my mouth, but I was already half-asleep, his words curling around me like a blanket. And then I was gone, drifting into sleep with laughter still echoing faintly in my head.

Chapter 28

I woke up to the pounding realization that my skull might actually crack open. Groaning, I rolled over, squinting against the pale winter light that filtered through the window. Every inch of my body felt heavy and sluggish, and my mouth tasted like a mix of frosting and regret.

Across the room, Allie was sprawled face-down on her bed, one leg hanging off the side like she'd just collapsed mid-motion. Sarah was curled in a tight ball, clutching a pillow over her head.

Sarah let out a low groan that turned into a muffled curse. She peeked out from under the pillow, her hair sticking up in every direction.

"Holy shit," she rasped. "Did we get hit by a truck? Or several?"

I snorted, then immediately regretted it as pain ricocheted through my skull. "Feels like it," I croaked.

Allie made a noise that might have been agreement, or just the sound of her soul leaving her body.

Somehow, we managed to drag ourselves out of bed and shuffle into the hallway, clinging to the railing as we made our slow, tragic descent. When we finally reached the kitchen, Cade was already there, standing by the counter like some annoyingly put-together guardian angel. He held a Gatorade bottle in each hand and nodded toward a third waiting on the counter.

"Drink," he ordered, his voice gentle but firm. "All of you."

I grabbed mine and chugged half of it in one go, nearly crying as the cold liquid hit my stomach. Sarah made a strangled sound and grabbed hers, sinking into the barstool like she might never move again.

Allie took hers and leaned heavily against the counter, her face pale. "You're a saint," she muttered to Cade. "Thank you."

Cade just raised an eyebrow, sliding a small bottle of ibuprofen across the counter like an offering.

A muffled snore interrupted the quiet. We all turned to find Hiro still slumped over the far end of the table, arms folded under his head, a thin line of drool trailing onto the wood. Someone had draped a blanket over his shoulders, and Biscuit was perched at the edge of it like she was standing guard.

Sarah started giggling, each laugh sounding like it might shatter her completely. "Oh my god," she wheezed. "He's been here all night?"

Cade sighed. "I tried to move him, but... well." He gestured vaguely.

Sarah chugged on her bottle, wincing. "We are never drinking that much vodka again," she croaked.

I managed a weak laugh, clutching my bottle like a lifeline. "Agreed. My soul hurts."

Allie dragged her free hand down her face. "I vote we move to the couches and do absolutely nothing today."

Sarah immediately nodded. "Movies. Junk food. Minimal movement. I'm not even wearing pants if I can help it."

I raised my bottle in solidarity. "Seconded."

Cade just shook his head, an amused, long-suffering sort of smile tugging at his mouth as he watched us shuffle toward the living room like a herd of half-dead zombies.

We collapsed onto the couches, limbs tangled, blankets dragged over us like we were nesting birds. Someone grabbed the remote and flipped through options until we settled on something dumb and comforting. Background noise to our collective groans and occasional giggles.

The day slipped by in a hazy, half-conscious drift. We barely moved from the couches except to grab more snacks or shuffle to the bathroom, groaning like the dead every time we stood.

Marcela and Alice wandered in around midmorning, both looking mildly regretful and deeply unamused by the sunlight. Alice muttered something about her brain being "too loud," while Marcela just grunted and curled up in the nearest chair with a blanket and a cup of coffee. Hiro eventually shuffled in too, blanket still wrapped around his shoulders like a giant cocoon, and dropped into one of the chairs with a resigned grunt.

By evening, the sky had changed into that soft winter twilight, the kind that made the world look quiet and pale. Someone had put on another movie. I was sprawled across the couch, Sarah wedged against my side, Allie's feet in my lap. My eyes felt heavy, but not in a bad way. More like I was finally letting my body rest after weeks of constant fight-or-flight tension.

The front door creaked open, and Cade stepped inside, his shoulders tense and his expression thoughtful. He closed the door quietly behind him, brushing snow off his boots before stepping fully into the kitchen.

He scanned the room, then his eyes landed on me. "Lena, can I talk to you for a minute?"

I carefully disentangled myself from the pile of blankets and limbs. Sarah gave me a sleepy little wave as I stood, and Allie just grumbled when I moved her legs.

I shuffled over to the kitchen, tugging my sweater sleeves down over my hands. "What's up?" I asked, leaning against the counter.

Cade glanced back at the living room, then lowered his voice. "I want to take you to meet someone," he said, his green eyes steady on mine.

I blinked, caught off guard. "Who?"

He hesitated, then gave a small shake of his head. "Someone I think can help you with your mark."

My stomach flipped with something between curiosity and unease. "Who is it?"

Cade's gaze softened. "His name is Reid," he said simply. "And... he's different. Trust me."

I looked away for a second, then back. "Why now?"

"I talked to Lorelei," he said. "She agreed it's time. You've been working hard. But I think this might be the push you need."

For a long moment, I just looked at him, my pulse ticking fast beneath my skin. Then finally, I exhaled, nodding.

"Okay," I said quietly. "When do we leave?"

"Tomorrow morning," he said. "Pack a bag. We'll be flying to Arizona."

"Arizona?" I repeated, my brows shooting up. "How are we supposed to do that? Can't Michael trace us?"

Cade shook his head. "Gage has it covered. He handled the tickets, the fake IDs... all of it. He's already cleared us through every system. Nobody will be able to trace us."

"Okay," I replied reluctantly.

• • •

I woke up before dawn, the sky still a deep, heavy blue outside my window. Frost clung to the edges of the glass, turning the world into a blurred, frozen painting.

I moved quietly around the room, tugging on jeans and a soft sweater, then threw my hair up into a high pony tail. My hands shook slightly as I packed a small bag, just the essentials. Toiletries, a change of clothes, the small bottle of ibuprofen I seemed to live on these days.

Downstairs, Cade was already waiting. He stood near the door, a dark jacket zipped up, hands tucked into his pockets. His hair was slightly damp, like he'd just showered recently. He looked up as I stepped off the last stair, his gaze moving over me slowly. A small, almost shy smile tugged at his lips. "Morning," he said softly.

"Morning," I managed, my voice rough with nerves.

He lifted a hand, gesturing toward the door. "Ready?"

I looked past him for a heartbeat, out at the snow-glittered yard, the faint glow of the moon still lingering on the drifts.

"Yeah," I said finally, though it sounded more like a question than an answer.

364

Cade moved first, stepping forward and brushing his hand lightly along my lower back as he guided me out the door. Outside, our breaths puffed into the icy air as we crossed to the Jeep. Its engine was already running, windows cleared. Of course he had it warmed up already.

Cade opened the passenger door, but I hesitated, glancing back at the warm glow spilling from the cabin windows. I thought of Allie and Sarah asleep upstairs. Of the echoing laughter in the kitchen the other night. Of Biscuit, probably curled in Cade's abandoned blanket on the couch.

Then Cade's hand came to rest gently on my lower back again. "Hey," he murmured, leaning in closer. "We'll come back. I promise."

I met his eyes, finding something steady there. A quiet certainty I couldn't name but wanted desperately to trust. I nodded, stepping up and sliding into the seat.

Cade closed the door softly, then rounded to the driver's side. When he climbed in, he gave me a sidelong glance before putting it in drive. The headlights cut across the snow, painting pale paths through the darkness as we pulled away. As the cabin disappeared in the rearview mirror, I curled my fingers into my lap, trying to steady my breathing.

The drive to the small regional airport felt endless and fleeting all at once. Cade's hand stayed on the gearshift most of the time, occasionally drifting to rest near my knee. Every time it did, something eased in my chest.

We didn't speak much. The dark roads were quiet, the world still waking up around us. By the time the first pale hints of sunrise touched the horizon, we were parking.

Inside the airport, everything felt too bright, too loud. The polished floors reflected overhead lights, and the murmur of early travelers pressed in from all sides. I clutched my small bag tighter against my chest, trying to keep my breaths even.

Cade stayed close, his shoulder brushing mine every few steps. He guided me through security, through check-in, moving with that calm precision I'd come to rely on. But once we stepped into the gate area, the press of bodies grew thicker. A child shrieked somewhere behind us, someone sneezed violently, a woman laughed too loud at a phone call.

The noise blurred into a single, pulsing wave. I felt it in my head first—like a thousand emotions slamming into me at once. Fear, excitement, impatience, irritation. The taste of someone's anxiety coated my tongue like ash. My fingers curled tighter around the strap of my bag. My heart picked up, faster and faster, until my vision started to tunnel.

I tried to swallow, but my throat felt too tight. My lungs dragged uselessly at the air, as if I'd forgotten how to breathe. I stumbled backward, bumping into a nearby pillar.

Before I could slip further under, Cade was there. He stepped into my space, blocking the crowd from view. His hands cupped my face, thumbs sweeping under my jaw. His eyes locked on mine, clear and sharp and achingly calm. "Breathe," he said. "Lena. Look at me. Right here."

I tried, my eyes darting between his irises, my breath stuttering in sharp, broken pulls.

"You're okay," he whispered. One thumb traced my cheekbone. "I've got you. Nothing else matters right now. Just us."

I gulped in another shaky breath. Then another.

Cade pressed his forehead lightly against mine. "In," he murmured. We inhaled together. "Out."

We did it again. And again. Slowly, the edges of the world softened. The noise faded, like someone turning down the volume on a chaotic song. My fists loosened, my chest finally expanding properly. My forehead stayed pressed to his, our breaths mixing.

"Good," he whispered, a hint of relief in his voice now. "There you are."

I let out a tiny, strangled laugh. Cade leaned back slightly, just enough to search my eyes. One corner of his mouth tilted up, the smallest, most tender smile.

"Ready to get on that plane?" he asked, his thumb brushing under my lip.

I nodded, breathless but steadier.

"Good," he said again, pressing a quick, gentle kiss to my forehead before stepping back. He reached for my hand, and I didn't hesitate before curling my fingers around his.

The flight itself blurred into a strange, suspended quiet. Cade and I sat side by side, our fingers entwined nearly the entire time. Every time I straightened or my breath hitched, his thumb swept across my knuckles, steady and sure.

He didn't sleep. Not once. While I dozed in short, shallow bursts, Cade stayed alert, his gaze darting around the cabin, scanning every movement like a silent guardian. Every so often, I'd open my eyes to find him already watching me. He'd offer a small, reassuring squeeze, and I'd squeeze back.

By the time the wheels touched down on the warm, sun-baked tarmac, my fingers felt almost molded to his. We got our luggage and made our way to the rental counter, the Arizona sun was already pressing down, making me squint even through the airport glass.

Cade handled most of the details, moving through the paperwork and keys with ease. I hovered beside him, still a little wrung out from the flight—the echo of other passengers' emotions lingering in my head like static.

When we finally stepped outside, the warmth wrapped around me in a way that felt almost cleansing after so many cold, gray days.

Cade paused beside the small, dusty SUV we'd been given, tossing our bags into the back. Then he opened the passenger door for me, his hand brushing lightly against my lower back as I climbed in. The interior smelled faintly of sunscreen and old leather. Cade started the engine and turned to look at me.

"You holding up?" he asked.

"Yeah," I replied. "Better than on the plane."

A small smile tugged at his mouth. He reached over, squeezing my knee before shifting into drive. The road out of the city quickly gave way to long, flat stretches of highway, framed by low, rolling hills and sparse desert brush. It felt like we were driving into another world.

Cade kept one hand on the wheel, the other resting close enough that our fingers brushed occasionally on the center console. At some point, I leaned my head back and closed my eyes, letting the motion of the car and the sun-drenched silence wash over me. When I opened them again, we were turning onto a narrow road lined with cactus and wildflowers. Ahead, I saw a small sign half-hidden by branches that said, *Welcome to Calverin.*

Cade slowed, his gaze scanning the quaint little street that unfolded before us—a handful of small houses, a dusty general store, a couple of wide porches strung with wind chimes and flowering plants. It looked more like a peaceful retreat than a town.

"This is it," he said, glancing at me. "Reid's place is at the end of the main road."

I swallowed hard, nerves twisting low in my belly. But Cade reached over, his thumb brushing my knuckles.

"You're okay," he murmured. "He's... you'll see."

The road narrowed into a sandy path lined with flowering desert shrubs and spindly trees casting pockets of dappled shade. We drove slowly, the tires crunching over the dirt, until Cade finally pulled off near a small, sun-bleached gate.

Beyond it stood a modest adobe-style house. Pale clay walls, a deep front porch draped in hanging plants, colorful pottery clustered around the steps. Wind chimes of all shapes and sizes tinkled softly in the warm breeze, filling the air with a peaceful, melodic hush. A stone walkway led from the gate to the door, where a simple wooden welcome sign hung.

Cade turned off the engine and glanced at me. "You ready?" he asked.

"I think so," I replied.

We got out but before we could even step away from the SUV, two neighbors came out from a nearby house, moving toward us with slow, deliberate caution.

One was a slightly older man wearing a simple t-shirt and khaki shorts, lines carved around his mouth and eyes. The other, a woman about my age, stood beside him, her arms folded tight, her eyes searching.

The man spoke first, voice calm but carrying an unmistakable authority. "Can we help you?"

Cade raised his hands slightly, palms open. "We're here to see Reid," he said evenly.

The woman tilted her head, her gaze narrowing. "Everyone says that," she said. "Doesn't mean they should."

The man's eyes stayed locked on me, unwavering and careful.

Before I could find words, a warm voice called from the porch—bright and gentle, somehow both young and endless.

"It's alright, Jim," the voice said. "They're expected."

My gaze snapped up. The man wore a soft gray sweater that hung loose against his slim frame and faded jeans rolled at the ankles, skin pale where the sun had yet to reach. His light brown hair curled lightly around his ears, soft and mussed as if he'd just woken up from a long nap. He looked to be in his early twenties. His face was open and untroubled, as if he'd never known a moment of pain or bitterness.

But his eyes—

My breath caught mid-step. Those eyes didn't belong to someone so young. They were wrong in the most impossible, beautiful way. Not wrong like unsettling. Wrong like finding an ocean in the middle of a desert, a vast, endless depth hidden behind an unassuming surface.

The older man, Jim, hesitated, still studying me. Then, after a slow breath, he stepped back. As he turned, a faint shimmer sparked along his forearm, a subtle ripple of light or energy, there and gone in a heartbeat. A warning, quiet but unmistakable.

Jim glanced at us one last time. "We'll be close by," he said.

The woman gave me a final sharp look before following him back toward their porch.

I could feel it as clearly as if he'd spoken it out loud. They weren't just neighbors. They were guards. Family. And they loved Reid enough to stand between him and anything.

Reid lifted one hand in a small wave, then opened both arms wide, as if he had been waiting for me.

Instantly, all of the tension vanished. My feet moved before my mind could catch up. I stepped forward, up the small path lined with desert flowers, toward that open embrace. Something inside me cracked wide open the closer I got, like a dam breaking after years of silent pressure.

Reid didn't hesitate. He met me at the bottom step, his arms wrapping around me in a slow, sure hug. The moment his warmth closed around me, the flood came. A shuddering sob tore from my chest, my fingers clutching at the soft fabric of his shirt. Relief, grief, exhaustion—every tattered edge inside me spilled out, and for once, there was no fight, no shame in it.

Reid held me firmly, one hand smoothing gently over my back, the other cradling the back of my head like I might collapse without him. "You're safe here," he said, his voice soft against my hair. "All of it is safe here."

I didn't know how long I stayed like that, shaking in his arms. Long enough for my breath to slow, for my fists to unclench, for my knees to stop threatening to give out beneath me.

When I finally drew back, Reid didn't let me go far. He kept his hands on my shoulders, his eyes searching my face.

"Better," he said softly, as though we'd shared some silent language only he and I understood.

I let out a broken, embarrassed laugh, scrubbing at my wet cheeks. "I'm sorry—"

"There's nothing to apologize for," Reid said immediately, his smile gentle and impossibly kind. "Tears are just proof you still have a soul."

Reid released my shoulders and turned to meet Cade's eyes standing beside me. "Good to see you again, Cade," he said, reaching out to clasp his arm.

Cade stepped forward, returning the gesture. "You too."

Reid's hand lingered for a second, giving Cade's arm a firm, knowing squeeze. "You've come a long way. They would be proud of you."

Cade's throat worked as he gave a quiet, sincere, "Thank you."

There was a weight to the exchange I didn't understand. Something unsaid that passed between them that was personal and private. I filed it away, even as questions stirred quietly in the back of my mind.

Reid turned back to me with a soft smile and gestured toward the open door. "Come on. Let's get you inside."

The moment I crossed the threshold, it felt like stepping into a different world. The air was warm, almost humming with a quiet, steady energy that wrapped around me like a thick blanket.

The space itself was simple but beautiful—smooth wooden floors, sunlit walls adorned with local art and small potted plants. A long shelf cradled rows of books, their spines well-worn. The scent of herbs and something sweet drifted lazily from the kitchen.

As I took another step, a sudden blur of golden fur bounded around the corner. A large golden retriever—older, with a soft white muzzle and big, soulful eyes—trotted straight to Reid's side and leaned gently against his leg.

Reid laughed, the sound like sunlight. He bent to ruffle the dog's ears. "This is Jasmine," he said. "She runs the place."

Jasmine turned toward me then, tail wagging in a slow, steady rhythm. Her eyes met mine, and before I could stop myself, I crouched down. Jasmine stepped forward and pressed her head firmly into my chest. A tiny, startled sound broke out of me as I buried my fingers in her thick fur.

Reid watched us with a gentle smile. "She has a mark too, you know," he said, almost conspiratorially. "The mark of unwavering devotion."

I let out a shaky laugh, my arms wrapping tighter around her.

Reid motioned to a deep, cushioned chair. "Sit," he said, his voice still gentle. "Make yourself at home."

I sank into the chair, the cushions soft and welcoming beneath me. Cade hesitated only a moment before sitting in the chair beside me, his eyes still scanning the room, protective even here.

Reid sat across from me, elbows on his knees, leaning forward slightly. He moved easily, pouring water into two heavy ceramic cups and handing them to us. I cradled the cup in my hands, feeling the warmth seep into my palms, the rhythmic weight of my breathing slowly matching the quiet pulse of the room.

Reid tilted his head, studying me—not invasive, just seeing. Really seeing. "Tell me what you carry," he said finally. "Or show me. You don't have to find the words."

I opened my mouth, then shut it again. My throat felt tight, a dozen things clawing to get out all at once. My fingers dug into the cup, my gaze dropping to Jasmine. Her big brown eyes watched me patiently, her tail thumping softly against the floor.

And somehow, I started to speak.

At first, the words came out in halting fragments—about Michael, the stolen marks, the guilt, the fear, the fury. About how each emotion felt like it would consume me whole, swallowing every piece of who I used to be.

Reid listened, never interrupting. He nodded sometimes, his eyes warm and knowing, like he could see every frayed edge inside me and still somehow wasn't afraid.

Finally, I trailed off, my breath shaky. I pressed a palm to my chest. "It's like… they're too big. These feelings. I can't hold them all. They crash over me and then I… I project them. Or I drown in them. I don't know how to be more than them."

Reid's eyes softened even more, impossibly gentle. He moved forward in his chair, his hand extending slowly until it hovered just above mine. "May I?" he asked.

I hesitated, but then nodded, my fingers trembling as they reached for his.

The moment our skin touched, it felt like stepping into warm sunlight after a long storm. A surge of energy moved between us—not just mine or his, but something shared.

"Close your eyes," he said softly. "Breathe with me."

I obeyed.

"Your emotions don't have to consume you," he said, his voice like a quiet current beneath my ribs. "They don't have to be your enemy. Let them move through you. Let them become a part of you, like a river shapes its banks—not to destroy you, but to carve you into something new."

I swallowed, my lips parting as a shiver ran down my spine.

"Feel them," Reid continued, his thumb brushing over my knuckles. "Each emotion is a note in a song. Your song. You can choose when to let them rise and when to let them quiet. You are not at their mercy. You are their conductor."

A slow, trembling breath left me.

Inside my mind, the chaos started to soften. The raging sea of colors and sensations melted. Not disappearing, but spreading, easing, finding channels instead of crashing in all directions.

I felt Reid's own emotions through the connection—an endless calm, a deep, steady warmth that loosened the knot inside me, like fingers unwinding a too-tight string.

Tears welled behind my eyelids, spilling silently down my cheeks. "It's so much," I whispered. "It's always so much."

Reid's grip stayed firm, unwavering. "And you are so much. That is your gift. You are not meant to shrink to fit the world's smallness. Let yourself be vast."

Something inside me trembled, then cracked wide open. I felt the grief, the rage, the love, the terror—and instead of pushing them away, I held them. Let them flow. Let them settle into me, threading into my bones instead of tearing them apart. A deep, shuddering exhale escaped me, my shoulders sagging forward. My forehead dropped to our joined hands.

Reid squeezed once. "There," he said. "You're not drowning anymore. You're sailing."

I stayed there, head bowed over our joined hands, as the last of the trembling worked its way out of me. My breath steadied, each inhale feeling fuller, each exhale leaving something behind.

Finally, I looked up, blinking at the warmth in Reid's gaze.

He studied me, then tilted his head slightly. "You've carried so much alone," he said quietly. "But the parts of you that were stolen? They are not truly gone."

A moment of confusion passed through me. "What do you mean?" I asked.

Reid leaned back a little but didn't let go of my hand. "Your marks... they were taken from your body, yes. But they were born of your soul. They are part of your essence, your deepest self. They can be severed, but they cannot be truly erased, not unless you allow it."

I shook my head, my brows pulling together. "I don't understand. How can I get them back? Is there a rune? Another dagger? Something I can use?"

Reid's smile was gentle and patient, but there was a deep certainty in it too. "There's no object that can give them back to you," he said. "No grand spell or secret chant. It is not about taking them back by force. You cannot reclaim them through violence or hatred, those are Michael's tools, not yours."

My mouth was suddenly dry.

Reid squeezed my hand. "You reclaim them by choosing yourself," he continued. "By refusing to believe that you are broken without them. By living, fiercely and fully, as though they are still yours... because they are."

My lips parted, but no words came.

"You have to stand in your truth," Reid said, leaning in slightly, his eyes impossibly deep. "To move forward as if they were never stolen at all. To act, to fight, to love as though you were always whole. Because you are."

A hot rush of tears blurred my vision.

"It sounds impossible," I rasped.

374

Reid's expression softened, and a small, warm laugh escaped him. "Most worthy things do."

I let out a shaky, disbelieving breath.

"It won't happen in a day," he added, his voice dropping to a near whisper. "It may not even happen in a single battle. But each time you choose to step forward instead of shrinking back, each time you claim your strength instead of mourning it… you will call those pieces home. Bit by bit."

Reid released my hand and sat back, his smile widening as he studied my face. "You're already stronger than you know," he said. "You always have been."

I sat there, my fingers still tingling from his touch, my mind trying to wrap around the impossible simplicity of what he had said. Reclaim them by choosing myself. By living as though I had never lost them. It sounded… wild. Naïve. And yet, as the words settled in my chest, I felt something inside me loosen, just slightly, like the first cautious crack of ice on a thawing lake.

My gaze strayed over to where Jasmine now lay sprawled at Reid's feet, belly up, snoring softly. Cade still sat nearby, his watchful gaze fixed on me.

I turned my eyes back to Reid, studying the relaxed curve of his shoulders, the warmth that seemed to radiate from him like a gentle flame.

"How…" I started, then faltered. "How are you like this?"

Reid's brow lifted slightly, amusement passing across his face. "Like what?"

I gestured vaguely at him, at the sunlit room, at the feeling of peace that clung to every surface. "This. All of this. You look… twenty, maybe twenty-two. But your eyes… they don't match. It's like they've seen centuries."

Reid's laugh was soft, airy, as though it had no weight at all. "Ah. The eyes always give it away," he said, shaking his head. He paused, as if debating whether to continue. Then he leaned forward, elbows resting loosely on his knees.

"I am over two hundred years old," he said simply. "Some call it a blessing, others a curse. My mark, Soul-Stillness, keeps me untethered from time. I don't age as others do."

My mouth fell open. "Two hundred..." I echoed, my voice barely above a whisper.

Reid only smiled, almost shyly. "I've watched the world change many times. Loved and lost many people. But there is always something worth staying for."

I swallowed hard, feeling my throat tighten. "That sounds... lonely."

His eyes softened again. "It can be," he admitted. "But I am never truly alone. There is always someone to guide, someone to comfort. And Jasmine, of course," he added, nodding down at the snoring dog.

A small laugh escaped me. "And your other mark... it's like mine, isn't it? But more..." I struggled for the word. "Alive."

Reid laughed, a sound like warm honey. "Yes. My other mark is empathy. Only, I've had over 200 years to perfect it."

Finally, I looked at him fully. "Thank you."

Reid's smile widened, slow and bright as a sunrise. "There is nothing to thank me for," he said. "I only opened a door. You're the one who walked through." He leaned back, his gaze still holding mine like a quiet promise. "You're not lost," he added. "You're becoming. And you're stronger than you know."

A tear slipped down my cheek, but this time I didn't wipe it away. Beside me, Cade reached over, his hand finding mine.

Just then I swear I felt it—a tug outside my body, my soul calling to what was stolen, telling me to bring it home.

Chapter 29

We drove back to the city in near silence. The sun slipped lower and lower, painting long streaks of orange and purple across the windshield. I watched the colors smear past without really seeing them.

My thoughts kept turning over themselves, looping in slow, heavy circles—Reid's voice, his touch, that strange quiet he left inside me. Each memory pressed against the next, too tangled to pull apart. I didn't notice the signs, the exits, the fading light. The world outside felt distant, like I was moving underwater.

When we finally pulled into the hotel lot, I realized I hadn't even felt the miles pass. My legs moved on autopilot as I followed Cade inside, up to a small room on the second floor.

Two beds. Plain, quiet. Neutral walls and a small table under the window.

Cade set his bag down and pulled out his phone. "You okay with takeout?" he asked.

I nodded, settling onto the edge of the bed like my body didn't quite belong to me. "Yeah. Anything is fine."

He ordered quickly, then sat across from me. We didn't talk. I ran my fingers along the seam of the blanket, my mind running in endless circles—not frantic, but constant, like a slow spin I couldn't stop. Reid's voice echoed inside me. His eyes, steady and endless. That feeling of my own emotions finally quieted enough to hear my heartbeat again.

Cade watched me without pushing, elbows resting on his knees. After a while, he stood and handed me a bottle of water from his bag. "Here," he murmured. "You need it."

I took it, our fingers brushing longer than necessary.

Dinner came not long after. I sat cross-legged on the bed, pushing food around more than actually eating it. Every so often, Cade's eyes met mine.

377

When we finally set the containers aside, Cade glanced at the clock, then back at me. "Try to rest," he said. "Tomorrow will be long."

I nodded and stood, grabbing a clean pair of pajama pants and a tank from my bag. I changed quickly in the bathroom, then crawled under my covers and turned to face the wall. My thoughts kept circling like slow tides, not panicked, just endlessly turning over everything, piece by piece.

Behind me, I heard Cade stir. The rustle of his sheets. A quiet sigh. I stared into the dark for a while, watching nothing.

I rolled onto my other side. Cade was already facing me, eyes open, watching quietly. Without thinking, I pushed the blankets back and crossed the small space between our beds. Wordless, I slipped under his covers and turned toward him.

He didn't say anything. He just moved closer, his arms folding around me like he'd been waiting. I pressed my forehead to his chest, breathing in the warmth of him. His hand slid up my back, settling between my shoulder blades.

Little by little, my thoughts began to slow. My breathing eased, my body softened. I felt safe enough to stop fighting my own mind for a while. I let myself fall into him. And then, finally, into sleep.

At some point in the night, I stirred, just enough to feel the weight of his arm tighten around me. The comfort was immediate, instinctive. I didn't fight it. I drifted under again.

I woke to warmth pressed all around me. My back was to Cade, his breathing brushing my neck, the solid weight of his arm draped over my waist. I stayed still, letting myself just *feel* it—the quiet, the safety, the soft rise and fall of his chest against my back.

I moved slightly, and his arm tightened, pulling me even closer.

"Morning," he murmured.

"Morning," I echoed.

We stayed like that for another minute, neither of us rushing to pull away.

Then I felt his forehead rest lightly against the back of my neck. "We should probably get ready," he said, though he didn't sound convinced.

"Yeah," I sighed, but I still didn't move.

After a few more minutes, I carefully slipped out from under his arm and sat on the edge of the bed, pushing my hair out of my face. Cade sat up behind me, his fingers brushing my shoulder briefly before he stood to stretch.

We got ready, gathered our bags, and made our way to the airport.

The flight back felt like a quiet test, and I passed it. At first, the emotions pressed around me. I sensed hints of fear, the low hum of exhaustion, bright sparks of anticipation. But instead of flooding me, they stayed at the edges, like birds just outside a window. I acknowledged each feeling, then let it drift away, just like Reid had shown me. I didn't drown in other people's storms. I held my own center.

Cade barely took his eyes off me the entire flight. His hand stayed wrapped around mine, his thumb brushing small circles against my skin every few minutes, a silent tether.

When we landed and stepped into the crisp night air, something inside me felt still. Ready.

We picked up the Jeep and started the drive back toward the cabin. The snow had deepened while we were gone. For a long stretch, Cade didn't speak. Then, as we rounded a bend, he finally glanced over at me. "I hope you know... I'm proud of you," he said. "Really proud."

The warmth of it moved through me, a different kind of glow than the one I'd found with Reid—sharper, more personal. It slipped under my ribs and settled there.

I turned toward him, unable to stop the small, genuine smile spreading across my face. "Thank you," I said.

He opened his mouth like he might say more, but then his phone rang, breaking the quiet. His expression changed instantly, tightening as he checked the screen. He answered on the first ring.

"Alice?" His voice sharpened, alert.

I felt the tension before I even heard anything else. I couldn't hear her words, but Cade's jaw clenched, his fingers flexing on the wheel. After a moment, he exhaled. "Say that again."

A beat.

"Fuck."

He ended the call and looked at me, his expression dark, protective.

"Sarah insisted on meeting Jack," he clipped. "She was worried he might report her missing or try to find her if she didn't see him face to face. The group was hesitant, but Alice went with her to keep watch."

My heart slammed against my ribs. "And?"

Cade's knuckles whitened on the steering wheel. "While they were talking, Chad appeared out of nowhere. Grabbed Sarah using his teleportation mark. Jack lunged for her, tried to pull her back, and got dragged with them. It all happened too fast. Alice couldn't stop it."

I stared at him, the words crashing over me in a cold, sickening wave.

"They're gone," I breathed.

Cade's jaw tightened. "We'll get them back," he promised. "We'll figure it out. But... they're gone right now."

For a moment, everything inside me went silent. Then it all hit at once—a suffocating wave of terror and rage so fierce I nearly doubled over. My heart slammed against my ribs, my ears rang, my vision tunneled.

Sarah. My person. My anchor. My sister in every way that mattered.

Gone.

My breath stuttered, my fingers clawing at the seatbelt like I might tear straight through it. A strangled scream ripped from my throat. "No," I gasped, shaking my head so hard my teeth rattled. "No. No, no, no—"

Cade's hand shot from the wheel, reaching for me, but I jerked back, pressing against the door. "She can't be gone," I choked out, my voice wild and raw. "We can't lose her. Not her. Not Sarah."

My pulse roared. My mark surged—heat, panic, something sharp enough to carve straight through me.

Cade's fingers closed firmly around my wrist. "Lena," he said, low and steady, threading through the chaos tearing me apart. "Look at me."

I couldn't. My chest felt like it might cave in, my entire body shaking.

"Lena," he repeated, his grip tightening. "We will get her back. Do you hear me? We will get her back."

I dragged my gaze up to his, my vision swimming, my breath broken and uneven. He didn't flinch. Just held my eyes as long as he could before jerking his focus back to the road. I collapsed forward, pressing my forehead to his shoulder, my hands fisting into his jacket like I might tear it apart.

"We have to get her back," I whispered, every word shattering. "She's my—she's my everything."

His arm came around me, fierce and protective. "And we will," he said again unwavering. "I swear it."

He hit the gas hard, the engine snarling as we surged forward.

"Fuck," he spat, his hand crushing the wheel. "Fucking Chad. I should've known—"

I lifted my head, my vision still blurred.

"They took her," I hissed, my voice trembling with something far beyond fear. "They fucking took her."

Rage flooded me, stronger than anything I'd ever felt. My fingers curled into claws against my thighs, nails biting deep. "I'll kill him," I snarled, each word vibrating from my chest. "I'll tear him apart with my own hands. I'll end every last one of them."

Cade's eyes flashed to me—sharp, dark, almost proud. "You will," he said. "And I'll help you."

The snowy trees blurred past, the world rushing by too fast to catch. I sucked in a shaky breath, the fury settling like molten steel in my veins.

"She's my person," I rasped. "He took my person."

Cade reached across again, his hand hot as it closed over mine. "And he made the biggest mistake of his life," he growled. "We're going to make damn sure of that."

I clenched his hand so hard I thought I might crush his bones, but he didn't even flinch.

We were over halfway back to the cabin when my phone lit up with an incoming FaceTime call. My breath caught. The name on the screen struck the air from my lungs.

Sarah.

Beside me, Cade snapped to attention, his entire body tensing. His hand shot out, hovering near my arm like he might grab the phone himself.

I slid my thumb across the screen without thinking.

The video opened and my entire body locked up. Chad's face filled the frame first, far too close, his grin wide and gleaming. His eyes were too bright, almost feverish.

"Hi there, sunshine," he drawled, voice dripping with mock sweetness.

He tilted the phone back, and I sucked in a sharp breath. Behind him, Sarah and Jack were tied to chairs that looked bolted into the floor. Rope cut into their arms and chests, duct tape twisted at the edges. Blood trickled from a cut on Jack's temple. Sarah's lip was split, one eye already starting to swell.

Sarah's gaze snapped to the camera—wild, furious, terrified. She started to shout, but Chad grabbed a fistful of her hair and yanked her head back hard, cutting her off mid-word.

Jack roared. His entire body lunged forward in the chair, muscles straining against the ropes until they creaked. "Get your fucking hands off her!" he bellowed, eyes blazing. For a second, I thought he might actually break free—his shoulders flexed, veins standing out in his neck.

Chad didn't flinch. He just turned, calm as ever, picked up a metal pipe from the floor and cracked it across the side of Jack's head with a sickening thud. He slumped in the chair, dazed, blood blooming fresh at his hairline. Sarah screamed.

382

Chad tsked softly and turned back to the camera, his grin never wavering. "Now. Where were we?"

Rage tore through me like a lightning strike. My fingers clenched so hard around the phone I thought the glass might shatter. "What do you want?" I spat, my voice sharp enough to cut bone.

Chad beamed, leaning in again. "Simple. You. We trade your pretty little friend and her boy toy for you. You come alone. No guards." He paused, eyes jerking sideways, barely able to contain his glee. "And you better hurry. Boss is back tomorrow, and I want to give him a nice surprise."

That last part slipped out too fast, too hungry to hide.

Behind him, Sarah wrenched against her bindings, her voice hoarse as she screamed, "Lena! Don't you fucking come! Don't—"

Chad jerked her hair again, laughing. "Shhh! You're ruining the moment."

"Sarah, I'm coming!" I screamed, my voice wild and cracking. "I swear to God, I'm coming."

My whole body shook, the screen trembling in my hand.

"Tomorrow. Sunrise," Chad continued, his grin splitting wider. "You show up alone. I'll send the location. Try anything stupid... and I'll carve a goodbye into her pretty skin."

Then he yanked her head back again and dragged his tongue slowly up her cheek, eyes fixed on the camera like he was daring me to challenge him.

Sarah thrashed, her whole body twisting in disgust and fury.

Chad winked, then abruptly ended the call.

The screen went black. I stared at it, my pulse roaring in my ears.

Cade's hand slammed onto my thigh, grounding me before I realized I was spiraling. His voice was sharp in my ear. "Breathe. Lena. Look at me. Breathe."

I dragged in a shattered gasp, then another, my vision swimming. Finally, I met his eyes—green, steady, burning

383

with the same fury. "I'm going to kill him," I rasped. "I'm going to rip him apart."

Cade's jaw flexed, his own breath rough. "We will," he said, his voice like iron. "But not on his terms. We're going to be smart about this."

Cade snatched up his phone, frantically dialing a number. His voice spilled into the space between us, a string of clipped orders and curse words. I couldn't make out the details, every word blurred under the roar in my head.

Sarah's face burned behind my eyes. Her voice rang in my skull, over and over: *Don't you fucking come. Don't—*

Cade snapped something into the phone, his tone urgent but contained, then hung up and tossed it onto the console.

I stayed folded in on myself, my nails digging into my palms so hard they might break skin. The Jeep tore down the road, the snow-blurred trees whipping past.

"We're almost there," Cade said.

The rage inside me pressed higher, hotter, crawling up my spine, begging to be unleashed.

When we pulled into the driveway, I immediately noticed another jeep parked beside the cabin. I threw open the door and bolted up the steps, the cold air biting at my cheeks.

The moment I stepped inside, Allie was there. She collided into me so hard I nearly toppled backward. Her arms wrapped tight around my shoulders, her face buried in my neck. She was shaking and her cheeks were blotchy and wet with tears.

"Oh god, Lena," she rasped, her voice trembling.

I clutched her back just as hard, my own breath catching. When she finally pulled back, her hands stayed on my arms as if she didn't trust herself to let go completely. I blinked past her, my gaze sweeping the main room. Everyone was still here, but now, it looked as though we had backup.

David stood closest, posture sharp and ready, eyes already on us. Logan lingered near the fireplace, his fingers tapping restlessly against his thigh. Mariah and Nicole hovered close together by the kitchen island, tense and alert.

Nick hovered near the far wall, his hands flexing like he needed somewhere to put them.

A tablet was propped up on the counter. Lorelei's face filled the screen, her expression fierce and focused. Behind her, Gage hovered, half-visible, his jaw tight.

The room felt electric, a live wire running through every person, every breath.

David stepped forward first, his eyes sweeping from me to Cade. His voice cut into the room. "Tell me exactly what was said," he ordered.

Cade didn't hesitate. "Chad said they wanted Lena in exchange for Sarah and Jack," he said. "He emphasized that she come alone. But then, I think he slipped. He said the 'boss' wouldn't be back until tomorrow. He seemed almost too excited to keep it to himself."

Gage's voice came through the tablet. "We think they tracked Jack's phone. Probably had something hidden on it for months, waiting to see if he'd lead them to Lena."

I felt my stomach drop.

"They got lucky," Gage added. "And they moved fast."

David's eyes narrowed, his mind clearly already moving miles ahead. He glanced once toward the tablet, as if confirming Lorelei and Gage were listening. "Chad's slip-up might just be our saving grace," he said finally. "If Michael isn't there tonight, we have one window—and it's now."

He turned to the others, his entire presence morphing into something even sharper, like a blade being drawn. "We move tonight," he said. "Before Michael gets back. We don't wait, we don't give them a chance to relocate or tighten security."

Without another word, David reached for a second tablet sitting on the counter. He tapped the screen quickly, and a detailed layout of Michael's estate lit up—building schematics, surrounding forest, entry points marked in sharp lines.

He set it down on the table and started outlining instructions. Fast, decisive, each point falling into place as

385

though he'd rehearsed it a thousand times. People leaned in immediately, drawn into the force of his focus.

Allie's eyes went wide. "Wow," she breathed. "That's... impressive."

Nick gave a short, dry laugh, shaking his head. "It's his mark," he muttered, almost under his breath. "Strategy. He doesn't just plan, he *sees* the plan before anyone else does."

Allie glanced back at David with new understanding.

David didn't pause to acknowledge them. He kept moving, gesturing sharply at routes, fallback points, guard rotations—each detail sliding into place like clockwork.

Beside me, Cade moved closer, his shoulder brushing mine. I felt the quiet burn of his readiness, coiled and waiting, echoing the heat pulsing under my own skin.

David finally straightened, gaze sweeping the room like a final check. "We move in twenty," he said, voice hard as iron. "We go in. We get them out before Michael returns. No heroics. No unnecessary risks. In and out."

He looked at me last, his eyes pinning me in place. "You okay?"

I swallowed, my pulse roaring, and nodded once. "Good," I rasped.

The room broke apart almost at once, people scattering like a sudden breath let out. Voices dropped to low murmurs, footsteps thudded against the floor. Someone grabbed weapons from a locked cabinet, others pulled on heavier jackets and tactical gear. The steady rhythm of motion felt like a pulse moving through the house.

Alice approached me quietly, almost hesitant, a bundle of dark clothes folded over one arm. My dagger rested on top, its handle catching the low light. She held it out to me, her gaze dropping to the floor before she forced herself to meet my eyes.

"I should have been faster," she said. "I should have seen it coming. I'm... I'm sorry, Lena."

For a moment, I just looked at her. At the exhaustion lining her face, the tension in her shoulders. Then I shook my head

386

slowly, my fingers curling around the clothes she offered. "It's not your fault," I said softly. "You couldn't have known. None of us did."

Her jaw trembled, her breath catching like she might argue, but then she just nodded and stepped back.

I went upstairs to the bedroom to change, my fingers moving fast despite the weight in my chest. I twisted my hair into a low ponytail, practical and out of the way. The dagger was warm in my hand, thrumming with quiet energy, like it already knew what was coming.

When I came out, Cade was already waiting by the doorway. He was fully geared up—tactical vest strapped tight over his chest, a long sword sheathed across his back, smaller daggers secured along his hips and thighs.

He looked lethal. Unmovable. Every bit the warrior he was.

His eyes scanned over me quickly assessing before they locked on my face. "I know you," he said, the words pressing into me like a hand on my chest. "And I know if things go sideways in there... you'll try to give yourself up. You'll think it's the only way to save them."

I started to answer, but he lifted a hand, stopping me.

"I know I can't stop you if you decide that," he went on, his jaw working hard, tension radiating from every line of him. "But I'm begging you. If it comes to that... don't. Don't give yourself up to save the others. Please."

The word *please* landed with a force.

Cade wasn't the kind of man who begged. He protected. Fought. Endured. But now, all that armor had fallen away. And in its place was something raw and open, something sacred. It struck me silent, the sheer weight of it. Like I was watching a storm fall to its knees.

I stepped closer, my fingers tightening around the dagger at my side. "I have no intention of losing anybody," I said. "Or handing myself over." I took another step until we were almost touching. "The only plan on my mind is getting Sarah back...

387

and making them choke on their own blood if they stand in my way."

Cade practically beamed with pride, his eyes glinting with a dangerous warmth. "So vicious," he said, his voice rough but almost tender, like it was the best thing he'd ever seen.

Slowly, he reached up, his hand coming to my cheek, his thumb brushing lightly against my skin. "I need you to come back," he whispered, so quiet it felt more like a vow than a request.

I leaned into his hand, my jaw tight, my heart pounding like a war drum. "I will," I promised.

From the main room, someone called out, breaking the moment. Cade let his hand drop, but his gaze held mine for a heartbeat longer before he turned away. I squared my shoulders, the final steel settling inside me.

Tonight.

Chapter 30

People were checking weapons, tightening straps, exchanging silent nods. Every motion felt precise, almost ritualistic. I turned to find Allie standing near the edge of the kitchen, arms wrapped tightly around herself. Vallerie hovered close behind her, choosing to stay back to watch over her. Allie's eyes met mine, and for a moment she just stared. Then she crossed the room in a few quick, tense steps and threw her arms around me.

Her grip was fierce, almost crushing, like she could hold me there and keep me from going. "This doesn't feel right," she said. "I can't stand you going out there and putting yourself in danger. I'm supposed to be the one protecting you. That's always been my job."

I pressed my face into her shoulder, breathing in the familiar scent of her hair. "Allie…" I started, but she pulled back just enough to meet my eyes.

"Promise me you'll come back," she demanded, her voice breaking on the last word. "Promise me."

My throat was as tight as barbed wire. "I promise," I whispered.

She studied my face like she was trying to memorize it, then nodded, her jaw clenched, eyes shining. Slowly, she let go, her hands sliding down my arms before falling away completely. Vallerie stepped forward then, resting a steadying hand on Allie's shoulder.

I followed the others out the door, glancing one last time over my shoulder to Allie. We all piled into the awaiting Jeeps.

The ride to the estate stretched out under a sky heavy with stars. David drove the Jeep I rode in, his focus absolute, hands steady on the wheel. Logan sat in the passenger seat, one boot propped up against the dash, his fingers drumming a restless beat against his leg.

In the back, I was wedged in the middle seat. Cade sat on my right, his broad frame taking up more space than seemed possible. Marcela was on my left, completely absorbed in her gear. She checked her knives one by one, each blade etched with careful sigils that glinted faintly in the dark. Small vials and tonics were lined up on her lap, liquid contents swirling with faintly glowing threads.

Without a word, Marcela uncapped a marker and shoved up the thick sleeve of my tactical jacket, exposing my forearm from wrist to elbow. I glanced down, surprised, but didn't stop her. She drew quickly, efficiently—tight, curved runes that wrapped from my wrist to my elbow, each symbol pulsing faintly as she finished it. "These will help ground you," she murmured without looking up. "And shield your empathy if it tries to spiral."

"You got any runes for hangovers?" Logan asked, dead serious but with a crooked grin. "Asking for a friend."

Marcela let out a sharp snort, shaking her head without pausing her strokes. "Pretty sure you're beyond saving."

Cade huffed a quiet laugh next to me, his hand squeezing my thigh gently.

Marcela finished the last rune and leaned back, studying her work critically. "You're ready," she said, capping the marker.

"Thank you," I said to her.

"Of course," she said, turning her attention back to her gear.

A couple hours later, we arrived. David killed the headlights and rolled to a stop at the edge of the trees.

Doors opened softly. Boots hit the snow. We made our way through the woods towards Michael's estate, moving like shadows. The trees were thick, the night too dark to see clearly, but Cade moved with perfect ease, guiding me with quiet nudges, his night vision cutting through the shadows like it was nothing.

David's final hand signal snapped through the dark: *Positions.*

390

I crouched low, Cade just behind my right shoulder, Kaylen poised on my left, Nick at our rear. In my mind, I pictured the others settling into place. Logan, somewhere along the southern wall, his fingers flexing against the cold ground, ready to rip the air itself into a concussive force. Mariah, further east, probably with her jaw set and her fists already glowing faintly with heat, seconds away from hurling a fireball that would set the night sky ablaze. And Alice, to the north, steady and unyielding, waiting to release a strike strong enough to collapse walls and send men flying.

At the exact same time, all three would hit. Chaos would follow—guards scattering, disoriented, unable to tell where the real threat was coming from. That was our opening.

I glanced at Nick as he checked the small vials on his belt that Marcela gave him, each movement precise and careful. Deep down, I couldn't shake the thought that Cade had made sure Nick was on our team for me. Another layer of backup, another silent insurance policy in case I got hurt. It felt exactly like him.

Cade leaned in close, his breath warm against my ear. "No matter what happens," he whispered, "you're not alone in this. I've got you." Then he pressed a slow, firm kiss to my temple.

Even now, with adrenaline roaring in my veins and the world about to burn, I felt a faint flush rise under my skin.

We all waited, breathless and coiled. Then a low, echoing rumble split the night as Logan's sonic blast tore through the south wall. Almost instantly, a roar of orange light flooded the eastern sky—Mariah's fireball igniting like a second sunrise behind the trees. A split second later, the ground shuddered beneath us, a deep, concussive thud as Alice's inertia strike snapped beams and sent parts of the north facade crashing down.

Screams rose in the dark, guards pouring from the estate in every direction, weapons out, shouts echoing into the trees.

Cade leaned in close. "Now."

391

I didn't hesitate. We slipped forward as one, moving like a single shadow over the snow. My mark thrummed hot and urgent beneath my skin. Then something hit me. Like the force of a hammer to the chest.

Fear. *Sarah's* fear. I had never felt an emotion so sharp, so perfectly traced back to one person. It was as if every beat of her panic lit up a path straight to her and instead of drowning, I breathed it in. Let it guide me.

We slipped inside through a side door, the chaos outside still echoing faintly through the walls. The halls were dim, lit only by a few scattered wall lamps that cast long, warped shapes across the floor. We moved in a tight line. Cade leading, Nick close behind, Kaylen sweeping our back, me in the center, every sense straining toward that thin, purple thread of Sarah's fear.

A sudden movement ahead—two of Michael's men stepped into the hall. Cade didn't even slow. He shadow-stepped forward in a dark blur, reappearing right in front of the first man. The guard barely had time to widen his eyes before Cade drove his dagger up under his chin, the blade punching straight through with a sickening crunch.

Kaylen lunged toward the second man, her arm sweeping out as she threw one of her curved daggers toward his chest. But just before it struck, the air shimmered and the blade twisted violently midair, spinning back toward her like it had been yanked by an invisible cord. Kaylen cursed, ducking out of the way just in time as the dagger sliced past her shoulder and buried itself in the wall behind us.

The second blast hit an instant later. It was like the hallway itself turned sideways, an invisible force slamming into us with bone-jarring strength. I was thrown backward before I could even register what was happening, my body striking the wall hard enough to knock the breath from my lungs. I heard Nick grunt somewhere beside me, and Kaylen staggered, one hand braced on the floor, her teeth bared.

The guard didn't hesitate. His eyes locked on me and he lunged.

I scrambled to rise, heart hammering, limbs still sluggish from the blast. I barely got my hands under me when he was suddenly there, towering over me, his outstretched hand plunging down toward my face.

But just before his hand could touch me, Cade appeared—sword already in motion—swinging down in a brutal slash that sliced clean through flesh and bone, severing the man's hand at the wrist. The hand hit the floor with a wet thud. Blood sprayed across the tile and on my boot.

Cade didn't pause. He grabbed the guard by the throat and lifted him off the floor like he weighed nothing, slamming him back against the wall with enough force to crack the plaster. His eyes were murderous.

Then he drove his sword forward, straight through the man's chest, the blade punching through with a deep, grating sound as metal scraped bone. The guard spasmed once, then went limp. Cade held him there for another breath, eyes locked on his face, as if daring him to keep breathing. Then he yanked the sword free and let the body fall.

Cade turned to me, his sword still in one hand, blood dripping steadily from the blade. Without a word, he offered his other hand—slick with blood, fingers curling slightly in silent invitation.

I reached up. He pulled me to my feet in one smooth motion. I swayed for half a second, breath catching, but he didn't let go until I was steady.

"You okay?" he asked, eyes scanning me.

"Yeah," I breathed. "Just winded." I hesitated, then added, "I'm sorry. I should've used my mark. I froze."

Cade leaned in, pressing a quick kiss to my forehead. "You're doing great," he murmured. "Next time, don't think. Just move."

Nick appeared beside us, already on his feet, dragging in a breath like he'd just shaken off a punch to the gut. Kaylen was close behind.

"We need to find them," Kaylen hissed. "And fast."

I closed my eyes for half a breath, feeling that raw pull deep in my ribs. "They're this way," I said, my voice certain. I didn't even wait for a response before moving forward.

Kaylen paused, a moment of confusion crossing her face, but she didn't question it. They all fell in behind me, boots silent on the floor. We rounded a sharp corner and three of Michael's guards burst into view, barreling straight at us.

The first, a tall man crackling with electricity, threads of pale blue light crawling over his arms and sparking across the walls. The second, a woman in fitted armor, her hands coated in a dark, oily sheen. The third, a short, hulking man gripping a heavy blade, his grin twisted and eager.

The electric man raised both hands and let out a roar—a wide blast of lightning exploded down the hall. I threw myself sideways, feeling the searing heat hit my side. Cade hissed in pain as a bolt scorched across his arm, burning through his sleeve. Kaylen stumbled, catching a shallow burn across her thigh. Nick took the brunt of a stray bolt across his shoulder, his teeth clenching as he staggered backward, one hand flying up to steady himself against the wall.

Cade vanished into the shadows in the same breath, reappearing behind the electric man and driving a blade deep into his lower back. The man convulsed violently, sparks dancing from his fingertips before he crashed to the ground.

The oily woman lunged toward me, her hands up as she reached for my throat—but Kaylen's arm snapped out, three daggers thrown into her chest in quick succession. The woman gasped, blood blooming across her skin before she collapsed forward.

The third man charged me, heavy blade raised, but this time, I didn't hesitate. I reached for my mark and slammed fear into him like a hammer. He faltered mid-step, knees slamming to the ground, blade clattering from his fingers as he gagged on a terrified sob.

I stepped forward, shoving my dagger up under his ribs without a moment's pause. His eyes rolled back, body crumpling at my feet. I yanked the blade free, already turning.

"This way," I said. And I kept moving, not waiting for anyone to catch up.

We kept moving, fast but silent, my boots whispering across the floor as I followed that thread of fear deeper into the estate. Cade stayed close at my side, his hand occasionally brushing my arm or my back.

My mark burned hot and bright, the sense of Sarah's terror pulling me forward like a live wire. We reached a narrow staircase leading down into a lower level. The air grew colder, the walls closing in around us.

Halfway down, a sudden warmth bloomed along my side where the electric current had hit me. I sucked in a sharp breath, glancing down. Nick was right behind me, his hand pressed gently over the burn. Warmth started sinking into my skin, knitting torn flesh and soothing the raw sting. Our eyes met. I gave him a quick, grateful glance, my lips parting in a small breath of relief. Nick just gave a slight, reassuring smile in return, as if to say *I've got you, keep going.* I smiled back, then turned, my focus snapping ahead as I surged forward down the last steps.

We reached the end of the hall, stopping in front of a heavy looking door. I could feel Sarah on the other side—her fear thrumming like a trapped bird against my ribs. Before I could reach for the handle, the door slammed open.

Two guards burst out, one man, one woman. The woman instantly split into multiple projections of herself, each copy mirroring her exact movements, her knives flashing from every angle.

The man lunged at us, his movements so fast my eyes struggled to follow. One moment he was halfway down the hall, the next he was right on top of Cade, slamming into him and knocking him sideways.

Kaylen barely dodged a slicing strike from the woman, her face twisted in concentration as she tried to track the real body among the illusions. I focused on the woman first, feeling my mark hum beneath my skin. I shoved raw, paralyzing terror straight into her mind. She froze for half a second, just long enough for the illusions to dissolve. Her eyes went wide, mouth dropping open in a silent scream. Kaylen closed the gap in one step and drove a dagger into her temple. She collapsed, her blade clattering to the floor.

Meanwhile, the man blurred forward again, almost a smear of movement. He lashed out at Kaylen, who ducked and rolled, flinging a dagger that skimmed his arm. Cade reappeared at his back in an instant, his sword cutting across the man's hamstrings in one vicious stroke. The man screamed, stumbling to his knees. Kaylen moved in, driving two short blades into his sides, ending it fast.

A sharp crack of energy split the air behind us. Chad materialized, gun already raised, his eyes wide and wild. Before he could even sight Cade, I reached for my mark and slammed terror into him with everything I had left.

He dropped the gun instantly, crashing to his knees, a high, choked wail tearing out of his throat. His hands clawed at his face as if he could tear the fear off his skin. I stepped forward, dagger steady in my hand, my steps calm and deliberate. I wanted to watch him bleed.

Chad's eyes snapped to me, wide and glistening with tears. At the last possible second, his body shivered, and he vanished with a sharp crack. I stood there, panting, the rage and adrenaline coursing through me like liquid fire. "Coward," I spat.

We moved toward the now-unguarded room. Inside, the air smelled of sweat and blood, a sharp metallic sting that hit the back of my throat. To the left, Sarah was tied to a chair, gagged, her head hanging forward, her whole body trembling. Jack lay on the floor beside her, unconscious. His face was battered, swollen, and covered in blood.

My heart almost split in two. I ran to Sarah, dropping to my knees and tearing at the ropes with shaking hands. The bindings bit into her skin, her wrists raw and bruised.

"Sarah—" I yelled.

She gasped, sobbing immediately. Her eyes met mine— wild, terrified, then flooding with desperate relief. I removed the ties and pulled her into my arms, crushing her against me. She clung to me so tightly it hurt, her fingers digging into my shoulders, her whole body shaking.

"It's okay," I choked out, pressing my forehead against hers. "I've got you. I've got you." We both cried, breaths shuddering and uneven, the room spinning around us.

Behind me, Nick rushed to Jack, dropping to his knees and pressing both hands over Jack's chest and temple. Jack jerked slightly, coughing as his eyelids fluttered open. Kaylen stood watch at the door, daggers drawn, her eyes scanning the hallway for any movement.

Jack's gaze darted around wildly as he struggled to sit up. He froze when he saw Cade, Kaylen, and Nick—then his gaze landed on Sarah and me. Realization that we were the rescue team washed over his face. "Do you... have a weapon?" he rasped, his hand trembling slightly as he lifted it.

Kaylen didn't hesitate. She lifted her hand without a word and a sleek handgun appeared in her palm. A second later, a combat knife solidified in her other hand. Jack's eyes went wide, a stunned sound escaping him—somewhere between a hoarse laugh and a shaky breath.

"Holy shit," he whispered, a glint of something like awed disbelief breaking through.

Kaylen didn't react, just stepped forward and dropped both weapons into his waiting hand. Jack's fingers closed around the knife first, gripping it hard. Then he took the gun, checked it with a practiced flick, and pushed himself shakily to his feet. Once standing, he immediately turned to Sarah, his eyes scanning over her.

He reached out, his thumb brushing gently along her lower lip where blood was smeared, his expression darkening as he took in every bruise and cut. "Hey," he said gently. "You okay? Did they—"

Sarah shook her head quickly. Tears welled in her eyes again, but she managed to breathe out, "I'm okay. I'm okay."

Jack exhaled, giving her a quick smile. Then he turned back to us, jaw set, weapon steady in his hand. I pulled Sarah closer, feeling her pulse still wild against mine. Cade gave a quick nod, turning toward the hallway that led back out of the estate. We all fell into step without a word.

We moved together through the halls, careful and quick. Each corner felt like it might hide another guard, but the building was empty—the chaos outside had pulled everyone away. At last, we reached the side door we entered from. Cade pushed it open, and a rush of freezing night air spilled over us.

We stepped outside as a group. Explosions and firelight flashed in the distance, The Severance's distraction still tearing Michael's estate apart.

Cade grabbed my shoulder. "Take them to the Jeep," he ordered. "Get them out. I'll help the others."

I hesitated, my breath catching. "Cade—"

"Go," he growled, already turning away.

"Don't you dare fucking die!" I shouted after him.

He lifted a hand in a rough half-wave, already sprinting toward the fighting. Kaylen and Nick followed without looking back.

I squeezed Sarah's hand tighter, and Jack stepped protectively to her other side, his weapon steady. We started across the snow toward the Jeep.

Then a man stepped out from behind a tree, blocking the path. Short and wide, eyes so dark they looked like empty wells. His lips curved into a slow, unsettling smile. Before I could react, he raised one hand, palm open. A crushing pressure slammed into my skull, dropping me to my knees instantly. My vision splintered into white shards, pain tearing through my temples. Beside me, Sarah crumpled with a strangled cry, her fingers clawing at the snow.

Jack let out a hoarse shout, stumbling forward a step before collapsing to one knee, his gun and knife dropping with a muffled thud. The man stalked closer to Jack, hand outstretched, pushing the invisible force harder. Jack's shoulders convulsed, his hands trembling as he tried to push up again. Blood streamed from his nose, dripping onto the snow in dark splatters.

The man advanced, his palm lowering closer to Jack's forehead, a sick delight gleaming in his eyes. Jack's fingers clawed blindly in the snow, closing around the fallen knife. He let out another strangled animal sound. Then, with a sudden burst of motion, Jack threw a handful of snow and blood up into the man's face. The man recoiled, sputtering, his concentration breaking for a heartbeat. Jack didn't hesitate. He lunged up with every ounce of strength left, driving the knife up under the man's ribs and shoving it higher, twisting savagely.

The crushing force vanished Instantly, my vision snapping back as I sucked in a stuttering breath.

The man gurgled, eyes wide, blood bubbling at his lips before he toppled backward into the snow. Jack fell forward over him, catching himself on shaking arms, his breaths coming in heaving, broken pulls.

I crawled to Sarah, grabbing her arm and dragging her upright.

Jack finally pushed himself off the body, staggering toward us, blood smeared across his face and hands. "You okay?" he asked, his eyes scanning our faces desperately.

I nodded, still shaking, my hand gripping Sarah's tightly. Sarah swallowed hard, tears spilling down her cheeks, but she managed to nod too.

Jack let out a shaky exhale, relief flashing across his face for a split second. Then he bent down, scooping up his gun from the snow. He straightened, jaw tight, his gaze sweeping the darkness around us. "Let's go," he ordered.

We broke through the last line of trees, stumbling toward the Jeeps. They sat half-buried in snow, their windows dusted with frost. Jack reached the first one, yanking open the driver's door and hauling himself inside. I followed, shoving Sarah into the back seat before sliding into the passenger seat. Sarah curled into the corner, her eyes wide and glassy as she scanned the treeline, her shoulders trembling.

I twisted around, frantically peering through the windows, searching for movement—any sign of the others. Explosions still echoed faintly from deeper in the estate, sharp cracks of sound that made my pulse jackhammer in my throat.

Maybe five minutes had passed, but it felt like hours. I couldn't sit here any longer. "I have to help them," I snapped, my voice too loud in the confined space.

"Lena, wait—" Sarah started, but I was already shoving the door open.

I sprinted into the snow, boots slipping as I tore toward the trees. I'd barely made it twenty feet before I heard rapid footsteps. I ducked behind a tree, dagger tight in my hand, every nerve alight.

Then I saw Hiro, Alice, and David charging past me through the snow, breath steaming in the moonlight. Relief crashed over me so hard I nearly dropped to my knees. I ran out from behind the tree. "Where is everyone else?" I shouted.

"Right here," a voice called behind me.

I spun. Cade jogged into view, his dark hair plastered to his forehead with sweat, his eyes locking on me instantly. The rest of the group spilled out behind him. Cade closed the distance in a few quick strides, his arm hooking around my waist and pulling me into his side.

"You okay?" he asked.

I nodded, my chest heaving, my fingers curling into the front of his tactical vest.

"We're good," David called out, scanning the perimeter. "Let's move before they regroup."

We ran back to the Jeeps together, packing in as fast as we could. I climbed into the backseat next to Sarah, who immediately grabbed my hand and squeezed it tight. Cade swung into the passenger seat up front, twisting to look back at us, his eyes sweeping over me and Sarah before turning his gaze out the windows. Hiro slid in beside me, his long legs squished awkwardly but not complaining, his eyes still scanning the treeline.

Jack gripped the wheel as he slammed the Jeep into gear. We sped off into the night, the estate shrinking behind us into a smear of fire and shadows.

My heart hammered so hard I thought it might split me open. I turned to Sarah and before I could stop myself, I pulled her into a fierce, trembling hug. She let out a sob, clinging to me like a lifeline, her whole body shaking so hard I could feel it reverberate through my own bones.

"We did it," I whispered into her hair, my own voice cracking. "We got you out. You're okay."

Sarah nodded against me, her tears soaking into my shoulder. I pulled back just enough to see her face, my hands cradling her cheeks, my thumbs sweeping her tears even as my own blurred everything.

"Are you okay? Did they hurt you?" I choked out. "God, Sarah, I was so scared—"

She shook her head quickly, her face crumpling. "I'm not hurt badly," she gasped, her voice so thin it barely sounded like her. "But I was so scared, Lena. I thought I was going to die there." She sucked in a breath, fingers curling hard into my sleeves. "I didn't want to go like that—not by that sadistic fuck's hands. Chad was horrible, Lena. He taunted me. Kept saying he was going to make me get on my knees right in front of Jack. And every time Jack tried to fight back, Chad just teleported around him, darting in and out, hitting him over and over while laughing like it was a game. He… he loved it."

Her eyes went wide, wild with terror as she kept going, the words spilling like acid. "Then… then he started talking about Abel. About how he wished he could've seen him go up in flames. Said he would have roasted a marshmallow on Abel's burning body." She dissolved into sobs again, her forehead dropping to my shoulder as her fingers dug into me.

A red-hot wave of rage surged through my veins, so sharp it felt like my skin might split open. My vision tunneled, narrowed to nothing but the echo of Chad's words and the image of Sarah crumbling in my arms.

I clenched my jaw so hard it ached, my hands curling tight around her shoulders. "He will pay for every fucking breath he took," I hissed. "I swear to you, Sarah. I'll make sure he dies screaming. I swear it."

Sarah sobbed harder, but she clung to me, her fingers tightening like she believed every single word. I held her as she sobbed, her whole body shuddering against mine. I didn't let go—not even when my own arms started to ache, not even when my throat burned from holding back my own tears.

Eventually, her cries started to slow, each breath coming in hiccupping pulls. She pulled back just enough to sit up, her eyes red and swollen, her hair sticking to her damp cheeks. She dragged her sleeve across her face, wiping at the tears, then took a long, shaky breath. Without a word, she reached down, found my hand, and squeezed it tight.

Hiro looked over at me. "There was a body in the snow not far from the Jeeps," he said. His eyes narrowed slightly, searching mine. "Was that you?"

I shook my head, still gripping Sarah's hand. "No," I said. I glanced at Jack, who was focused on the road, jaw set hard. "That was Jack. Thank God he was with us. That man had a mark—something that attacked our minds, almost crushed us from the inside. It dropped all three of us to our knees in seconds."

The memory rippled through me again—the static, the splitting pain behind my eyes. I shivered, and Sarah squeezed my hand tighter. "If Jack hadn't acted when he did… we wouldn't have made it," I finished.

Cade's gaze snapped back to me, remorse sharpening every line of his face. "I shouldn't have left you," he said quietly, like the words cost him. Guilt shone in his eyes, raw and unguarded. "I'm sorry."

Before I could respond, he reached over and grabbed Jack's shoulder. "Thank you," Cade said, his voice full of something deep and unwavering.

Jack glanced over, his mouth parting like he might deflect, but then he let out a shaky exhale and gave a half-shrug. "I almost wasn't able to stop him," he muttered. "That... mark, is that what you call it? It was extreme. I've never felt anything like that before. Somebody's gonna have to fill me in on what the hell is actually going on," he added, a faint edge of disbelief breaking through.

Sarah reached forward from the backseat, her hand settling on his shoulder. "Careful what you wish for," she said, her voice hoarse but carrying a spark of humor. Then, softer, "I'll tell you everything. Promise."

Jack let out a rough snort, almost a laugh, but he didn't take his eyes off the road.

"What happened out there?" I asked Cade. "Did anyone get hurt?"

Cade shook his head, a small, tired smile tugging at the corner of his mouth. "No serious injuries," he said. "Unless you count Logan's hair getting singed—which, to be fair, he absolutely does count as serious."

I let out a shaky laugh, my shoulders dropping just slightly.

Cade's smile widened, dark and a little wild. "We took out a lot of his people," he continued. "Destroyed a good chunk of his estate, too. It was a good night."

"Estimated at least twenty five down," Hiro added. "We hit them hard before they even knew what was happening."

I stared at him, stunned. "Twenty five..." I repeated. I turned back to Cade, the question burning on my tongue. "Why do you think he has so many people? What's his plan?"

Cade's expression sobered, his gaze dropping to the floor of the Jeep for a moment before finding mine again. "I don't know," he admitted. "But we're working on it."

Jack's voice cut in from the driver's seat. "Maybe he's trying to build an army," he said, eyes fixed on the road. "It's the only thing that makes sense. Gather enough people, loyal fighters... he could be planning something big. Something that goes way beyond this here."

403

Cade's expression darkened, his gaze dropping for a moment before he glanced back at me. "It does seem that way," he said quietly. "But why? What does he want to take with that army? What's the endgame?"

I didn't answer. I turned to the window, the rushing snow outside matching the roar in my head. Whatever Michael was planning, it wasn't just about me anymore. But I had a feeling it was going to end with me.

Chapter 31

We pulled into the driveway just as the first gray sliver of dawn started to bleed across the sky. The second we stepped inside, warmth and noise swallowed us. It didn't matter that it was nearly morning—everyone was up, wide-eyed, buzzing with adrenaline and relief.

Allie let out a strangled sound the moment she saw us, nearly knocking Sarah off her feet with how hard she hugged her. Then she reached for me, yanking me in without hesitation. "You did it," she said. "You both came back."

Sarah pulled me tighter into the hug, burying her face into Allie's shoulder. For a moment, the three of us just stood there, tangled together, breathing each other in like we were trying to prove we were all real.

Nick stepped up quietly then. He rested a hand lightly on Sarah's shoulder. "May I?" he asked gently.

Sarah hesitated, her eyes wide and shining, then finally nodded.

Nick pressed his hand against her side, then up to her split lip and the bruises shadowing her cheek. Sarah gasped, tears spilling fresh down her face as the pain ebbed away. "It's okay," Nick murmured, his own expression calm and steady. "Breathe."

She did, her shoulders sinking as she sagged deeper into Allie's arms, relief flooding every line of her body. "Thank you," she said hoarsely.

Nick gave her a soft, reassuring smile. "Anytime," he said simply, before stepping back to give us space again.

Around us, the rest of the room pulsed with cautious celebration—claps on shoulders, quiet laughter, heavy sighs that felt like whole weights being dropped.

But exhaustion was creeping in fast. We had extra people to shelter tonight. Nobody seemed to mind. Everyone just started pulling out spare cots and blankets, moving them into any room with floor space to spare. Cade, as always, claimed the couch, settling in with practiced ease. Jack dropped heavily onto the other one, barely even bothering to tug a blanket over his chest before his eyes closed. Mariah and Nicole slipped into our room with a couple of cots, quietly setting them up at the far side of the wall. Our room was big enough, and nobody complained. Not tonight.

I lay in bed, exhausted, but my mind wouldn't still. The images kept flashing behind my eyelids on an endless, stuttering loop—the hallways, the blood, the gurgling gasp as I drove my dagger into that man's ribs. The way his blood swirled down the shower drain.

I didn't regret it. But I felt a deep, heavy crack down the middle of me. I'd spent my life saving people, stitching them back together. Tonight, I had ended someone. Deliberately and brutally. I turned onto my stomach and pressed my forehead into my pillow, trying to quiet the roar in my head.

Sarah's soft whisper cut through the dark. "You okay?"

I hesitated, my throat tightening. "Yeah," I lied softly, forcing my voice steady. "Just a headache."

She made a quiet sound, almost like she wanted to say more, but I didn't give her the chance.

"I'm gonna grab some ibuprofen," I added quickly. "I'll be right back up."

Sarah mumbled a sleepy "okay," already half-asleep again.

I slipped out of bed quietly and made my way downstairs. I crept into the kitchen, my bare feet whispering against the wood floor. The house was quiet now, everyone sleeping after the exhausting night. I pulled open the fridge and grabbed a bottle of water, twisting the cap off and taking a long, slow drink. My hand trembled just enough to make the plastic crinkle. After a moment, I moved to a cabinet, opening it slowly. I wasn't even sure what I was looking for, maybe a sleep aid. Something.

"You looking for something?"

His voice was gentle, but it still startled me enough to make me flinch. I turned to find Cade leaning against the edge of the counter, arms crossed over his chest, eyes fixed on me.

"I—" I started, my automatic lie bubbling up. "I have a head—" But I stopped. The words caught in my throat suddenly felt too small, too false. "Actually," I said. "I keep thinking about the man I killed tonight."

Cade didn't move or interrupt.

"I don't regret it," I said, the words coming out fast. "Not for a second. But… I've never taken a life before. I've spent my whole life trying to save people. And tonight, I…" My breath shuddered. "I just keep replaying it in my head, and it's kind of eating at me" I finished, my voice barely above a whisper.

Cade pushed off the counter, stepping closer. He didn't rush, didn't reach for me too soon, just moved with that same calmness he always carried. "You did what you had to do," he said, voice unwavering. "It doesn't make you less of who you are. It doesn't erase all the lives you've saved. You're still that person."

"But it does change you," he continued, almost like he was admitting a secret. "Taking a life… it leaves a mark on you, too. It always will."

He lifted a hand slowly, curling his fingers lightly around the side of my neck. "The fact that it's eating at you?" he said, his eyes locked on mine. "That's proof you're still you. That's what makes you different from them."

Cade's hand slipped down to mine, his fingers closing around it. "Come on," he murmured. He led me over to the couch. When he sat down, he didn't wait. He pulled me down next to him immediately, wrapping his arms around me in one smooth motion. I curled into his chest without thinking, burying my face into the warmth there, breathing in the quiet strength of him. His hand drifted up to the back of my head, fingers sliding into my hair, slow and careful.

407

"You're allowed to feel it," he whispered, his voice rumbling low against my ear. "And you don't have to carry it alone."

I felt my shoulders loosen, my fingers twisting lightly into his shirt. But the fight was already leaving my body, my mind finally sliding toward something softer, heavier. His other arm tightened around me, holding me like he meant it—like he wasn't going to let go. And before I could even try to resist, the exhaustion swallowed me whole.

I fell asleep right there in his arms.

· · ·

My eyes barely fluttered open before a soft shadow crossed my face. I blinked, squinting upward.

Logan was leaning over the back of the couch, a steaming mug clutched in one hand. He squinted playfully, taking a slow sip of his coffee. "So... was there a classified briefing on this new... arrangement? Or did I just not get the invite?"

Cade let out a low groan, stirring beside me without opening his eyes. "Logan," he muttered, voice gravelly with sleep. "Shut up."

Logan raised his mug in mock surrender, backing away with a sly grin. "Hey, just making an observation. Carry on with your... tactical bonding. Happy for you. Really. Adorable. Disgusting, but happy."

I let out an incredulous laugh and grabbed the nearest pillow, hurling it at him with all the force I could muster. It smacked him square in the chest, making him nearly spill his coffee.

"Hey!" Logan barked, catching the pillow before it hit the floor. His grin only widened.

I sank further into Cade's chest while his hand drifted slowly up and down my back. The rhythm was so steady, I thought I might actually fall asleep again.

After a few quiet minutes, he let out a low chuckle. "We should probably get up," he murmured, his fingers pausing against my spine.

I let out a muffled groan, pressing my forehead harder into him. "Don't wanna," I muttered.

He laughed softly, the sound rumbling through his chest. "What if I offered you a cup of coffee?" he teased, his tone mock-innocent.

My eyes snapped open. I tilted my head just enough to glare up at him. "Damn it," I grumbled, and rolled off the couch in defeat.

As I stood, I glanced over and saw Jack still sprawled on the other couch, one arm flung over his eyes, completely dead to the world. Biscuit sat curled in the recliner like a wronged queen, her gaze locked on me with the slow, deliberate disdain of someone who'd been replaced. She just stared, as if she wanted to make sure I knew I'd stolen her rightful place beside Cade last night.

I followed Cade into the kitchen, where he poured two cups of coffee, sliding one into my waiting hands before he picked up his own.

At the table, Logan was sprawled in a chair, mug in hand, looking far too pleased with himself. Vallerie sat beside him, her eyes clear despite the early hour. Mariah and Nicole were hunched over opposite sides, both sipping quietly. David sat at the end, a laptop open in front of him, the screen throwing bright light across his face.

"What's that?" I asked, nodding toward the screen.

David didn't look up at first, his fingers still tapping quickly across the keys. "Hiro slipped a backdoor program into Michael's security system when we hit the estate," he said. "Some really elegant code, practically invisible. Gage picked up the signal on his end and looped me in this morning."

He finally glanced up at me, clearly pleased. "Long story short? We've got eyes inside Michael's house now."

That piqued my interest. I moved around to stand behind David, peering over his shoulder at the screen. "What's been happening?" I asked.

"Nothing yet," David replied, his eyes still fixed on the footage. "Just Michael's minions trying to clean up the mess we made last night. Michael isn't there yet."

The screen held several small boxes, each showing a different angle of the house. With a few quick clicks, David switched to the exterior feeds.

I couldn't help but let a small, fierce smile tug at my lips when the images came into focus. The damage was glorious. Holes punched straight through outer walls, shattered stone and splintered boards littered everywhere like confetti after a storm. I straightened up, admiring the disaster like it was a masterpiece in a gallery. Out of the corner of my eye, I saw Cade watching me, his own mouth tugging into a small, crooked smile.

He leaned in close. "God... that wicked little smile," he whispered, almost like it was the sweetest thing he could say. "You're dangerous."

I snorted softly, my eyes still on the screen. "I didn't even do that," I said, a hint of mock innocence in my voice. "But... I kinda wish I had."

Cade's quiet laugh vibrated through me.

Jack shuffled into the kitchen just then, his hair sticking up at wild angles.

"Morning," Cade called, his tone easy and friendly. "You want some coffee?"

Jack paused, then nodded, still looking half-asleep. "Yeah... sure."

Cade grabbed a mug and started pouring, glancing back over his shoulder. "You want anything in it?"

Jack shook his head. "No. Black's fine."

I watched them quietly, my fingers absently drumming against my mug. Cade seemed almost warm toward Jack, like saving us last night—saving me—had earned him that.

"I'm gonna go check on Sarah," I said. "Yell if anything happens on the cameras."

Upstairs, Allie was just stepping out of the bathroom, towel-wrapping her hair, when I slipped into the room. Sarah was just starting to sit up, her eyes still puffy but clearer than last night. I stepped over and sat beside her on the bed.

"How're you feeling?" I asked softly.

Sarah paused for a moment, actually thinking, her brows drawing together. "Homicidal," she said, dead serious.

I let out a sharp laugh, shaking my head.

But then her face softened, her voice lowering. "I'm okay," she added more quietly. "Really."

Allie moved over, dropping onto her own bed with a huff. She eyed me carefully, one eyebrow arched. "So," she started slowly, "I noticed you didn't sleep in here last night."

My mouth opened, then closed again. "I—"

Sarah leaned forward, her eyes suddenly bright with mischief.

"Oh my God," she breathed, a grin tugging at her lips. "You stayed with Cade, didn't you?"

"I did not—"

They both burst out laughing, cutting me off.

"Seriously?" Allie snorted. "You expect us to buy that? You're clearly falling for him."

I threw my hands up, my face burning. "Okay, maybe I am. But... God. You don't understand." I let out a shaky breath, my voice tightening. "The last man I fell for turned out to be the devil incarnate. I was so madly in love with him, I would have died for him. Killed for him. I thought he was everything. My world. And look how that ended."

Allie's face softened. She leaned forward, her voice steady. "Cade isn't anything like Michael."

My jaw clenched. "Are you sure about that?" I snapped, my voice sharper than I meant it to be. "None of us in this room—none of us—would have ever guessed what Michael really was. We were all fooled. How am I supposed to know it's different this time?"

411

Allie looked at me, one eyebrow lifting like I'd said the dumbest thing she'd ever heard. "Seriously?" she said. "You can literally feel what people are feeling. You have a built-in lie detector, an inside trade no one else gets. Just use your mark, dummy. See how he feels about you."

I opened my mouth—then snapped it shut again, the retort dying on my tongue.

Sarah snorted, covering her mouth like she was trying to hide a laugh. "She's got a point," she mumbled through her fingers.

I got up and walked to the dresser, pretending I was looking for something. Why hadn't I done that? Why hadn't I just *felt* him? Because I was scared. Scared of what I might find if I reached too far into him. I had felt him that one time, after we slept together. But it had been all heat and arousal, nothing else. What if that was all there was? Just lust. Just strategy. A tactical move to keep me stable enough to finish what we started. What if all I felt was duty? An obligation to protect the broken girl who couldn't control her mark?

And maybe worse... What if I found something real? What if he *did* feel something for me? That's what terrified me. Because if it was real, if I let myself believe in it, I wouldn't know how to stop. I'd fall so hard there'd be no coming back. And I don't have it in me to risk that again.

But could I walk away from it? From him? I wanted him. God, I wanted him. Not just the way he touched me, but the way he looked at me like I was more than the mess I'd become. And if I let myself have that, if I opened that door and it turned out to be temporary? It would break me in ways Michael never could. It would completely destroy me.

The thoughts tangled like barbed wire in my head. I turned, desperate to change the subject before they could push any further. "How about we talk about Jack," I said. "Sarah... he literally got beaten unconscious trying to protect you. And the way he kept scanning your face last night to make sure you were okay? Now *that's* a man with feelings, no mark needed."

Sarah's eyes dropped to her lap. She twisted her fingers together, her voice so soft it barely reached me. "I know," she said.

Allie and I stayed quiet, waiting. Sarah drew in a breath, her hand moving briefly to the pillow beside her—resting there, just for a moment, where I knew Abel's badge was tucked.

"I just... I feel so ashamed," she admitted. "Jack was Abel's friend. He's been texting me every day since Abel died. At first it was just... checking on me. Then we started talking about Abel. It was nice, having someone who actually knew him, who didn't treat him like some perfect memory."

Her shoulders curled inward as she kept going. "Then it just... veered. We started talking more. On the phone and through text. About music, movies, favorite foods, our families... stupid shit. And I like him. I really do." She paused. "But how unfair is that to Abel? I feel like I'm... stabbing him in the back."

"Hey," Allie said softly. "You are not stabbing Abel in the back. You loved him. You always will. But you're allowed to keep living. You're allowed to find comfort and connection and... whatever else you need."

Sarah's eyes shimmered with tears, but she nodded slowly.

Then Allie leaned back, her voice twisting into a sharp, teasing edge. "And for the record," she continued, her voice suddenly changing into that bossy big sister tone, "both of you need to get the hell out of your heads and just enjoy these ridiculously hot, loyal, sword-wielding men who keep throwing themselves at you."

My mouth fell open in shock, and Sarah choked out a wet, surprised laugh.

Allie rolled her eyes dramatically, tossing her damp hair over her shoulder. "Honestly, I'm starting to feel personally attacked by the universe for not getting my own tragic, emotionally tortured warrior to pine after me," she grumbled, crossing her arms.

Sarah let out a strangled giggle, and even I couldn't stop the sudden burst of laughter that broke free.

Allie shook her head, rolling her eyes dramatically. "I'm gonna go find some coffee before I start charging you two." She gave us both one last look, then turned and slipped out of the room.

"She's right, you know," I said. "You're not betraying Abel if you decide to... explore things with Jack." Sarah looked at me, her eyes still a little watery.

"You loved Abel. You always will. But he wouldn't want you to stay frozen in that grief forever. He wouldn't want you to stop living just because he's gone."

She swallowed hard, her fingers twisting in the blanket again.

"And Jack..." I went on, my voice gentler still. "He's not trying to replace Abel. He's just... someone who cares about you. You're allowed to let that happen. To let someone care."

Marcela's voice called up from downstairs, sharp and urgent. "Guys! You need to come see this!"

Sarah and I exchanged a glance, then hurried down the hallway and stairs, our feet nearly tripping over each other.

In the kitchen, everyone was crowded around David's laptop. David looked up. "You need to see this," he said.

I moved closer, Cade already at my side. The screen showed a live feed from an office inside Michael's estate.

Michael stormed into view on the camera, his movements sharp and wild. He wore a tailored black suit, the shirt beneath unbuttoned just enough to look careless instead of formal. His hair was slicked back, but strands had started to fall loose, giving him a slightly unhinged edge.

Chad was on his knees, hands up in a useless shield.

Michael's voice rose in a violent crescendo. "Nobody was supposed to make a move without my say so! Not only did you disobey me, you let them humiliate me! And you destroyed my house!"

His hand shot out, a fireball bursting to life and smashing into Chad's side. Chad screamed, crumpling, trying to crawl away. Michael only stalked forward, grabbing him by the hair, yanking him upright again.

My eyes locked on Michael's face. I was staring at those soulless eyes when suddenly I felt a violent yank tug inside me, like an invisible hook buried beneath my ribs, jerking me forward so hard I nearly stumbled. My hand instinctively flew to my chest.

At that exact instant, on the screen, Michael jerked violently too, his hand slamming to his own chest in a perfect mirror of my movement.

Gasps shot around me. Cade immediately pressed in close to me, his hand steadying my elbow. "Lena," he hissed, his voice taut with alarm. "What is it?"

I couldn't move. My eyes locked on Michael's as he froze, then turned his head slowly—almost sniffing the air, like he could *feel* me.

Then his gaze snapped to the camera. A slow, razor-edged smile crawled across his face, so deliberate it felt like it reached straight through the screen and wrapped around my throat. "Lena, darling," he drawled. "Is that you?" Michael tilted his head slightly, as if listening to a private joke. "You feel it, don't you?" he murmured, his words almost gentle, taunting. "That little tether between us... humming so beautifully."

His lips curled wider, eyes glittering with a sick excitement. "You think you can hide? That your little army will protect you?" He chuckled—a dark, broken sound. "I will peel you open, piece by piece... and when I do, everyone you love will watch."

Then, his mouth stopped moving, but the words didn't stop. They flooded into my mind, slick and poisonous, only for me. My hands shot up to my head. I could feel Allie's hand grab my shoulder.

"I can't wait to get my hands on you again... to feel you squirm while I tear you apart. Maybe I'll take my time... enjoy every inch of you before you break."

415

A feral snarl ripped up my throat. My hands clamped into my hair, shaking with a rage so hot it nearly blinded me—and then out loud, I *screamed.* "I will carve your fucking heart out and feed it to you before I ever let you touch me again!"

On the screen, Michael recoiled violently, his hands flying to his head, eyes wide with shock, like I'd struck him straight through the screen. His face twisted in rage, his lips curling back over his teeth. He said nothing more—just stared, eyes burning with a wild, silent fury.

Then he waved his hand, knocking the camera off the wall before going blank.

I let out a shaky laugh, startling everyone. "They were calling to me," I said, my voice bright with a fierce, breathless energy. "My marks, they were *calling* for me. I felt it at Reid's, but this… this was stronger. Like they were tearing forward, trying to break free."

I looked up at them, my eyes wide, almost shining. "And Michael—he used the mind weaving mark to get into my head," I went on, breathless now. "I don't know how… I pushed back. I gave it right back to him. I used *my* mind weaving. Mine."

They all stared, stunned and unmoving.

A wild grin curled across my face. "He felt me," I breathed, my voice low and alive with a dangerous joy. "Oh, he *felt* me."

Then, a promise. "And he'll feel me again."

Chapter 32

The afternoon sun cut across the snow, turning everything into a field of sharp, blinding white. The yard had been plowed that morning, as always, but thin sheets of ice still glittered in the patches of shade. My breath curled in front of me, fast and bright, each exhale making me feel more alive.

We all gathered in the yard. It had started as a joke—Mariah teasing me, Nicole chiming in with a mock battle challenge to see how my training was coming along. But now it was happening for real.

David gave me a long, considering look. He glanced at Cade, then at Logan, who stood bouncing from foot to foot like an overgrown wolfdog waiting for a ball. Kaylen was already spinning a pair of wooden practice swords in quick, smooth arcs, her expression sharp with anticipation.

"Three on three," David finally called, voice ringing across the yard. "Lena, Logan, Nicole—you're one team. Cade, Mariah, Kaylen—you're the other. Everyone else stays clear."

A current of energy shot through the group. Logan let out a whoop, his grin going feral. Nicole rolled her eyes but grinned, wind already curling around her legs. Mariah's fingers sparked with small tongues of fire. Kaylen cracked her neck and rolled her shoulders, already dialed in. Cade just watched me, one eyebrow slightly raised, a quiet dare in his eyes.

We spread out across the snowy yard, the ice crunching and squealing under our boots.

"Ready?" David called.

I closed my eyes for a breath and reached in. Logan's thrill burned bright. Nicole's tight, humming focus thrummed at the edges of my mind. Cade's careful, controlled calm pressed steady against me. Mariah's fire-laced excitement sparked like a match. Kaylen—hers hit me hardest, sharp joy, wild hunger for the fight.

I swallowed it all down, didn't push it away, didn't let it crash me. I let it guide me.

"Go!" David shouted.

We exploded forward.

Logan's sonic blast cracked through the air. Nicole darted sideways, a blast of wind spinning toward Mariah. I moved too, a second too slow, but moving

Kaylen came at me hard, her wooden blades blurring. I tried to project anxiety into her, to make her falter—but instead, it ignited something deeper. Her energy snapped into a wild, almost feral exhilaration. She let out a sharp yell, surging forward faster. The blade cracked into my side so hard it sent me skidding across the ice and crashing hard into a drift.

"Shit," I hissed, my ribs screaming.

Kaylen just grinned, all sharp teeth and wild eyes. "Bad move, sweetheart," she taunted as she ran forward.

Before I could move, Cade was suddenly there, his shadow falling over me. I twisted up onto my knees, snow sliding down my back.

Cade stepped in close, towering over me, his breath heavy and white in the cold air. His eyes dropped to mine, sharp and dark and burning. His mouth curved into a slow, wicked grin.

"You know," he drawled. "I really like you in this position."

Heat roared up my spine. My mark surged. I felt that molten gold swirl of arousal inside him—thick, hungry, throbbing.

A wild idea flashed through me, dangerous and electric. I grabbed that feeling—that hot, liquid desire—and amplified it. Just a little.

Cade shuddered, his breath stuttering out of him in a shocked sound. His eyes widened, mouth falling open just enough for a sharp curse to slip free.

I lunged. I slammed into his chest, catching him completely off guard. We crashed together onto the ice, Cade hitting the ground with a heavy grunt. I landed on top of him, both of us panting, steam curling into the cold air. His hands instinctively caught at my hips, fingers digging in tight. His eyes locked on mine. A low laugh tore out of me, bright and wild.

"Clever girl," he panted, his eyes wild and bright.

I pushed up, my whole body trembling with cold and adrenaline and something hotter, sharper, coursing straight through me. Cade stayed sprawled on the ice for a moment longer, still laughing, his chest heaving. Finally, he sat up, running a hand through his snow-damp hair, his eyes still locked on me. "You're trouble," he said, a crooked grin twisting his mouth. "Beautiful, dangerous trouble."

I rolled my shoulders, every muscle screaming—but my grin stretched wide enough to split me open. "Again," I said.

The afternoon unraveled in a blur of breath and snow and bruises.

Teams changed and changed again, David barking new combinations every time we started to settle in. Mariah and Nicole traded off between groups, always quick with a taunt or a laugh. Logan seemed to land on everyone's team at least once, crashing into the fray like a battering ram. Hiro fought with sharp, calculated precision, his movements efficient and controlled. Alice moved like a dancer—quick, fluid, and annoyingly hard to hit. Marcela didn't even need to touch anyone to leave them gasping, half the time her alchemy potions had us stumbling through sudden bursts of light or disorienting pulses of sound. Kaylen was everywhere at once, her wooden blades whirling, wild grin flashing even as she cursed the cold. Nick stood just off to the side, arms crossed but alert, ready to step in if anyone got seriously hurt.

Vallerie didn't join. She never did during mock battles. Once, she quietly explained to me that memory weaving wasn't something you could just *practice*, not without consequences. In a real fight, she could use it to rewrite loyalties, make enemies turn on each other, or forget their own names mid-attack. But in training? One slip could shatter someone. And when she told me that, I felt it through my mark—the deep, lingering guilt of what she'd done to Corinne.

The rest of us pushed harder, sweat and snow mixing as the afternoon wore on. Allie, Sarah, and Jack watched from the porch, bundled in coats, yelling out encouragement and completely unsolicited pointers.

I fell. Over and over, I hit the ice, ribs screaming, elbows scraping across the hard-packed snow. But every time, I got back up faster. My mark, once a wild crashing sea, now felt more like a river under my skin—strong, fast, but following my lead when I demanded it. Each time I shoved emotion into an opponent, it got smoother, sharper. Not perfect—sometimes it backfired, sometimes it fizzled, but it was improving.

Cade slipped in and out of my orbit like a dark star, a gravitational pull I couldn't escape. Every time his hand brushed my arm to shove me aside or steady me, every time he caught my waist before I could slam into a tree or hit the ground too hard—a spark shot through me so fierce I nearly forgot to breathe. And through my mark, I felt it mirrored in him. That molten gold, low and heavy, curling hotter each time we collided.

Once, he shadow-stepped behind me and I felt him before I saw him—a surge of dark amusement, threaded with something sharp and hungry. I spun just as he grabbed me, his fingers catching around my wrist and hip, yanking me off balance. I crashed into him chest-first, our breaths clouding between us, hands tangled. For half a heartbeat, we just stood there—faces inches apart, hearts hammering, that liquid gold surging between us so strong I nearly choked on it. Then I shoved him backward, breaking the moment with a sharp, wild laugh.

Later, he caught me mid-dodge, one hand splayed across my stomach, pulling me flush against his chest. My head dropped back against his shoulder, a sharp moan ripping free. "Distracted?" he murmured low against my ear, his voice dark and amused, but rough around the edges.

"Not at all," I said, forcing my voice steady, refusing to give him the satisfaction.

He dipped his head, lips brushing the side of my neck, right over the frantic beat of my pulse. His breath was warm against my skin when he spoke. "Liar," he whispered. "Your pulse is screaming my name."

The heat that shot through me was instant. I twisted free with more force than finesse, elbowing him in the ribs before slipping forward on the ice. His low laugh followed me, sending a shiver racing down my spine.

Hours slipped by, the sky changing slowly from bright, cutting blue to soft gray as the sun began to sink lower. We only paused for quick gulps of water, snatched breaths, a few barked instructions from David. But we kept going, muscles screaming, knees bruised, gloves soaked.

Every time Cade's eyes met mine across the yard, that gold wave rolled over me—hot and urgent and coiling tighter each time.

Focus, I told myself. The mark. The battle.

But Cade. He was everywhere—in my head, in my ribs, under my skin.

By the final round, my entire body throbbed with exhaustion, but I stood taller, my grin still sharp. I felt alive, raw, and buzzing at every edge.

Cade stood across from me again, steam curling from his shoulders into the evening cold. His eyes found mine and held, bright and dark at once.

"Last one?" he called, his voice gentle, but threaded with that same wicked promise.

I straightened, every muscle aching, my mark humming bright under my skin. "Last one," I echoed.

We launched forward at the same time, a blur of snow and ice and breath. He dodged my first swing, his arm catching around my middle, hauling me tight against him.

For a moment, everything stopped. Our chests heaved together, that shared molten gold roared up between us.

Then without meaning to, I seized it… and amplified it. Not gently. I poured fuel on it like a spark begging for a wildfire.

The hunger exploded. It wasn't just arousal anymore, it was feral. A heat that felt like it could strip skin.

His grip spasmed against my side. For a second, he looked like it hurt. Then his mouth twisted into a slow, dangerous grin.

That was all it took. I pushed forward at the same time he did, my hands fisting in his shirt, his arms banding around me in a bone-crushing grip. Our mouths collided, all teeth and heat and desperate noise. My nails clawed up into his hair, yanking him impossibly closer. I couldn't breathe. I didn't want to. There was only him, his taste, the molten roar between us.

Somewhere far off, someone shouted our names.

We didn't stop.

A second shout, louder this time.

Cade's eyes snapped open, wild and dark. His head jerked up toward whoever shouted, a murderous glare slicing through the cold air. Without a single word, he grabbed me tighter, the world twisting and folding around us in a rush of shadows.

I landed on solid ground, my boots scraping on wood. I barely had time to glance around—just enough to see we were alone, inside, somewhere warm—before Cade was on me.

His mouth slammed into mine, brutal and hungry, like he was starving and I was the only thing in the world that could save him. I answered with a moan that turned into a snarl, my hands flying to his hair, yanking him closer, closer, until there was no air left between us.

My fingers clawed at his jacket, tearing at the zipper, shoving it off his shoulders. He ripped at mine too, yanking it down so hard the fabric strained and tore at the seams, falling to the floor in a heap.

His hands gripped at my shirt and sports bra, tearing them apart with such force the cotton shredded under his fingers. I yanked at his shirt, nails scraping across his stomach, dragging it upward until I could shove it over his head.

His hands clamped onto my hips, shoving me back into the nearest wall so hard my skull thudded against it, a gasp tearing out of me. He pressed in, his whole body caging mine, heat radiating through my skin, every inch of him hard and unyielding with molten, restless need.

"You're mine," he snarled, the words more like a promise than a claim, and before I could respond, he surged forward again, his mouth devouring every sound I tried to make.

Then he dropped to his knees so fast I nearly fell. Rough hands gripped my legs, yanking off my boots with a speed that stole my breath. Then he was tearing my pants and underwear down in one violent motion. The warm air barely kissed my skin before his mouth was on me—tongue flicking, lips sealing over my clit with ruthless precision that made my whole body jolt.

I screamed, my head dropping forward, hands fisting in his hair so hard I felt the vibration of his groan rattle straight down my spine, pooling hot and dangerous between my legs. His tongue flicked and pressed, relentless, savage, each movement so precise and so fucking sharp I felt my legs start to buckle.

He hooked my thighs over his shoulders, holding me open as he fucked me with his tongue. I sobbed his name, my nails raking his scalp as he devoured me, my hips rolling against his mouth without shame. I felt his growl vibrate straight through me, echoing so deep I nearly blacked out.

Without breaking contact, he surged up, lifting me effortlessly—my legs still locked over his shoulders, my back sliding along the wall. He turned, carrying me across the room, and I barely had time to realize we were moving before he dropped me onto a bed, sprawling me out beneath him.

His mouth never left me. His face stayed buried between my legs, licking and sucking until my thighs clamped around his head and my entire body bowed off the bed.

My orgasm crashed through me like a lightning strike, my scream ripping from the deepest part of my chest, hips jerking against his face, so feral and desperate it sounded like an animal being set free.

He didn't stop. Even as my orgasm tore me open, ripping my scream from deep in my chest, Cade's mouth stayed locked to me. His tongue worked me through the aftershocks, pushing me even higher, so high I thought I might break apart completely.

My thighs trembled violently around his head, my hips jerking as if trying to escape—but his hands clamped down hard, pinning me in place with a fierce grip. When I tried to squirm away, he growled into me, the vibration sinking straight into my bones.

"Cade—please—" I sobbed, my voice high and broken, my entire body shaking so hard I thought I might black out.

His head finally lifted, his lips slick, his eyes black with hunger. "You're going to stay exactly where I put you," he murmured darkly. "And you're going to come for me again, and again, until I decide you've given me enough."

Before I could drag in air, his mouth crashed back down— licking, sucking, plunging so deep I saw stars burst behind my eyes. I came again so violently I nearly curled up around his head, my entire body locking, my scream strangled into a silent, shuddering collapse.

I thought he'd stop. He didn't. His tongue kept working me, fast and ruthless, until a third wave slammed into me, tearing a strangled cry from my chest. My legs shook uncontrollably around his head, my hips jerking as if they didn't know whether to push him away or pull him deeper.

He pulled back just long enough to let me see the wicked, feral grin on his face—and then he surged up, grabbing my wrists and slamming them above my head, pinning me to the bed with one strong hand.

His other hand dragged down my stomach in a hard line, fingers sliding straight back between my legs, thrusting in so deep and suddenly I wailed, my hips bucking up helplessly.

The sudden fullness was almost brutal, the slick slide of his knuckles pressing against every aching nerve until I wailed.

"Look at you," he rasped, his face inches from mine. "Fucking beautiful. Falling apart for me."

His fingers curled inside me, finding that spot instantly, stroking it until my back arched like a bow. My breath broke into helpless gasps, my legs kicking against the mattress. "Cade—" I choked, tears sliding hot into my hair.

"Tell me," he growled, his thumb dragging slow, merciless circles over my clit. "Tell me who you belong to."

"You—fuck—you—" My body was convulsing, the pressure shoving me higher with every brutal stroke. "Yours, I'm yours—"

"Again," he ordered, his fingers driving deeper, his thumb grinding in perfect time.

"Yours—yours—I'm yours—" I screamed, the orgasm tearing through me so hard my vision went white, my whole body clenching tight around his fingers. He kept working me through it, stroking until I was shaking and gasping, nails digging into his wrist above my head. When he finally pulled his hand away, the emptiness made me whimper.

"Please—" The word slipped out of me.

He caught my face in his free hand, fingers still slick from me, the scent of my release sharp in the air. His grip was firm, tilting my head so my eyes locked on his.

"Please what?" he growled, his thumb pressing into my cheek, his touch rough and claiming.

"I... I need—" My voice caught, my hips already rolling against nothing.

"Say it," he demanded.

"I need you inside me," I gasped, my throat tight, the plea pouring out of me without thought. "I need your cock—please, Cade—"

Something in him snapped. His eyes went dark, his jaw flexing like he was holding back the last thread of restraint—then it was gone. "I'm going to fuck you," he snarled, his voice both a vow and a threat, "until every part of you is branded by me—including your fucking soul."

Then he tore his pants down with a savage yank, his cock flushed and hard. He grabbed me like he was claiming prey, dragging me to the edge of the bed so fast the frame groaned. Then he was inside me—one brutal, claiming thrust that stole every ounce of air from my lungs—his snarl breaking against my skin like he was ready to tear me apart and keep every piece.

I felt it everywhere—every inch, every pulse—like he was carving his name into my bones, etching himself into every cell so I could never forget. He didn't pause. He pulled out and slammed back in, over and over, each thrust harder, deeper, tearing me apart and stitching me back together all at once.

I clawed at him desperately, but he caught my wrists again, pinning them above my head in one big hand, his entire body a feral cage over me. "Take it," he growled, his forehead pressing to mine, sweat dripping from his jaw onto my lips.

I could only sob, my nails scraping the air, my body bucking up into him in mindless surrender.

"Fucking take it, Lena," he snarled, his thrusts turning brutal, each one sending electric shocks of pleasure-pain ricocheting through me.

When my next orgasm hit, I screamed, my voice cracking, my body seizing so violently I felt the whole bed shudder beneath us.

He didn't slow down. Didn't stop.

Even as my legs shook uncontrollably, even as tears soaked my hair and my voice fell into silent, breathless sobs—he kept going.

He released my wrists, his hand sliding down to my throat, fingers wrapping tight enough to steal a breath—not cruel, but commanding, forcing my gaze to lock on his. My pulse thundered under his grip, trapped, owned.

I moaned, my hips arching up, offering myself to him completely, my hands flying to his back to claw and grasp and

426

hold. "More," I begged, my voice so hoarse it barely sounded like mine. "Please—don't stop—more—"

His hand closed tighter around my throat, the pressure forcing my pulse to thunder against his palm. His eyes were wild, locked on mine like I was prey that had finally stopped running. "More?" he growled, his hips crashing into me so hard the bedframe screamed. "You'll take more until you can't fucking breathe."

"Good," I gasped, nails biting into his skin. "Then die with me."

A dark, feral sound tore from his chest. "Happy to. I'll die buried inside you so deep that even death will have to fight to pry us apart."

His grip at my throat kept me pinned as his other hand clamped down on my hip, dragging me into each brutal thrust, forcing me to take every inch whether I could handle it or not. I could feel him everywhere—deep in my core, thick and unyielding, hitting that spot that made my vision stutter. The stretch burned and fed me all at once, the heat of him searing into places no one else had ever reached. My body clenched around him without permission, like it was trying to keep him there, to wring every drop from him.

God, he was *so deep* I swore I could feel him in my ribs. Every nerve lit up, my pulse synced to his, my mind unraveling under the ruthless rhythm. He wasn't just fucking me—he was *owning* me, grinding his name into my body so I'd never forget who had been here, who had filled me this way.

"Cade—" I cried, voice breaking.

"Say it again," he snarled, driving harder. "Say my name every time I fuck into you."

"Cade—Cade—oh God—Cade—" It fell apart on my tongue, each thrust tearing another broken syllable from me until I couldn't breathe, couldn't think, could only sob the sound of him into the dark.

"That's it," he panted against my lips, his gaze wild. "Nothing else exists. Just this. Just me."

And I shattered for him again, my whole body locking and breaking under his hold, my voice gone but my mouth still forming his name like a prayer I couldn't stop.

His breathing turned ragged. Each thrust lost a little of its precision, breaking into frantic, almost violent jerks that shoved me higher on the bed. I could feel him swelling inside me, the tension winding through his body like a bowstring about to snap.

A brutal roar tore from his throat, his whole body locking as he slammed in to the hilt and stayed there. The first thick spurt of his release hit so deep I swore I felt it in my spine— heavy pulses pumping into me like he was trying to brand me from the inside. Cade snarled against my ear, grinding deeper, forcing every drop as far inside me as it could go.

When he finally pulled free, his cum poured out slow and obscene, sliding over my swollen folds and down towards the sheets. Cade caught it with his fingers, scooping the hot spill without hesitation. His daring gaze locked on mine before he shoved his fingers against my lips.

"Open," he commanded.

I did, shuddering when his fingers pushed past my tongue, smearing the mess across it.

"Swallow it," he ordered, his voice a low, dangerous growl. "Every fucking bit of me stays in you one way or another."

I obeyed, my eyes closing on a moan as he watched, his jaw tight, chest still heaving like he hadn't quite come down from the high. And the way he was looking at me told me he wasn't anywhere close to done.

"Fuck," he growled, watching my lips close around him, his jaw tight. "You just earned yourself more."

Before I could breathe, he yanked his fingers free, gripped my hips, and slammed back into me—hard enough to make the headboard crack against the wall.

I choked on a sob, my head snapping back, tears spilling fresh. "Cade—" I gasped.

His eyes met mine—dark, wild, unhinged. "We're just getting started, Lena," he growled, each word hitting me like a physical blow. "So fucking take it."

And I did. I screamed for him, arched for him, gave him everything until I wasn't a person anymore—just heat and need and the brutal, beautiful weight of him above me.

He dragged me upright, barely giving me time to breathe before flipping me over, pushing my face into the mattress, his hand sliding up to fist in my hair and yank my head back. He fucked into me from behind, each thrust a violent punch that made the whole bed crash against the wall.

He ripped me upright against his chest, one hand across my throat, his other clawing across my ribs, his teeth sinking into the side of my neck in a brutal bite that made me convulse violently around him.

Then he shoved me forward again, yanked my hips up, and split me open over and over, so deep and relentless I saw sparks behind my eyes. When the next orgasm ripped through me, I couldn't even scream—my entire body locked, shaking so violently I thought I might never stop.

Hours blurred into a fever dream. I lost count of how many times he spilled inside me, how many times I shattered around him, my voice gone, my mind dissolved into a haze of ecstasy and pain and worship.

At one point, I was on my knees in front of him, my jaw aching as he fisted my hair, forcing me down his cock until I gagged—tears streaking down my cheeks as he fucked my throat like he couldn't get close enough.

I clawed at his thighs, desperate, needing every brutal inch, every savage thrust. When I looked up, my eyes wet, I saw him staring down at me, his face twisted in pleasure so violent it almost looked like agony.

"Fuck, baby," he snarled, his hips jerking forward, his hold tightening. "That's my girl—taking me so deep." His voice dropped lower. "Swallow all of me, Lena. Every drop. Show me you're mine."

He came down my throat with a hoarse roar, his whole body locking. I swallowed everything, the taste sharp and searing, and when he finally let me breathe, I sagged forward, gasping, saliva and tears slick on my chin.

But even then, it wasn't over. He hauled me up, carried me back to the bed, threw me down, and drove back into me before I could beg, before I could even breathe.

Over and over, he claimed me until my body felt molten and my mind gone, my screams echoing off the walls, his name a broken prayer on my lips.

By the time he finally collapsed, we were both trembling, sweat-soaked, bruised, our bodies marked by each other in every possible way. We lay tangled, hearts still racing, breaths shallow and uneven.

A ruin. A worship. A promise sealed in flesh and blood and fire.

I managed to drag in a shaky breath, my voice hoarse and wrecked when I said, "So... I think it's safe to say that amplifying our arousal can be... dangerous."

Cade let out a low, rasping laugh—the sound vibrating through his chest where my face was pressed. "Dangerous?" he repeated, his hand coming up to slide lazily through my hair, tugging just enough to make my scalp tingle. "Or do you mean... exhilarating?"

I snorted, too exhausted to fully laugh, and lightly slapped his chest. "You're insatiable," I mumbled, though the warmth blooming low in my belly at the word *exhilarating* betrayed me.

His arm curled tighter around me, his lips pressing to the top of my head in a slow, claiming kiss. "And you love it," he breathed against my hair, smug and certain.

And God help me... I did.

His hand stayed tangled in my hair, his breath still rough against my forehead. "Did you mean it?" he asked, his voice almost hesitant, but still edged with that quiet certainty that was so him.

I blinked against his chest. "Mean what?" I asked, my voice barely more than a cracked whisper.

His hand stilled. "When you said you were mine," he said, his words barely above a breath. "Did you mean it?"

I froze.

The words echoed in my head, cracking me open from the inside. *Did you mean it? When you said you were mine.*

The question slammed into me, and all the walls I'd put up since Michael began to splinter. The last time I opened myself fully to someone, I paid for it in blood and screams and loss. I gave everything and was left hollow. He betrayed me in a way so complete it carved out pieces of my soul... literally.

Could I deny that I felt something for Cade? No. But did that mean I was ready to hand him every shard of myself? To surrender completely, to risk that same kind of devastation all over again? I didn't know.

My lips parted, my pulse roaring in my ears. I felt the hesitation, the instinct to pull back, to protect what was left of me. I started to shake my head, the words tangling in my throat. "Cade," I started, my voice breaking as I forced myself to look up at him.

But the moment our eyes met, it hit me—a violent, shattering surge of feeling that almost knocked the breath from my lungs. I felt it. Not just the lust, not just the molten hunger that always roared between us.

I felt his love.

It crashed over me like a tidal wave—hot, heavy, endless. It was raw and wild, so pure it almost hurt. A devotion so deep I could barely breathe under the weight of it. He loved me. Every piece. Even the broken parts, even the pieces I still hated. I could see it, taste it, feel it right down to my bones. And somewhere in that flood, the realization hit me like a blade straight through my ribs.

I loved him too.

I think maybe I had, even in those earliest moments. That first time his eyes locked on mine across the room, bright and steady and endlessly patient. When he offered safety without demands. When he stood between me and every threat like it was simply the only thing he knew how to do.

The sob tore out of me before I could even think, raw and violent, like something ripped from the center of my chest. My vision blurred, tears streaming hot and unrelenting, blinding me in trembling waves.

"Lena," he said, panic flaring in his eyes as his hand flew to my face frantically brushing my tears. "Lena, talk to me— what's wrong?"

I choked on another sob, my fingers curling tight around his wrist. "Nothing," I managed to gasp out, shaking my head violently. "Nothing is wrong. Everything is... everything is perfect."

I dragged in a breath, my vision blurring, my heart splitting wide open in my chest. "And to answer your question," I said, the words tearing straight from my soul. "Yes, Cade. I'm yours. I'll forever be yours."

His lips parted, his eyes going impossibly wide, like he hadn't dared to believe it.

And then the final words slipped out, so raw and true they nearly undid me. "I love you too," I whispered.

He exhaled, the sound almost broken, like it had been trapped in his chest forever. His forehead dropped to mine, his breath trembling against my lips. "Say it again," he whispered, the plea cutting through me. "Please... say it again."

I laughed and sobbed at once, the tears still streaming as I cupped his face in my hands. "I love you," I said again, firmer now. "I love you, Cade."

A shudder rolled through him, his eyes squeezing shut as he pressed closer, his arms wrapping around me like he could fuse us together.

"I love you, Lena Merrow." His voice was steady but threaded with something raw. "I've loved you since before we even met. Back when all I had were stories... pictures... pieces of you. I loved you before I heard your voice. Before I

432

touched your hand. Before I knew you'd be the one I couldn't survive losing. And when I finally saw you…" His breath hitched, something raw cutting through his voice. "It was the first time in years I wanted to survive. I'd spent so long chasing vengeance I stopped caring if I lived through it. Most days, I hoped I wouldn't. But then you were there, and suddenly, dying felt unbearable."

His hand slid up, fingers curling lightly at the back of my neck, holding me there as his breath trembled against my lips. "So I'm yours," he said like a vow carved into bone. "All of me. Every mark, every scar, every dark, fucked-up piece. Yours."

I whispered, my voice shaking. "All of it. All of you. Always."

Then he kissed me—slow, deep, nothing like the feral hunger from before. This was gentle, reverent. A promise. A surrender.

When we finally pulled apart, we stayed close, our foreheads still touching. I felt his heartbeat echo against mine, steady and sure.

Without another word, Cade pulled me against his chest, his arms locking around me like a shield. He pressed one last kiss to the top of my head.

"Rest," he murmured.

And I did. I drifted into sleep wrapped in warmth, safe and wholly his.

Chapter 33

I woke slowly, my body a map of aches and bruises that felt like the sweetest kind of possession. But the moment I reached out and found empty space beside me, my body jolted upright, heart slamming into my ribs.

Before I could even swing my legs off the bed, the door opened. Cade stepped in wearing only a pair of sweatpants, a glass of water in each hand.

Relief crashed over me.

"Hey, easy," he said, his voice laced with amusement. "I didn't go far." He crossed the room in three long strides and offered me one of the glasses. The second I wrapped my fingers around it, I realized how parched I was—my throat felt like it had been scraped raw.

"Drink," he murmured, the corner of his mouth tilting up in a small, fond smile.

I didn't need to be told twice. I practically chugged it, cold water spilling a little at the corners of my mouth. When I finally lowered the glass, I sucked in a deep breath and wiped my lips with the back of my hand.

Cade laughed, taking the empty glass from me. "Better?" he asked.

I nodded, swallowing hard. "Yeah. Much."

My eyes swept around the room for the first time—soft light pouring through the old curtains, the faint smell of pine and something older, familiar. A single floor lamp glowed in the corner, casting a shadow across simple walls and a plain wooden dresser. A few folded blankets sat neatly on a chair, and the bed itself felt old but solid beneath me. The space felt quiet and lived-in.

I turned back to Cade, my brow furrowing. "Where are we, anyway?"

"My childhood home," he said quietly.

My eyebrows shot up. "Your... childhood home?"

I looked around again, really seeing it now—the simple walls, the old bed, the worn floorboards that felt sturdy but carried a hush of history. "But... how did we get here?" I pressed, confusion tightening in my chest. "I thought you had to see the shadow you wanted to step out of?"

Cade's mouth curved into something small and bittersweet. He set the glasses down and pointed to the corner of the room. "I told you I needed to see it—or have a crystal-clear memory of it," he said.

I followed his finger to the wall. The small lamp cast a single, distinct shadow—a sharp shape, warped gently by age and time.

He drew in a slow breath, his eyes distant. "After my family was killed, I spent so many nights lying in this bed, staring at that shadow. I couldn't sleep. Could barely even breathe some nights. That shadow... it's burned into my memory."

My throat constricted, my fingers curling around the edge of the quilt.

"I kept this house after I joined The Severance," he continued. "Nobody lives here. I come back every now and then to check on things, fix what needs fixing. Change the bulb in that lamp."

He paused, glancing at the light, something haunted and soft glared behind his eyes. "I always leave it on," he murmured. "So it can cast that same shadow... so I can always find my way back home."

My chest ached. Not for the house, or the story, but for the boy who had stared at that wall, night after night, just trying to survive the silence. I didn't know what to say that wouldn't sound small compared to what he'd just given me. So I reached out, found his hand and gave it a gentle squeeze.

"Where exactly are we?" I asked, glancing around the quiet room again, trying to piece together the feeling in my chest. "Are we even still in Maine?"

Cade offered a small smile and met my gaze steadily. "We're in Vermont."

436

My brows lifted. "Vermont?"

Cade nodded, a small, almost teasing smile playing at his lips. "Vermont. Just over the border. Not too far away."

"Well," I said. "At least it's warmer than the clearing."

"Careful," he said with a mock-serious tone. "You're talking about sacred ground now."

"Oh?" I teased. "Because you almost froze your ass off out there with me?"

A crooked grin spread across his face as he stepped closer. Then he bent down, crouching in front of me so our eyes were level. He lifted a hand, his fingers sliding along my jaw, thumb brushing lightly across my cheek. "Worth it," he murmured.

Before I could respond, he leaned in and kissed me. When he finally pulled back, his eyes stayed locked on mine, his thumb tracing slowly down to my chin, holding me there like he was memorizing every inch of my face.

I cleared my throat, glancing away for a moment. "Allie and Sarah... we should call them before they think you kidnapped me for real."

"I already texted them," he said. "They know you're safe. Now come on. We need a shower."

He turned toward the dresser in the corner, pulling open a drawer and rummaging for a moment. After a second, he pulled out a plain black t-shirt and a pair of old gray sweats with a drawstring, both looking comfortably worn and much too big for me. He walked back, holding them up with a small, almost shy smile. "These should work," he said.

I took them without hesitation, hugging them to my chest. The soft, faded fabric smelled like him—pine and soap and something deeper, uniquely Cade.

"They'll be huge on me," I said, a small laugh slipping out.

His eyes crinkled, a warmth blooming there. "Good."

I wrapped the quilt from the bed around my shoulders before sliding off the mattress. Cade waited, then reached out and took my free hand, threading his fingers through mine. He led me across the hall, the floor cool under my feet.

The bathroom was small but clean, a bit outdated, with pale tiles and a mirror that looked like it had seen decades of quiet mornings. Once inside, he turned to face me, his fingers brushing lightly at the edge of the quilt. Slowly, carefully, he slid it off my shoulders, letting it fall to the floor in a soft, heavy puddle.

I stood there, completely bare before him. My breath caught in my throat as his gaze swept over me. Not hungry this time, but soft and intent, like he was reading every part of me. He lifted one hand and began to trace his fingers over my skin, following each mark from the night before—the scratches along my ribs, the bruises blooming on my hips, the faint bite at my shoulder. His touch was so gentle it almost ached. When he reached my face, his thumb brushed softly across my swollen lower lip.

"I'm sorry," he said. "If I got carried away last night."

I felt my lips curve into a small smile. Slowly, I lifted my hands and began to trace along his chest, over the scratches I'd left on him, the small bruises scattered along his sides, the faint half-moons from my nails.

"Don't be," I said. "I love every single mark... which is why you'll have to replace them when they fade."

His mouth twitched into something dark and satisfied. "Gladly," he said. He hooked his thumbs in the waistband of his sweatpants, pushing them down in one smooth motion before stepping free of them.

Without another word, he guided me backward, stepping us into the shower.

We actually started trying to get clean—him putting shampoo in my hair, his fingers massaging my scalp with a tenderness that made me weak. I helped him wash, my hands sliding over his shoulders, his chest, down his back. But every touch sparked between us like electricity, sharp and irresistible. It didn't take long before the practical scrubbing turned into wandering hands, breathless kisses, soft laughs swallowed by steam.

By the time he pressed me back against the wall, his mouth claiming mine again, any thought of getting clean was gone. I could still feel the raw and tender soreness between my thighs from the night before—an ache that should've made me flinch, but instead had me hungry for him all over again. It was quick and passionate, but still somehow gentle, both of us lost in the slick warmth and the rush of each other.

After, he held me close under the water, his hands steady at my hips, his forehead resting against my temple as our breathing slowly returned to normal.

Once we got dressed and managed to find some coffee in the old kitchen, Cade gave me a tour of the house. It was bigger than I'd expected, stretching back into long, narrow hallways and sunlit rooms that felt somehow both outdated and timeless. The walls were covered in soft, faded wallpaper, and the hardwood floors creaked in a comforting, familiar way.

A big stone fireplace dominated the main living room, stacked with neatly cut wood and surrounded by mismatched chairs that looked like they'd been collected over decades. Family pictures covered nearly every wall—snapshots in old wooden frames, some sun-bleached and curling at the edges. I trailed my fingers lightly along them as we moved from room to room, my chest tightening at the warmth in each captured moment. A young Cade appeared again and again—grinning with missing teeth, arms slung around others, cheeks smudged with dirt and summer sun.

Then, halfway down the main hallway, I stopped. My breath snagged hard in my throat as my eyes locked on a large family portrait. Dozens of people crowded together in front of a wide porch, faces bright with laughter and summer warmth.

And there, right in front, stood a young teenage Cade. Beside him, smiling, hand resting lightly on his shoulder, was Michael. My fingers hovered just inches from the glass, frozen there.

439

Cade stepped up beside me. For a moment, he didn't say anything—just stood there, staring at the photo with me. "We were like brothers," he said finally. "Not just cousins. He was... everything to me when we were little. We did everything together—fishing, climbing trees, getting into trouble we swore we'd never tell our parents about."

"That's them," Cade said, pointing to a couple in the same picture. "My parents."

I studied the photo, a lump rising in my throat. "You look just like your dad," I said.

He gave a faint, bittersweet smile. "He would've liked you. Mom, too."

That statement made my chest ache. "My parents would've liked you too," I said. "My mom would've tried to feed you the second you walked in the door."

His gaze settled on me. "I wish I'd gotten the chance to meet them," he said.

Then his eyes returned to the picture and he pointed to two little kids, a boy and a girl. Both wide-eyed and grinning, tangled up in each other like best friends. "They were Michael's little siblings," he said, his voice thinning. "Sam and Lila."

He didn't say anything else. He didn't have to.

I couldn't look away from them. Their joy. Their innocence. The way their cheeks were still full and round, their eyes lit up with the kind of happiness only children carried. My vision blurred. I reached out without thinking, fingers hovering just above the photo—above Lila's tiny face—like I could touch her, protect her somehow. A sob clawed at the back of my throat. I bit it back, but the tears still flooded my eyes.

"Somewhere in our early teens... Michael started changing," he continued. "I thought it was just growing pains at first. We all did. He got moodier, started sneaking off on his own, started talking about power in these... weird, obsessive ways. I thought he was just trying to act tough. Be the big man."

440

His fingers curled lightly at his side. "I didn't realize how deep it went," he said. "Not until it was too late."

"I should have seen it," he whispered. "I should have stopped him."

Slowly, I reached for his hand, sliding my fingers through his and squeezing tight. "It wasn't your fault," I said. "None of it was your fault, Cade."

He didn't respond, but he squeezed my hand and leaned in, pressing a kiss to my temple. "We should probably think about heading back to the cabin soon," he said looking down at me.

I let out a quiet protest, my fingers tightening slightly around his. "Or... we could just stay here. Forget the rest of the world exists."

A low laugh rumbled from his chest. "Maybe some day," he said, with a soft, hopeful expression. "But for now... you've got more training to do. And a soulless parasite to make bleed."

"Right," I said, nodding solemnly. "The important things."

He chuckled again, shaking his head before letting go of my hand and stepping back.

"How are we even getting back?" I asked, glancing around as if a car might magically appear in the hallway.

Cade's grin turned a little smug. "I have a truck here," he said. We'll drive back."

I lifted an eyebrow. "Of course you do."

He shrugged, "always prepared," he said, glancing over his shoulder with that same faint smirk. "Comes with the territory."

• • •

The drive back felt like stepping into a soft blur, a pocket of time that didn't quite belong to the real world. We talked about nothing and everything all at once. Random stories from our childhood, dumb hypothetical questions, half-formed confessions that spilled out in the hush of the cab as we

441

picked at greasy fast-food breakfast and sipped coffee hot enough to burn. I found myself laughing more than I had in months, the sound surprising and bright even to my own ears.

At one point, Cade pulled off at a tiny gas station to fill up. He went inside to prepay—cash only, so we wouldn't leave a trail—and came back out carrying a small plastic bag. He slid back into the driver's seat and handed it over to me, casual as ever.

I looked down and saw a pack of Skittles. "These are my favorite," I said. "How did you know?"

Cade just shrugged, stepping back out of the truck to start pumping the gas. Over his shoulder, he called, "Heard you talking with Marcela about them once. Figured you might want something sweet."

I shook my head, a quiet laugh slipping out as I tore open the bag, my heart hammering in a way that had nothing to do with sugar. By the time he climbed back in, I was already sorting the colors, a small, giddy smile tugging at my lips.

The rest of the drive slipped by in a haze of candy colors, shared glances, and a quiet, easy kind of closeness. Sometime in the afternoon, we made it back to the cabin.

Kaylen was the first to look up from where she was perched at the kitchen table, a knife in her hand, slowly peeling an apple. Her eyes gazed over us once—my baggy clothes, flushed faces, the easy way Cade's hand hovered at the small of my back.

A sharp, humorless laugh broke from her mouth. "Nice of you two to finally come back," she drawled, raising an eyebrow. "What happened? Decided to abandon us all so you could fuck your way through Vermont?"

My cheeks flared hot with embarrassment. Marcela, leaning against the counter, tried to conceal a laugh with her hand. Alice let out a sharp snort, her shoulders shaking with silent laughter.

Cade didn't miss a beat. He just shot Kaylen a flat, unimpressed look. "You're just mad we didn't invite you."

442

The room went quiet for a split second. Then Kaylen barked out a single laugh, tossing the apple peel onto her plate. "Fair enough," she muttered, shaking her head.

I just stood there, my face still burning, torn between wanting to melt into the floor and laughing until I couldn't breathe. Cade's hand slid up to my shoulder, squeezing gently, and when I glanced up at him, he gave me the smallest, wickedest grin. Then he scanned the place.

"Where are the others?" he asked. "Did they go back to the main compound?"

Marcela pushed off the counter, wiping the last of her laughter from her face, her expression sobering quickly. "Yeah," she said, nodding. "They left this morning. Lorelei called them back. She thought having too many people here would draw attention—too many supplies going in and out, too many energy signatures in one place."

Kaylen crossed her arms, her mouth twisting. "She was worried it would raise suspicion. And suspicion means Michael could catch wind of where we are."

"Smart," Cade muttered, though I could hear the edge of worry buried under the word.

After a few more tense glances and quiet updates in the kitchen, I slipped away, my steps almost automatic as I climbed the narrow staircase.

When I pushed open the bedroom door, I found Sarah, Allie, and Jack all sitting around—Sarah sprawled across the foot of her bed, Allie perched in the corner chair with Biscuit curled on her lap, and Jack leaning against the dresser, arms crossed.

The moment Sarah saw me, her face lit up. She scrambled up and crossed the room in a few quick steps, throwing her arms around my shoulders in a quick, fierce hug. She leaned in close, her voice dropping to a conspiratorial whisper. "You better believe I need all the details later," she breathed, her grin wicked.

A small laugh tumbled out of me and I shook my head as she pulled back, her eyes glinting.

"What's going on?" I asked, glancing past her toward Allie and Jack.

Allie scratched behind Biscuit's ear, then looked up at me. "We've been filling Jack in," she said. "Everything. The marks, Michael, what really happened to Abel... all of it."

Jack's eyes glanced up to meet mine, something heavy and haunted in them. Sarah stepped back to hover beside Allie, her expression softening as she watched me take it in.

"I'm just... trying to process it all," Jack said. He paused, his gaze dropping to the floor for a moment before lifting back to me. "And Abel... I knew damn well a faulty gas line wouldn't have taken him out. I just didn't know it was... this," he finished quietly, his hand dropping to his side in a helpless, almost defeated motion.

I swallowed hard, my fingers curling into the edge of Cade's oversized hoodie I was wearing. "I'm sorry, Jack. I'm so sorry," I said. "I know this all happened because of me... and that's a shame I'll carry for the rest of my life."

Jack's eyes snapped up to mine. For a moment, he just looked at me. Then he crossed the space, stopping right in front of me. "You did nothing wrong," he said. "This was all Michael. Every bit of it. And he's going to pay. I'll make sure of that."

A beat of silence.

Then Allie let out a sharp, humorless snort from her chair. "Get in line," she muttered, her mouth twitching into a grim, almost feral little smile.

Then a voice cut up from downstairs, sharp and impatient. "Lena!" Kaylen called. "We still have some sunlight left. Ready for another round?"

A slow, confident smile tugged at my mouth.

"Absolutely," I said.

Chapter 34

The next couple of months slipped by and before I knew it, it was spring. I trained every single day, sometimes until my muscles shook and my knuckles split open. But I wasn't drowning in my mark. I was thriving. Each day, I felt it settle deeper under my skin, no longer an enemy but a living, breathing extension of me.

Most nights, I fell asleep curled against Cade on the couch. It was cramped, never spacious, but it was the most comforting thing in the world to drift off wrapped in his arms. Somehow, even on that lumpy couch, I slept deeper than I ever had in my life.

Jack stayed at the cabin, taking the spare bedroom. Sarah started spending some nights there too, though she insisted, loudly and often, that they hadn't slept together. "I'm not ready," she'd say, almost defiantly. But then she'd glance at him—and a quick, unmistakable heat would flash across her face, a look that said maybe… she was closer to ready than she let on. She told me they spent their nights talking, sometimes falling asleep wrapped around each other on the small bed. It wasn't a relationship, but it was something. A start.

Jack, ever the quiet motivator, eventually talked Sarah and Allie into training too. Hand-to-hand, basic defense moves, drills that left them panting and laughing. Sarah officially dubbed them the "Markless Wonders Squad," and the name stuck so fast even Kaylen started using it.

Sometimes, Kaylen and Cade joined their sessions, offering pointers, pushing them harder. Other days, Allie and Sarah disappeared into the kitchen with Marcela, who taught them all about her potions—what each one did, how to use them, how to tell if they were charged or not.

Vallerie gave me updates about Corinne. She was safe, still tucked away in the new facility, hidden from Michael's reach.

Cade and I found slivers of time alone. An occasional stolen shower together, steam curling around whispered laughter and soft kisses. A quick escape to the clearing when the weather turned milder, the sun warm enough to let us forget, just for a moment, how close everything still hovered to danger.

Kaylen started to soften too. She cracked jokes—real ones—and even tossed out occasional words of encouragement to Allie and Sarah during drills. Coming from her, it felt like a hug.

Sometimes I caught moments of something between Hiro and Alice—a lingering glance, a quiet, private laugh in the corner of the kitchen. The start of something new, something delicate and sweet that no one dared point out too loudly.

Meanwhile, Michael stayed on the news—still traveling, still performing for cameras and reporters. But otherwise…it stayed quiet.

The members who'd returned to the main compound checked in regularly. Short messages, quick video calls, steady pulses of connection that reminded us we weren't alone.

And beneath it all, I felt my own edges sharpen and solidify. I wasn't running anymore. I wasn't falling. I was becoming something dangerous.

This morning started out like the rest. We were all crowded around the table, eating breakfast before heading out to train. Then the tablet on the counter buzzed. Cade was the first to move, swiping the screen. David's face filled the display, his expression tense but focused.

"Morning," he said, without the slightest hint of warmth. "We've had a development."

Cade's jaw ticked. "What happened?"

"We believe we found one of Michael's safehouses," David replied. "We sent the twins to check it out. Shortly after they arrived, a man showed up. One of Michael's people."

He paused, glancing off-screen for a moment before looking back at us. "Mariah and Nicole managed to take him," David said, his voice clipped. "Alive. We have him here in the interrogation room now," he finished. "Thought you guys would want to see this."

David tapped something off-screen, and the tablet feed changed. Suddenly, a new image took over most of the screen—a security camera view of a stark, concrete room. Harsh overhead lights cast sharp shadows along the walls.

In the center sat a man bound to a heavy metal chair, his ankles strapped down, his chest cinched tight against the backrest. Thick metal glove-like devices swallowed his hands completely, bolted into the arms of the chair.

In the corner of the screen, David's face stayed visible, watching the feed with us.

Sarah leaned forward, squinting. "What the hell is on his hands?" she asked, her voice sharp with curiosity—and a little horror.

David's eyes glanced up, catching the question. "He can shoot shards," he said evenly. "Not sure what kind. We didn't have time to analyze it, but it's sharp enough to kill. The gloves are reinforced so he can't use them."

A tense silence fell, our eyes all glued to the screen. Allie's arms tightened around her middle as she watched the man struggle slightly against the restraints, his head still bowed. She looked at David. "So... what now? You're going to torture him to see if he talks?

"Oh, no," Vallerie said, her voice smooth and almost teasing. "This is Lorelei's time to shine."

Allie looked at her, confused.

"Her mark is truth telling," she continued, her tone turning almost casual, like she was explaining a recipe. "She can force someone to tell the truth if she touches them. But even without contact... she always knows when someone is lying."

447

Sarah's mouth fell open, then snapped shut again. She shook her head once, then muttered under her breath, "Poor Nick."

Cade let out a low chuckle beside me, shaking his head. "Yeah," he said, a wry smile tugging at his mouth. "He's had to watch himself at home more than any of us."

On the screen, the man suddenly jerked upright, his head snapping toward the door as he strained against the restraints. His voice cracked through the speaker, raw and defiant.

"I won't say a fucking thing!" he shouted, spit flying. "You might as well kill me now, because I'll never talk!"

A slow, quiet hush settled over the kitchen as we all leaned closer.

Lorelei stepped into view then—calm, collected, moving with the kind of quiet authority that didn't need to announce itself. Right behind her came Nick. He didn't say a word, but the way he hovered a step closer to her, the way his eyes darted constantly to the man in the chair—it was clear he was there to stand guard, to be close in case anything went wrong.

Lorelei didn't flinch at his outburst. She barely even looked at him at first, her gaze sweeping the edges of the room like she was checking for dust.

Then she finally turned, fixing her eyes on him. She lifted one hand and flicked her fingers dismissively, her voice smooth and clipped. "Oh, you'll talk," she said simply, almost bored. "You don't have a choice."

His breath caught, his eyes going wide as if he could already feel the mark taking hold. Lorelei stepped closer, her hand coming down to rest lightly on the side of his face, almost like a caress. The man's entire body went rigid. A strangled sound tore from his throat, his chest heaving as if he couldn't breathe.

The room back at the cabin was dead silent. Beside me, Cade's hand slid to my lower back

"What's your name," Lorelei said, her voice quiet but carrying like a crack of thunder.

448

"Callum," he spat. "Callum Decker."

Lorelei nodded once, as if she'd expected nothing less.

"How did you end up with Michael?" she asked next, her tone still low and almost patient.

Callum's eyes twitched, his throat working furiously. His breaths came faster, like he was fighting each syllable.

"I… I joined him a couple years ago," he gasped out eventually. "He promised power… supremacy over the unmarked. Said they were worthless. That we deserved to rise above them, rule them. He said… he said we were chosen."

I swallowed hard, bile rising up my throat. My vision blurred for a moment, and I forced myself to focus on Callum's face, on Lorelei's hand.

Lorelei's eyes narrowed slightly—a small, lethal focus. Behind her, Nick stood still as a statue, his eyes locked on Callum, fists clenched at his sides.

"What is Michael planning?" she asked. "Why has he been traveling?"

Callum's entire body convulsed once, like he was trying to wrench the words back down his throat. His head thudded against the chair as he let out a broken sound.

Finally, he choked out the words, each one slicing the air like a confession. "He… he was looking for the books," Callum gasped. "Ancient alchemical texts. They… they hold the rituals and runes for soul harvesting. Ways to bind souls, consume them. Make him… immortal. All-powerful."

Lorelei didn't move, her eyes drilling into him with relentless precision. "How many books?" she demanded.

Callum shuddered, his breath coming out in pulls. "Two," he rasped. "There are two. He… he has them both now. He found the second one last week."

Lorelei's hand moved slightly on Callum's face, her thumb pressing just enough to make him flinch. "What is the ritual?" she asked, each word razor-sharp.

Callum let out a shuddering exhale, his eyes rolling back briefly before snapping forward again. "It's… it's a soul harvest," he gasped. "The books...they describe a way to collect souls, but not just any souls. They have to be...willing. Given freely. Powered by love and belief."

He coughed, his whole body trembling in the chair. "That's why he needed the public. The hero image. He made them love him...worship him...it's the only way it will work. It will make him immortal and untouchable."

Callum's breaths came faster now, almost panicked, but the words kept spilling out like he couldn't stop them. "It...it doesn't matter if they're marked," he continued, his voice cracking. "The ritual, it only needs the willing and devoted soul. That's what makes them pure. That's what gives him power."

Lorelei's fingers stayed firm on Callum's face, her expression as calm and cold as moonlight. "When is he doing this?" she asked.

Callum gave a strangled sound, his whole body jolting. "Next Saturday," he choked. "At sunset. It has to be twilight...between day and night. The veil is thinner then. The energy is stronger, more malleable. Easier to...to take them all at once."

Lorelei's gaze narrowed further. "Where?"

Callum's head jerked back, eyes wide and wild. "His estate," he choked. "He's been preparing it all week since we got the second book. The runes... they're carved into the cement... everywhere. They channel the souls, bind them to him. It all has to be exact, or it won't work. He's invited around two hundred people. All supporters. All people who love him."

"And how does he plan to make the runes and rituals work?" Lorelei pressed.

Callum's head jerked violently, and for a moment he looked like he might pass out. "He... he has an alchemist," he choked out finally. "In his ranks.

Lorelei paused, tilting her head slightly, studying every twitch of his face. "What happens after?" she asked, her voice almost too quiet to catch.

Callum's mouth opened and closed. "He…he ascends," he whispered. "Becomes immortal. Untouchable. The power makes him unstoppable. Once it's done…no one can kill him. He'll be everywhere. In everything. He'll be…a god."

Lorelei's grip tightened, making him flinch. "Why do this? Why now?"

Callum's eyes darted around wildly, but he couldn't escape her gaze. "He…he needed proof first," he stammered. "Lena…she was the prototype. The test to see if a soul tied by love could be harvested. Once it worked…once he took her marks…he knew it was possible on a bigger scale."

His voice turned thin and almost hysterical. "She was just the start. Now he wants them all. The supporters…they think they're coming to thank him. They'll give themselves willingly, not knowing they're handing him their souls."

Lorelei watched him for a long, heavy moment—her eyes as sharp and cold as glass. Then, slowly, she drew her hand away from his face. The instant her touch left him, Callum's head dropped forward, his chin thudding against his chest.

On the tablet, the security feed disappeared, switching back to David's face. He looked exhausted, shadows deep under his eyes, but his expression stayed steady as he glanced off-screen, likely checking on Lorelei.

No one moved. No one even seemed to breathe. Then, almost as if by some unspoken agreement, everyone turned to Marcela at once. She stood near the end of the table, her eyes wide and her hands twisted tightly together at her waist.

Sarah was the first to speak, her voice rough and trembling. "Marcela… did you know about this? The books? Any of it?"

Marcela swallowed hard, her throat working. She shook her head quickly, almost frantically. "I knew…I knew there were forbidden rituals and runes," she said. "Dark techniques. Things we were warned about as children. But I had no idea there were actual books that contained them. I was always told that knowledge had been destroyed centuries ago. Erased so no one could ever try it again." She let out a shaky breath, her eyes darting between us all. "I didn't think it was even possible," she whispered.

Lorelei joined David on screen. Gage stood just behind them, arms crossed tightly over his chest. Nick hovered protectively near Lorelei, his hand resting lightly at her back. A few others—people I didn't recognize—moved purposefully in and out of frame, voices low and urgent.

Cade didn't waste a single second. He stepped forward, his jaw tight, eyes locked on David. The warmth of his touch left my back, and suddenly the kitchen felt colder, emptier. "What's the plan?" he demanded.

David's gaze snapped up, meeting Cade's without hesitation. "I don't have enough yet," he said, his voice steel. "I need to send Lorelei back in to question him further about the security measures for the event."

"I'll go in with her this time," he added. "Once we have all the information, I'll figure it out and call you back."

"And after that," David said, "we'll have to eliminate Callum. He can't be left alive. If Michael's people realize he's missing, they'll get suspicious. They might move the event, tighten security, or even activate the runes early. We can't risk it. We'll place his body back at the safehouse where Mariah and Nicole found him—make it look like he was never captured. No trail. No questions."

He gave one last hard glance around the room, as if silently daring anyone to argue, then looked straight at Cade. "Stay ready," David said. Then the screen went black.

I felt myself slowly backing away, the edges of the room blurring as I processed the new information.

Michael. Immortal. A god.

I had known he was dangerous—a monster—but this… this was so much bigger than I'd ever imagined. I found myself staring at them—at these people who had somehow become my family. My chest tightened painfully. What if we didn't make it? This fight would be brutal. People would die. I couldn't lose them. Not a single one.

452

Voices exploded around me the second the screen went black—tangled, clashing, no one pausing, everyone desperate to be heard at once.

Marcela started first, her voice sharp and tight. "We need to find a way to cut him off before the ritual. Or maybe I can create a spell that disrupts the ritual—"

Vallerie shook her head, eyes dark with a sharp spark. "If I could get my hands on him...I could wipe his memories clean. Erase everything. He wouldn't even know who he was, let alone finish a ritual."

Alice snorted, her arms folding across her chest. "And how exactly do you plan on doing that? He has the shield mark, remember? There's no way he's dropping that during the event. Our marks can't penetrate a shield, not even mind marks."

Vallerie's mouth pressed into a thin, frustrated line.

Hiro leaned forward, his hands braced on the table. "What if we find a way to trap him? Maybe with a rune," he said, looking over at Marcela.

Marcela's eyes went wide, her fingers twisting together. "I...I don't know of any runes that can actually trap a person," she said, her voice low and hesitant. "At least, none that have ever truly worked. Those are more legends than anything else."

Allie frowned, her arms crossed tight over her chest. "But even if they did exist... how would we get him in one place long enough to use it?"

Sarah jabbed her finger against the table. "We blow up the estate! We end it all in one hit."

Alice let out a short, harsh laugh. "Oh, sure. Because we've done such a great job stopping him so far," she snapped. "But I'm sure this time we'll just waltz in and take him out. Easy."

My head spun, each idea crashing into the next—each one desperate, each one already crumbling before they finished saying it.

Cade stayed a few steps back, his eyes fixed on me.

453

Then Kaylen's voice cracked through it all. "Enough!"

It wasn't just loud—it was commanding, the kind of sound that cracked straight into your bones. The room shuddered into silence, like she'd sucked all the air out of it.

She stepped forward, eyes sweeping over each of us, her dark hair falling into her face. She didn't bother to push it back. "You're all missing the point," she said, her voice sharp enough to cut glass. "None of this matters—the spells, the traps, the bombs—if he still has those marks."

Kaylen turned, her eyes moving deliberately from one person to the next. "He's already damn near unstoppable now. Even if we managed to blow him up, he'd heal. Even if we found a way to trap him, he could use mind weaving to make us let him out. And his shield? It'll stop every single one of our marks from touching him. You all know that."

Kaylen's gaze locked on me then, sharp enough to pin me in place. "The only one who can stop him is Lena. She's the one who can take the marks back. That's it. She's the mission. Everything else is noise."

I heard someone inhale sharply—maybe Vallerie, maybe Allie.

Kaylen shook her head, her voice lower but somehow even harder. "Our only job now is to keep her alive long enough to do it. Otherwise, none of this matters. He'll win. And every single one of us dies for nothing."

The silence that followed felt like a physical weight pressing down on my shoulders, on my ribs, on my skull.

Kaylen didn't look away. "She's the only shot we've got," she said, final and absolute. "So we stop pretending it's anything else."

"I..." The word broke in my throat. I forced myself to try again. "I... I don't know if I can do it," I said, my voice cracking. "But I'll try. I swear I will."

My eyes moved first to Allie. She stood there, her jaw clenched, tears welling but refusing to fall. Her hands curled into fists at her sides, her shoulders squared like she was ready to charge into battle for me.

For a moment, we just looked at each other. All the years, all the arguments, all the fierce love between us pulsed in that single look. A tiny, trembling smile tugged at her mouth, and she gave me one small nod—not permission, not encouragement, but a promise that she was still with me, no matter what.

Then Sarah. Her chin lifted the moment our eyes met, her eyes bright and unflinching. She looked like she was already halfway to throwing herself in front of a blade for me without a second thought. Wild, loyal, and so impossibly her.

One by one, I looked at the others. Marcela, her fingers twisted together but her eyes fierce. Kaylen, solid as a mountain, her steady gaze sharp and sure. Alice and Hiro, standing close, ready. Vallerie, her face calm but her resolve shining through every line of her body.

And then Cade. Always steady, always watching me like I was the only thing that mattered in any room. My anchor. My wildness and my calm, all tangled up in one.

They were all with me. Already in.

Cade stepped forward, slow and careful, like he was approaching something wild and wounded. His eyes locked onto mine. "It was always going to be you," he said. "And you won't be alone. I promise you that."

A small, knowing smile tugged at my lips. "I know."

Chapter 35

The call came in just after lunch. Cade stepped forward first, swiping the screen. David's face filled the tablet, but this time, he wasn't alone.

A dozen smaller squares framed the edges of the screen, each showing different people. Some were older, some young, all with the same sharp focus and haunted exhaustion. Behind them were cluttered rooms, supply racks, weapons propped against walls, quiet hallways. I didn't recognize any of them.

David didn't waste time. "We've called in backup," he said, his voice sharp and clipped, cutting straight to the bone. "These are leaders and operatives from Severance teams across the country. This is bigger than any of us can handle alone. We pulled everything Lorelei could extract from Callum before he shut down. Michael isn't at his estate. He's staying in a separate safehouse. Completely hidden. Nobody, not even his closest guards, knows where it is. He's kept it as an insurance policy. Which means we cannot move on him before the event."

A sharp, cold dread twisted through my chest.

David tapped something to share his screen. An aerial image of Michael's estate backyard filled the display— sprawling and unnervingly beautiful, the kind of place that might have once hosted garden parties instead of mass manipulation.

My eyes swept over the scene. Wide cement walkways curled across perfect emerald grass, precise and cold. Four massive fountains anchored each corner like silent sentinels. A grand gazebo sat closer to the center, ornate and elegant, its roof catching the light like a crown. Statues dotted the yard, posed mid-stride or mid-thought, like guests frozen forever in a moment of false serenity. Above everything, a balcony jutted from the second floor of the mansion, overlooking it all like a throne—the perfect vantage point for a god playing king.

David's voice cut into my thoughts. "These fountains—each one has runes carved into the base," he said, his tone clipped and surgical. "Together, they create a massive protective shield, spanning several miles out from the estate. Once all of Michael's guards are inside, they'll activate the runes. After that, no one with a mark can cross the barrier. The guards and Michael will be locked in, but it means we can't get in either. It's a total lockdown. We'll need unmarked people to infiltrate first as guests, get close to the fountains, and corrupt the runes."

Gage's voice cut in and a moment later his face took over the screen. "I'm already working on cracking Michael's guest list," he said, fingers flying across a keyboard just out of view. "It's a pain. He's kept this event private, only sending invitations to his top supporters. But as soon as I find out who's invited, I can hack in and get their digital credentials. Then we just have to make sure the people whose invites we take don't make it to the party."

Jack was the first to move. He stepped forward, his jaw set. "I'll go in," he said.

Sarah's head snapped toward him. She opened her mouth, then snapped it shut, her eyes narrowing. After a beat, she turned to Gage. "Get three tickets," she said. Her gaze glanced to Allie, then back. "We're going too."

Jack went pale, like all the blood had been vacuumed straight out of him. "No," he barked, reaching for Sarah's hand. "It's too dangerous, Sarah. Absolutely not."

David kept talking on the tablet—some calm, clipped tactical explanation about infiltration timing and fallback points—but it washed over me like distant ocean waves.

I was locked on Allie and Sarah now, my pulse crashing in my throat. Allie's eyes burned when she looked at me, her chin already tilted stubbornly. "You can't go," I said, my voice breaking halfway out. "You don't have marks. You're not trained for this. You can't—"

Allie cut me off with a sharp shake of her head. "I'm not sitting on the sidelines while you go in there to face him."

I turned to Sarah, my voice rising. "What if you get recognized? What if Chad sees you? He knows what you two look like."

Sarah snorted, tossing her hair back like she was on a runway. "Please. This is an elegant event. I'll be so glammed up that even my own mom won't recognize me. Chad will be too busy drooling to realize it's me. He'll probably ask me for a dance before he figures it out."

Jack turned on her, wild desperation in his voice. "Sarah, you don't understand. Once you're inside, if something goes wrong—"

Sarah's murderous glare snapped to Jack, her words slicing the air. "If she's facing death, I'll be there to flip it off with her. We're going."

The three of them faced each other, the air between them vibrating with all the things they couldn't or wouldn't say out loud.

Finally, Jack closed his eyes, shoulders slumping in defeat. "Goddamn it," he muttered, voice almost a growl. He looked up at Sarah, eyes resigned, but burning with something fiercely protective. "Fine. We do it together."

Sarah's mouth split into a victorious, feral grin. "I knew you'd see it my way," she crowed.

Before anyone could respond, she threw her arms around him and yanked him into a kiss—right there in front of everyone. My eyebrows shot up so fast they nearly flew off my face. My mouth dropped open, words scrambling in my head but refusing to form. When Sarah finally pulled back, Jack's face was completely flushed, his eyes wide and a little dazed, like he'd just been hit by a truck he might happily lie in front of again.

I blinked hard, trying to find my voice. "So... is this officially a relationship now?"

Sarah shot me a wicked look, breath still heavy. "Considering we're all probably going to die next week? No time to lose, babe."

Jack let out a strangled laugh then surged forward and grabbed her again, crushing his mouth to hers with a grin so big it split his whole face open.

Everyone in the room was watching them. I glanced toward the tablet—now dark and silent on the table—and realized the call had ended at some point.

Hiro's eyes went wide. He turned to Alice so fast it was almost a blur. "Wait... are we doing love confessions now? Because if so—"

He didn't even finish before he grabbed Alice and pulled her into a sudden, heated kiss.

Marcela let out a sharp whoop from across the room, her hands shooting into the air. "Oh my god, finally!" she cheered, laughter spilling over her words.

Then Kaylen snorted, shaking her head. "Fantastic," she drawled, her voice dry as sandpaper. "Everyone's making out while we plan a war. Priorities, people."

Marcela stepped forward, sliding in beside Sarah, Allie, and Jack. "Alright," she said. "Since you three are going to be the first ones stepping into the lion's den, we need to make sure you're prepared. I want to arm you with potions and runic weapons. The only problem is, I don't know if they'll pass through Michael's barrier. So you can't carry them in at first. But once those are disarmed, we'll find a way to get them to you."

She glanced between them, her tone softening slightly. "That means I want to make absolutely sure you know how to use them properly, which ones do what, and decide which will work best for each of you. No fumbling. No second-guessing. So let's go outside and go through everything together."

"Okay, let's get our magic murder cocktails ready," Sarah quipped, throwing Allie a wink that drew a snort of laughter.

Marcela turned on her heel, grabbing a heavy canvas bag from the corner before leading the others out the back door.

Allie and Jack followed close behind, but Sarah paused just long enough to toss me a crooked grin and a wink before jogging after them.

Then Cade moved to me, his eyes locked on mine. He reached out, brushing a strand of hair from my face. "We'll find a way," he murmured. "No matter how ugly this gets. We'll walk out the other side. Together."

A small, shaky breath escaped me. "Promise?"

"I promise," he said. "Now come on. Let's go make sure they don't accidentally blow themselves up."

We stepped outside together, the afternoon sun washing everything in a soft, golden haze. Marcela, Allie, Sarah, and Jack were gathered on the far side of the yard, a collection of boxes and crates lined up in front of them like a makeshift practice range.

Just as we crossed the porch, Sarah launched something at one of the boxes—it hit with a sharp crack, followed by a burst of vivid orange light and a small explosion that rocked the box backward.

Sarah threw her hands up with a wild cheer that echoed across the yard. "Hell yeah!"

I couldn't help but laugh, the sound catching somewhere between relief and disbelief.

Marcela leaned forward, adjusting something in Sarah's hand, likely explaining another trick or fine-tuning her throw.

Jack stepped up next. He weighed a gleaming blade in his hand—a runic knife, faint markings glinting along the edge—then whipped it forward in a smooth, practiced motion. The blade slammed dead center into a painted target nailed to a fence post beyond the boxes. Sarah let out a loud cheer, punching the air. Marcela gave Jack a sharp nod, clearly pleased.

Allie stepped forward next, her eyes narrowing in concentration. She hurled a small glass vial—it arced high, spinning once before shattering against another box. Smoke curled up in thick tendrils as the box began to dissolve, its edges bubbling and collapsing inward like melting wax. A smug grin pulled at Allie's mouth as she turned back to Marcela, who clapped her on the shoulder approvingly.

Cade and I settled down on the edge of the porch steps, close enough to watch but far enough to feel separate from the chaos. He leaned back on his palms, one knee bent, his eyes fixed on the group.

"They're naturals," he said, amusement and something almost proud weaving through his voice.

"Yeah," I said, my eyes following Sarah as she took another vial from Marcela, practically bouncing in place. "They really are."

For a while, we just watched in silence—the occasional whoops and laughter drifting across the yard, mingling with the soft rustle of early spring leaves.

"Come on," Cade said, that spark of challenge lighting up his dark gaze. Before I could protest, he pushed himself up and turned, reaching down with both hands.

I slipped my fingers into his without hesitation. He led me across the yard, opposite the side from where the others were practicing with Marcela. Once there, he turned to face me.

"Michael is a coward," he said. "He's always hidden behind manipulation, behind stolen power, behind the illusion that he's untouchable. But he's not."

His thumb brushed lightly along my cheek. "He'll underestimate you. He always has. He thinks you're something small, something fragile, something he already broke." Cade shook his head, his gaze burning straight through me. "But I know what you're capable of. I know how strong you are, how stubborn, how relentless, how... vicious."

My hands came up to wrap around his wrist. "He thinks he's already won," Cade continued. "But he doesn't realize you're going to be the end of him."

A pause, just long enough for the words to sink in. Then Cade dropped his hand, stepping back slightly. He tilted his head, that familiar spark of challenge lighting up his eyes. "Ready to prove it?"

A slow, fierce smile curved across my lips. "Ready," I said.

462

We started slow at first. Cade circled me, his steps measured and quiet, his eyes locked onto mine like a predator. I lunged first, a quick feint to my left, then a real strike toward his ribs. He blocked it easily, his hand snapping up to catch my wrist. But instead of pulling me in close, he pushed me back, forcing me to reset.

A spark of laughter slipped out of me. Cade grinned in answer, that quick, crooked smile I'd started to crave more than air. Then he came at me fast, but I met him head-on, my mark crackling under my skin, humming with that new, dangerous harmony I'd finally learned to trust. We moved across the yard in a blur of strikes and counters, kicks and dodges, until my breath burned in my lungs and my pulse pounded in my ears.

At some point, Kaylen slipped in behind Cade, jumping into the fray without a word. Hiro joined a moment later, then Alice—all three weaving in and out, testing me, pushing me, forcing me to stay sharp. It wasn't an organized fight, it was chaos and rhythm and challenge, a dance made of bruises and laughter and grit.

Every hit I landed sparked cheers from the far side of the yard, where Marcela, Allie, Jack, and Sarah had paused their own drills to watch. By the time we finally dropped to the grass, breathless and grinning, my arms ached, and my legs felt like they were made of molten lead. But I felt alive. Strong. Ready.

After the sparring, we all went back inside the cabin, sweat cooling on our skin as twilight crept in. We gathered around the big kitchen table for dinner, shoulders bumping, forks clinking against plates, the soft hum of conversation filling the spaces between us.

Everyone seemed sharper somehow, more present. Like they were all silently counting each heartbeat, each laugh, each passing moment. It felt like we were all trying to carve these small pieces of normal into our bones before they could be taken away.

Over the next week, during the day, everything was preparation. Drills, strategy talks, endless briefings with the main compound over video calls. The screens filled with faces from faraway chapters, all tight-jawed and serious, each voice adding layers to the plan.

But the evenings... those were ours. We reclaimed them fiercely, like they were a precious commodity we might never see again. We played cards, shared stupid jokes that left us wheezing, passed around mismatched mugs of tea or whatever strong liquor Marcela found hiding in a back cabinet.

And then, almost before I realized it, it was the day before the event. The tension in the cabin buzzed like a live wire. Conversations trailed off mid-sentence, hands fidgeted at weapon straps and mugs, glances shot around the room like tiny, sharp arrows. By evening, it had settled over us so thick it was hard to breathe.

Sarah was the first to snap. She slammed her hand down on the table so hard that Vallerie flinched. "Alright! Enough," she barked. "I'm not spending what could be our last night alive acting like a bunch of mopey ghosts."

I lifted my head, blinking at her. Then I nodded slowly. "You're right," I said. "What do you have in mind?"

Sarah threw her hands up. "I don't know, but not this. Not sitting around like we're already dead."

I glanced around, then snapped my fingers as an idea sparked. "There's a fire pit in the side yard we haven't used yet... How about a fire?"

Sarah's eyes lit up instantly. "Yes! Perfect!" Without waiting for another word, she spun on her heel and marched straight onto the porch, grabbing the nearest chair and dragging it noisily down the steps toward the side yard. Jack shot up after her, grabbing another chair before she could make it far, falling in beside her to help.

The rest of the group exchanged glances—then, one by one, everyone pushed back from the table and went outside, grabbing chairs, small side tables, whatever they could carry.

They dragged them down to the side yard, arranging them in a loose circle around the fire pit.

The night settled around us, warm and close, the fire crackling and spitting little sparks into the dark. Sarah ended up in Jack's lap on one of the lounge chairs, her head tipped back against his shoulder, legs draped lazily across his. Every so often, she'd lean up to say something that made him snort into her hair, his arms tightening around her like he still couldn't believe she was really there.

Alice and Hiro had pushed their chairs so close they were practically sharing a seat, knees touching, heads angled in as if they were trading secrets too soft for the rest of us to hear.

Allie sat cross-legged in her chair, a mug cradled between her hands, her gaze sweeping over all of us with that protective, quietly fierce energy she carried like armor. Every so often, she'd lean over to nudge Marcela or toss a dry comment that had Vallerie cackling.

Cade sat on the ground in front of my chair, one arm draped easily across my leg. Every now and then he'd tilt his head back to look up at me, eyes catching the firelight, his thumb brushing slow circles against my skin.

Biscuit made the rounds from chair to chair, shamelessly accepting scraps, scratches, and quiet praise. Eventually, she settled beside Cade, her head resting on one big paw, eyes half-closed in bliss.

Marcela handed out mugs filled with something strong enough to make our throats burn, laughing when Sarah nearly choked on hers. Vallerie argued with Kaylen over the best way to roast marshmallows, their bickering sharp but edged with rare, genuine smiles.

The world beyond our small circle felt impossibly far away.

After a while, Cade squeezed my knee gently before standing. "I'll be right back," he murmured, his voice low enough that only I heard.

I watched him slip into the house, his broad shoulders momentarily lit by the warm glow inside before he vanished from view. The conversations around the fire carried on—

465

laughter bubbling up as Sarah teased Jack about his "serious soldier face," Allie pretending to gag at their sweetness.

A few minutes later, Cade reappeared at the edge of the circle, a thick blanket hooked over his arm with a bag dangling from the same hand. The firelight caught on his hair as he stepped forward, his eyes locking on mine like he'd only ever had one destination. "Come with me," he growled—quiet, but so full of heat and authority it made my heart stutter and my thighs clench.

I didn't even hesitate. I stood, and the moment I did, his arm slid around my waist, pulling me flush against him. He stepped forward into a shadow cast by the moonlight at the edge of the yard.

The world blinked around us, and then we were in the trees, the smell of earth and moss rushing up to meet me. Another step. I stumbled a little when we landed. I looked up at him, a slow, knowing smile spreading over my lips. The clearing—*our* clearing. My heart thudded once, sharp and heavy, heat already starting to pool low in my belly.

Cade stepped a few paces away, his silhouette barely visible in the moonlight. He crouched with the bag, and unzipped it. He pulled out a candle and lit it, the flame catching with a soft flare. Then another. He moved in a wide arc, lighting each one as he went, the flickering glow building gradually around the clearing like stars awakening.

When he was done, he spread out a blanket in the center, the candlelight glowing gently around it. I stepped forward without thinking, my fingers sliding into his. Cade's fingers tightened around mine, leading me into that soft circle of light like it was a sacred place built just for us. We stood facing each other, the moonlight slipping through the trees and catching on his hair, his shoulders—making him look almost otherworldly.

I lifted my hands to wrap around his neck, needing to feel him. But before I could touch him, he caught my wrists in his hands. Slowly, deliberately, he raised my arms above my head, holding them there with a firm but gentle grip. My pulse roared in my ears.

His fingers released my wrists, sliding lightly down the length of my arms, feather-soft, leaving goosebumps in their wake. He kept going, tracing down the sides of my ribs, over my hips, until he reached the hem of my sweater.

He paused for a moment, his eyes meeting mine. Then, with careful slowness, he tugged the sweater upward. Inch by inch, the fabric peeled away from my skin, until he lifted it fully over my head and tossed it aside, his gaze never once leaving mine.

He stepped forward, close enough that I felt the warmth of his breath on my collarbone, and reached behind me. His fingers unclasped my bra with patient ease, then slid the straps slowly down my arms, letting it fall away before tossing it aside.

He lingered there, his hands hovering just above my bare skin. Then, lightly, he traced his fingertips across my breasts, a delicate, reverent touch that sent a shiver rolling down my spine.

His hands drifted lower again, skimming along my waist until they found the button of my jeans. He took his time, unfastening it with excruciating slowness, then sliding the zipper down, the sound impossibly loud in the quiet clearing.

He knelt as he worked the denim over my hips, then lower, pulling my underwear with it. His fingers brushed along my thighs, the backs of my knees, my calves, as he guided the clothes all the way down, finally slipping them off along with my shoes.

When he stood again, he stepped back a pace. For a moment, he simply looked at me.

I stood there, bare and trembling. With his perfect night vision, I knew he could see every curve, every line, every tiny mark on my body. His eyes roamed slowly, hungrily, reverently.

Then, with that same slow, deliberate grace, he reached for the hem of his shirt and pulled it up over his head, revealing the lean, powerful lines of his torso. The candlelight and moonlight played across the ridges of his muscles, the scars that spoke of a thousand battles—and the tattoo that wound over his skin like a living shadow. Under the faint glow, it looked almost alive, like it was shimmering just beneath his skin.

He dropped the shirt to the ground beside him without a second thought. His hands moved to the waistband of his pants next, unbuttoning them with a careful patience that made my pulse skitter wildly in my chest. He eased them down his hips, sliding them all the way off along with his boots, leaving him completely bare in front of me—broad, powerful, and already hard, his arousal unmistakable in the soft candlelight.

My breath caught. He was the most beautiful thing I had ever seen—every scar, every ripple of muscle, every line of ink telling a story I had only just begun to understand. Something deep in me ached at the sight, a wild, molten warmth flooding my veins. In that moment, it felt like nothing else existed—not the looming battle, not the fear, not even the clearing around us. Just him. Just us.

He stepped forward, closing the small space between us. He reached for my hands, his fingers curling around my wrists with a firm but gentle certainty. He guided me down, easing me carefully onto the blanket until I lay flat on my back, the cool night air brushing across my bare skin.

I instinctively lifted my hands to wrap around his shoulders, wanting to pull him close, but he caught them easily, his long fingers wrapping around both my wrists in one strong hand. He pressed my arms gently but insistently above my head, pinning them to the blanket. The dominance of the gesture, mixed with the soft warmth in his eyes, made my breath hitch in my throat.

He lay half beside me, half over me, his chest pressing lightly against my ribs, his hips angled so that the heavy, hot length of him brushed along my hip. The feel of him there, thick and solid, made my pulse hammer deep in my belly.

His free hand came up to brush a strand of hair from my forehead before he bent down and pressed a soft, lingering kiss there. His lips drifted lower, brushing over my temple, then the curve of my cheek, the tip of my nose. Each kiss was deliberate, like he was memorizing me piece by piece.

When he reached my lips, he paused, hovering so close I could feel his breath feather against my mouth. Then he kissed me—deeply, thoroughly, his tongue sweeping slowly against mine before he pulled back just enough to leave me chasing after him.

His hips pressed closer, and the thick, rigid line of him dragged against my side, pulling a sharp sound from my throat.

He moved lower, his mouth sliding along my jaw, down the side of my neck. Each kiss burned into my skin, making me writhe beneath him.

I tried to lower my hands, to touch him, but he only tightened his hold, keeping me pinned, making me feel exposed and worshipped all at once.

His mouth drifted lower still, gliding across the slope of my collarbone. He paused to suck lightly, his teeth grazing me just enough to make me gasp, my hips lifting off the blanket. He pressed me gently back down, a low sound rumbling in his throat—a soft warning, or maybe a promise. Then he dipped even lower, his lips closing around one nipple. He drew it into his mouth, slow and hot, his tongue flicking over it before he sucked harder.

A broken moan tore out of me, my back arching despite his steadying grip. I tried again to pull at him, desperate to touch, but he squeezed his hand harder around my wrists.

His mouth moved to my other breast, lavishing it with the same torturous, exquisite attention—licking, kissing, drawing it into his mouth until my breathing turned shaky and my thighs trembled with need.

When he finally pulled away, every inch of my skin felt electric, each nerve thrumming under his touch. Then, he let go of my wrists. Instantly, my hands shot down, burying into

469

his hair, desperate for more. But he caught them gently, guiding them down to rest beside me on the blanket.

He rose up onto his knees, leaning forward over me now. The hard length of him brushed across my thigh as he bent over me, and I felt my legs tremble with anticipation. His mouth traced a line down the center of my chest, over my ribs, lower still, each kiss leaving a trail of heat across my skin.

Then he began to move even lower. He kissed along the gentle curve of my belly. Each time his lips touched me, my hips twitched upward, but he only pressed me gently back down, his palm firm against my stomach to hold me in place.

I let out a shaky, desperate sound, my fingers curling uselessly in the air beside me.

He paused just below my navel, his warm breath ghosting over my skin. I could feel how wet I was already, could feel the ache building so strong it almost hurt.

Then he dipped lower still, pressing a feather-light kiss to the inside of my hip. I whimpered, my body trying to move toward his mouth, craving more, but he only laughed softly— a low, gentle sound that made my heart stutter.

He kissed the other hip next, his mouth lingering there for a long moment. My thighs trembled, my toes curling into the blanket beneath me. Then, finally, his mouth drifted even lower, kissing just above my clit. My whole body jolted, a strangled cry breaking from my throat.

But instead of giving me what I so desperately wanted, he moved again, sliding down to kiss the sensitive skin of my inner thigh, then the other, slow and teasing, like he had all the time in the world.

My breaths came in helpless gasps. I tried again to thread my hands into his hair and guide him where I needed him most, but he gently pushed them back down beside me, his fingers soft but unyielding. Every kiss felt like a spark lighting me up from the inside, building me higher and higher without ever letting me tip over the edge.

When his lips finally brushed over the crease where my thigh met my center, I nearly sobbed, my hips lifting in a desperate plea. But he only chuckled again, low and warm against my skin, before moving on to press a gentle kiss to the inside of my knee, then down my shin.

I felt wild under him, completely undone and yet held so carefully, like I was something fragile and priceless. My entire body felt like it was vibrating beneath him. Every nerve was lit up, raw and aching in the sweetest way, my thighs trembling against the blanket.

Cade's lips moved lower still, kissing my ankle softly, then tracing along the top of my foot. Each kiss felt like a brand, a soft, searing promise that left me breathless.

When he finally reached the end of my foot, he paused, then began to work his way back up—so slowly it felt like torture. He pressed a kiss to my shin, his fingers skimming lightly along my calf as he went. The gentleness of it made my chest ache, made my eyes sting with the threat of tears I didn't even understand.

Higher. Another soft, lingering kiss to the side of my knee, his palm sliding up the outside of my thigh to steady me when I twitched beneath him.

His mouth moved again, brushing up the curve of my thigh with an agonizing slowness. I was shaking now, my breaths coming out in tiny, gasping whimpers.

Then he paused above my hip, hovering. His fingers traced lightly over the scar Michael had left—that rough, puckered line that marked where the blade had gone in, the place I almost lost everything.

I felt my entire body still under his touch, my chest clenching tight.

Cade lowered his head and pressed his lips to it—soft, lingering. He didn't move away quickly. Instead, he stayed there, his breath warm, his mouth gentle and reverent as he kissed the scar again.

I felt something in me break open at that, my eyes burning as I tried to swallow the sob clawing its way up my throat.

Then he moved higher, kissing my ribs again, my sternum, my collarbones—every part of me that had been

471

hidden and guarded for so long, now laid bare under his worshipful touch. As he moved closer to my throat, I felt my hands instinctively lift again, reaching for him, desperate to hold on.

But he caught them gently, his fingers wrapping around my wrists. He pressed them firmly back above my head, pinning them to the blanket once more. Then he lowered his mouth to my throat, kissing softly along the delicate line of my pulse, feeling it hammer wild beneath my skin.

I arched up instinctively, my body straining for more, but he only pressed me back down gently, his hand firm and patient. A small, strangled sound slipped out of me—half-plea, half-surrender.

Cade paused, lifting his head just enough to meet my eyes. In the candlelight, his gaze looked almost feral with devotion, dark and hungry and so gentle it made my heart stutter. His eyes stayed locked on mine as he lay half on, half beside me, his free hand slowly drifting down to trace a heated line along my ribs, then across my stomach.

My breath hitched, my muscles jumping under his touch. I tried to move, to press up into him, but his other hand kept my wrists pinned gently above my head, grounding me in place.

When his fingers reached the curve of my hip, they paused—just long enough to make my pulse riot in my throat—before sliding lower. His touch skimmed over my lower belly, feather-light, making my whole body shiver. I could feel how slick I was already, the need building so fiercely I thought I might come apart just from the anticipation.

Then his hand slid further, dipping between my thighs. He moved them apart slowly, carefully, like he was unwrapping something fragile and precious. A groan slipped from my lips as he settled his hand there, palm warm, fingers teasing just at the edge of me.

He started to stroke, so slowly I thought I might scream. His fingers glided over every inch, circling and tracing, exploring every slick, swollen line but never pushing inside.

I felt my hips twitch and lift, desperate for more, but he kept the pace steady, refusing to give in. I whimpered, the sound high and strangled, my thighs quivering around his hand.

Cade's lips curved into a small, knowing smile.

My fingers flexed uselessly above my head, nails scraping at the blanket as another moan tore out of me.

He rubbed slow circles, every movement deliberate, maddening, each pass lighting me up from the inside out. But he didn't rush. He just kept worshipping me—slowly, thoroughly, like he had all the time in the world.

"Look at me," he growled.

I forced my eyes open, dragging them up to his. His gaze locked onto mine, deep and unflinching, holding me there like a tether. The moment our eyes met, he finally pushed his fingers inside me. A raw moan ripped out of me—so loud it echoed into the trees around us. My hips bucked, my thighs trembling, but his hand on my wrists kept me pinned, grounded, completely his.

He moved his fingers slowly, deliberately, filling me inch by inch. The stretch was perfect, maddening, and I felt my walls clench around him, desperate to pull him deeper. My breath shattered, my chest arching up against his. I felt like I was burning from the inside out, every nerve lit up and hungry. His thumb brushed against my clit, and I nearly sobbed, my body straining toward him helplessly.

"Cade—" His name tore from my throat.

His lips curved into a faint, wicked smile. He moved deeper, his fingers curling just right, sending sparks exploding behind my eyes.

I couldn't look away. Even as my vision blurred with tears, even as my body trembled on the edge, I kept my gaze locked to his—wide open, raw, completely laid bare. And he never looked away.

It only took a few more seconds. The slow, perfect curl of his fingers. The relentless brush of his thumb. The way his

473

eyes stayed locked to mine—dark, intense, like they were seeing every secret I'd ever tried to hide.

A sharp, broken cry ripped out of me as it hit. My entire body arched, my muscles locking tight before they snapped, a blinding wave of pleasure crashing through me so hard I thought I might shatter beneath it. I felt myself clamp around his fingers, my thighs shaking, my breath tearing out.

He didn't look away. "Good girl," he said roughly.

My vision went white at the edges, my head tipping back as I sobbed out another cry, my hips twitching helplessly against his hand. By the time the wave finally began to ebb, I was trembling all over, my chest heaving, sweat and tears mixing on my cheeks.

And still, he watched me. Every single second. Like there was nothing else in the world but this—but me. I barely managed to drag my gaze back to him, my lashes heavy, my lips parted around shaky breaths.

A small, satisfied smile curved at his mouth, and he began to ease his fingers from me, moving achingly slow, like he wanted to savor every last tremor.

His eyes stayed locked on mine as he slid his hand up, palm dragging lightly over my lower belly, up between my ribs, over the curve of my breast. I felt every gentle sweep like a brand, my skin buzzing beneath his touch.

His hand moved higher, cupping my chin firmly, his thumb brushing over my bottom lip. He bent down, his eyes burning into me. "Do you have any idea," he rumbled, "how fucking good you feel?"

A whimper slipped out of me, my lips parting under his thumb.

He kissed me then—deep and slow, his tongue sweeping into my mouth like he was tasting me for the first time. When he finally pulled back, his eyes looked to my hands still pinned above my head. Slowly, he released my wrists. He took the hand furthest from him, curling his fingers around mine.

Without breaking eye contact, he guided my hand down my own body, over my stomach, lower still, until my fingers brushed against my own slick, swollen core. I gasped, my hips jolting up, but he held my hand steady, his larger hand wrapped firmly around mine.

"Feel that?" he whispered, his breath hot against my mouth. "So fucking perfect." He guided my fingers in slow circles, pressing them against that aching, throbbing bundle of nerves until my head fell back, a sharp cry breaking from my lips. Then he pushed my fingers lower, coating them, slipping them just inside—only barely—before drawing them back up again. With every small, deliberate movement, his hand stayed over mine, controlling each stroke, each press. My breath stuttered, my hips jerking up into our joined hands, my lips parted on a helpless cry.

Then, slowly, he let his hand fall away—leaving my own fingers pressed between my thighs. For a second, I froze, my mind blank with shock. But then I moved. I kept going. My fingers slid over my clit, dipped lower, circled back up again, my movements shaky and desperate.

His eyes locked onto my hand, wild and hungry, his chest heaving. "Fuck…" he rasped, voice breaking like he couldn't take it. I watched him watch me, every nerve in my body burning under that fierce, reverent gaze. "Don't stop," he ordered, his voice ragged, almost pleading.

I didn't. I couldn't. My fingers moved faster, chasing that sharp edge that hovered just out of reach, my hips rolling helplessly beneath me.

"Look at you," he snarled. "Fucking yourself for me… so desperate… so perfect."

I felt him pressing against my hip—hot, thick, so hard it almost hurt—the weight of it a silent threat that had my whole body sparking with need. Then it hit. A sharp, blinding orgasm crashed over me, tearing a scream from my throat as my entire body clamped down, my thighs shaking violently around my own hand.

He watched every second, his eyes glued to me, his breath crashing and uneven. When I finally collapsed back against the blanket, gasping and trembling, he grabbed my wrist and pulled it up between us. Without breaking eye contact, he wrapped his mouth around my slick fingers, sucking them deep, his tongue curling to catch every last drop.

A deep moan rumbled in his chest, his eyes fluttering shut for just a heartbeat as he savored me. When he finally pulled back, I was already moving—wild and unthinking, driven by the brutal, singular need to have him buried inside me.

I lunged at him, pushing hard enough that he stumbled back, landing flat on his back. A few candles crashed to the side, wax spilling as shadows danced wildly around us. I scrambled over him, my hands grasping, desperate, lining him up. My body shook so hard I could barely see, every nerve screaming for him, for the stretch and heat of him filling me.

But just as I started to lower myself onto him, he moved. A sudden, violent twist and I was thrown to the side, landing hard on my stomach with a choked gasp.

Before I could even push up, his weight was on me, heavy and unyielding, his chest pressed to my back, his hand sliding up to wrap firmly around my throat. I froze beneath him, my breath coming in shallow bursts, my entire body pulsing with frantic, electric need.

He leaned down, his mouth at my ear, his breath scorching. "So hungry for me," he murmured, and I could hear the dark amusement twisting through every word. "So greedy... couldn't wait another second, could you?"

Another whimper tore out of me, my hips pressing back into him instinctively, desperate for any contact. His fingers tightened just enough to keep me exactly where he wanted.

"Tell me how much you need it. Tell me who makes you this desperate." He growled softly, almost like a purr—dark and reverent and taunting all at once.

"Please," I gasped, my voice so wrecked it didn't even sound like my own. "Please, Cade... I need you—fuck, I need you so bad I can't breathe—" My hips bucked back against

476

him, frantic and helpless, my entire body shaking like I was coming apart at the seams.

"Please," I sobbed again, the word dissolving into a shattered cry. "No one else—no one—only you... you're the only one who can make me feel like this... I belong to you... I'm yours... please, please, I need you inside me. Please—take it. Take all of me."

The words poured out like a confession, each one sharper and more desperate than the last, like I was begging for my life, for my soul, for every piece of me to be taken and held.

Above me, I felt him freeze. "Good girl," he rasped, shaking with barely controlled need. His hand tightened once more around my throat—then he slid it up, curling into my hair at the base of my skull. In one sharp, commanding motion, he yanked me upward, forcing me up onto my hands and knees beneath him.

A cry tore out of me, my arms shaking so hard I nearly collapsed again. His fist stayed tangled in my hair, holding me upright, my back arched, my head tipped back into him—completely exposed, completely his.

"Mine," he snarled, his voice a vicious growl that shivered straight down my spine. Before I could even suck in a breath, he slammed into me—deep, brutal, claiming. A scream ripped from my throat, my fingers clawing at the ground beneath me as my body rocked forward under the force of him.

He didn't pause. He drove into me again, and again, each thrust harder than the last, the slap of skin echoing out into the dark night around us. My eyes rolled back, my jaw dropping open around broken sobs and cries, every inch of me burning alive under him. His fist twisted in my hair, holding me exactly where he wanted me, dragging me back into each punishing stroke.

"Say it again," he growled, his voice breaking as he pounded into me. "Tell me who you belong to."

"You," I sobbed, my voice splintering. "You—only you—fuck, Cade—please—"

His fist twisted tighter in my hair as he slammed into me again, a feral, guttural sound ripping from his throat. Then he let go of my hair just long enough to grab my hips, yanking me back into him so hard I nearly screamed.

Somewhere between the gasps and the curses, he dragged me back down onto my stomach, his chest pressing over my back as he kept pounding into me. I could barely catch my breath, the world dissolving into white-hot sparks behind my eyelids.

Then he flipped me again, fast and rough, shoving my knees up to my chest and driving into me from above, his face inches from mine, his breath crashing into my mouth.

"Look at me," he snarled, voice so low it sounded almost broken.

I forced my eyes open, sobbing out his name, my fingers clawing at his shoulders as he pounded into me, each thrust deeper than the last. I lost track of time completely—minutes or hours, I didn't know.

We rolled again, dirt and twigs sticking to our sweaty skin, the blanket long forgotten somewhere behind us. I straddled him, sitting up straight on his hips, my hands braced against his chest as I bounced on his cock, every thrust sending shockwaves up my spine. My hair clung to my damp skin, my breath coming in broken cries as I rode him, wild and desperate.

"Fuck, look at you," he growled, his hands gripping my waist, dragging me down harder with every slam. Then one hand slipped lower, his thumb finding my clit and rubbing rough, relentless circles as he thrust up into me at the same time. The combination wrecked me. My body jolted, my thighs trembling as the orgasm ripped through me. I screamed his name, my back arching, my vision fracturing into white-hot sparks as I clenched tight around him, grinding helplessly against his hand.

"That's it," he snarled, pounding up into me, his eyes burning into mine like he wanted to memorize every second of me falling apart. "That's it, strangle my cock while you come. Fuck, I can feel every twitch."

His words tore through me, and I could only sob harder. The orgasm tore me open until I collapsed forward, shaking, my nails digging into his shoulders.

Before I could catch my breath, he flipped me again, pressing me into the forest floor, the scent of earth and sweat filling my head as he took me all over again. His thrusts were ruthless, each one grinding me deeper into the dirt, leaving me clawing for something to hold onto that wasn't him.

By the time his rhythm began to falter, I was a trembling, filthy mess beneath him, my body covered in scratches and dirt, my skin humming with pain and pleasure so intense I thought I might break apart completely. His hand snaked down between us, rough fingers finding my clit again, circling with brutal insistence.

"Come with me," he growled, his voice shredded, desperate, commanding. "Now—fucking come with me."

The words shattered what little control I had left. My body obeyed like he owned every nerve, sobs breaking out of me as I clenched around him, the orgasm tearing through me in violent waves.

He slammed in one last time, burying himself to the hilt as a feral, raw sound ripped out of him—a sound so deep it vibrated through my bones. His entire body shuddered above me, his hips grinding down as he came hard, pulsing deep inside me, filling me until I thought I'd drown in him. I sobbed his name, my fingers clawing at his back, my entire body locking around him as if I could keep him there forever.

When he finally stilled, he collapsed forward, pressing me into the dirt, both of us gasping, our bodies slick and shaking, tangled together and covered in twigs and leaves. Cade lifted his head first, his breath still labored. His hand rose to brush my cheek, fingers shaky. A low, strained laugh rumbled out of him—more an exhale than anything else, like he couldn't quite believe himself. "This... this wasn't how I planned tonight," he said.

479

His thumb traced my lower lip, his eyes roaming over my face like he was trying to commit every scratch and tear-streak to memory. "I wanted to… fuck," he murmured, his jaw flexing like he was fighting for the right words. "I always think I can slow down with you. Be patient and gentle."

A shaky, breathless laugh slipped out of me, tears burning hot behind my eyes.

His eyes locked on mine, fierce and soft and wrecked all at once. "But I can't," he finished, his thumb still hovering at my mouth. "I have no fucking control when it comes to you."

I let out a broken, breathless sound and turned my head to press a trembling kiss into his palm. "Good," I whispered against his skin.

Then he slid his arms beneath me—one under my back, the other behind my knees. I let out a soft, startled gasp as he lifted me easily, my arms instinctively looping around his neck, my head dropping to his shoulder. His chest was still heaving, his skin streaked with dirt and sweat, but his hold on me was steady, careful, like I was something fragile and priceless.

He carried me back toward the blanket—the soft glow of the scattered candles flickering around us, some still upright, others toppled and guttering. When he lowered me onto the blanket, he kept me close, guiding me down beside him, pulling me against his side. I curled into him automatically, my head finding the crook of his arm, one leg tangling over his.

Above us, the stars stretched endlessly, bright and cold and impossibly far away. Our breaths slowed together, the wild storm inside my chest settling into something warm and heavy and achingly sweet.

His fingers drifted lazily over my arm. After a long moment, he let out a soft laugh. "Next time," he said as he pulled out a twig from my hair. "Next time, maybe we keep it on the blanket. Or at least try not to roll halfway across the forest floor."

The words hit me like a blow straight to the ribs.

Next time.

The reminder crashed over me all at once—that there might not be a next time. That tomorrow could be the last morning either of us ever sees. My fingers froze on his chest. I felt my whole body go tense, a tremor running through me that I couldn't stop.

Cade went still beneath me. He didn't have to ask—he felt it instantly, like my thoughts were echoing straight into his bones. His arm tightened around me, squeezing me so hard it almost knocked the air from my lungs. "Hey," he said softly. "Hey. There will be a next time. I promise you. There will be a lot of next times."

He turned his head slightly, his hand sliding up to cradle my jaw, his thumb brushing over my cheek. "There'll be a small house," he murmured, his voice soft, like he was laying each brick of that dream right into my chest. "Surrounded by woods. A big porch you'll fill with too many potted plants, and you'll yell at me for watering them wrong every damn time."

A laugh tore out of me, my chest heaving.

"We'll have Biscuit," he went on, his mouth curving against my hair. "Obviously. She'll still be in charge of everything, bossing around some big, dumb dog we adopt. He'll weigh twice as much as her, but she'll still show him who's boss."

I laughed again, the sound turning into a sob, my fingers fisting into his skin.

"Sarah and Allie will live close by," he continued. "Close enough to just show up without notice. We'll have dinner together all the time. You'll roll your eyes when Sarah brings three bottles of wine instead of one, and Allie will complain about the food even though she eats every bite."

More tears slipped free, and I pressed my face into his neck, breathing him in like I could memorize him into my blood.

"And we can't forget drunk baking nights," he added, a small laugh rumbling in his chest. "You and Sarah will make some ridiculous cake at two in the morning, and the kitchen will look like a bomb went off. I'll pretend to be annoyed, but I'll eat half of it before you even frost it."

He tipped his forehead to mine, his hand cradling my jaw like he was terrified I might vanish. "Maybe," he whispered, "maybe there'll be a little me. Or a little you. Running around that porch. Laughing. Safe."

The tears poured out of me now, soaking his skin. His eyes searched mine, dark and fierce and so unbearably soft I thought I might fall apart right there.

"There will be a next time," he repeated, his voice so low it felt like it echoed through my bones. "I swear it. I swear it, Lena."

"I love you," I whispered, the words tearing straight from my ribs, raw and truer than anything I'd ever said.

His breath caught, his hand fisting gently in my hair, pressing me closer.

"I love you," he rasped back, his voice cracking right down the center. "God, Lena… I love you more than anything."

I pressed my forehead harder into his, tears slipping hot and fast down my cheeks, soaking into his skin.

"I want all of that," I choked out, my voice splintering. "The porch… the plants… the dog… the late-night baking… all of it. With you. Only you."

I pulled back just enough to see his face, my tears blurring him into something almost unreal. My chest ached, but I still found the strength to hold his gaze. "And the little one," I whispered, the words catching, breaking me open. "I want that too."

A deep, shuddering exhale shivered through him, and he nodded, like he was making a promise he'd carve into the world if he had to.

We stayed like that, pressed together under the stars, until my tears finally slowed, my breath settling into something almost peaceful. My eyelids grew heavy, every bone in my body sinking into the warmth of him, the safety of his hold.

I barely registered the soft press of his lips to my forehead, the gentle stretch of his arm beneath me as he started to move. I felt the blanket wrap around me, his hands lifting me to his arms. Then that familiar, gentle pull of his magic.

When I opened my eyes again, it was only for a moment. We were just outside the cabin now, moonlight brushing across his shoulders as he held me tight against his chest. I felt him start to walk, each step slow and steady. Then the door creaked open, warmth spilling over us. He laid me on the couch beside him. His arm tightened around me, one last fierce squeeze that felt like a promise.

I drifted under again, safe and warm and so full of him I thought I might float away.

Chapter 36

The cabin felt charged, every breath taut with quiet dread and defiance. No one moved quickly. Each action was careful, deliberate—like every step might be the last on solid ground before the storm swallowed them whole.

Our upstairs bedroom had become a makeshift dressing room. Two dresses lay spread across the bed like relics waiting to be claimed. Sarah's was a deep midnight blue, fitted tight to her curves, with a high slit that promised movement and danger in equal measure. A fierce statement, all sharp lines and dark glamour. Allie's was a deep emerald green—elegant, powerful, understated. The shape was simple but cut in a way that demanded attention, echoing the quiet, sharp force she carried in every breath. Marcela had them sent a few days ago, after the plan was set in motion.

Allie stood close to Sarah, carefully tilting her chin up as she lined her eyes. Her fingers were steady, but her jaw worked tight, like she was grinding each thought into dust. With her free hand, she smoothed back a loose curl and tucked it behind Sarah's ear, then adjusted a silver pin anchoring the soft twist at the back of her head.

Sarah's hair had been pulled into a low, elegant knot—just messy enough to look effortless, with dark tendrils left loose to frame her face. It was the kind of style that made her look regal and dangerous all at once.

Sarah tried to joke, her voice strained but bright. "When did you become a secret makeup artist, huh? You gonna open a salon after we save the world?"

Her voice shook, just a little. I caught it. So did Allie, though she didn't say anything. She just rolled her eyes and focused on smoothing out the line, her thumb brushing lightly under Sarah's lower lashes.

Marcela moved around us in circles, counting vials, setting out small blades. She didn't say much—just the occasional muttered number or curse under her breath.

I stood back against the wall, already dressed in my black combat gear, the weight of daggers snug in my vest and strapped tight to my thigh. My hair was pulled into a low braid, a few wisps already working free around my face. My arms crossed so tightly across my chest it almost hurt as I watched them, like I might have to memorize every moment, every tiny detail, in case I never got another chance.

When Allie finally stepped back, Sarah leaned closer to the cracked mirror and let out a low whistle. "Dangerous," she murmured, and for a second, that old spark flared bright behind her eyes.

Allie rolled her eyes and turned to the bed, fingers brushing over her own dress.

Marcela stepped forward then, guiding Sarah into her gown first. Sarah set her hands on Marcela's shoulders, steadying herself as she stepped in. Marcela zipped her up slowly, her hands lingering at Sarah's shoulders for a long, quiet moment before she stepped back.

Then it was Allie's turn. I stepped in, lifting the green dress and helping her step into it, careful not to let the fabric drag. I zipped it up in one smooth motion, my fingers pausing at the top, resting against her shoulder.

Her hair was half-up, twisted back from her face in soft waves that spilled down her back—controlled but not severe, like everything else about her. The kind of style that looked composed even when everything else was falling apart.

She looked at me in the mirror, her eyes catching mine— fierce and stubborn and so full of love it nearly cracked me open. My voice wavered as I said softly, "Mom and Dad would be so damn proud of you."

Allie reached up and covered my hand with hers, squeezing tight. Her reflection met mine with a steadiness that made my throat ache. "They'd be proud of us both."

486

I gave the smallest nod, pressing my hand a little firmer against her shoulder before finally stepping back.

Marcela picked up two small, slim blades from the dresser—sharp, almost delicate. She moved to Sarah first, slipping the blade into a hidden pocket sewn into the side of her dress. "Quick, clean line through the rune," she said softly. "Then get out. No hesitating."

Sarah nodded, her fingers brushing the hidden seam as she let out a shaky exhale. Then Marcela turned to Allie, sliding the second blade into her dress just the same. Allie didn't flinch. Marcela's hand stayed at her side a moment longer before she stepped back.

At the doorway, I heard a sharp inhale.

"Sarah...?"

Jack stood there, half in the hall, his hand braced against the doorframe like he needed it to stay upright. He was wearing a very flattering black tux that suited him well. His eyes locked on Sarah, and for a moment, he didn't breathe.

Sarah turned toward him, one eyebrow arching, that crooked, defiant smirk sliding across her face. "Don't stand there drooling, soldier," she drawled.

Jack shook his head, his gaze moving over her slowly, like he was seeing her for the first and last time all at once. "God... Sarah," he breathed.

He stepped into the room and from his jacket pocket, he pulled a folded strip of black lace with a familiar glint of silver fastened to the center.

Abel's badge.

"Vallerie helped me sew it in," Jack said quietly, his voice catching at the edges. "So it won't get lost. Thought maybe..." He trailed off, shaking his head. "It just felt right."

Sarah didn't speak. Her hand trembled slightly as she reached for the hem of her gown and lifted it, just enough. Jack crouched without a word. He fastened the garter around her thigh, his fingers careful, tender. When he was done, he stayed there a moment longer, one hand resting gently on the badge, his head bowed. When he finally stood, he didn't meet her eyes right away. He looked at the floor, then up—his expression raw, like someone trying to hold back a lifetime of grief.

"He would've wanted to be here," Jack said, his voice breaking. "And I know he can't be. But this... this is a piece of him. And it's going with you."

Sarah's eyes shimmered as she reached down and touched the badge.

"He loved you more than anything, Sarah. That kind of love—it doesn't end. It stays. And tonight... he's watching. He's with you."

She nodded, pressing her lips together tightly.

Then Jack added, softer, as his hand brushed hers. "Now we both get to look after you."

"Jack... thank you," she said as she stepped forward and wrapped her arms around him, pulling him in without hesitation. A single tear slipped free, catching on his shoulder before she could stop it.

I glanced toward Allie. She stood perfectly still, one hand at her side, the other swiping a tear from her cheek before it could fall. Her face was otherwise composed—jaw set, shoulders back—but that tear said everything.

Marcela's voice cut through the stillness. "All right. Let's move downstairs."

Allie shot me a quick look, her chin tilting up in that stubborn, protective way of hers, before she turned to follow Marcela out the door. Jack hovered for a second, his eyes still locked on Sarah like he didn't want to look away.

Sarah just flicked her fingers at him, smirking. "Go on, pretty boy. I'll be right there."

Jack hesitated, then finally turned and stepped out into the hall. I started to move after them, but Sarah's hand shot out, catching my wrist.

"Wait," she said.

"Last night," she started, her voice barely above a whisper. "Me and Jack... we finally..."

My eyes went wide. A shocked laugh punched out of me, and I clapped a hand over my mouth to stop it from echoing down the hall. "Oh my god," I hissed. "Sarah—"

She squeezed my wrist harder, her mouth twisting into a shaky, wild smile. "Yeah. And it was… Jesus, Lena. It was so fucking good."

I felt something bright and wild spark in my chest, pushing against all the fear and grief sitting heavy there. I reached for her, pulling her in without a second thought.

She let out a shaky laugh against my shoulder. "Had to tell you," she mumbled, her voice muffled. "I couldn't… couldn't walk into this without you knowing."

I pulled back just enough to look at her, my hands gripping her arms tight. "I'm so happy for you," I said, my voice fierce and thick all at once. "You deserve that. You both do."

"God, I'm gonna fuck up this eyeliner," she muttered, half-laughing, half-sobbing.

I laughed too, shaking my head, my braid brushing against my shoulder. "You look perfect," I told her. "And you're going to survive this. We all are."

She sucked in a breath, her lips pressing together. Then she gave me one last hard squeeze and shoved me lightly toward the door.

"Let's go," she said. "Before I make this a full-on Lifetime movie moment."

I gave her one last squeeze of her hand, then stepped into the hallway. Everyone was already gathered in the main room when Sarah and I stepped downstairs. I couldn't help but take in the stark contrast. Jack in his dark, sharp suit. Allie in her emerald dress, all quiet strength and grace. Sarah a living blade of midnight blue beside them. And the rest of us—dark, tactical gear layered tight, weapons and runes hidden in every fold and strap. We looked like shadows ready to swallow the room whole.

Sarah went straight to Jack and Allie without a word, her hand sliding naturally into Jack's, her other arm brushing against Allie's side. I moved to Cade. The moment I reached him, he turned slightly, his arm brushing my waist.

Biscuit sat perched on the back of the couch like a little sentinel, her body upright, tail wrapped neatly around her paws. She looked regal and unbothered. Like she'd seen centuries of chaos and decided we'd be fine.

No one spoke. We all just stood there for a long breath, the silence heavy and electric, every unspoken fear and promise hanging in the air like a held note.

Then Kaylen's voice cracked through it. "Mount up!" she barked.

In an instant, everyone moved—a sudden rush of motion, boots scraping, doors swinging open. Cade squeezed my hand before heading for the first jeep. I followed, heart pounding, blood roaring in my ears. We filed out together, a silent, tight formation stepping straight into the unknown.

• • •

We met Gage and his team at a small, abandoned rest stop just a few miles from Michael's estate. The sun was already sinking low, staining the horizon in streaks of orange and violet.

He was already waiting when we pulled in, leaning against the hood of a dark large van, his arms crossed tight over his chest. The second we stepped out, he pushed forward, holding up two delicate looking necklaces. Each one had a small, elegant pendant—a silver heart, polished to a soft shine. Pretty enough to blend in at an upscale party. "Cameras and mics," Gage said. "Signal goes straight to us. You'll be our eyes and ears once you're inside."

He didn't wait for questions. He stepped up to Allie first, looping the chain around her neck, his fingers quick but careful. Then he turned to Sarah, and did the same.

Then Gage reached into his jacket and pulled out three slim phones, holding them out one by one. "The tickets are all digital," he said. "You'll use these to get in."

He tapped quickly on the screen of the first phone, showing them how to pull up the tickets. "Once you're at the gate, swipe here. Don't overthink it. Just act like you belong." "You," he said, pointing at Allie, "are Riley Jones." His finger switched to Sarah. "You're Gia Bennett." Then to Jack. "And you're Henry Brooks."

They each glanced down at their phones, committing the names to memory.

Sarah snorted lightly, breaking the tension for half a heartbeat. "Gia Bennett? Sounds like a reality show star."

Gage didn't even blink. "Good. Play into it."

He reached into his pocket one last time and pulled out a set of keys, the metal jangling sharply in the quiet. He held them out, his gaze steady. "You're ready," he said simply, nodding toward a sleek, red car parked a short distance away.

Allie stepped forward first, taking the keys from his hand without a word.

Gage's eyes swept over them one last time, his jaw tight. "Get in. Get close to the fountains. Do what you need to do. And come home."

Allie, Sarah, and I all looked at each other, holding that gaze for a long moment. No words. Just a thousand things packed into a single look—love, fear, defiance, promise. Then, slowly, we all smiled.

Allie turned first, slipping into the driver's seat of the car. Sarah followed right behind her, tossing me one last wink before ducking inside. Jack climbed in last, shutting the door with a quiet, final thud.

I watched as the car rolled away. I blinked rapidly, trying to clear the sudden sting burning behind my eyes, but it didn't help. The tears threatened anyway.

A warm hand slipped into mine, squeezing tight. I looked up at Cade. His eyes were steady, fierce, but soft just for me. He squeezed again, his thumb brushing the side of my hand.

"Come on," he said gently, tugging me forward. He led me to the back of the surveillance van, where Gage and two women and one man were waiting. The back doors were open, cables and monitors crowding the space inside, the whole setup buzzing faintly like a living creature.

Gage gestured to the people in the van. "These are the tech leads—Tania, Jess, and Emilio—from the other chapters."

I barely glanced at them, my focus locked on the large screen above. A split feed was there, the left half showing the view from Allie's necklace pendant, the right from Sarah's. The images moved as they settled into the car, the world rolling past outside their windows.

Cade's hand stayed wrapped around mine as we watched. Then, I heard the crunch of gravel as a car pulled up beside the van. Cade moved first. He squeezed my hand again before letting go, then pushed the back door open.

Muted voices drifted in. I heard Cade's tone first. Then a woman's voice, clipped and confident. Another, deeper voice rumbled something in response. A few heartbeats later, Cade leaned back inside. "Lena," he called, motioning with a small tilt of his head. "Come meet them."

I pushed myself up, moving carefully past the clutter of tech equipment, the cords snaking across the floor. A woman stood closest. She was about my height, maybe a little taller, with blonde hair pulled back into a messy braid that looked like it had been redone a hundred times on the road. Her features were strong but kind, a small scar cutting through one eyebrow like an old story she didn't bother to hide.

A man stood just behind her. He was tall and lean, his dark hair cropped close to his scalp, a black hoodie hung loosely over his frame. He had a quiet, watchful presence, his eyes glancing constantly across the lot, like he couldn't stop checking every shadow.

"This is Melanie," Cade said, his hand brushing lightly at my back. "And that's Matthias. They're the other empathy-marked. They're here to help you."

Melanie met my gaze first. She looked me over in one long, assessing sweep. "Good to finally meet you," she said.

Matthias gave a single, quick nod, his fingers drumming lightly against his thigh. "Hello," he added.

We had gone over the plan a hundred times with David, with everyone. Every risk, every fallback point. But standing here, seeing them in front of me, it finally felt real. Once the runes were corrupted, we would breach the estate grounds. But Michael's two hundred guests would still be inside. They had to go first. Melanie, Matthias, and I would move to the tree line behind the estate. Together, we would project a single, unified surge of pure, primal fear—a psychic rupture strong enough to force them to flee, scattering into the night, away from the ritual site.

Then Gage announced, "They're going in."

We climbed back into the van, my eyes immediately going to the screen. Both feeds showed them in line, inching forward between velvet ropes under golden lights. Around them, clusters of guests chatted quietly, heads dipped together, laughter bright and brittle.

Allie's camera dipped as she glanced down at her phone, her breath steady in the mic. Sarah moved, her camera catching a glimpse of Jack just ahead. She let out a quick, shaky sigh. When they finally reached the front of the line, I felt my own breath lock in my chest. I pressed closer to the screen, fingers curling into fists.

A guard stepped forward and took Allie's phone first. A small scanner flashed across the digital ticket. A beat. Then the guard nodded sharply and stepped aside. Allie moved forward, her camera catching a dizzying swirl of black tuxedos and shimmering gowns.

Next was Sarah. The guard took her phone and scanned it. A moment that felt like a lifetime stretched out. Then another nod. She stepped forward, a small, triumphant huff of air slipping out through her mic.

Jack followed after, disappearing into the crowd just beyond the entrance. As they stepped inside, both camera feeds shook—quick turns, fast glances.

I could see small groups clustered along the edge of the lawn, drinks in hand, their elegant dresses and polished shoes catching the low lights strung along the hedge walls. But some of them—the ones in darker suits, standing straighter, eyes constantly moving—were clearly Michael's guards. Even through the tiny, shaky cameras, you could feel the tension radiating off them.

Allie's feed tilted toward the bar. Sarah's followed a second later. Through the mics, I heard Sarah's voice. "Good. I need a drink," she muttered.

At the bar, they each grabbed something—champagne flutes, I thought, from the thin stems and pale shimmer. Music drifted in through the mics, warm and polished, some soft classical string arrangement made sharp by the jagged nerves underneath it all.

Then a voice boomed overhead, echoing across the yard from hidden speakers. "Ladies and gentlemen, thank you for joining us tonight for what is sure to be a truly unforgettable evening. Our host will be with you shortly. In the meantime, please enjoy the open bar and take this time to mingle and connect."

The voice cut out. A ripple of polite applause spread through the crowd, quick and shallow. On the screens, I saw Sarah lift her glass and tilt her head toward Allie in a silent toast. Allie bumped her glass back, the motion careful, almost tender. They were in.

I watched as Allie and Sarah leaned against the bar, their camera feeds tilting slightly with each breath. They looked casual—almost bored—but I knew them too well. I saw it in the set of Allie's jaw, in the way Sarah's shoulders rose and fell just a little too fast.

A flash of movement caught Allie's camera—Jack stepping closer, his glass cradled in his hand. For a moment, they all just stood there, a small cluster in the sea of glittering strangers. My nails bit into my palm. My mind conjured every horrible possibility at once—a guard catching them, a mark, a gun, a blade, a single slip that would mean I would never see them again.

I leaned forward, my forehead almost brushing the edge of the monitor. Please. Please be safe. Then I saw Allie's feed tilt slightly toward the far side of the yard. A wide cement path, shimmering under the soft lights, snaked past the sculpted hedges. And at the end was the first fountain.

Sarah's camera followed a second later, tracking Allie as she started to move. They slipped away from the bar, merging into the flow of guests milling across the lawn. The mics picked up scattered bits of polite laughter, the clink of glasses, a woman complimenting another's dress in a honey-sweet voice.

Allie reached the edge of the first fountain, pausing to lift her glass as if admiring the water. My entire body locked up, every nerve screaming. On screen, I saw her hand slip down, just out of view of the main crowd.

Sarah's camera angle moved—she glanced back, her lips moving, though the mic only caught fragments. "... all clear... go..."

Allie's fingers moved again, subtle and quick, slicing through the first rune line with the hidden blade Marcela had given her. Nothing really happened. Just a faint shimmer that rippled once across the surface of the water and then vanished.

Allie turned away, moving back toward Sarah and Jack with a small, easy shrug, as if she'd simply been fixing her dress. Sarah's camera turned, catching a fleeting glimpse of Allie's face—her lips curved into the smallest, fiercest smile I'd ever seen.

They did it. One down. They started moving again, weaving toward the next fountain.

Cade's arm slipped around me, pulling me back against his chest, his chin lowering to rest at the crown of my head. "They've got this," he murmured against my hair.

I swallowed hard, my eyes still locked on the screens. "Yeah," I whispered. "They do."

I forced myself to breathe as the second fountain came into view. Sarah's camera tilted, catching Jack bending down beside her. "Shit," he muttered under his breath, just loud enough for the mic to catch. "Laces." His hand slid inside his jacket as he lowered fully to one knee. In the same movement, he drew the blade out, slicing it cleanly through the rune line at the fountain's base on his way down. Another ripple on the water. Then he stood, tugging at his shoe like he really had tied it, and they moved on.

My fingers dug into Cade's thigh where my hand rested, but I didn't even notice.

Third fountain. Sarah moved, angling the camera toward it. I saw her stumble forward, her hand shooting out to catch herself against the fountain's edge.

"Shit!" she yelped, the word sharp and convincing. Her palm smacked right over the rune. A split-second pause. Then she pushed herself back up, brushing off her dress with a loud, exasperated huff. Through the camera, I saw Jack's shoulders shake—probably laughing—but he turned away, guiding her quickly back toward the center of the yard.

My pulse roared in my ears as the final fountain came into view.

Just then, a guard moved in front of the camera. He stepped directly into the path between them and the fountain, scanning the crowd. They stopped. Hovered together in a small, awkward huddle.

"Shit," Allie's voice hissed into the mic.

"How the fuck are we gonna get past him without looking suspicious?" Sarah muttered, her voice a thin, nervous thread.

There was a beat of silence. Then Allie's voice. "I'll handle it."

Before anyone could argue, she broke away, her camera bobbing slightly as she moved.

I watched, breath strangled in my throat, as she approached the guard, a smooth, practiced sway in her step.

496

She stopped in front of him, her hand sliding up to rest lightly on his arm. "I was hoping you could help me find the bar again," she purred, her voice syrup-sweet. "I think I got a little turned around…"

The guard, glancing down at her with a reluctant, nervous smile. "I really should stay here."

Allie's hand moved higher, her fingers brushing the inside of his elbow. She leaned in, her mouth close to his ear, too quiet for the mic to catch.

I watched the guard's shoulders soften. A crooked, almost embarrassed smile spread across his face. Then he nodded once. Allie turned, hooking her arm through his, and guided him away from the fountain without a backward glance.

The camera on Sarah's necklace jerked—she and Jack moved quickly, stepping around the now unguarded fountain. Sarah's hand shot out, knife glinting in the faint light. One quick, silent slice. A shimmer. Gone. They pivoted away immediately, merging back into the flow of guests like nothing had happened.

Cade pressed in closer behind me, his hands coming to settle firmly on my shoulders.

"They did it," I said.

Cade bent down. "Yeah," he murmured. "They fucking did."

"Markless Wonders mission successful," Gage announced in a microphone attached to his head. "Runes are down. All units move in. Phase two"

I shook my head, a small smile tugging at my mouth despite the tension. I still couldn't believe Sarah had actually talked them into using that name. The brief moment of humor was gone just as fast, swallowed by the weight of what we were about to do.

We climbed out of the van in tense, focused silence. Cade guided me toward the jeeps where the rest of our team was still waiting. Melanie and Matthias fell in with us without a word, their steps syncing naturally to ours. We drove slowly until we were closer to the estate, but still out of view.

Cade took the lead, moving easily through the darkness, his hand brushing lightly at my back whenever the ground dipped. The rest of the team followed in tight formation—Kaylen's sharp gaze sweeping the woods constantly, Hiro moving with his quiet, coiled energy, Alice ghosting through the underbrush as if she'd been born to it. Marcela and Vallerie kept close together, their steps careful and deliberate. Melanie and Matthias flanked me, both eerily calm, their presence a steadying hum at my sides.

We moved until we reached the final tree line—the last cover before the manicured edge of Michael's backyard. Beyond the trees, lights spilled across the grass like an invitation, music drifting faintly in and out on the breeze.

I could see the tops of the four fountains gleaming, the balcony above catching the light like a blade. Statues, guests milling in tight clusters, waitstaff weaving between them with trays—all of it felt dreamlike and fragile, like something that might shatter at the slightest touch.

We dropped into position, low in the brush. Cade signaled for us to hold. He pressed a finger to his earpiece, listening. The others settled into a silent line, eyes trained ahead.

I crouched down, my heart hammering so loud I felt it in my teeth. Then, from above, Michael appeared. He stepped out onto the second-floor balcony, hands braced on the ornate railing.

The moment I saw him, I felt that familiar tug in my chest. My marks, sensing me, reaching for me to bring them home. I forced my gaze down, away from him. If I looked too long, if I let that connection flare, he might feel it. He might know I was here.

Melanie's hand found mine first. Matthias's fingers wrapped around my other a moment later. I felt their marks slide over mine—cautious at first, then bolder, merging together like warm currents. My empathy surged up to meet theirs, weaving through me, around me, becoming something bigger, more focused.

I shut my eyes for a second, letting the sensation anchor me. Then, carefully, I reached out with my mark. Like extending a hand into a dark room, feeling for warmth.

I found Allie first—a sharp, steady focus, her mind taut like a drawn bowstring. Then Sarah—hot, reckless energy simmering just under the surface. And Jack—solid, protective, his presence curled protectively around them both. I could almost hear them in my head, almost feel Sarah's muttered curses, Jack's frantic check-ins, Allie's quiet steel.

I shielded them instinctively, a soft mental nudge that wrapped around their presence like a cloak. The other two felt it, and I felt them nod in silent agreement. Those three would stay untouched.

Above us, Michael's voice finally rose, rolling over the crowd. "Tonight," he began, arms spreading wide, "is for all of you—"

Cade's head snapped up, his fingers tapping twice against his earpiece. The signal. He turned to us, his eyes locked on mine, voice a low, steady rasp. "Now."

We didn't hesitate. Together, hands locked tight, the three of us unleashed. My mark roared out of me like a tidal wave, crashing forward and spreading wide, amplified and sharpened by Melanie and Matthias. Fear—primal, gut-deep, overwhelming. The kind of terror that seizes your throat and sends your legs sprinting before your mind can catch up.

It ripped through the estate like fire in dry grass. People stumbled back, drinks shattering at their feet, wide-eyed screams slicing the night air. Clusters scattered, shoving past one another, clawing for the edges of the yard. Guards spun wildly, weapons half-drawn, but even they weren't immune— two broke first, bolting down the path, their panic snapping the rest like a flock of startled birds.

Allie, Sarah, and Jack moved fast, slipping through the chaos with practiced precision—herding guests toward the gates, pointing frantic hands toward the road. One woman in a red dress tore off her heels and bolted across the grass. A man in a crisp tuxedo hurled his glass aside, face white as chalk as he barreled into the hedges. More shapes streamed past, shadows breaking apart into the night.

Chaos. Pure, consuming chaos. I could feel the panic building, rolling outward like a storm surge. Every second, more bodies surged toward freedom. Through it all, I kept that small, bright shield tight around Allie, Sarah, and Jack.

Above us, on the balcony, Michael straightened sharply. His head snapped in our direction, his eyes scanning the darkness beyond the treeline.

For a split second, I thought he might see me. Then Cade's hand clamped over my shoulder, reassuring me. I stayed hidden. We all did. But the first blow had landed. And the war had finally begun.

Chapter 37

The yard was chaotic. Screams still echoed through the trees as guests fled in every direction. A few stumbled, crashing into each other in their gowns and tuxedos, shoving past statues and knocking over chairs in blind panic. But already, the space was clearing. The once-polished, perfect lawn now looked like a storm had blown through.

Melanie and Matthias finally let go of my hands. Melanie's fingers gave mine one last tight squeeze before she stepped back. Then, without a word, they turned and jogged down the treeline, slipping into the shadows to join their own squad.

Shouts were rising from the house. Dark figures spilled onto the lawn, weapons gleaming in the dim light. Guards poured from every doorway, their formation fractured by the stampede of fleeing guests.

Cade moved in beside me, close enough that I could feel the heat coming off him. We didn't speak. We just looked at each other for one long, unguarded heartbeat.

Then he leaned in, his hand catching lightly at the side of my neck as his mouth brushed mine—a fleeting, desperate kiss, gone as quickly as it came. His voice followed, low, meant only for me. "Do it for all the next times."

My chest squeezed so tight I thought it might break open. He held my gaze one second longer before he tapped his earpiece. Then his voice rang out, louder this time, steady and commanding. "Go!"

And just like that, we moved. Figures burst from the trees—shadows and steel, fire and wind. The compound roared alive with screams and thunderous crashes as Severance fighters collided with Michael's guards.

I ducked under a low branch, sprinting toward the yard, Cade close by my side. My heart pounded so hard it rattled my teeth, every nerve lit like wire.

Through the tangle of bodies and flashing blades, I caught sight of Sarah, Allie, and Jack. Marcela was there too, ducking a blast of flame as she skidded to a stop. She heaved a heavy canvas bag at Sarah, who caught it without hesitation. Marcela vanished back into the chaos without a word, swallowed by smoke and sparks.

Then, a solid line of guards flooded out from the main house and side halls. Some carried guns, others held blades that crackled with electric light or shimmered with magic so thick I could taste it in the air. Their faces twisted with that same fanatical devotion, eyes wide and unblinking, as if they no longer belonged to themselves at all.

They surged forward in a tight wave, war cries tearing through the night, gunfire and sparks splitting the air. A haze of energy glimmered around some of them—flickering shields, living flame, shimmering force fields that made my skin crawl just to look at.

Cade stepped in front of me without hesitation, his stance low and coiled like a predator about to strike. He moved like a blade swung by a vengeful god, his sword flashing in lethal swipes. The first guard rushed him head-on and Cade's strike split him open shoulder to hip, the body folding before it hit the ground. He pivoted on the next, steel singing through the air as his blade cleaved clean through a raised assault rifle. The guard didn't even have time to scream before Cade's follow-through took his head.

A shot cracked through the chaos. Cade jerked as a bullet tore through his shoulder, blood spraying hot against his shirt. He didn't even flinch. His eyes never left the next target.

Another lunged from the side. Cade shadow-stepped, reappearing behind him with a dagger already in hand. One sharp thrust slid between the ribs, puncturing deep, before he let the body crumple and drew his sword again.

Every movement was brutal and precise, a dance meant to end lives, not save them. Blood slicked across his forearms, his jaw set, eyes already cold and locked on the next target before the last even hit the ground.

I launched forward beside him, my dagger catching moonlight as I ducked under a guard's swing and drove my dagger up through his ribs. Another came at me with a blade glowing red-hot. I pivoted, barely feeling the heat scorch my side before I buried my blade in her throat.

Around us, the compound dissolved into pure mayhem. To my left, Mariah and Nicole moved like a storm given flesh. Fire coiled around Nicole's slicing gusts, becoming a living inferno that burned guards alive where they stood. Mariah's face was split in a wild grin, flames dancing along her arms like living jewelry, while Nicole's eyes stayed cool and calculating, pushing her sister's fire exactly where it would cause the most destruction.

Logan stood on a crumbled statue base, head thrown back, laughter reckless and wild as he unleashed sonic shockwaves. Each pulse hit like a cannon blast—guards staggered, dropped their weapons, some vomiting blood as their insides ruptured from the force.

Kaylen darted through the yard like a shadow stitched from rage and steel. Knives appeared in her hands only to vanish again before plunging into soft places—eyes, throats, the soft gap under the jaw. Blood splattered across her face, her braid whipping like a black lash behind her, and she never once paused to wipe it away.

Farther back, Alice moved like a conductor orchestrating a deadly symphony. She flicked her wrist and guards flew into walls, bones shattering on impact. A blade aimed for Kaylen reversed mid-flight and tore its thrower open instead. By her side, Hiro was a quiet echo—"Left! Drop now! Roll!"—each word threading her movements into something impossibly precise, impossibly alive.

Vallerie stood at the edge, eyes hard and distant as she sent waves of mental chaos into the enemy ranks. Guards turned on each other without warning, eyes wide and glassy as they hacked their own allies apart, screams tearing free in hoarse, animal pitches.

Lorelei held the center line, her presence a bright iron anchor amid the swirl. Her voice cut above the noise— "Kaylen! Behind you! Hold that line! Push forward on my signal!" —each command hitting like a bell in the dark, undeniable and clear.

Nick charged through the middle, a wild gleam in his eyes. A bullet tore through his chest, blood spraying across his body. He stumbled, then straightened, grinning as the wound knitted itself closed. He lunged forward and gutted the shooter with a single clean strike, already pivoting toward the next injured ally. He clamped his hands over open wounds, sealing flesh in seconds before sprinting onward.

At the rear, Evangeline knelt in the grass, eyes gone milk-white. Her voice cracked and shivered as she called warnings only she could see—"Now! Move left! Duck!"—saving fighters by split seconds. When a guard lunged toward her, two Severance members leapt between them, cutting the threat down before it ever reached her shaking hands.

Farther out along the east side, Melanie and Mathias stood back to back, eyes closed, hands linked for a moment before they broke away. Waves of raw, searing terror burst outward from them like ripples in a pond—guards stopped mid-charge, screams strangled in their throats, some dropping weapons and bolting into the dark without a backward glance. Others collapsed, clawing at their own faces, unable to escape the emotions pouring into them.

The yard had become a living nightmare, a churning mess of screams and heat and blood. Sparks from mark impacts drifted through the air like dying fireflies.

A guard slammed into me from the side, his blade catching my forearm and opening it to the bone. I cried out, vision going white for a moment. Another figure stepped into my path, hands glowing with a cold, electric shimmer. Before I could move, my body locked tight—arms pinned, breath frozen in my chest, feet rooted to the ground. Panic clawed up my throat. I couldn't move. Her eyes met mine, a cold sneer curling across her lips. She started toward me, slow, savoring.

But my mind, my mind burned. I reached for my mark, that raw, half-feral core inside me, and hurled it at her. Panic. Sheer, undiluted terror. Her face twitched. The sneer faltered. Her hands dropped, glow flickering like a dying bulb.

I shoved forward the moment my muscles snapped free, my blade slicing across her throat. Hot blood fountained against my chest as she fell gurgling at my feet. I didn't stop to watch her die.

Cade reappeared beside me, blood smeared up his arms, a gash along his cheek weeping crimson. Our eyes locked, breath heaving. Then he pivoted and took off again, a blur of muscle and violence tearing a path toward the main house. I followed.

Around us, The Severance kept pushing, a wall of moving death and defiance, every breath soaked in blood and magic and rage.

A new wave of guards started tearing across the lawn toward me, eyes wild, weapons raised. Cade was farther off now, his body a blur as he fought three, no—four—at once, blood pouring from a deep gash along his ribs. His eyes darted toward me, frantic, but another guard slammed into him, driving him back.

I turned just as one guard raised his hands. Light gathered between his palms, swirling tighter until it formed a pulsing orb that hummed with violence. With a sharp thrust, he hurled it at me.

It struck square in my chest, detonating with a crushing force that drove me to my knees. Air fled my lungs in a single exhale. My head spun, darkness clawing in at the edges of my vision. I tried to rise but my arms trembled and gave out. The world tilted. Something inside me felt like it was collapsing, bones grinding, organs folding in on themselves.

Then—

"PRIORITY DOWN! FULL COVER, NOW!"

The voice split the air, undeniable. Vallerie.

The guard's palms flared again, light sparking between them, building faster this time into another orb. Hotter, brighter, and deadlier. His eyes burned with cruel delight, certain one more strike would finish the job.

Allie's scream tore through the chaos. She sprinted forward and flung herself over my body, shielding me with every inch of hers. The force pinned me into the dirt, her breath ragged in my ear. "I got you," she said.

"N-no..." The word scraped out of me, weak and useless.

The orb left the guard's hands in a blinding flash. It missed us by inches, detonating just beyond my hip. The earth buckled under the crushing impact, a concussive wave tearing through me as debris pelted down.

Allie pushed up, wild-eyed, and snatched a fallen blade from the ground. She charged straight at him, reckless and furious, her grip clumsy but her steps unyielding. The guard's hands flared, light sparking wildly as he tried to summon another orb, frantic and sloppy in his haste. He almost had it—

But Allie was faster. She swung like her life depended on it, the blade carving a messy, jagged line across his throat. He staggered, choking, the light guttering out between his fingers as he crumpled to the ground.

For a heartbeat, her eyes met mine, fierce and unyielding.

Behind her, more guards barreled closer, their weapons flashing.

The next instant, I was surrounded.

Figures tore across the lawn. Sarah hurled a potion point-blank, the glass shattering as fire roared up to consume a man's scream. Jack intercepted a blade meant for my head, his own knife burying deep into an attacker's gut.

Out of the smoke behind them, another figure surged forward, breaking through the chaos. Chad. He started to advance straight toward me, that familiar cruel intent twisting across his face.

"CHAD!" Sarah's voice rang out, sharp as a blade.

506

He snapped his head toward her, surprised, just in time to see the shimmering vial already flying.

She hurled it with every ounce of strength left in her. Jack moved at the same instant, grabbing Sarah and yanking her back, shielding her with his body.

The vial slammed into Chad's chest and he screamed. A guttural, terrified sound, ripped from him as he staggered back, clutching at the spreading fire. Then he exploded. A roaring blast of blood, bone, and flame tore outward, the ground quaking beneath my knees and shuddering through my bones. When the smoke cleared, there was nothing left of him but a scorched crater and wet, scattered ash.

Sarah stumbled against Jack, eyes burning with wild triumph. Our eyes met for a split second, and despite everything, I couldn't help the quick smile that tugged at my lips. She mirrored it instantly.

Kaylen then staggered into view, blood soaking her braid, knives flashing even as her legs shook beneath her. With a feral snarl, she lunged past Sarah, driving her dagger into a guard's gut and twisting it hard enough that I heard bones crack.

One by one, more of the cabin crew pressed in, forming a tight wall in front of me, bodies tense, weapons dripping.

Marcela was last, emerging from the smoke like a phantom. She raised one hand, hurling a vial that exploded in a blinding flare of green fire. The final guard dropped instantly, his body writhing as acid ate through flesh and bone in seconds.

They stood shoulder to shoulder, breathing hard, weapons dripping, eyes fixed on the next threat. I forced my eyes up. My braid was half-unraveled, pieces plastered to my cheek, dripping with blood. It ran from my hair, down my arms. My chest felt caved in, each breath a fight.

Kaylen turned, her gaze finding mine through the haze. "Get up," she snarled. "You're not done yet."

I dragged in a breath, every muscle screaming. But I planted my foot. Then the other. Slowly, like pulling myself up

507

from the bottom of a deep, black sea, I rose. My vision narrowed to a single point: forward.

High above the chaos, on the upper balcony that overlooked the carnage below—a new energy pulsed through the night, sharp and cruel, a vibration that clawed across my skin like broken glass.

Michael stood at its center, ringed by a twisted pile of fallen Severance fighters—bodies broken and scorched, some still twitching, others unnaturally still. He hadn't joined the main fight below because he couldn't. He'd been held back—distracted, forced to stay on the balcony as wave after wave came at him. And still, he stood.

Dozens more Severance members surged from every direction—through the balcony doors, across the lawn, even dropping from the roof. Shouts rose as they hurled everything they had—fire, wind, sound, steel, mind. Each wave crashed against him and fell away, only for another to follow.

Michael stood at the eye of it all, a wild, jagged grin splitting his face. His hands flicked out, carving the air in vicious slashes, each movement leaving new bodies in its wake. Flames whipped around him like a living cloak, shards of telekinetic force tearing through anyone who dared close the gap. A fighter dove from the roof toward him, blade raised, but Michael's power caught him mid-air, snapping his body sideways into the stone wall with a sickening crack. Another group surged through the balcony doors only to be hurled back like rag dolls, screams trailing as they plummeted to the lawn below.

For a single, suspended moment, he looked like something holy and monstrous all at once—an avatar of raw, stolen power.

Around me, Cade was still tearing through guards trying to close ranks. Kaylen staggered nearby, knives still flashing as she fought to keep moving. Logan bellowed somewhere beyond, his voice hoarse from shouting, from calling for fighters already fallen. Mariah's fire flickered and shrank as she dropped to one knee, Nicole's wind folding around her

508

protectively. Hiro's voice rose in a sharp, desperate scream—
"Alice!"—but I couldn't see them. My focus was on Michael.

Then his gaze cut downward—to me. When our eyes met, the grin widened, lips pulling back to reveal a feral, gleaming snarl. My empathy mark bucked hard under my skin, rage and grief and terror hammering through me like war drums. My heart crashed so loud I thought it might tear itself apart.

Then I heard Reid's voice. A memory, but not just a memory. A pulse, a thread woven deep into my bones.

"You reclaim them by choosing yourself. By refusing to believe you are broken without them. By living, fiercely and fully, as though they are still yours... because they are."

My breath faltered, a tremor running through my hands.

"To act, to fight, to love—as though you were always whole."

I saw it then. Michael wielding my marks like stolen jewelry, dancing through power that was never his. My power. And then I saw them—invisible to anyone else, but clear as sunrise to me. Threads of shimmering gold, thin and trembling, snaking out from his core. My marks. My soul.

Mine.

A hot surge flared up my spine, burning through the terror, the grief. I wasn't broken. I had never truly been. He hadn't taken *me*. These marks weren't just pieces of power—they were threads of my soul. And they had always known the way home.

I reached for the threads—not gently, not hesitantly. I *seized* them. I felt the change like a sun breaking through a storm. The terror snapped like a brittle branch. The rage solidified, no longer chaos but a blade in my hand.

I took a step forward. Michael's arm lifted, fire coiling in his palm, heat shimmering around him as he drew power from the stolen mark, as he aimed it directly at me.

Cade saw it. Even bloodied and outnumbered, his eyes found the fire and the intended path. In a blink, he was gone. Then he was behind Michael on the balcony, slamming into him with the full force of his body.

They went over the edge together, crashing down to the stones below in a tangle of limbs and snarled curses. The sound of it echoed through the yard like a gunshot. They rolled, Cade's fists a blur of pure, savage rage, each hit shaking Michael's head back, blood spraying. The fall must have shocked Michael, just enough for him to lose focus and drop the shield.

As they fought, I felt the marks surging into me, those golden threads embedding themselves in my bones, burning into my veins.

Michael roared, shoving Cade back with a savage telekinetic blast. Cade flew, skidding across the yard and slamming into the low wall, his body crumpling.

Kaylen burst forward, knives appearing in her hands like silver lightning. She hurled blade after blade, each one a heartbeat of rage and vengeance. Michael turned, fire blazing in his palm, and threw it.

The explosion slammed into Kaylen, lifting her off her feet. She crashed to the ground yards away, her scream ripping the night open. Smoke curled off her clothes, her face scorched and bloody as she struggled to rise.

That final scream, that pain, it shattered the last fragile thread inside me. I felt it. The marks snapped home, all at once—like a thousand doors slamming shut, like a star igniting in my chest.

I could feel them in every part of me—my veins, my marrow, my very essence—glowing with a quiet, comforting heat.

My wounds—the deep gash across my arm, the burn along my side, the bruises blooming across my ribs— shivered, then began to heal. I watched, almost detached, as torn skin knit back together, heat fading into smooth, unbroken flesh.

Michael started laughing, a wild cracked kind of laugh. "Do you think this is going to stop me?!" He raised his arm, fingers twitching like a conductor calling for a symphony.

Nothing.

Confusion flashed across his face, replaced instantly by rage. He tried again, twisting his hand in a savage jerk, as if to throw someone across the yard.

Nothing.

Desperation crawled into his eyes. He flung his other hand out, trying to summon fire.

Nothing.

He froze, the truth crashing down on him.

I stepped forward, power humming beneath my skin. I lifted my hand, and instinct rose with it—a memory deeper than thought, older than fear. My fingers curled, and the fire answered, coiling into my palm like it had always belonged there.

Hot. Alive. Mine.

A slow, cold smile spread across my lips. "Looking for this?"

Michael turned, wild-eyed, his face blanching as he saw me. Behind him, Cade pushed up to one knee, blood covering every inch of his body. His face split in a savage, awestruck grin. His eyes glimmered as they locked on me, pride radiating from every broken, shaking inch of him.

Kaylen rolled to her side, coughing, her face scorched and streaked with blood. She dragged her head up, squinting through the smoke. When her gaze found me, a cracked, triumphant smile tugged at her lips.

Somewhere behind me I heard Logan's ecstatic voice roar out. "FUCK YEAH!"

I didn't take my eyes off Michael. Not for a single, perfect, triumphant heartbeat.

Michael stood frozen, eyes wild, chest heaving. His hands twitched uselessly at his sides, fingers flexing like he still believed he could summon something.

I held the fireball, watching the light dance across his blood-smeared face. "Wow," I said, my voice carrying across the yard. "I get it now. I really do."

His eyes locked on the flame, horror crawling slowly across his features.

I turned my hand slightly, watching the fire curl and dance around my fingers like a living thing. "All this power. All this... *possibility*. It's exhilarating, isn't it?"

Around us, the fighting had gone still. Severance members circled the edges, weapons still raised but breathing hard, watching, waiting. A few guards had dropped to their knees, heads bowed in surrender.

Cade was getting up and making his way towards me.

I tilted my head at Michael, smiling faintly. "But you know what, Michael?"

He staggered back a step.

My smile widened, slow and sharp. "You're so weak... I don't even *need* my marks to end you." I let the fireball snuff out, the flames disappearing in my palm as if they had never existed. "I could do it with my bare hands."

Then he jerked his gaze sideways, pointing at Cade as he moved to stand just behind and to my side. "Yeah," Michael spat, his lip curling. "Like your little guard dog there would ever let you fight me on your own."

Cade gave a low, humorless laugh. "You really think she needs me? Watch."

I turned my head, just enough to meet Cade's eyes for a brief moment. Then I turned back to Michael.

"And by the way," I said, tipping my head slightly. "He is sooo much bigger than you. Like... *so much*. And better. In every possible way."

Somewhere behind me, I heard Sarah yell "WHOOP!"

Michael's face crumpled, rage igniting so fast it looked like a physical crack splitting across his features. With a snarl, he lunged.

We slammed together like two crashing waves, the impact knocking the breath out of my lungs. His hands clawed at my shoulders, fingers digging for my throat. I twisted, slamming my elbow into the side of his neck. He choked out a gasp, but his other hand grabbed my braid, yanking me downward so violently my knees almost buckled.

Pain shot down my spine—then vanished, my mark already knitting it away. I surged up instead of pulling back, my forehead crashing into his nose with a wet, brutal crack. Blood spattered across my cheeks.

He howled, staggered back, but swung again—his fist crashed into my jaw, snapping my head sideways. Stars burst behind my eyes. I tasted blood. I spat it out and lunged forward, grabbing his wrist mid-swing, twisting hard until he screamed. I used the hold to jerk him forward, smashing my knee up into his gut.

He folded, retching, but still lunged. His hand shot upward, nails clawing across my cheek. The skin split open, already beginning to knit itself back together before his hand fell away. I let out a snarl, punching him across the face once, twice—each hit splitting skin and spraying blood. His head snapped back, mouth open, teeth red.

He clawed at my forearms, desperation in every trembling movement. I felt his fingers catch my earring, yanking it out— a sudden sharp sting that vanished as quickly as it came.

I roared, grabbing a fistful of his hair. This time, I dragged his head down and rammed my knee up into his face. Something crunched. Blood poured down his chin, his breath coming in wet gasps.

He shoved at my shoulders, trying to topple me, but I held firm, boots braced against the shattered boards of the gazebo—splinters stabbing up into my ankles, already healing before the pain could root itself.

He threw a wild punch that glanced off my cheekbone. I rocked back just an inch, then came forward again, driving my fist into his temple. He crumpled backward, collapsing onto the splintered boards beneath us.

He turned over like he was going to try to crawl away, but I didn't give him a chance. I lunged after him, grabbed his shirt, turning him onto his back. I straddled his chest hard, knees pinned against his side on the shattered floor of the gazebo.

He thrashed, spit and blood foaming at his lips. I loomed over him, breath steady, my hair hanging in blood-streaked strands around my face. Above us, the open sky gaped through the roofless, skeletal remains of the gazebo, stars like cold pinpricks of judgment.

His hand clawed across the splintered boards, fingers closing around a jagged shard of wood slick with his own blood. With a wild, desperate motion, he swung it up toward my side. I caught his wrist before it made contact. Almost bored, I grabbed a dagger from my vest and slammed it through his hand, pinning it to the floorboards.

A garbled shriek tore from him, spit and blood spraying from his ruined mouth. His other hand shot toward the dagger trying to pull it free. I drew a second dagger from my vest and rammed it through his other hand on the opposite side, spreading his arms wide beneath me like some grotesque crucifixion.

He writhed beneath me, legs kicking weakly, boards groaning under our weight. Blood soaked through his shirt, pooling beneath us, warm against my knees.

And then he looked up at me. And he started to laugh. Wet and gurgling, full of blood—but still laughing. "You think this makes you strong?" he rasped. "You're nothing but a scared little girl playing dress-up—pretending you're something more than the broken, weak *thing* you've always been."

His chest heaved. Blood ran from the corner of his mouth, but he kept going.

"You think they give a fuck about you? When this is over, they'll bury you with the rest of the mistakes. You're not power. You're not vengeance. You're just a sad little *bitch* who got lucky."

He leaned his head back and spit in my face. "Fucking *cunt*," he said through gritted teeth.

I tilted my head, studying him. Slowly, I reached down to my thigh and drew my dagger—the one that I spent months training with. I smiled. "You always did talk too much."

514

Before he could spit another word, I shoved the dagger into his mouth and sliced. His tongue hit the boards with a wet slap. His scream ripped through the night—high, broken, spraying even more hot blood across my chest and face. It hit my lips, flooding my tongue with the bitter tang of iron.

I didn't flinch. I watched him. His body bucked beneath me, his eyes wild and rolling in panic. He tried to scream curses I'd never hear—all that came out was a bubbling, choking gurgle.

I kept my weight solid on his chest, knees digging in, unmoving. I felt every weak, frantic spasm ripple beneath me, the hot blood pooling around my knees, the sharp iron tang thick in the air.

I pressed my blade to his throat, his pulse fluttered wild and rabbit-fast against the steel. He arched, eyes bulging, his gurgling breaths rattling in the pit of his chest. I leaned in close, my lips brushing his ear. "You never broke me," I whispered. "You just taught me exactly who I am."

Then I straightened, looking directly into his wide, shattered eyes. I pressed the blade to his throat and drew it across, slow, deliberate, feeling every shudder, every stuttering breath leave him beneath me.

His wild, broken eyes found mine one last time, shining with terror and disbelief. Then a sharp, desperate jerk—like he was trying to take a breath, but his body couldn't find an airway. Another shudder ran through him, a final, useless fight. His mouth worked silently, red froth bubbling at the edges.

I watched every second. I didn't look away. The life drained from his gaze, leaving his eyes wide and empty, staring up at the open night sky. I waited, listening for another breath, another twitch. But there was nothing.

Michael was gone.

Chapter 38

I stayed there for a long moment, straddling his chest, my knees aching against the splintered boards. His blood soaked most of my body. I kept watching his empty eyes, almost expecting some last trick, some final, pitiful gasp. But there was nothing.

Finally, I moved my weight back, my hands bracing on my thighs. I glanced down, feeling the dagger still warm in my grip. Slowly, I lowered it to the holder on my thigh.

When I looked up, the yard was a ruined tapestry—bodies strewn across the torn grass, weapons glinting where they'd fallen, small fires still spitting and sputtering in the churned earth. Smoke curled through the air in thin, drifting ribbons, carrying the sharp sting of burnt magic and blood.

Severance members moved everywhere, their silhouettes weaving through the haze—some limping, some helping each other to their feet, others kneeling beside fallen friends. Shouts cut through the smoke, some urgent, some relieved, all raw.

I went to stand, my knees creaking as I planted my hands on my thighs and pushed up. My legs trembled, sticky with blood—his blood—but I stood.

Then I saw Sarah and Allie. They were running toward me, feet pounding over torn grass and broken boards. Their once beautiful gowns were shredded and streaked with dirt, blood, and ash. Sarah's hair was half fallen from its style, wild curls bouncing around her shoulders. Allie's hair whipped behind her, the end frayed. Their eyes locked on me—wide and shining, somewhere between relief and disbelief.

Sarah's arms flung around my shoulders first, her momentum almost knocking me backwards. Allie slammed into us an instant later, her arms circling both of us, forehead pressing into my collarbone. Sarah let out a sound between a sob and a laugh, her fingers gripping my back like she'd never let go again. Allie's breath hitched sharp against my neck, her whole body shuddering. I wrapped my arms around them both, pressing my face into their hair, the smell of smoke and blood clinging to every strand. Finally, slowly, we pulled apart.

Sarah's eyes swept over me, taking in the blood, the soot, the rawness. "I can't believe you actually cut out his tongue!" she blurted, her voice uneven from leftover adrenaline and something like gleeful disbelief.

A slow, shaky laugh broke out of my chest. I shrugged, still catching my breath. "He wouldn't shut up," I said simply.

Sarah threw her head back and let out a wild, triumphant laugh, the sound echoing through the smoky yard. Allie snorted beside us, wiping at her face with shaking fingers.

I felt him before I saw him. A solid presence at my back filled with warm admiration and love. I turned to face him.

Cade was barely standing. What skin wasn't smeared in blood was pale as bone, his face a ruin of cuts and bruises, a long gash snaking across his brow and vanishing into his hairline. Blood streaked his jaw, dripping from a split lip. His left arm hung useless at his side, bone clearly broken beneath the skin, while fresh crimson still leaked from the gunshot in his shoulder and the deep gash in his ribs. He looked half-dead, but his eyes were still alive—burning, unbroken.

My breath caught. But before I could say a word, Cade stepped forward—his good arm snapping out and pulling me hard against his chest. His mouth crashed into mine, fierce and desperate, tasting of sweat and blood and something so purely him it sent a hot rush spiraling down my spine.

I pressed closer, my hands flying to his face, his shoulders, sliding across his back, his ribs—every cut, every bruise, every tear. Heat poured from me in a wild flood, spilling into him under my fingers. I felt the bones knit, the split skin seal, the shallow gashes close like quiet exhalations.

By the time he finally pulled back, his eyes were wide with something like awe. "You're... incredible," he said, his voice hoarse but full of wonder, like he was seeing me for the first time all over again.

"So are you," I replied. I touched his jaw, my thumb brushing over the now-smooth skin. "I need to help the others," I said.

I turned, ready to sprint toward a cluster of Severance members collapsed on the grass. But before I could take a step, a strong hand clamped around my forearm. I whipped around and Kaylen was there.

She stared at me for a heartbeat, her chest rising and falling fast. Her braid was half-burned away, her clothes scorched and torn, but her skin—healed. No trace of the flames that had torn into her. Then, without a word, she yanked me forward and wrapped her arms around me in a tight, sudden hug. For a second, I froze—the shock of her warmth, the strength in her hold.

Behind us, I heard Hiro's voice crack across the yard. "Holy shit!"

I turned my head just enough to see him standing a few yards away, eyes wide, mouth open. Alice stood beside him, hand clapped over her mouth, eyes bright with shock and something like laughter. Further back, I saw Marcela and Vallerie—all of them watching, dirty and battered, but smiling. Big, real, unstoppable smiles. I looked at them all, my chest aching in the best possible way, then I looked at Kaylen and squeezed her fiercely.

She let go first, stepping back with a sharp nod, her mouth twitching at the corners like she was fighting her own private grin. I took one last look at all of them—my family—and then turned, sprinting toward the downed fighters who still needed me.

I sprinted across the yard, weaving between fallen guards and bent metal, sliding to my knees beside the first group of Severance members I reached. Their faces were pale, clothes soaked through with blood and ash. I didn't hesitate.

I pressed my hands over wounds, feeling the rush of warmth surge out of me and into them. Skin stitched closed under my fingers, bones clicked back into place, breath shuddered back into lungs. One by one, they gasped,

519

coughing, their eyes snapping open in stunned relief. I pressed a hand to the last fighter's chest, felt the final wound seal beneath my palm.

"Over here!" Logan's voice ripped across the yard, high and fractured, edged with a sharp panic I had never heard from him before.

I bolted toward the sound without thinking. When I skidded to a stop, I saw them. Mariah was on the ground, her face ashy and slack, a deep red bloom soaking through her top just below her ribs. Nicole knelt over her, hands clamped hard over the wound, her entire body shaking. Logan hovered behind them, eyes wide, blood streaked across his arms and face.

I dropped to my knees so hard it rattled my bones. Nicole's head snapped up, her eyes wild. "Please—" she choked out, her voice nearly gone.

I didn't answer. I pressed my hands over Nicole's and shoved healing into Mariah in a single, burning wave. Mariah's back arched under my hands, her mouth opening in a silent gasp. The wound closed, skin knitting smooth in seconds. She sucked in a shaky breath, eyes flying open, head jerking up like she'd just woken from a nightmare.

"Holy shit," she rasped, staring at me with wild eyes.

Nicole let out a sob that turned into a strangled laugh, throwing her arms around her sister and nearly knocking her back down. Logan hovered just behind them, his hands flexing open and closed at his sides. His eyes darted frantically between their faces, scanning for any sign of pain or injury.

Once he saw both sisters breathing, his shoulders sagged. He let out a long, shaky breath, then his mouth twisted into a crooked, manic grin. "Damn, Mariah," he panted, shaking his head, "you just gotta be the center of attention everywhere we go, huh?"

Mariah let out a wet laugh, collapsing back into Nicole's arms.

I pushed myself up from Mariah's side, my breath still sharp in my chest, my hands sticky with drying blood.

Most of the yard had quieted now. Fighters sat slumped in small circles, heads bent together, some laughing through tears, others simply staring at their hands like they still couldn't believe they'd made it.

I kept moving.

Nick caught my eye. He was slumped over a broken chair, his hair plastered to his forehead with sweat, his hands hanging limp between his knees. His clothes were torn and smeared with blood. Lorelei knelt beside him, one hand on his back, her other arm braced on the chair as she leaned in close, murmuring something.

I started toward him, something instinctive rising up inside me, the same pull that had sent me to every wounded fighter. Could I heal a healer?

Nick's head lifted slowly, and he managed a tired, crooked smile. He raised a shaky hand, palm out. "I'm just drained," he said. "I'll be fine. Go help the others."

I hesitated, my hands half-raised, but Lorelei turned to me then. Her eyes were bright, shimmering even through the exhaustion etched into her face. "You did exactly what you were meant to do tonight," she said, her voice clear and steady as a bell ringing through the smoke. "Go finish it."

I gave her a short nod, my fingers curling at my sides and kept moving.

I passed David, who was leaning heavily against a broken railing, his head tipped back, a rag pressed to a cut above his eyebrow. When he saw me, he gave me a quick two-finger salute, his grin crooked but real.

Evangeline stood a few paces away, her eyes distant and milk-white. Her sightless eyes seemed to pierce straight through me, her words trembling at the edges. "This is the vision that I saw all those years ago. Your flames, your wrath, tearing through the dark. I thought it was the end of us, that you were the ruin I was sworn to stop. But it was never ruin.

It was vengeance. And it was the hand that would save us all."

Her words hung between us, fragile as glass. Slowly, she dipped her head, a shadow of regret—or maybe understanding—passing over her blind eyes. I didn't answer. There was nothing left to say. I turned and kept moving.

Near the edge of the yard, I caught sight of Gage. He stood surrounded by a small cluster of fighters, his tablet tucked under one arm, his glasses askew. When his eyes landed on me, he flashed a broad, relieved smile and lifted one hand in an easy wave.

I felt something warm and steady curl through my chest, my steps growing a fraction lighter as I pushed forward, scanning for anyone else who still needed me.

Through the haze and drifting smoke, I spotted movement at the far edge of the yard. A Severance member staggered backward, arms hooked under the armpits of a fallen fighter, dragging the limp body across the torn ground. The fighter's boots bumped and scraped over dirt and debris, leaving a dark, jagged trail behind them.

I sprinted over without thinking. As I reached them, I dropped to a crouch, slipped my hands under the fallen fighter's legs, and lifted.

The Severance member glanced at me, eyes wide, sweat and soot streaking her face. For a second, she just stared. Then she gave a sharp, shaky nod, and together we hauled the body toward a small clearing where a few others had already been laid out. We lowered the fighter gently, arranging their limbs as best we could, brushing dirt and ash from their hair.

I stood again and walked back into the wreckage to help find more bodies. Cade appeared beside me, his hands sliding under the shoulders of another fallen fighter. Sarah and Jack moved in next, Allie right behind them, each one stepping into place without a word.

Hiro and Alice emerged from the smoke, helping lift another body between them, their faces pale and set. Vallerie,

Marcela, and Kaylen joined in too, moving between the wreckage, bending to lift, supporting the weight without hesitation.

Logan came last, stumbling forward with a quiet curse, sweat dripping off his brow. He grabbed the legs of a body David was already dragging, his mouth twisting into a grim line. Body after body, we carried them to a clearing. Each one placed gently, arms arranged, heads turned to the sky.

We left Michael's body and the bodies of his guards where they lay.

As the pile in the clearing grew, someone started sorting them, moving each fallen fighter toward small groups so they could be returned to their home chapters, to be mourned properly in the days to come.

No one spoke. There was only the rustle of fabric, the grunt of strained breaths, the dull thud of boots on scorched earth. I wiped sweat and soot from my forehead with the back of my arm, my shoulders screaming with exhaustion, but I didn't stop. None of us did.

When the last body was laid down, we stood together in the clearing. The air buzzed with quiet sobs, trembling breaths, the small shuffling sounds of people holding each other upright.

Some reached for hands. Others pressed their foreheads into shoulders. A few dropped to their knees, arms wrapped tight around their middles, as if trying to keep the pieces of themselves from spilling out.

I felt the grief. It hit me like a slow, rising wave—heavy and vast, pressing at the edges of my ribs, curling cold fingers around my spine. I felt every shattered sob, every quiet prayer whispered into torn sleeves, every sharp ache that pulsed in the gaps where friends and lovers and siblings had once stood. It moved through me, bright and brutal and endless.

But I didn't drown in the sorrow. I let it move, let it echo through my bones and thread into my lungs, each breath a quiet testament to every soul we had lost.

I felt Melanie step up beside me, her fingers wrapping around mine. On my other side, Matthias's hand landed on my shoulder. Their empathy marks pressed into mine. I understood instantly. Together, we reached outward—not to erase the grief or silence it, but to hold it. To soften the sharpest edges, to let everyone breathe through it instead of being swallowed by it.

A wave of warmth rolled through the clearing, slow and steady. Around us, shoulders loosened. Clenched fists uncurled. Heads tipped back, breaths coming easier, quieter. A few cries changed into shaky, relieved laughter. Others pressed their foreheads into each other's shoulders, sobbing freely but not alone.

The grief stayed. But it was cradled now, held safely among all of us. We just stood together, connected by that fragile, powerful thread—a single, steady heartbeat in the wreckage.

• • •

By the time we reached the cabin, dawn had begun to creep over the trees, painting the sky in streaks of bruised lavender and soft gold. We moved as one, silent and heavy-footed, each step echoing with exhaustion and relief.

The moment we opened the door, Biscuit let out a sharp, offended mrrrow—the kind that made it very clear we were late, and she was unimpressed. I reached out and brushed a hand over her head as I passed. "Missed you too, drama queen."

No one moved toward the bedrooms. We stood scattered in the main room, shoulders drooping, hands hanging at our sides, eyes darting from face to face like we were all waiting for something.

Then Hiro cleared his throat. "Fire pit?" he said, glancing toward the back door.

Sarah let out a weak laugh, scrubbing a hand over her face. "God, yes. I am not closing my eyes yet."

524

Allie sighed, leaning back against the wall. "Please. Anything but just... going to bed alone right now."

Marcela nodded, her shoulders sagging as she murmured, "I think we could all use that."

Cade let out a soft grunt of agreement, his hand brushing mine as if answering for the both of us.

Vallerie and Alice exchanged a quiet look, then Alice muttered, "I'll bring the blankets."

Before we went out, we each took a quick shower and threw on soft, comfortable clothes. When we met again at the back door, we looked like ourselves again—still battered, still raw, but human. Together, we stepped out into the pale dawn and made our way to the fire pit.

Cade moved first, hauling logs over one by one. When he finished stacking them, he crouched down and reached for the matches in his pocket. I stepped forward, laying a hand gently on his shoulder. He paused immediately, tilting his head up to look at me.

"Let me," I said, with a small smile tugging at my lips.

Cade's mouth twitched, that soft, reverent wonder flickering across his face. I lifted my hand, summoning a small, bright ball of flame into my palm. I guided it forward, letting it slip into the logs. The wood caught instantly, a low, hungry whoosh echoing across the quiet yard. Sparks leapt up, swirling like fireflies in the dim light.

Cade stayed crouched there for a moment longer, his head tipped back to watch me, a slow, crooked smile curving across his lips. "I don't think I'll ever stop being amazed by you," he said.

"Then don't," I replied.

We settled around the fire. I could still smell the blood on my skin, even though I'd scrubbed as best I could. I wasn't sure that scent would ever really leave me.

Vallerie nudged a piece of wood with her boot and said, "I'm going to miss this place. But I guess it's time to get back to normal."

Allie let out a short, rough laugh beside me. She pulled her knees in tight, her arms wrapped around them. "Normal," she echoed, her voice tinged with disbelief. "I don't even know what normal is anymore. How am I supposed to go back to my office, listen to people talk about their everyday lives, and just... nod along? File paperwork? Like none of this happened?"

Sarah groaned, leaning back on her elbows and tilting her face up toward the lightening sky. "I mean... I don't think I can go back to editing books after this," she said, her voice threaded with a spark of humor. "Maybe I'll switch careers and become a spy. I've got the moves now." She shot Allie a crooked grin.

Allie snorted, rolling her eyes. "God help us all."

Jack, perched on a log nearby, let out a soft snort of laughter. "You'd blow your cover in about two minutes flat," he said, smirking. "You can't even keep a straight face when you're lying about stealing my hoodie."

Sarah flipped him off without even looking his way, a small laugh slipping out of her.

Marcela hummed quietly, her head tipped back, eyes closed as if she were listening to some private music only she could hear. "You'll all figure it out," she murmured. "Whatever 'normal' is now... maybe it's not about going back. Maybe it's about going forward, and finding something new that fits."

Hiro moved closer to Alice and said, "I think I'm going to talk to Lorelei about transferring to the Maine chapter. Feels like it might be time to stick around here a little longer." He nudged Alice gently. "Someone's gotta make sure you don't keep sneaking all the pastries from the kitchen."

Alice let out a laugh, shoving at his shoulder. "I do not sneak them," she protested, but she didn't let go of his arm.

Kaylen scoffed from her spot nearest the flames. "You're all idiots," she muttered.

Everyone was still talking around the fire, voices weaving over each other in that easy, comfortable way that only came after surviving something big together.

Allie leaned forward, hands gesturing as she said something to Vallerie that made her laugh, that deep, rare laugh that always felt like a small victory. Hiro and Alice sat pressed shoulder to shoulder, heads tilted in close as they spoke in low voices. Sarah leaned into Jack's side, snickering at something he whispered in her ear.

Through all of it, I stayed curled on Cade's lap in one of the lounge chairs, his arms wrapped snug around my waist. He moved beneath me, his arms tightening almost painfully. "Stand up," he growled against my ear, the sound more animal than human.

My heart slammed against my ribs as he guided me to my feet. Before I could catch a full breath, he stood too, towering over me, his gaze wild. He didn't say another word, just grabbed my waist and stepped. The shadows swallowed us, and a heartbeat later, the clearing unfolded around us.

Cade slammed me back against the nearest tree, his hands caging me in, his mouth a breath away. "You have no idea," he snarled, "how fucking unstoppable you looked tonight. You fought like a goddess. Like something the universe couldn't even dream up. I watched you take everything back. I watched you become everything you were meant to be. And I have never—" His voice cracked, his hands trembling where they caged me in. "—never wanted you more than I do right now."

"Then don't make me wait," I whispered.

He didn't.

Epilogue

Five Years Later

The porch creaked as I rocked in my chair, one hand curved around my swollen belly, the other flinging a piece of crust toward the bushes. The squirrel darted out, grabbed the offering, and disappeared back into the underbrush with his usual flair.

"You better be sharing that," I muttered. "I saw you chase off a chipmunk last week."

Wind chimes tinkled gently above, catching the sunlight. Our house was small, just one story with a big porch that wrapped around the back and side. It was back from the road, surrounded by trees, quiet as ever.

The air smelled like pine and dirt, and the garlic Cade had been dicing in the kitchen.

The door eased open behind me. "You're feeding him again," Cade said, stepping onto the porch.

"He stared at me for twenty minutes," I replied. "I gave in."

He bent to kiss my cheek, then my stomach. "How's she treating you tonight?"

"Like she's training to be a kickboxer." I winced as another jab landed low. "She's got your attitude."

He smirked and eased into the porch chair beside mine. "Perfect. I was starting to worry she'd be too sweet."

"Not a chance." I poked my belly. "This one's all fire and vengeance."

"So basically you," he said grinning.

A high-pitched squeal shattered the stillness.

"UNCA CAAADE!"

Little Abel hurtled barefoot across the yard, curls flying, limbs flailing, a wooden spoon clutched in his hand like a weapon. Cade stood just in time to catch him as he launched himself upward.

"Hey, monster," Cade said, scooping him up. "You bringing trouble?"

Abel nodded like it was a badge of honor.

I put a hand to my chest, feigning offense as I looked at Abel. "Traitor. Just yesterday I was your favorite."

Cade's mouth tugged into that slow, crooked grin. "Careful, kid. Betraying her comes with consequences."

Sarah stepped up then, holding a foil-covered dish in one hand and a bottle of wine in the other. "He refused shoes. I picked my battles."

Jack followed close behind with a diaper bag slung over one shoulder and a tired grin.

Sarah leaned down and kissed my forehead. "God, you look *huge*. I love it. Glowing and terrifying."

"Your child's using cutlery as a war club," I said.

"Balance," she replied, waving it off.

Cade adjusted Abel higher on his hip. "You're getting heavy, champ."

"I'm strong," Abel said, patting his chest with the spoon.

"You are," Cade agreed, smiling as he set him down.

Abel took off across the porch, chasing a butterfly with the spoon still clutched in his fist. Sarah watched him for a moment, then handed the casserole dish to Cade. "Hope you're hungry."

"Always," he said, disappearing inside with it.

A few moments later, the gate creaked open. Allie walked through hand-in-hand with Garrick, a towering wall of muscle and menace at her side. He was the kind of man who looked like he'd kill you if you disrespected her... and smile while doing it.

Allie had taken a job with The Severance not long after everything settled, working as a trauma psychiatrist helping the fighters cope with the battles. That's where she met Garrick. Allie said they barely spoke for weeks, just long stares and the occasional grunt. Honestly, I think that was his version of courtship. Whatever it was, it worked. Now he looks at her like she hung the damn moon, and he's got a knife for anyone who disagrees.

I joined The Severance around the same time Allie did, fighting side by side with Cade. The two of us were a force—quick, ruthless, and terrifying when we had to be. For a while, it felt like we were always on the move, always chasing the next threat. But once I got pregnant, we stepped back. Now we only go in when something urgent comes up or they really need us.

"We brought banana bread," Allie said as they reached the porch. "Corinne made it."

I smiled. "Of course she did."

It still caught me sometimes how far Corinne has come. There were whole months where we weren't sure she'd ever come back to us. But between Vallerie's memory weaving, Marcela's delicate enchantments, and my own mark reaching gently into her mind, piece by piece, we'd found her again. Not all at once. But enough. She lives nearby now, in a small house tucked just down the trail. Vallerie visits her often. Sometimes they spend hours together in the garden or inside baking.

Allie stepped close, resting her hand on my stomach. "How's my niece doing?" she asked.

"Feisty," I said. "She's been practicing roundhouse kicks for the last hour."

Allie grinned. "She's gonna fit right in."

We all went inside and sat around the table. Cade passed around plates while Jack poured drinks. Abel circled the table once, wooden spoon still in hand, before spotting Biscuit perched on a chair. "Kitty!" he shouted, charging toward her.

Biscuit hissed, leapt down, and vanished into the next room with her tail puffed like a bottlebrush. Abel didn't seem to mind. He pivoted immediately and made a beeline for Garrick instead. Without hesitation, he clambered into his lap.

Garrick froze. His hands hovered in the air, unsure where to put them, like the concept of toddlers was a threat assessment he hadn't trained for.

531

Sarah laughed. "You're fine," she said. "He only bites when he's tired."

Garrick glanced at her, then slowly, awkwardly rested one massive hand on Abel's back. Abel grabbed a piece of garlic bread off Garrick's plate and took a triumphant bite, blissfully unaware of the tension radiating off the man beneath him.

Dinner was loud and easy, pasta and garlic bread disappearing faster than Cade could refill the plates.

"You ready for Alice and Hiro's wedding next weekend?" Allie asked, glancing over at me.

"As long as I don't go into labor in the middle of it," I said.

"You better not," Sarah added. "Marcela's already threatening to make a rune to seal your cervix shut until after the wedding."

"She's serious," I said. "She tried to draw a rune on my ankle last week with eyeliner."

Cade gave a quiet laugh from the other end of the table. "She's got backup. Kaylen said if your water breaks, she's not pausing the ceremony. She's just going to hand you a towel and tell you to walk it off."

"That won't be a problem," Sarah said, popping a piece of banana bread into her mouth. "She's going to have the fastest recovery in birthing history. Her body will probably heal right after the placenta's out."

I smirked. "Didn't hear you complaining when I healed you five minutes after Abel ripped you open like a feral badger."

Sarah raised her glass. "And I never will. Cheers to magical best friends."

She clinked her glass against mine, then leaned into Jack, who pressed a kiss to her temple and murmured something low in her ear that made her smile.

It was because of Jack the world finally saw Michael for what he really was. He had taken the evidence Gage spent years collecting, the parts that didn't show magic, and passed it through the right hands using his military ties. He dismantled Michael's image overnight. And now, instead of a hero, the world saw a monster. A murderer. Exactly what he'd always been

The rest of the evening blurred into easy conversation, the kind that ebbed naturally until plates were cleared and goodbyes were said.

Later, after everyone had gone and the dishes were done, Cade and I curled up on the back porch in the oversized lounge chair. The sun was just starting to set, and cicadas were humming somewhere in the distance.

Out beyond the trees, a familiar warmth stirred. For a breath, I saw her—grandma, smiling at me through the fading light. It wasn't the first time she had come like this, quiet and steady, her way of letting me know she was proud and that she was at peace. My chest ached, but the ache was sweet.

The vision faded, leaving only Cade, his arms wrapped around me, his hands rubbing slow circles over the curve of my belly. "You still want to name her Margot?" He asked.

I nodded. "She's definitely a Margot."

"Do you think she'll be marked?" I asked.

His answer came without hesitation. "Doesn't matter. She's ours. She's already perfect."

I turned my head just enough to meet his eyes. "Even if she's all fire and chaos?"

He smiled. "Yeah. Even then. We'll just teach her where to aim it."

I settled into his chest, a smile curving on my lips because I knew that whatever waited for us, for her, we'd face it together. Always.

Author's Note

The character Reid in this story was inspired by my nephew, Reid Brewer. He was only seven when we lost him, yet he carried the heart of an old soul—wise, kind, generous, and deeply loved by everyone who knew him. Team Reid Charities was created in his honor to carry forward that spirit of love and compassion. If you'd like to learn more or contribute, please visit
https://www.facebook.com/teamreidbrewer/

www.ingramcontent.com/pod-product-compliance
Lightning Source LLC
Chambersburg PA
CBHW060810120726
47909CB00006B/1849